The Shadows Within

Hannah Till

Trigger Warnings

Adult Sexual Content

Depression

Self Harm

Gore

War

Death

Published in the United States by Hannah Till

Cover design and all associated artwork by Marcia Godfrey of PlusInfinityArt

Editor: Marcia Godfrey

Developmental Editor: Rachel Bunner of @rachels.top.edits

To receive special offers, bonus content, and all other information related to works completed by Hannah Till, please visit the following websites and sign up for the newsletter.

www.hannahtillauthor.com

www.instagram.com/hannahtillauthor

THE SHADOWS WITHIN

To the ones who felt they weren't enough.

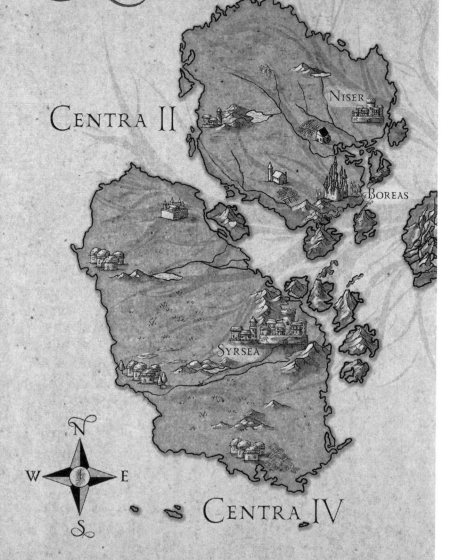

ITHESIN

CENTRA II

NISER

BOREAS

CENTRA IV

SYRSEA

N
W   E
S

CENTRA III

THE
CABIN

SEA OF CARRIGAN

THE
CAVERNS

MULARA
FOREST

HALABAR

CENTRA I

Act I

- The Deceptions -

I

"I'm so sorry," the familiar voice echoes through my ears. Sadness is wrapped like a ribbon around the phrase.

My eyes blink rapidly in an effort to open, but I'm so damn tired. There are only flashes of light and darkness and stilted movement, yet nothing comes into focus. Then I feel it. The featherlight touch against my cheek and the warmth radiating from it threatens to pull me back into a dark, dreamless sleep.

The world is blurry. A secret veil floats between me and the unknown. My body feels as heavy and cumbersome as the surrounding sticky air. Every muscle, every bone, every inch of skin feels like lead as the weight of movement becomes too much. Even my thoughts swirl just out of grasp.

My eyelids are thick and heavy, and I long to vanish within the depths of the darkness that hovers just out of reach. Yet something in me fights back against that obsidian pit below, and I use every ounce of strength I have left to keep from falling back into it.

"I didn't mean for it to end up like this," the voice continues as warm fingers brush across my forehead. The touch is so soft, so gentle, that for just a moment, I think lying here in this inbetween, somewhere in the midst of a cruel reality and a merciful new beginning, may be where I belong.

Even with the veil, I find I can hardly turn my head enough to take in my surroundings. But I feel movement—a rocking motion—and I know we're riding within something. The swaying teeters between a gentle lull and something a little more . . . *nauseating*. I can't decide which sensation to give in to first.

The sudden jolt of this body, somehow both detached from and belonging to me, is what breaks that rift, shattering the glassy veil, and finally revealing the world that lies just out of reach.

The warm hand begins to trace the outline of my features, and I inhale the delicious scent of mint and dirt which linger in the air. It instantly brings forth a wave of ease and calm—something I have so desperately missed over these last weeks spent confined in that pretty palace Koreed calls home.

Without warning, the realization of what that scent means hits me hard, and the air is sucked from my chest as everything finally comes crashing into view.

"Tarak?" my voice crackles on the word, so I try to clear my throat.

He places a straw to my lips, and I drink the cool water, letting it soothe the soreness, and thankfully, it calms my nervous stomach—if only a little.

I push back when my eyes finally meet his.

"Don't." He counters my movements and places the straw to my mouth once more. "You'll get dehydrated; you need to drink." His plea is soft and soothing as his warm fingers continue their path of exploration across my face, mapping out each and every freckle as he once did not so long ago. A sensation wraps around my body, soothing me and telling me I am finally safe.

It sends me back into oblivion, and when I open my eyes again, I find an oddly familiar room in front of me. An unusual dusting of snow covers the previously carpeted floor.

"Where would you like this one?" Tarak holds out a book, and I twist forward to meet his familiar face.

"What?" I blink, trying to remember what it is we're working on.

"It says Medieval Studies, but I don't know what that means." Confusion covers his features.

I stare a little longer, and he eyes me warily. His clothes are all wrong. Instead of his normal attire, he's wearing jeans and a t-shirt. When I look down, I find snow blanketing the floor under his sneakers.

"Nera?" Taylor says as she comes from behind me. "Are you going to help him?" Her tone is almost accusatory.

"O– of course." I attempt to shake the fog away as I try to stand, but my body is too heavy and my hands won't move.

"Help him!" Taylor admonishes, her tone more forceful than I've ever heard before.

"I am, but I can't get–" I try to throw my hands out for balance, but they're frozen, and my feet feel as if they've sunk into the fresh cement of a new city sidewalk.

"I asked you to train him!" she all but seethes and I recoil at the harshness in her words.

"I'm sorry." Tears sting my eyes at the thought of disappointing the only person who truly cared for me after I walked out of that hospital.

"Help. Him." Her voice is more frantic.

"I am!"

But her form starts to blur and then the bookstore I know and love fades away, leaving me alone with Tarak looming over me.

"Where are . . . " My gaze searches, but that familiar sight is gone and a new wooden contraption surrounds me. I shift forward, but find I can't move my arms. It's as if my body is almost immobile. I have just enough energy to twist a small amount, but it takes everything I have to force the movement.

After a brief struggle, Tarak's hand gently pushes me back down against the soft pillow. I don't fight it, all but collapsing when the side of my face grazes against the soft, warm material.

"Don't struggle. *Please*," he begs. "I don't want the vines to cut you." His warm breath tickles my skin as he whispers quietly against my ear.

Cut me?

I blink again, determined to fully wake. My eyes shift through blurred surroundings until I finally locate my hands; only, I find them bound and enclosed within a singular cream-colored cloth, which is drawn together at my clasped wrists. The fabric seems to shimmer in the wavering sunlight seeping in through the cracks in the wooden walls.

I can't see any vines, but from the small, needle-like stings on my wrist which cause me to wince with even minimal movement, I know they're there, binding my hands and wrists together. I frantically shuffle the rest of my body, and relief fills me when I find only my hands now remain immobilized. My heart rate spikes as a thunderous tempo rams against my chest. My breathing seems to pause as my entire body shifts from the clutches of that comfortable daze into sheer panic.

"Untie me. Tarak, untie me!" I attempt to yell, but my voice is too raw, and all that comes out is a barely audible pleading whine.

It only takes a second of staring at his still form before I understand he's not going to release the binds. He doesn't even budge; he barely even breathes as I watch waves of hurt burst through his sapphire gaze, and feel further confusion bubbling up within me.

My eyes crease, wondering if I'm still caught somewhere in between, somewhere not quite real, thinking perhaps this is some cruel dream. Maybe I'll wake up soon. But, the more he comes into view, and the more I smell his scent and feel the warmth radiating from his body, I come to the realization that this is no dream.

As we stare at each other, I struggle with what his refusal means. He did rescue me, *right*? Did Koreed, or maybe a palace guard have me tied up? That doesn't make any sense. I don't remember them restraining me at all. Though, I can't say I remember much of anything at the moment. The last few hours, maybe even days, seem to be one large obsidian blur with only tiny fragments of light inching their way in to allow the smallest hint at my memories.

As I continue to stare at him, my eyes are freed of the clouded veil, and a war of emotions barrels through me.

I want to scream at him. I want to reach up and slap him across that beautiful face. But as his full frame appears through the mist, his hand strokes my arm, and a sigh of contentment makes its way past my lips.

Tarak.

He's here.

He's really, truly *here*.

My breathing slows, the sight of him easing my ragged breaths, and all other thoughts are left behind. With him here, I know I must be safe. My lips rise in a small smile just as a painful pinch surges into the back of my arm and the warmth, once again, seeps through my bones.

I welcome the underlying darkness and sink back within the shadows of the veil.

Little Mary runs between the aisles, her two small braids flying behind her.

"Slow down!" I call to her with no conviction whatsoever.

Her giggle fills the room.

When I look up hoping to see her blue eyes peering out from between the books, I see wisps of smoke curling along the ceiling.

"Mary!" I jolt forward in an attempt to reach her, but my legs won't budge. "Mary!"

The smoke fills the expanse, followed quickly by her cries of pain.

"Mary!" I struggle against whatever holds me back.

"Nera! Help! Help me!"

"I'm trying baby girl. I'm trying!" Visions of a blistered, bloodied form I'm sure to find race through my mind and tears spring to my eyes.

"Help me." Her small voice sounds so foreign, and for a moment I wonder if I've ever heard it before. "Help them!"

"I'm coming." I cough through the words as the smoke fills my lungs. A loud banging reverberates through the room, and I watch as shelf after shelf falls over. Dust and smoke billow outward and cloud my vision.

But the dark room suddenly brightens so much I have to shield my eyes. When I look back up, I find my worst fears realized as Mary burns, her entire body covered with flames.

"NO!" I cry out as she fades from view.

"Save me! Save them!" she begs, but her voice crackles on the last word as her body turns to ash. Then the ceiling caves in.

My head bobs in an effort to lift from the pillow as the world around eases back into view. This time, when I meet his gaze, Tarak is no longer at my side but pacing the rickety floor.

How did he get up so fast? Why is he so far away?

I want . . . no, I *need* him. I need his scent to fill every crevice of my body. I need his taste to linger on my tongue. I need his body pressed tightly against mine.

I lick my lips, hoping the dryness will dissipate and allow me to tell him what I so desperately need. But not a sound emerges. I try to reach out to him, but no matter how much I command my body to move, nothing happens, and when the haze of the veil returns as his warm fingers trail along my jaw, the side of my face finds the pillow once more.

There is only a momentary high that barely even begins. The second it's over, the nameless man's hands turn my stomach as a visceral sensation settles in.

"That was good." He plops to the side, fully out of breath. His deep voice is as unfamiliar as his hands felt, and I feel the sudden urge to flee as disappointment surges through me. "Thanks."

"You're welcome," I reply as if on instinct. The same phrase I have stated so many times after empty nights such as these. Even in the pitch black of this room I stare up at the ceiling, counting the seconds before he passes out.

True to form, I hear his snoring start before I even get to fifty.

My rigid muscles roll with effort when I try to slip away as silently as possible. I scurry around in the dark and on my knees, locating each item of clothing thrown about. I'm just sliding on my shirt when I feel a vice-like grip on the back of my arm.

"Where are you going?" the now familiar voice says, and I twist to find a faint glow covering the previous room and a welcome face in front of me.

"Tarak?"

"Where are you going?" He tightens his grip.

"I'm not sure," I answer honestly, knowing he'd be able to tell if I tried to lie.

"You are mine," he commands as he yanks me upward.

"I know." I forcefully stumble to my feet. "Tarak, let go." I try to pull my arm away. "You're hurting me."

"You are mine," he commands once more as I stare questioningly into those comforting eyes.

"Tarak, let me go," I plead once more, but his grip tightens.

I open my mouth to speak once more, but stop when cold droplets land atop my hands. When I look up, I find ice covering the ceiling of this city apartment.

"What is–"

"You're mine," he cuts me off with a menacing tone, and when my gaze jolts back to his, I find those sapphire eyes transformed into burning orbs, and streaks of fire surging through his veins.

"Tarak!" I scream out, yanking my hand from his hold to find a burning ash-covered handprint where he once held me.

When the shifting light comes into view, I find Tarak sitting on the bed, or cot—*maybe pallet?*—with me. His fingers barely graze the skin of my arm as he tugs the blanket up a little higher. I nearly melt into the heat surging through me.

I missed him.

I missed his touch and his smile and his dimples. It's an odd feeling; missing something I *actually* have. I think I hear a chuckle and, by the confused look he sends my way, I would have to bet the sound came from my own lips.

I want to see his dimples. I want to see his smile. I want him to laugh and to smirk and to annoy me, but most of all, I just want him. I spent far too many days living within the hellscape of his death and the sadness which came with it not to reach out and grasp this moment before me. Now, I want nothing more than to revel in the knowledge that he is alive. He is here.

But he looks sad. So devastatingly sad. I want to take the sadness away from him. *Need* to take it away. My hand reaches up to soothe away the thoughts plaguing his mind, but I can't get to him.

My hand is stuck. And it hurts.

I try again, but as before, it doesn't move. I feel a sting burrowing deep within my wrist and a groan seeps past my lips.

The pain sends a jolt through me, and my eyes finally focus on the room around us. For just a moment, I thought this was his home. But that's not right. His home is gone. My home is gone. We're no longer in the safety of the wooden dwelling so high within the canopy of the trees. I'm no longer within the golden and bejeweled walls of the palace. We are most definitely, instead, riding inside something. And I don't think it has wheels.

Are we on a boat?

I try to scoot my body up, but the piercing sting hits me again, and my eyes shoot down to find the source of the pain as another groan seeps out.

My wrists feel as though I'm being stabbed by a thousand tiny needles all at once.

Vines. That's what he said before. *I don't want the vines to cut you.*

And then it fully hits me.

I'm tied up.

"What . . . " My head jerks up to meet his gaze, and that shimmering veil finally vanishes again. "What's going on?"

His chest heaves as he sucks in the stagnant air and his head rapidly shakes from side to side. "This was not part of my plan," he whispers. It sounds almost like a plea as his eyes meet mine.

"Correct me if I'm wrong, but this was *exactly* the plan." I hear Jaxon's voice come from somewhere behind me. I attempt to turn, but between the vines securing my wrists and the overwhelming exhaustion I still feel, I can barely move.

"Please, just shut up!" Tarak yells from above me. His gaze is trained behind me, and my eyes widen in shock at his use of the phrase.

Jaxon barks out a laugh. "Come on. Using her words now? Don't act so remorseful. This was the plan, and *it worked*. Your timing was off, so I had to kill a few more Halabarians than I expected. But, honestly, I liked that part. Maybe I should thank you." I hear Jaxon's small snicker.

He walks into view and I finally get a glimpse of his face. The same face that helped me, that went with us to the springs, that introduced me to the bow. The face of a friend now turned foe. He balances a knife on his finger, letting it teeter from one side to the other before deftly twisting it in a circle and sliding it back into the sheath at his belt. The trick feels more like a warning than anything else.

But his words bring it all back. My time in Halabar. The bombs. The fight. Oh god, my Celestra gifts. *Mina.* I choke out a strangled sound at the thought.

Mina. My grandmother. The one and only person I felt truly connected with on this godforsaken planet outside of *him*. The person I was just starting to know again. The person who was teaching me my history—teaching me who I was.

An ache I've never known before fills my chest. It's too much. The memory of her death hits like a lightning bolt straight to my heart.

But, it's not just her death. It's *all* the death. All the soldiers who are now gone because I foolishly ran into a forest instead of facing what was ahead of me in the palace.

My sight blurs as my eyes rim with unshed tears, but even in the mess of confusion and betrayal, I still look up to find *him*.

Tarak appears as though he might tear Jaxon in two. They spit words back and forth at each other which don't fully reach my ears, and I wonder how much time has passed since all the devastation, the death . . . . Since I learned the truth.

"Why am I tied up?" I cut in, my thick voice now frantic. I thrash against the restraints, and *damn*, the vines hurt, but I don't care. *I have to get out of this.*

"Stop." Tarak's warm hand grabs my chin, bringing my panic-stricken eyes to meet his and, for just a moment, the pain dulls. He bends down on his knees so our faces are at the same level. "You are going to bleed. If you haven't already caused cuts, then you will if you keep struggling. There is no use in trying to get these off. Don't fight it." His expression is one I haven't seen before. If I thought the soul hidden behind those sapphire eyes was tortured before, what lies behind them now is inexpressible.

He pulls his fist toward his mouth as his breathing becomes labored and his eyes shut in frustration. Jagged lines mar each corner as he fights not to look at what lies before him—not to look at me.

"Elders!" he screams to the air as he stands.

Stunned silence fills the space as his fists pull at the curls covering his head, and I look between the two men, waiting for someone, anyone, to talk. But neither of them do.

"Someone needs to explain this right now!" I scream out as I yank on the vines. "Dammit!" I all but cry as the pain surges through me.

Jaxon sucks in a breath, then shakes his head and walks away, as if he wants no further part in dealing with this—with me.

"I told you to up her dose. Now we're going to have to listen to this nonsense the rest of the way," an unfamiliar voice barks out from behind, but I can't turn to see who it is.

Tarak finally turns back to face me. Anger, fear, regret all mar his perfect features. "If you don't stop moving, I'm going to have to knock you back out." This time when he speaks, I find his voice flat and void of emotion. His fists open and close at his sides.

And then the truth sinks in.

I am his captive.

Maybe I always was.

I look to my hands once more, or better yet to the cloth binding them together and hiding the torn skin I know lies below, as if I need to see them again to fully comprehend what is happening. My sight blurs as more tears begin to gather. I open and close my mouth, trying to find the words to say, but the quivering of my bottom lip stops me. There is nothing I can say. I am completely and totally useless. I am at his mercy, and he won't help me.

My breaths come in pants I can't control, and I feel my rapid heartbeat shaking against my chest. I haven't had a panic attack in so long, but I don't think there is any way to stop this one from coming.

Koreed was right. Tarak and all those out within the trees are the enemy.

Maybe Himerak is the mastermind behind all the deaths. Maybe he's the puppet master. Koreed may have been his first puppet when Himerak caused all those deaths with mind control, but it seems as if Tarak's taken up that mantle so very easily.

I may not be able to fully move, but I twist just enough to face him head on before I gather what little spit I have and hurl it at him.

It lands on the boards between his feet.

He jolts back as if the action physically scars him. "Nera?" His voice almost breaks. My name is an unimaginable pain.

But no amount of pain can compare to the stab of betrayal which now pierces me. This time when I twist the vines, I welcome the agony, hoping it might drown out the torture ripping through my soul.

"Nera, stop!" *His* hands clasp over mine, stilling any movements. But I yank them away from his touch, causing more pain to sear through my wrists. I wince as a patch of red oozes its way into the fabric.

Tarak flinches, and my heart almost breaks at his sharp inhalation of distress.

Then I remember he caused my pain.

"You lied to me." The words are barely audible as they pass my lips. My breathing becomes more and more labored as the seconds tick by. He turns and grabs something behind me as I speak. "You lied to me!" My voice shakes. My body goes numb at the betrayal.

It was all a lie.

The stories he fed me. The way he made me feel. The . . . *more.*

It was all a lie.

"I'm sorry. I'm so very sorry." His voice cracks as he speaks, and a shuddering breath escapes his lips.

I catch sight of his sapphire eyes, swearing a glint of moisture collects there. Then he shifts his body over mine, and I still.

"I don't want to do this," he calls out through gritted teeth.

"Do what? Get off me!" I buck up as I try to dislodge him, but my strength is no match for his. In one swift move, he deftly rolls me over, and I call out as my hands are trapped between my body and the hard surface I've been lying on.

My sleeve is shifted upward, and I scream as a thick needle is thrust into my arm.

The darkness instantly settles over me, and I hear his muffled voice in my ear just before it takes me under.

"You promised you would wait for me. Wait."

"Come on. I need you to wake up."

I barely register the soothing voice as I feel a shake to my shoulders. My eyes peek open to find the most beautiful face, and I feel a smile spread across my features. It's only when I notice his expression, full of detachment and devoid of emotion, that I feel the air shift, and recall our previous moments together.

Desolation comes rolling in.

Everything I know is a lie.

Everything about him—about us—was a lie.

Every time my heartbeat became rapid or my skin prickled with the warmth from his touch was a *lie*.

A murderous, vicious lie.

For just the slightest of moments, the taste of this pain rings familiar. I think this is why I never truly gave in to love before. Somehow, even with my rattled and broken mind, I knew. I *knew* what grief followed this pain. The pain which has no physical wound, yet burns a cavity so deep nothing will ever be able to fill it. No amount of shiny things or distractions will ever replace this giant void.

This is the pain of a broken heart.

"Come on. I'll help you sit up." Tarak reaches behind me, and this time I jerk away, desperate never to allow his hands on me again. He tries once more, and I all but fall backward in my determination to get away from him.

I don't want his warmth flooding my veins.

I don't want to give in to what I know was just a pretty lie.

I want the hate.

I want his touch to sting like the vines around my wrists.

He cringes at my recoil.

Good.

As I sit, still and waiting for his next move, my eyes catch sight of my arms, my dress, and my bare legs. The gown I planned to wear to dinner with my father is a disaster. Burnt holes litter the bodice, and there are entire pieces missing throughout what used to be a beautiful cream-colored skirt. My arms are covered in what at first appear to be bruises, but upon further inspection, the bruises are mingled with ash and soot. My legs are a mess of the same. I can't even begin to imagine what my face must look like. But I don't care. Not really. Not now.

Not when my entire world has once again shattered around me.

I sink back down into the hole in my mind I methodically dug for myself during those first few days in Halabar. I'd buried myself deep within its cold walls, and shut out the world around me. It was the only way I could survive, and I know I can do it again.

I thought the depths of my despair those first days back in my Halabarian prison were hell. Now I wish I could run back to them and let their flames consume me whole.

Maybe if I dig a little deeper this time, burying myself just a tad bit farther down, no one will ever be able to reach me.

But no matter how much I will myself to disappear, my body remains taut and aware.

The most abundant feeling surging through me at the moment, outside of the hatred which seems to ooze from my every pore, is unimaginable pain. Though my hands are still hidden beneath the crimson-stained cloth, I can only imagine what gruesome scene lies within.

Tarak stands to my side with a hand placed against the wall near my shoulder. My eyes find Jaxon poised in front, leaning against a beam with his arms crossed over his chest. He's wearing an outfit almost identical to Tarak's, to the one he was wearing when I first met him. Brown leather pants, fitted green shirt, but with a strap across his chest. He stares at me for just a moment, but his eyes don't linger for very long before he reaches out his hand to grab me by the arm, pull me forward, and shuffle me through a narrow hallway to the deck of what I now know is a boat.

Or maybe it's not. The two room vessel, built from deep brown woods and twisted vines, is just tall enough for one to stand in.

"Where are we?" I ask with no acknowledgement from anyone.

Jaxon opens a door and blinding white light surges in. He pushes me across the threshold and I trip over the singed edges of my dress as I move. Falling forward onto my knees, I throw out my bound and bloodied hands as a brace.

I instantly regret the decision as a thorn pierces so deep into my palm, a cry tears from my throat.

"Aww, don't scream, darling. It gets me all excited."

My head jerks up at the crude voice to find an unknown man standing in front of me, a pale hand placed between his legs in a lude manner, and a wide, menacing grin is plastered across his ash and dirt-covered face. Stringy blonde strands of unwashed hair stick to the lingering grime. My gaze turns back to the ground, unwilling to allow this filth to look upon me any longer, and a tear splashes against the wood grain below. There's a moment of confusion before I realize it fell from my eyes.

The man starts to chuckle at my weakness. "I wonder if that's how you sound when–"

"I suggest you quickly forget whatever was about to pass your lips," Tarak warns as he pushes past Jaxon to lift me from the floor.

I cringe at the thought of his hand on me again, and uselessly try to jerk my arm from his grasp. He holds steady.

"What?" the man asks with an incredulous smirk. "No one told me she looked like *that*," he quips with a disgusting lick of his lips as if I were a meal he can't wait to devour.

"Casin. I swear to every Elder, one more word and I will sever your head from your body before you can take your last breath." Tarak's hand is gripping my arm so tightly I begin to wonder whether he's trying to hold me steady or keep himself from attacking the guard.

Perhaps it's both.

I jerk away, but the movement is useless. Tarak doesn't budge and for the first time I curse his stupidly beautiful muscular physique.

Casin throws his hands up in mock surrender and takes a few steps back, still eyeing me as he moves. His gaze trails my body, lingering on places he has no right to, and I tense as I fight the urge to wrap my arms around myself. Not that I can anyway, bound as I am.

"If anyone else so much as *thinks* of behaving in a similar fashion, they will find the same fate. Do not tempt me." Tarak glares, and I turn my head to find a dozen or more guards standing behind us, spread across an old pier. "Not a hand touches her." They all nod in silent agreement.

"Except yours, right?" Jaxon adds in a whisper only we can hear as he saunters around us, hands placed calmly in his pockets, a cool but deadly look in his eyes.

"Jaxon–" Tarak's warning is cut short as Jaxon ignores his friend and continues away from us, walking down the broken and splintered pier to the nearby shore.

"Let's go," Tarak says to me as he violently pulls me along. But then he stops, turns to place his back toward the others and blocks me from their view. His skilled hands fuss with the fabric encircling my wrists, but they don't do anything of use. And from the way we are positioned, only I can tell his movements are purposeless.

"Keep your promise. There is more. Wait for me," he whispers as his eyes meet mine, and then he roughly grabs my arm again, yanking me forward.

II

*W*ait for me.

Wait for me.

Wait. For. Me.

That simple three word phrase circles my mind. Each repetition causes more and more anger and resentment to build.

Wait. For. What?

Wait for him to *kill* me?

Wait for him to *love* me?

Wait for him to *save* me?

But, I think I'm done waiting for others. Especially now. Especially him. I think, from here on out, I will only trust the one person who I know won't disappoint me, even if she barely knows herself.

A familiar hardness forms in my chest, and I will it to spread within every inch of my body. I steel my breath and square my shoulders in the light cast down from the blazing sun above, ready to meet whatever end these people have in place for me. I let one foot guide itself in front of the other, focusing on the only thing I have control of in this moment.

Right foot.

Left foot.

Right foot.

As I walk, I pray my resolve remains steady and the turning of my stomach contents doesn't make itself known. But with each step I take along this pier and closer to the group before me, the stench of unbathed filth fills my nostrils. I slow my breathing to reduce how much of the offending aroma reaches me, then block off my senses and tune out the world around me.

But one sense lingers.

One would think that going from the teetering movement of the small vessel to the stable footing of the pier and then the solid ground would curb the overwhelming nausea which seems to always hover over me. But, sadly, the vomit now threatens to emerge along with the overwhelming feeling of dread as I take in the sight of what lies ahead . . . and consider what may lie beyond.

Behind me. I know there is a beach covered not by sand, but with the same green, seaweed-like protrusions I once saw at Koreed's palace . . . my palace. The only memory I can call on is from a book on southern marshes at Gram's.

I feel another tear seep past the well-constructed barrier at the thought of those I have lost.

Further away from the water's edge, the weeds grow thicker until they fade into a broad forest. Vines fall from the trees in bunches, threatening to entrap anyone within, and inky moss lurches across the ground as if slender fingers are reaching up from the depths of hell, willing and ready to pull one down to their doom.

While this is nowhere near the most frightening scene I have encountered since my arrival on this godforsaken planet, my body almost falters. Every inch of skin along my bones tightens, and those sensations, the ones I have fought to free myself of, scream at me in alarm, warning me that this is not where I should be.

A silent signal—an urgent plea—to run and never look back.

But I've never been one to listen to reason.

I refuse to withdraw. I won't falter.

I will continue to keep my head high and my sight straight ahead. I'll show him, show all of them, I am better than this. I don't even acknowledge the burning embarrassment that bubbles upward each time I trip over the twisted pieces of my dress. The singed ends, burned away by the furious power which unraveled at my own fingertips, now gather and tangle beneath my feet.

What a perfect metaphor for how I now feel.

But somehow I know that, this time, thinking about how I feel and what I see, or hear, or taste won't have the same calming effect it did before. The fury I have long kept buried now rushes forward, threatening to consume me. Had they not placed this binding over my hands, sparks promising death and destruction would be flowing outward in all directions.

My only defense is to let my mind drift elsewhere as I continue my trek forward, never letting them see what lies beneath the shadows . . . what secrets remain hidden within my soul.

I find it hard to imagine exactly what someone's soul might look like. Or if they even exist at all. If they do, I imagine mine as a once beautifully swirling ball of light which has long since dimmed. I'm not sure if my soul was ever whole or beautiful, but now I picture it as a dull and shattered globe, its surface scarred where pieces have broken away.

I rush through the small number of memories I do have in order to distract me. But that too only leads to more hatred, loathing, and regret. I spent my time on Earth wishing to be a part of something while maintaining a repetitious and, admittedly, tedious routine which kept me just on the edge of life. But here . . . oh, here, on this wonderfully beautiful, awful planet . . . Here, I am in the middle of it all.

Here, I am the missing piece which seems to bind it all together.

Here, I am the remnant of the past which is currently tearing it into pieces.

Here, I am nothing and everything, all at once. And that notion just depends on whom you ask at what moment.

I don't fit. And *that* is what hurts the most.

During these long weeks since I arrived on Ithesin, I've had ample time to delve deeper into how I fit into this world, how it makes me feel knowing I don't.

I *am* different.

Different from Tarak. Different from Koreed. Different from Riann. No matter how much they've all tried to make me feel as if I was finally home, I never felt I was.

That realization claws at my very soul. No matter how far I have traveled, I still have yet to find a home—my home.

The last few weeks have become a messy, confusing, and downright contradictory blur of memories now running through my mind as my feet continue to move forward.

The memories come in waves. Waves of happiness, fear, anger, frustration . . . love. Memories of moments which made me, even for just an instant, feel as though I was finally becoming something, someone. Moments which made me think that maybe I was finally finding where I belonged and who I was. When I felt as though I'd finally broken out of that shell I had cocooned myself within for those three years on Earth, and could finally become who I never knew I longed to be.

But now those memories are tarnished with the weight of truth.

I always thought knowing one's truth would mean finding oneself. I now wish I had never discovered the reality of my situation. I wish I'd stayed cocooned within that lie of forgetfulness.

Lies are pretty. The truth is messy.

I've found that most lies start out with some form of truth embedded deep inside them. Then, just like stones which tumble down the stream to the mouth of a river, the tiny lies which were so miniscule to begin with tumble and bang into one another along the journey. They strike the barricades, then fill the leftover holes with small bits of falsehood to fit a narrative or a desire.

My story was always outlined with a thinly veiled coating of lies. A coating which, at one time, I chose to look beyond in order to see only what I wanted. Now, my story no longer has that shiny veil to shield me from the pain of my truth.

My truth is that, at some point in time, I was a murderer. And that point in time wasn't even long ago. My heart threatens to shatter at the thought of all those souls lost on the palace grounds. The ones no longer breathing due to my arrows piercing through their beating hearts. The memory is a punch to the gut which takes my breath away.

I can no longer say I *was* a murderer. I still am. No wonder my soul has dimmed and frayed.

As we walk in a silent line through the unforgiving jungle, the sounds of the sea fading, a shuddering breath slips out as I try to rein in my wayward emotions. It's one of the few sounds disrupting the ominous silence, causing a few of those in front of me to cut their gazes in my direction. By the looks on their faces, I know my moment of weakness brings them far too much joy.

I steel my features. I refuse to let my captors think they've won. I would rather die a thousand deaths than to let any of them know the extent of the storm raging within my mind.

But the wayward tears which continue to fall sell me out. I blame it on the lingering haze of the drug which took me under, which is still fighting me at every turn. It takes all my strength to keep one foot moving in front of the other.

But even I know that's a lie. These tears aren't from the drugs. They're the evidence of the torrent in my mind.

I seal my lips as I focus on inhaling deeply but silently through my nose, keeping my eyes trained ahead.

Which brings me back to my feet, my dress, *my soul*.

The only sounds I hear outside of the crashing waves disappearing behind me are quiet rips of fabric being yanked from the hem of my dress as they are snagged on fallen branches and rising roots as we venture further into the forest.

I pretend little pieces of myself are falling away with it, now to be trodden into the ground and forgotten. Maybe if I imagine I am no longer me—if I see myself as a cracked orb, a torn dress—I can no longer be hurt by any of it. A person can feel pain; an object cannot.

Right foot.

Left foot.

Right foot.

The thick green vines which stretch across the ground and soar into the sky catch my attention more than once. The expanse of the twisting knots seems endless. But if I can keep my focus on the forest around me, perhaps the others will truly fade away. Or at least, I can pretend they are little more than a fading hallucination for a while. Maybe if these people aren't real, and this place isn't real, and what I see is all just a figment of my fractured mind, then I can slowly slip into a welcome oblivion.

Unfortunately, I don't get that reprieve. My mental tricks are nothing but that, a mirage. What's happening to me is real.

I turn back to look at those I can see and count. If I can't bury myself within the depths of darkness to drown this out, maybe it's time to choose another path.

There are fourteen guards—including Tarak, Micel, and Jaxon—in this line with me. Both men and women, and based on their dress and the emblem which is seared onto the breast of their leathers, I assume they all belong to Himerak's settlement within the trees.

My eyes shift around the brooding men and women to find they each—with the exception of Tarak—have some version of colorful strings wrapped into the intricate braids which appear as a crown atop them. And just as before, after that first individual meeting with Himerak, I wonder which color means what. Who holds the highest rank outside of Tarak? Who will decide my fate?

There is something else I notice that wasn't there before. Each wears a small silver like pendant around their necks. It isn't gaudy like the jewelry in Halabar. If anything, most of the small circular pieces appear to have seen better days and I can't tell if it is better suited for uniform decoration or a tool.

If it's the latter, my best guess is it will somehow be used on me. Against me.

Most of the guards are covered in scars or burn marks of various severities, and all meet my gaze with complete and utter contempt.

Their narrow eyes seem to drink me in from top to bottom, and a few even slow their step to match mine and spit at my feet.

A plethora of what I assume are vulgar words and gestures are thrown my way. If my bound hands aren't obvious enough, their actions prove I am definitely an unwelcome outsider this time.

But there is one person I cannot find.

Ranya.

My only guess is she's no longer living. Her unwavering support and protection of those within the settlement became her end.

I think I knew, even then. Even in the throes of the attack from Halabar, I knew. When Micel fitted us with weapons and quickly shuttled us out of *his* home, he said Ranya was holding them back. She was fighting them off. She was standing against Halabar. Maybe we should have stayed and done the same. Maybe, we shouldn't have run like the cowards we were. The coward I still am.

I shake my head as confusion barrels through me. That is wrong. I shouldn't have stayed and fought against Halabar because from what I now see, they were never the enemy. Maybe those within the settlement were truly my enemy all along. I was just too caught up to see what was right in front of me.

Still, the thought of Ranya and what she has sacrificed holds true. There was a moment in time when I was jealous of her; jealous of the fact she and Tarak once shared something I now know we never will. I now know I never want.

I couldn't care less about the miniscule contest over a man not worthy of my nightmares, let alone my dreams. Now, I'm jealous of the fact she was brave enough to go down fighting for something she believed in. I am jealous because she did everything I wasn't brave enough to do myself.

But now I see the reality staring me down, even if I don't want to fully accept it. And this time I get to choose my path.

Determination solidifies as racing thoughts of my next moves take hold. I will show them no weakness. I will keep my head high and meet each one of their gazes.

Right foot.

Left foot.

Right foot.

When Jaxon eventually falls into line beside me, I find his eyes, once warm and gentle, have been replaced with a steely, hate-filled stare. I mirror the look and though he quickly recovers, there is just a moment where he falters and a hint of the man I once knew breaks through the crack.

When I look behind us again, I find the barrage of guards following closely; mere footsteps separate us. Many, if not all, have some form of weapon in their hands. Any one of them could easily take me down from behind. A quick slice of a sword through waiting flesh, the stab of a knife to a well-placed location, or even the blow of a fist at my temple could end me at any moment and I wouldn't even see it coming.

Heat surges through my hands at the thought. And though pain rages forth with each movement, I clench my fist in effort to drown out what I know will soon be released.

They think I am their prisoner.

But the truth is, I am about to become their worst enemy.

Right foot.

Left foot.

Right foot.

I look to the side. To *him*. I want him to see the steely determination now focused in my stare. But he doesn't even look my way, and instead I catch a glimpse of the features of someone else I have come to know and then lost.

I turn back, facing ahead and away from his traitorous nature.

Rhea's face now fills the void, and it is all I can do not to collapse to the ground at the memory of her. For just a moment, I wonder if she, too, was in on the deception. Was she also a culprit in this scheme? Was kind, sweet Rhea my enemy? Was it my action—or better yet, inaction—which killed her?

No.

No. No. No. I will not allow my mind to shift in such a direction. I will forever believe nothing but love filled her heart.

My presence in the settlement may have been the catalyst for the attack, but the only reason I was even there was because of . . . because of *him*.

I look up once more, silently begging him to acknowledge what he did only to find his weathered hair is long and unkempt, his dark-rimmed eyes allude to sleepless nights, and though it may seem he is parading a captured prisoner before his crew, he bears no triumph in his stature.

If anything, he appears defeated.

Dejected.

A small shell of the man I once believed him to be.

He should.

He should feel every ounce of pain which I wager is surging through him. He deserves it. He caused it. He is the *enemy*. My enemy.

I only stare a moment more, and then I set my gaze forward, promising myself not to take a chance on looking his way again.

Not to take a chance on trusting him again.

On loving him.

On missing him.

On waiting for him.

Not to take a chance on *him* again.

III

We silently continue deeper into the jungle, weaving between vines and trees, disturbing the unseen small creatures who are scared out of their hiding spots as we approach. Déjà vu surges through every sense I possess as I recall my first venture through a wooded paradise with this man.

My eyes sweep across the area, and though we are once again trekking into dense trees and brush, this jungle is unquestionably different from the settlement forest. The ground, while still somewhat green, seems lifeless compared to the forest I became used to those first weeks in this world. This place is less colorful. Almost as if all the life has been sucked out of it, leaving only the tortured memories of a once vibrant world in the wake. The inky moss is splayed out in patches along the tree bases. The birds, if there are any, are silent.

I question my eyesight, wondering how much of the drug still lingers within me as I watch the low-hanging branches and scattered vines part to reveal a path through the brush. The dead jungle is leading the way, as if it knows exactly where we are meant to be going. There is no breeze, and yet the vines tense and shift as if moved by a thought. Or, perhaps, they recoil in fear of the unknown woman heading in their direction.

For just a moment, I wonder if something more sinister is lying within these towering trees. Something from this world that I have yet to encounter.

Just as the thought goes through my mind, the once-still air wraps around me in a cold breeze, causing a chill to race down my spine and goosebumps to form along my bruised and battered skin. My stomach fills with acid and my feet become leaden as they sink into the ground. As my lips begin to tremble with the frigid burst, I hear a high-pitched whistle spear through the surrounding brush. The piercing noise rattles my mind, fracturing my thoughts.

It starts on my left and then curls around the trees to my right. Even the leaves seem to recoil at the notion of what this could mean.

"Find me."

The tortured whisper seeps inside my mind, its voice so old and withered, and yet fresh and new.

"Save me."

Its sound grates against my bones as it makes its way inside my body. It courses through my veins and makes a home deep within my heart.

"Become me."

The urgent plea is somewhere between a river of pleasure and a pit of agony. It swirls in my mind and settles heavily in the pit of my stomach.

There is no warning when the nausea that I have been holding off finally consumes me and the contents of my stomach spill forth as a lancing heat spreads through me. A battle within surges forward and my body feels as if it is being ripped in two.

Then a blinding white anguish swallows me. A dark, icy cloak of despair ensnares me—*becomes* me. A whirling gust of wind surrounds me, blinding me from those around. The cold takes over, piercing every square inch of my body with a thousand shards of ice.

"Become me."

I scream out and fall forward as the last words cause grief and anger like I have never known to hurtle through my body. Every vein, muscle, hair, and bone threatens to shred into tiny fragments at the sound. My sight is stolen, and no matter how much I try to force the air inside, my lungs won't allow it.

When heat comes barrelling upward from deep within, I cry out in relief, but the cry quickly turns to a scream as the battle rages on. My body is being boiled from the inside out as it tries to melt the frost covering my skin, tries to break free of the glacial wind which surrounds me.

And then, as if the sound was merely a figment of my own demented imagination, my sight returns, the wind dies out, and the grief and icicles, the boiling heat within, they all subside. Through the fabric of the cloth, my surely bloodied hands fist the crumbled, vomit-covered leaves. The dead forest slowly comes back into view and my body is yanked upward and back to meet the confused stares of those around me.

"She's insane," a woman declares as she shakes her head in annoyance.

Tarak pays her no attention as he stares at me, worry in his eyes. "What was that?" he whispers as his hands cup my cheeks.

In my stunned confusion at what just occurred, I momentarily forget the hatred I now hold for the man, and don't push away before my still weak mind falters at his touch. A sense of calm surges into me, and I silently berate myself.

One touch from him and I almost forget everything that has happened. But then I directly push away the thought.

He is no longer my ally, and I will no longer allow him to be the one I cling to. If there is one thing I have learned, it is that there is no one I can trust. Only myself.

I keep my trembling lips shut as I bend forward in order to remove myself from his touch. To save face, I make a clumsy attempt to wipe away the sweat forming at my brow and falling onto my shoulder.

My body is such a contradiction. I'm a mixture of internal burning flames and glacial rivers of ice, and when I look down to my arms, I find them covered in goosebumps and sweat as my body shivers.

Though the cool air is a relief to my lungs, it is torturous to my body. And then I hear it once more. The piercing scream surges forward. But this time I'm ready, and I brace myself for the onslaught of agony which is sure to come. My eyes catch on Tarak and Jaxon at my side, but neither seems to notice what I now feel as the icy breeze crashes through me, through my ears, my body, my mind . . .

"Find me . . . "

My chest expands and I go still, my breathing becoming labored as I push the words away. A second pain lances through my hands. A burning sensation covers my palms as I watch the golden cloth glow from within. An eternal struggle of light and dark, heat and cold, fire and ice consumes me.

"Become me!" It screams out in horror at not being able to surge past my defenses.

But I continue to fight back. I don't let it take hold as something inside me I can't quite understand remains steady and strong. This time my senses aren't overrun by the unknown attack, but remain unbreakable.

For the first time, I smile at the thought.

The others become frantic with worry as they catch sight of the now glowing cloth, and I hear their pleas to end me—to end what they can't understand.

"Find me . . . "

The rasping voice coos, a soft melody meant for a child. It tickles my ear and soothes the lingering pain, but I know its game and I don't let it in. Finally, the light dulls and the roaring in my ears dampens as the frantic pleas to end my life increase in veracity.

But Tarak pays no heed to their words. He just looks my way with questioning, concerned eyes. I meet his stare with conviction.

The crew is confused. I can hear their tones of frustration, but the words slither around my region of consciousness as I focus on what just occurred. The only thoughts my mind allows in are those six words. A tender melody on repeat.

Find me.

Save me.

Become me.

"Nera?" Tarak finally voices. But it doesn't truly register. The words are muffled and far away.

I'm too engrossed in the breath of warning which tickles my neck, and how in God's name I was just able to stop it from taking hold. But it doesn't give up. One last valiant effort as it skirts along my skin, noting I have every defense locked down, before spreading out to surround me as the words fade away.

Maybe I should thank my rattled brain for that horrid pit I buried myself within all those weeks ago. It may have just saved me.

The world stands still, unmoving, as my captors assess my odd behavior, and I fully realize only I was privy to whatever just occurred. I wonder if they even noticed the wind or felt the chill or if they only witnessed a prisoner going mad.

Something is happening. Something I don't quite understand, but hell if I'm going to give voice to something in front of the one person I know I can never trust again.

"Nera?" Tarak calls to me again, but my only reply is a glare of warning. It causes him to pause for just a moment, but when I don't answer, he quickly reclaims that face devoid of emotion, tugs my arm, and beckons me forward.

But my feet are immobile . . . suspended in that inbetween. As if a frozen block of ice stands mere inches before me, holding me still, telling me to turn back and retreat as the warmth from my body desperately tries to melt away that which keeps me frozen in place.

And then I'm jolted forward by a man from behind.

"Move, *queen.*" The man's voice is as smooth and menacing as a slithering snake, the words rippling off his tongue. I fight the momentary sense of betrayal that Tarak has told them more about me—about us—than I had known. His stupid little nickname for me, the same one that once caused welcome sensations to race along my skin, now does nothing but further build that wall between us.

Tarak's arm leaves mine as he grabs the man, nearly lifting him off the ground from the neck of his shirt.

"Do not touch her," Tarak grinds out through gritted teeth. The man balks in annoyance, but I hear his feet slam to the ground and then his shuffled steps as he slowly sinks farther behind.

I try a forward step, unsure if my body will allow the motion. With my movement, the heat crashes through the ice, shattering it into a million tiny shards of light which flicker as they fall away into the abyss of my mind.

And then the cold is gone, and with my arm pulled forward once more, my feet continue on.

Right foot.

Left foot.

Right foot.

It is a long and silent walk. One filled with just my inner thoughts to keep me company, and sometimes those are exponentially worse than what any enemy could throw my way. Mostly those thoughts circle around what in the hell just happened to me. How did I hear something that obviously no one else did? And why could I feel it in my bones? There are even a few moments in which I almost convince myself it didn't happen.

But then that begs the thought I'm not sure what's worse; the idea that it was real, or the idea that it was just me.

Broken and shattered me.

After trekking for far too long over uneven ground, we finally come to a stop.

Instead of guiding us up into a tree as I was expecting, *he* pushes the vines away from a large boulder, revealing the stone to be a trap door, exactly the same as the boulder which led underground that first day in the Mulara Forest.

As soon as the door is fully open, the light from the sun exposes a ramp-like path to the world below. I wonder how many of these passageways lie hidden around Halabar, and say a silent prayer of thanks that there is not a ladder this time. I wouldn't be able to steady myself with the way my hands are bound.

Déjà vu hits once again.

But this underground world is quite different from the passageway Tarak and I ventured down before. I can see it's a massive, well-lit hallway with various doors built right into the dirt. I'm sure it was once a pristine location. Now it appears to be a long-deserted bunker, meant only to be utilized for the most dire of situations.

Acid fills the pit of my stomach once more, the bile inching its way upward, burning as it moves. The silent warning I can no longer ignore.

My attention shifts to the cloth covering the design on my wrist as a strange sort of muted prickling caresses the area. My body—my mark—is somehow connected to this world, and it is warning me as to what is to come. I just don't yet understand enough to discern what exactly it's warning against.

Then, as if set forth by some unknown cue, the sinister feeling which has hovered over me during the last few miles dissipates. It sinks away the farther we go underground. At first, the lightness in the air is a welcome reprieve, but it slowly turns to emptiness, as if a shield I didn't know was there has finally solidified.

He never leaves my side, or even strays more than a few inches from me. At this point, despite my more than constant attempts at shrugging off the touch, his hand might as well be glued to my arm. Even when we walk through a passageway barely wide enough for two, he never lets me go.

Instead, I find his body practically flush with mine. I tense as I await the heat which is sure to come. I don't want to feel anything he has to give me, not now or ever again. And then it hits me. That heat pouring from him, the kind that lured me in so completely all those weeks ago, has dulled to a barely discernible note. I wonder if it has anything to do with the damp cold of the underground.

My body further tenses as an eruption of anger at all the death he has mostly likely caused bubbles up and then a rush of serenity floods through me. I grunt in frustration at the warring emotions. Anger, calm, confusion, certainty. Again and again, they all come and go with no care as to how exhausting it is for me. I want to scream out. If my hands were free, they would surely be clawing at my hair or skin, trying desperately to set free whatever this is that's stuck inside me.

There is a slight yank on my arm, and in the midst of my own agony, I lift my eyes to find *his* face. Pinched brows and uncertainty meet my gaze. I quickly turn away, unwilling to spend any more time on that traitorous visage, now yearning for the chaos I felt only moments ago.

We continue on.

The echoes of footsteps become less and less, and I realize the men and women behind me are each splitting off into various rooms along the way. *He* lets me go only after he leads the two of us through a door and places me into a barely stable wooden chair. Dust swirls into the air, and my tired body sinks into the hard seat as he finds his own chair in front of me.

My eyes stay trained on the floor below. I don't even look up when I catch sight of two sets of boots moving into the room, the door quietly shutting behind them. They slowly cross the floor, flanking my sides as they move to stand behind me.

"What do you need?" Tarak inquires, clearly annoyed. At first, I'm unsure which one of us he's questioning. If he's addressing me, the answer would probably be a maniacal laugh, so, in an effort not to appear any more crazed than they likely already believe me to be, I stay as silent as possible.

Besides, what I need he can no longer provide.

Safety.

Security.

Hope.

All the things I once thought *he* embodied. I have since come to realize this man is the furthest thing from the man I thought I met that first morning. That Tarak was a pretty-faced lie designed to draw me in at every turn.

"Just making sure the plan continues on and nothing else happens . . . " Jaxon trails off as I hear the soft thud of his body leaning against the dirt-covered wall behind me.

"I don't need you two watching over me. Wait outside," Tarak commands.

"We're not leaving," the other man answers, his voice unfamiliar.

"I am your commander. You–"

"Tarak," Jaxon quickly cuts him off, but then I hear him deflate, as if the sting has finally left. "I'm not here as a fellow guard. I'm not even here as an enemy of Halabar—or of . . . her," he adds, my chest tightening. "I'm here as *your* best friend, and I'm not leaving."

Tarak eyes the man standing behind me before he takes a deep breath, letting his shoulders settle and turning his attention back to me.

"Are you going to use it?" His tone is dejected, and at first I'm not sure why he's asking me this.

What is it that I could use?

"Nera?" he urges.

I close my eyes at the sound of my name on his lips. Before, it caused waves of heat to course through my body. Now, all it causes is ripples of cold pain to expand where his warmth once filled the chasm.

"Nera?"

My eyes squint in confusion and my body tenses. No matter how much I want to deny him the satisfaction of an answer, I can't bear to hear my name pass his lips again.

"What?" It's barely a whisper. I'm not even sure how he heard it. But if I speak any louder, I know my exhausted voice will betray me. And I can't let him hear that. If I am to promise myself only one thing in this unfortunate life, it is that I will remain unyielding when it comes to him. I am no longer going to lean into the role of the pitiful girl trapped in an impossible situation. I will take this situation and make it mine.

"Are you going to try to kill us?" Tarak questions in exasperation, and my eyes finally meet his.

"I should," I seethe. And I mean it.

His body almost imperceptibly recoils at my words, and I can't quite figure out why. But he quickly recovers, a bored expression covering his features once more.

"That wasn't the question I asked."

I huff in indignation, rolling my eyes, and then cringe as another traitorous tear falls to the ground below.

"Killing you *is* the only appropriate answer," I retort.

He reaches out to brush a finger along my cheek, and I jerk backward at the unwanted touch. "I'm not done with you yet," he purrs into the air, and I scoff at the implication. But he squares his shoulders and leans in closer, now mere inches from my face. "I need to check this wound. I can't have you dying on me. Not yet, at least." He smirks as he looks to the two others and then refocuses on me. "I'm going to have to unwrap this to do so. Are you going to try to kill us or not?"

"I don't even know how." My shoulders deflate in what I hope gives off the impression of bored annoyance as my eyes once again hit the floor. I shouldn't want to kill him, but I do, and he knows it. Because of Mina. The lies. The betrayal. Everything he has taken away from me.

"Did your deflecting skills improve during your time in Halabar?" He chuckles, and my sight again finds his sapphire gaze. His brows lift and a smirk hints at the corner of his lips. It causes my blood to boil. "If I remember correctly, you were already well versed in–"

"Don't," I spit the word out.

"Don't what?" he counters while his smile continues to grow, and with it, my anger.

"Don't do that. Don't try to play with me. The ruse is over. The game is finished. You won. No need to pretend any longer."

He again catches sight of the two men behind me and then abruptly straightens as I watch the mask free of emotion slide back into place.

"You're wrong, Nera." I swallow at his callous tone. "The game has just begun." His stare is piercing. "And *you* are the final piece to the puzzle."

IV

"I'm going to ask you one last time, and this time you will give me a straight answer. Do you understand?"

I nod my head in agreement, knowing there is no other alternative from here on out.

"Will you use it? Will you try to kill us?"

"No. I won't use it. I won't try to kill you."

He pauses for a moment as if my words didn't quite catch. Confusion mars his features. But he quickly refocuses, "Thank you." He reaches out to grab my hands, but I quickly pull back, wincing at the pain which flares with the movement, and his face tightens.

"But only because I don't know how," I add through gritted teeth as my quivering voice betrays the strength I'm so desperate to exude. He chuckles slightly at the words, and for some reason, that sound—the sound of his amusement at my pain—is the worst thing I have ever heard.

"At least you're being honest." He shrugs, and I hear a note of warning seep from Jaxon before Tarak quickly gives him a silencing glare. He reaches toward me once more, but again, I pull away.

"No. Not you. Someone else can check them." No longer able to hold in the emotion, my cheeks slowly become a river-stained canvas. I blink as I unsuccessfully will my body to comply just this once. It never does.

His eyes crease at the sight, but with a quick shake of his head, he gets back to the matter at hand.

"No one else. Only me," he retorts, as if I have no say in the matter, and once again reaches out to grab my wrists. I quickly yank my arms back.

"Find. Someone. Else." I bite out the words through clenched teeth as I try to conceal the pain I feel. The small needle-like thorns continue to bring waves of agony as they cut and pierce my skin with even the tiniest motion. But it's nothing compared to the torment racing through me at the feel of his touch.

He watches me for just a second before his eyes focus on mine.

"I don't think you understand, Nera. No one touches you but me."

"I would rather rot!" The words come barreling out of my mouth before I even have time to think, and he chuckles, not giving them a second thought.

"You're still bleeding." He gestures toward the ground with indifference, my statement having had no effect on him.

I cast my attention to my hands and pull back, a gasp leaving my lips. I knew the cuts were bad, based on the constant pain which surged through me with even the most minimal of movements. Still, the small pool of blood forming between my feet is shocking.

"My guess is you've nicked a rather large vein." He stands to retrieve medical supplies from a kit nearby.

It's not enough blood loss to kill me, but with the combination of the drugs still lingering within and my already exhausted state, I'm sure I will become even more woozy as the minutes tick by. Something I cannot allow, not if I'm going to find a way to get out of here and back to–

My body jolts at the realization I haven't yet seen the two other captives.

"Where are Riann and Alesia?" My voice, sharp with panic, bounces off the walls of the small room.

Tarak goes still at the table. His fingers flex as his shoulders rise with deep breaths, and the frayed edge of his resolve almost gives way.

"Don't worry, Nera. Your friend and betrothed are perfectly fine."

At his words, an ease rushes along my bones, and I sink further into the chair. He turns back to face me, supplies in hand, and I catch the smallest hint of an emotion I can't quite place flash across his features. For a heartbeat, I see the Tarak I encountered that first day. But a mere second and one deep breath later, he's gone. The man who stares me down now is not the Tarak I met in the forest, but a trained killer on a mission.

The only problem is, the focus of that mission is me.

He mumbles something under his breath as he carefully removes the blood-soaked coverings, placing them on a nearby table. Though I've felt the pain for hours, now is the first time I can actually assess the damage. I go still at the sight of my wrists tangled within the crimson-stained vines. Everytime he unwraps a cord of the binding, I feel the thorns pierce into flesh as they drag across, further marring my skin. When my wrists are finally free, I all but heave at the mangled sight.

I can't help but wince as he flips my wrist over. When his eyes land on my mark, he stills, and I recoil as he runs a thumb over the intricate design which has somehow escaped the jagged cuts now outlining it.

When our eyes meet, I swear there is a silent plea hidden within them. He doesn't say a word as his eyes linger on mine and his breathing picks up in rhythm. I don't back down as I meet his stare, hoping he understands the message I am sending through my gaze.

You did this to me.

You lied to me.

You hurt me.

You made me BLEED.

"Hurry up. I need a drink," the soldier behind me urges in annoyance, breaking the trance Tarak and I were stuck within. Suddenly his words cause the pain of hunger to settle in my stomach.

"So does she," I hear Jaxon add.

"I'm not wasting good ale on—"

"I'm not talking about ale. I'm talking about food, water," Jaxon quickly counters. "Tarak, she hasn't eaten or had water in too long. You said yourself we can't kill her yet."

I almost turn to give Jaxon a grateful glance at his somehow backward way of assisting me, but before I can move, a loaf of bread is shoved into my waiting hands.

"You have two minutes before I re-wrap this around you." Tarak holds up the crimson cloth. "Use it wisely," he commands before tossing it on the table behind him, reaching into his pack, and setting a canteen before me.

I'm certain it takes me less than thirty seconds to down the water and bread, not even caring when my stomach almost protests at the urgency of delivery.

Then he gets to work. This isn't anything like the first time he bandaged my cuts. He isn't gentle, kind, or loving. If anything, I think he is yanking and pulling a little more than is necessary, and he's definitely adding extra solution to cause the burning to linger.

But what he doesn't know is this is exactly what I need. This physical pain is the only way to outrun the devastating heartache he's caused—the invisible pain I refuse to let him see. So I grit my teeth, let the sting sink in, and welcome the waves of torment which wash over me, knowing I am finally feeling something real, even if it is agonizing.

He takes his time. I refuse to watch as he meticulously pulls out each thorn which has wedged its way into my skin and wipes away the blood seeping from each tiny hole. By the time he's finished, my hands are on fire from the burn of the solution, and the white rag he used to wipe the blood away has turned a deep scarlet.

He then covers my hands in a soothing balm, and rewraps the same blood-stained cloth back around my wrists. This time there are no thorn-covered vines.

I barely have a moment to register my relief before my world is once again shattered.

"I'll take her to the pit," the unknown soldier volunteers, and my eyes flit up.

The pit? That sounds like somewhere I definitely do *not* want to be.

I almost expected Tarak to balk at the statement. He appears to be the one in command, but he doesn't say a word. He barely even glances in my direction as he puts away the supplies.

"Jaxon, go with Kies and meet me at base after. We have some things to discuss."

Jaxon steps forward and nods in agreement before Kies roughly yanks me out of the chair and to my feet. My attention snaps to where his white-knuckled fingers are squeezing my upper arm, and I know there will be a handprint-shaped bruise there soon.

My eyes catch Tarak's just as I pass by. In an instant, he shifts his stare to the wall behind me as I'm marched out of the small room and into a new maze of hallways.

Neither Kies nor Jaxon utters a word as we move. Kies's death grip only tightens with each passing curve in the hall, and I swear Jaxon is wound so tightly he barely breathes. I keep a steady stride, matching theirs and refusing to let them notice the shaking in my legs, which seems to increase with each step we take. It's not until we turn the corner into a darkened passageway that I falter.

The only noise in the empty underground hollow is a faint rushing of water I can only hope is far in the distance. But with each step forward the sound increases and that feeling of dread further settles in.

"I can't see anything," I object when Kies tries to pull me forward into the unknown.

"Nothing for you to see." His voice is even and direct, laced with an air of amusement. He yanks me into the darkness, this time keeping my feet half a step in front of his, guiding me from behind.

My heartbeat picks up at the loss of sight, and even in this cold underground, I can feel the sweat starting to form at my brow. Panic builds within me. I expect the heat to come and for flames to burst forth as dread expands to fill every inch of my being, but nothing happens.

I reach out the only way I know how, hoping against all odds my once friend still holds at least the tiniest amount of warmth for me.

"Jaxon, I–" My would-be plea ends in a scream as I'm shoved forward onto a rickety slab of wood barely a foot wide and two feet long. It creaks under my feet as water sloshes up from what I guess is something like a moat below and then fall into pitch-black nothingness.

V

There's no time to brace before my left hip and shoulder crash into the hard, dirt-covered surface of the pit. The air is purged from my lungs, and my exposed skin is sliced by the razor sharp bits of dirt and gravel coating the ground.

I desperately try to inhale as my body fights the pain, but the wind has been knocked from my chest.

I can't breathe.

I can't see.

I can't *move*.

A silent scream pours from my lips just as solid hands reach out to grasp me. I yank away as the air finally enters my lungs, sending a roaring pain through my chest.

When I twist upward, my eyes catch sight of the barely illuminated air as Jaxon quickly leans down and over the edge of the pit, a lantern now in his grip and a look of shock and concern etched across his features.

"Let's go. She'll be fine, and if she isn't, then that's an even better outcome," Kies says as he spits down into the pit, saliva landing on my face.

Disgusting.

Then they're gone, and with them the small amount of light which afforded me any sight.

"Nera!"

The whispered but urgent voice comes as a sweet surprise, but it still takes a moment for me to recognize who it is in the inky darkness.

"Nera?" He pulls me closer, small shards of dirt nicking along my skin as I move. "Are you okay? I need you to say something. Tell me you're okay!" Riann's voice is weak, but his words are frantic and rushed as he coughs through the swirl of dust stirred up by the force of my impact.

As he speaks, his hands are skimming every part of my body, blindly assessing my condition. My only answer is a muffled laugh at the memory of someone else doing this not so long ago. Except *then* I was hiding in a tree, my legs were covered in blood, and my body was screaming for more.

He stalls at the noise, as if my slight chuckle is an indication I have truly gone mad.

Maybe I have.

That might be easier to bear.

"Nera?" His hand finds its way to my face, and he wipes away the damp curls plastered to my skin.

"I'm okay." The words are barely a whisper before I suck in another breath, so very thankful for the air which now easily makes its way in, and I use my upper arm to swipe away the foul-smelling spit which runs down my cheek.

"Thank the Elders." He gathers me in his arms and buries his face against my neck, gently rocking me. I almost lean into his touch, nearly giving in to the need to feel something real. "I thought they had killed you." His voice breaks as he whimpers in relief. My body tenses. That mist of warning which wrapped itself around me when we first arrived at this underground bunker lingers in the air.

"They won't kill her. They need her." My head spins, trying to discern the location of Alesia's voice. Just as I'm about to ask where she is, I feel her hands reach out in search of me. She finds my foot and sighs, relief filling the empty void which surrounds us and an inkling of calm surges through me at the nothing that she is okay. Even she needed to physically touch me to make sure it was real.

But her words bounce through my head, causing a myriad of questions to resurface, one echoing over the others.

They need me?

I heard Tarak say that before I ended up on that boat. And he just mentioned I was a missing piece. But why?

"Are you hurt? Can you move?" Riann slowly adjusts my position, shifting my train of thought and allowing me to sit awkwardly before him. I twist and move as much as I can manage given the fact my hands are all but useless, wrapped as they are beneath the heavy cloth.

"I think everything's in working order." I chuckle again, but the noise ends in a sob as my voice breaks, and the dam which has done its best at holding back the river of tears finally breaks.

The resulting torrent might be enough to drown out the world.

At least I'm afforded the shield of darkness. It helps to conceal just how broken I have become—just how shattered my body and mind are after the hell of what has happened.

I expect four hands to find me in the darkness, and I steel myself for the awkward embrace, but neither Riann nor Alesia reaches out. Instead, Riann reluctantly releases his hold on me, and I hear the dirt and rocks shift as he moves backward. Maybe they do know me more than I seem to know myself. They wait patiently as the tears start to slow. Eventually, all that's left are the hiccups which come after.

I only speak when I'm sure I won't fall back into the weak person I am now so desperate to break free of.

"Can you get this cloth off?"

I push my hands forward, hoping one of them will know what I'm referring to, even if they can't see it. Even without the vines, the binding is tight enough that I can't manage removing it by myself.

"The gold one on your hands?" Riann questions. I hear him scoot closer to me and feel his soft fingers grab the underside of my arms, pulling me back to him. I decide not to correct him. It's true, the cloth once held a beautiful golden hue which shimmered in the wavering light on the boat. What he doesn't know is the previous sheen has been dulled, drowned out. It is now covered by a deep crimson, filled with the remnants of a physical pain I long for.

Thank *fuck* for the dark.

"Yeah. They wrapped this cloth around my hands, and I can't–"

"It's useless to even try," Alesia cuts in. "We won't be able to get it off." Unwanted icy tendrils run down my spine, and I stiffen at the thought that whatever came for me on our journey here has found me once again. "It can only be removed by a Celestra." Her tired voice creeps across the darkened space. I almost sigh in relief when the sudden cold slowly dissipates.

"I'm a Celestra. Why can't I get it off?"

"The cloth nullifies your powers. You won't be able to use your gifts while it's on," she clarifies, not waiting for my next question.

Joke's on them. I wouldn't know how to use my gifts, anyway.

"They think I'll use my gifts—the fire—to kill them?"

"Wouldn't you?" Riann adds through gritted teeth. The words are spat out as if each leaves a sour taste in his mouth. But I don't answer. And they don't question me further.

Even with the minimal use of my hands, I find the cool, dirt covered wall of the pit and lean against it, letting my head fall back.

Maybe it's the fact we're underground, or maybe it's because it's so dark, but I want nothing more than to just wrap my arms around my middle as I hold on tight. But with the bindings on my hands and wrists clasped together, I can barely even move. Frustration and hatred toward my captors grow.

"Why?" I ask the dust which dances around me, begging for an answer.

"Nera." Alesia breathes out my name in an exasperated sigh.

"Why is all of this happening to me? I'm no one special. I don't have any answers to give them."

"They're worried you could end it all. They're worried you are the key to ending this centuries-long war between the centras." There is so much truth hiding behind her words.

Still, I furrow my brow in confusion. "Wouldn't that be a good thing?"

I'm still not yet sure how I would end a war which has been raging on for far longer than I've been alive. And even if I could, that's what Tarak wants. I know it is. He told me so himself. As did Koreed. They want it to end. They want peace. I just wish they were on the same side of the flipping coin which has become my life as of late.

Alesia shuffles around as if trying to find the most comfortable spot in the darkness, and then reaches out to find my arm. Even though she can't see it, I feel her swipe her thumb across the mark which has determined the course of my life thus far.

"Do you remember what heartstone is?" she tentatively asks.

Riann quickly cuts her off. "Alesia?" His tone is edged with frustration and fear—a warning in itself—and I wish I could see what secrets his eyes hold.

"She has to know. If she's going to fight this and be on the right side of history, she must know. She's ready," Alesia all but commands, leaving me further confused by Riann's response.

"Ready for what?" I plead.

I hear Riann's quick grunt of irritation. He's not happy with where this conversation is about to lead. Then Alesia finally speaks.

"The trees in Centra I—the ones which fill the Mulara Forest—are not like the trees across the rest of Ithesin. They are not like the trees which fill the other centras. The trees of the Mulara Forest are sacred. They were once the center of our world. They're not born from the dirt as the others. They are born from the souls of our ancestors."

"I don't understand?" I'm not sure whether I voice the question aloud or if the astonished sounds are just in my head.

"The cloth wound around your hands is made from heartstone. It's the mineral at the center of the trees. It can be harvested, but to do so requires a delicate process. Heartstone is what powers our world. It gives this planet and its people life. But in the wrong hands, it will bring nothing but death," she warns as I feel her squeeze my arm in emphasis. "It's what made Halabar and the homes Himerak's settlement is built from. It's magical in an alluring way, and if used correctly, it's invincible." She breathes life into every word.

I think back to the way Rhea's home seemed to have come directly from the tree itself. As if it grew into the form of the shelter they needed. There were no nails or grooves I could see. It was all so perfect it felt unreal.

"These trees . . . they're only in Centra I?" I inquire.

"Yes. And the other centras have been vying for them for years. Hundreds of years. They want the heartstone mineral found deep inside to power their nations. They want to build unspeakable weapons, and right now, Koreed and our people in Halabar are all that stand in their way. Those other nations would wipe out our sacred forest if they had the chance. And if Himerak hadn't fled into the trees so many years ago and kept our people from accessing what is rightfully ours, this war would have long since ended."

"That doesn't make sense," I counter.

Alesia laughs lightly as if she almost agrees. "Which part?"

"Are they alive? The trees, I mean?" I shake my head at the realization of my odd wording. "I'm sure they're alive like any other plant, but are they alive like you and me? Do they have a soul inside them?" I clarify.

"Yes and no," Riann interjects. "They are made from the souls that leave our world. When someone dies, there's a ceremony. We give the body back to Ithesin, and in doing so, the soul attaches to the land and they bring what is needed for our world."

"So those soul-filled trees give Ithesin what is needed?"

"Yes," they answer in unison.

"There is a prophecy from long ago," Alesia adds, and Riann lets out a low grunt of continued frustration she pays no mind to. "There are not only four centras, but also a fifth lying in wait, preparing for the time to come when the world will be bound together again."

Tarak said just the same. He used almost those exact words that night in the cave.

There is said to be a fifth centra that has the tools and power to bring all the people together once more.

"Is that true? Is there another centra?" I wait for them to speak, but their silence is all the confirmation I need. "Where is it? Where is the other centra?" I don't know why I whisper the question. We are alone. But speaking those words aloud seems somewhat traitorous.

Alesia reaches out in the inky blackness, one hand splayed across my beating heart, the other gripping my wrist just below my mark. "Right here."

VI

There's a moment in which I can't feel my heartbeat. My fingers and toes become numb, and my stomach twists as far too many emotions settle within. The darkness blurs with the rim of unshed tears, and my mind dulls out all other thoughts.

"Me?"

"You are the key." Alesia's voice is so low it's almost a whisper on a wayward wind. But I hear it now, just as I heard it from Mina not so long ago.

"How? Why?" Fresh tears fall with the weight of everything this revelation brings forth. "Why me?"

"Why any of us?" Riann counters. "Who are we to question the will of the Elders? Who are we to alter the path set forth for us?" He sounds almost angry.

"*I* am the fifth centra? That doesn't make sense. Centras are made of land, and I am a person. Besides, how am I supposed to bind this world back together when I barely know anything about it in the first place?" My words are no longer a quiet whisper, instead they are a frantic ramble. "And I'm supposed to do this all by myself, while having no memory of my past or knowledge of what I need to do?" The incredulous revelation is forced out as the mountain of what my future has now become settles on my shoulders. "This is insane. I can't do that. I am not–"

"You are not alone. You were *never* alone," Alesia all but argues. "We have been with you every step of the way, and we will continue standing by your side until we win this. Until we–"

"We *must* find the stones," Riann urgently cuts in, his words frantic. "That's what we were doing before everything was destroyed. We can't finish this until we find the stones."

"I have a feeling that *is* what we are doing—what *they* are doing," Alesia counters, and for the first time I note lingering angst in her words. It's also now that I remember Tarak's words just after the battle.

We can't kill her. Not yet, at least. She is the key to the stones.

"What happens after they—after we find these stones?" I implore. "What do they do? Why are they so important?"

I feel Riann lean in just as his sweaty hands grip my cheeks. He is so close I can almost make out his features as he speaks.

"Right now we need to stop worrying about telling stories and start finding a way out of here. We already have one stone, and we know Himerak holds another. We have to find them all before *they* do." Riann's growing disgust is evident in his tone, though I can't discern who he's most angry with. "It's just the three of us from here on out. Just us. Until we get back to Halabar and with my people. You understand me?" His hold on my face grows tighter with each word, and I quickly nod, not sure he would even allow another answer. "Nera!" He urgently whispers my name, making sure I follow along with every word, and although I can barely move with the vice grip he has on me, I frantically nod once more. "We can't let Tarak and those from the settlement get the stones. We can't let him get them either."

He drops his hands in exhaustion as his words sink in. Tarak and Himerak and Micel—all those in the settlement—they believe the Halabarians are on the wrong side. And I am absolutely positive the Halabarians feel the same about those in the settlement. A mutual hatred for a people neither even know.

But, if the heartstone is feeding this world what it needs, if this magical entity is somewhat providing aid to the *right* side, to me, then why has it also provided so much to Halabar's enemy? Why did it give Tarak and those in the settlement exactly what they needed?

"There's something I don't understand." My voice is no longer at the level of a whisper, but I'm still cautious in case someone is lingering above us. "Four centras are in a centuries-long war, fighting over those trees, or rather, what is *inside* those trees, because this 'heartstone' can power their civilizations and build weapons, and basically every single one of these nations is just populated by power hungry individuals."

For some reason, neither responds, and I have a sneaking suspicion that they, along with everyone else I have encountered, may be among the group I just mentioned.

"Why did Himerak defect?"

"What?" Riann's voice is laced with confusion.

"He was the sovereign of Halabar and Centra I, the largest nation on Ithesin. *He* was the sovereign. And from what Tarak said, Centra I is the most powerful of the four." I hear a barely discernible balk come from Riann. "Why would

Himerak give up his sovereignty to wage a secondary war for something he already had in the forest? And don't tell me it's because he fell in love. I don't doubt that, but I don't see Himerak running away from all that power if he knew about the trees and the heartstone."

"I don't have an answer for that," Alesia admits, and I feel a tingling sensation crawl down my spine.

"It doesn't make any sense," I counter.

"Himerak is evil. Sometimes evil motives are not built on the foundation of reason," Riann notes, and for the first time in this conversation, I feel his fingers brush against my covered hand, settling there.

I look up, expecting to see his dark eyes directly in front of me, and yet all I see is unending obsidian. "You said the heartstone provides the people with what's needed? How?"

"This world was built by our Elders long ago," Alesia explains before Riann can answer. "And, while they are no longer here in the way you and I are, they can still influence what happens. They use the trees, the stones, the Celestras, and the heartstone to help guide this world toward something better."

Though they can't see it, I nod my head along in agreement. "They give the people what they need."

"Exactly." Alesia breathes a sigh of relief as I finally seem to put together all the pieces to the puzzle. "Just like they gave us *you*."

I know my next words will cause some strife, yet I can't stop myself.

"The settlement which Himerak needed to house those who escaped the city of Halabar came from the trees." I expect some sort of retort, but neither speaks a word. "I lived in the rooms, I ate at the tables, I ran along the branches. Why would the Elders allow the forest to give Himerak exactly what he needed? Why would it build a city for his people from the ground up if he was the enemy?"

I wait for an answer I know will not come. Stating the truth would mean that, in the history they are outlining, Himerak made at least one right decision. And that notion will never feed well into the idea that he is, and always has been, nothing but a hateful tyrant.

"Nera." I swear Riann's voice is a barely discernible warning, and I can't quite tell who he is fighting against.

It's not lost on me that Riann is hiding something. I can tell from the frustration in his words and the ire he directs at Alesia. Something isn't right. And I may not know much, but I have at least learned not to easily trust those around me.

"What are you hiding?" The blatant implication in my words is clear.

"Why do you believe I'm hiding something?" His tone eases too quickly into effortless grace.

"Riann." I peer out into the darkness, hoping the sound of his name on my lips will bring forth some kind of honesty.

But nothing comes. The silence stretches on.

"You are hiding something from me," I urge.

He scoffs in annoyance. "I am only trying to get you to understand the implications of your actions should you choose the wrong side." That twinge of ice slithers down my spine once more. Anger blooms within my core.

"No. You are hiding something from me." I ignore the pain that seems to linger and lean forward, inching myself in the direction of his voice.

"Stop it, Nera. You're tired and weak. Rest while you can and–"

"I am not *weak!*"

His scoff of indifference grates along my bones. "I just meant you shouldn't take on things you don't need to worry about. Let us handle it."

Heat surges through my veins. "No! I will not sit by and let others lead the way. I'm done being a pawn in everyone's game. I am a fucking Celestra!" My voice starts to shake, but this time it's not from fear but determination and sheer will. "I am a goddamn queen! Now stop hiding shit and be honest!"

There is a stunned silence as both seem too shocked to even respond. I heave the much needed breath as I fall backward, unsure of exactly where that sudden surge of anger and confidence came from. I close my eyes at the silence that is their answer.

We sit in complete stillness for the better part of an hour—maybe more, maybe less—as I let my mind wander through all the questions I want to ask, all the answers they have and haven't provided, and try to wrestle with the idea that maybe even these two are just as untrustworthy as the others.

VII

"Alesia?" I call out into the darkness and promptly hear her quick shuffle over to where I sit.

"Yes?" Her voice is much more subdued than earlier and I know it's because of my previous outburst.

I still don't know who I can trust, but maybe I can get some useful information while we're trapped down here.

"You said I'm the fifth centra?" I ask the words as if I still don't believe them. In all actuality, I'm not even fully sure what it means. How can I *be* a centra?

"Yes."

"Does everyone know this? Is that why Tarak took me?"

"No. I don't think Himerak and the others even know exactly what you are. They just need a Celestra to harness what lies within the stones. Himerak is too old, and being as you are–"

"They already *have* a Celestra," I blurt out the confession without even thinking.

The second the words pass my lips, I swear I can feel Riann tense from the other side of the pit. It is only now that it occurs to me.

They don't know about Tarak.

The air shifts, and I know there's no turning back.

I should've kept my damn mouth closed. Or maybe I shouldn't have? It seems like I'm bouncing back and forth between sides pretty frequently these days.

"What do you mean they *have* a Celestra?" Riann questions, and for some reason the sound of his voice causes my hair to stand on end.

This would be much easier if I could see them. But all I find when I open my eyes is the dark expanse of nothing. I hesitate a moment more before realizing

I don't care. I don't know who to trust at this moment, and I don't owe any of them blind loyalty, especially when almost everyone around me has proven themselves unworthy. I'm *done* keeping other people's secrets for them. So, I rip off the bandaid.

"Tarak's a Celestra," the words come racing out. Straight to the point.

There's a moment of silence when I contemplate if they even heard what I said, but then I hear twin gasps of surprise and–

"*What?*" they ask in unison, the shock evident in their tone.

"Tarak is a Celestra." I repeat it once more, each syllable more enunciated than before. But, again, I'm met with silence.

After a few moments, Alesia is the first to speak. Her words are filled with bewilderment.

"The man who tricked you into falling in love with him, blew up your home, kidnapped you, drugged you, tied you up, and carried you to the boat; then had you placed in this pit. *He* is a *Celestra?*"

My heart threatens to tear apart with each revelation she states.

"Yes. *He* is."

I can't—no, won't—say his name again. I refuse. Acknowledging the one who put me in this literal pit of despair might undo what mental fortitude I have built up. He may have abandoned me in this darkness, but I'll claw my way back to the light.

We don't speak again. My guess is the news of a second Celestra is more shocking than the idea of our capture, and they need a little time to process it.

I have no idea how long we have been sitting here in the dark when a muffled noise from above pierces through the silence. My head snaps up, and the sound grows closer just as a gentle haze of light begins to flicker through the blinding darkness. I blink my eyes as it draws near, and realize the soft, rhythmic noise is the shuffling of approaching feet.

When the lantern leans over the edge of the pit, *his* illuminated face follows close behind.

"We need to talk," *he* commands.

When none of us responds, he opens his mouth to continue, but Riann cuts him off.

"You aren't taking her up there without us." He stands, and with the muted light from the lantern, I can see him position himself between our captor and me.

He huffs out an annoyed breath. "I'm going to lower a lift. Step on."

Riann gives a maniacal laugh. "Not without–"

"I will decide where I go. Not you or anyone else," I bark back at him and almost instantly regret my tone.

It's the first time I can actually see him, and instead of finding a menacing glare, I see the man who showed me so much kindness when I felt so alone.

"I . . . " The apology is on the tip of my tongue, but slowly fades out, and I realize I'm done apologizing for things I can't control. "I am going up there with him and I am figuring this out. I will come back for you."

"You will not!" His voice is so loud and boisterous, I swear the walls begin to shake.

"You are not my keeper. I make my own decisions."

"Nera! Stop!" He grabs my arm and I yank away.

"I swear to God if one more person attempts to grab hold of me, I will burn this damn hideout to the ground!" I look between the two men. Riann still heaves with unreleased anger, but Tarak just looks confused.

Within seconds, a lift is lowered down into the pit, a lantern hanging from its side. From this view, I can tell I fell at least ten feet if not more. I'm surprised I didn't break anything.

"My hands are bound. I can't hold onto the rope." I speak while not looking at the man above.

The wooden bench of the lift hits the bottom, sending a plume of dust swirling through the air.

"How did you get down?" he questions.

"Kies *threw me* in here," I spit.

"*What*?" His frustrated expression changes to seething anger.

"He. Pushed. Me. In." I'm direct. Confident.

Tarak's glare is murderous, and I can see the slight raise of his shoulders as his breathing increases. But I know the only reason he's concerned is because I'm only useful when not injured. Though I don't yet know how useful one can be while their hands are bound and imobile.

"Are you hurt?" He leans down toward the pit.

I steel my shoulders and raise my chin as I speak.

"No worse than the injuries you've given me." That statement halts him, and I watch as his gaze shifts to the ceiling far above. When he finally meets my eyes, there's a hint of sadness lurking within his sapphire stare.

"Nera, please step onto the lift. Lean against the rope, and I'll *gently* pull you out." His tone sounds defeated. I know it's a trick of the light, but I could swear I see just the slightest quiver of his lips as he speaks.

I hesitate for just a moment. "If I come with you, will you promise not to hurt them?"

He pauses a moment, looking at the two beside me before finding my gaze. "I promise."

His vow is unwavering.

Riann's chest expands with the inability to control what I do, and I watch as Alesia reaches out to grip him by the arm just in case he decides to lunge, either at me or the lift. I make it onto the rickety boards and all the way up without a word or movement from either of them. I think even they know we have no way of overtaking Tarak or the guards, not without weapons or the use of my untrained gifts.

Thankfully he follows my instruction and instead of placing a hand on my arm he motions forward in a silent plea for me to walk. I keep my gaze straight ahead through the dark turns as we make our way into the dimly-lit hallway I was first brought through. He cautiously peeks his head around each corner, and when he's convinced no one is coming, guides me into a room, shutting and locking the door behind us.

It's small and mostly dark, with shadows playing along the walls as the sparsely-placed candles flicker. One bed sits off in the corner, and a table and chairs flank the other wall.

It's obviously someone's room. My bet would be his. And I don't want to be here. His smell covers every surface, every inch. Once, I would've delighted in being surrounded by the scent, but things have changed. I have changed.

"What are–" I begin as I turn, but I don't get to finish the thought.

He crashes into me, pushing me backward and against the adjacent wall with overwhelming strength. I can do nothing but sink into his touch as he holds me steady against him, his right arm slung around my back and his left bracing the wall mere inches from my face. He pulls me to him, his body pressing flush against mine and I tilt my head upward to find his dim sapphire eyes staring down at me.

There are too many conflicting emotions wrapped up in this and my body can't seem to decide which to give into.

Before another thought can occur, I feel the vibration of his lips as they tentatively touch mine. I'm too stunned to move. The physical whiplash of this man is absolutely infuriating.

He pushes against my lips and whispers a growl at the contact.

It takes a moment for my muddled brain to register the stark contrast between what's happening now and what happened only minutes and hours ago. But I recognize the war between what my body craves and what my heart knows is a lie. It's only when I try to reach for him, to fist his shirt or slap that stupid, victorious grin off his face, that the war is won.

I'm still bound.

The last few hours come roaring back into my mind like a splash of cold water to my face, and I raise my hands, pushing him away. His only response is a drunken stare, lust lifting from his gaze as he, too, stands frozen at the realization I'm still confined.

Bound because of him.

His fingers grasp the cloth, and within a mere second, the covering falls to the ground, allowing my hands to move freely.

"I'm sorry." His voice sounds so soft and kind, just as it was before . . . "I forgot you were still bound. I would have taken it off earlier, but with Kies following us in there, I . . . "

The slap of my palm against his face reverberates throughout the room.

He stumbles, but quickly regains his posture. Recognition flashes through him with my utter stillness and he takes a deep breath. It's as if he's seeing me for the first time. *Truly* seeing me. Seeing what he has done to me.

My eyes stay locked on his, but he inches slightly closer, and before I can form all the words I want to hurl at him, his hands are cupping my cheeks and his lips surge forward to make contact with mine. But this time, I'm ready.

I duck before he can reach me, latching onto the hand that just seconds ago was rubbing the sting out of his cheek, twisting it backward. I may not be an expert when it comes to hand to hand combat but at this moment, I have the gift of surprise in my corner.

"What the fuck are you doing?!" I bite out from behind him and he jerks forward, easily escaping my hold.

"Nera? It's me! What are you–" The palm of my hand stings as it again makes contact with his face, and this time he bellows out in pain. Before I can even register what I've done, I push him back with as much force as I can muster, moving as far away from him as the small room will allow.

"No," I whisper as I look back at him.

"Nera–"

"No," I grit my teeth, swallowing down all the anger washing over me.

"Nera–" His voice breaks as my name passes his lips, and I almost give in to the soothing comfort which seems to always surround him. But I can't. Not when he's done such horrible things. Not when he has killed so many innocent people.

Not when *he* has been my enemy all along.

His feet inch closer to me until I throw a threatening glare, causing him to pause.

"No." My voice, now much stronger with newfound resolve, echoes through the room.

No. No. No.

He doesn't get to come in here and think his kiss, his touch, his apology will take it all away. He doesn't get a pass on the horrible things he has done. He doesn't get to use his touch to weaken me further than I already am.

"Please." He is begging now, dropping to his knees before me. "Please let me explain. I thought you understood. It was all a ruse. I had to. I had to act like that or they would've killed us both." The words are rushed out in a frantic, garbled mess.

My lips tremble at the sight of him kneeling before me. "Don't ever touch me again."

"Give me time to explain," he implores, reaching out for me once again. His eyes fill with unshed tears, and I watch as this once-strong man crumbles in front of me.

"Don't touch me or, so help me God, I will use every last ounce of power I have to burn this entire structure down with all of us inside." I repeat my previous threat as my seething words hiss through gritted teeth, and though I don't know how to fully use my gifts, I hope my tone convinces him otherwise.

"Okay," he finally surrenders, hands in the air and inches away from me, while still kneeling down on the floor below. "Your rules. You tell me what happens from here on out."

VIII

I stare at him for far too long, gauging whether or not to kill him. How I am supposed to stand in this room with the man who took away every ounce of trust and courage I had built back up over the last few weeks. How can I manage to say anything to him without completely losing every shred of self-worth I have left?

We are frozen in time as he patiently waits for my cue. Waits for me to say or do something, anything.

I strain to keep my stare as menacing as possible, but his form becomes blurred as traitorous tears rim my eyes. How long does he plan to stay here waiting?

"I . . . " My voice shatters the invisible barrier I've placed between us, and with it, both of our resolves. I watch as a tear slowly inches its way down his perfect, golden skin.

"Nera." His voice breaks, and it's a booming crack against my body. "Ask me anything. I promise this time. No lies. No deception. I am fully and completely open to you."

A dreaded weight settles deep within my bones.

I open and close my mouth, stammering while I try to decide what to say first. What can I ask that won't cause my already fragile mind to disintegrate from the answer?

Then I jut my hands out and watch as he recoils with the movement, waiting for me to finally and irrevocably end him.

"Why? Why did you put that on me? Do you not trust me?"

His guilt-filled gaze shifts from my eyes to the floor. "The vines weren't my idea—that was Kies. Just give me time to explain," he frantically begs as he begins to stand, but I push myself further against the wall at his movement, shuffling outside of his reach, and he slowly sinks back to the ground.

Still glaring at him, I find a defeated look etched onto his face. He doesn't speak, but deflates right before me. This strong, capable man has been reduced to a mound of grief and sorrow.

And for some reason, I can't find the will to care any longer. I don't ache to reach out to him, to soothe his pain. Instead, I feel a fiery drive to find out *why*. To seek answers to the countless questions running through my head. I brace myself for the words which I know will come, knowing that, despite his proclamations, they may just be more lies served to me on a pretty platter.

"You have five minutes before I march out of this room. If I have to burn my way through this place to get out, I will. And I don't care how many bodies I leave in my wake. Explain," I state firmly, my mind catching up to reality, and the venom-laced order seems to jolt him back to life.

"It wasn't planned."

"What? The part where you deceived me? How long were you going to continue to lie to me? To your crew? They all think I'm some traitorous monster because of *you*," I retort.

He reaches out to grab my arm and pull me to him, but I yank away just in time.

"Don't touch me." I spit the words out, my chest heaving, and watch as he continues to deflate. With all my resolve, I burrow down deep beneath the wards I've built around my heart. I can't reach back out to him. I won't.

He shakes his head, as if trying to discard all the horrid truths I've laid before him. "I didn't lie about . . . about *everything*. At least, not in the sense you're thinking. And it was only so I could save you."

An incredulous laugh bursts from my lips before I can stop it. Everyone I have ever known has walked on eggshells around me, not wanting to say or do the wrong thing in case they trigger an episode, a panic attack. Their neverending assumption of what I am thinking and feeling only caused further resentment and pain. Why does everyone presume to know what is best for me when they barely even know me?

God, I'm on another planet and it's still the same way.

I thought he was different. I thought *we* were different together. I thought by finding him I was somehow finding myself along the way. But that was just another myth my heart fabricated. He's simply doing what every other person in my life has always done.

"I promise it's not what you're thinking," he pleads on bended knee.

"Please, go on." My upper lip curls in disdain as I gesture with undeniably sarcastic flourish for him to continue. "Inform me as to *what* I am thinking."

He swallows as if readying himself for battle, but I'm nowhere near patient enough to allow him time.

"Four minutes, Tarak! *Explain it!*" I scream.

He turns his head sharply to stare at the door, holding his breath as if the volume of my voice will call the attention of his crew. When the seconds pass and no one shows, he turns back to me and takes a deep, steadying breath. Then the words come out in a garbled rush, as if he can't figure out how to say them fast enough.

"I did stumble upon you that first day. I was out hunting; that part is true. I didn't realize you were a Celestra until I saw the mark, and I had already alerted Himerak of your existence by that point, so I couldn't pretend I never saw you." He stands and begins pacing the small space between us.

"Someone with your training should know better than to act before you have all the information at hand." I counter, my words filled with hatred. He doesn't even take note.

"I watched you sleep for a while—*after* I realized what you were. I tried to fix it. I– I spent hours sitting there, watching you and trying to figure out a way to keep you from them."

I huff, frustration further building inside me.

"When I let Himerak know what I found, he–"

"Me. I am the '*what*' you found."

His lips tighten in a taut line. "Are you going to interrupt me every time I speak?"

I quirk my head to the side, feigning contemplation. "Maybe. Three minutes." My voice is dripping with sarcasm. His hands fist in his blonde curls. They're too long and keep falling in his face, covering up his eyes. An image flashes in my mind of another time his curls brushed over his forehead, and I get the urge to push them back. I want to–

No.

I can't let my thoughts wander down that road. Not now. Not anymore.

He shakes his head and takes a long inhale, as if readying himself for the fight to come.

"Himerak gave an order. He is my sovereign, and I have to follow his every command. It is the *law*. He is the law. I was told to bring you to him first thing in the morning. That you could become very useful to us. To our cause."

"So I was—no, I *am*—just a piece in your game. I'm a pawn." My shoulders drop, and I close my eyes, not wanting him to see the sting of his words. But when I open them, the steel in my spine is reforged, my determination along with it.

"No. Not for me. *Never* for me." His hands lift up in surrender as he sits in a nearby chair. Taking a deep breath, he leans forward, hanging his head in defeat, then continues to pull at his golden curls. Watching him work through this, seeing him in utter agony, feels like a thousand tiny blades piercing my heart, but I relish it.

"I . . . You . . . " He takes a moment to breathe, as if willing the words to come. "I couldn't . . . It was just that . . ."

"Tarak, two minutes. Speak. Form a sentence. Say *something of substance!*" I scream in frustration.

"It was a way out for me," he blurts. His hands cover his eyes as he rubs his temples. "You were a way out. That's what it was at first. If they had *you,* then maybe they wouldn't need *me* anymore."

"Need you for what?" I ask, even though I already know the answer.

"The stones. I– I didn't realize you were Koreed's daughter. I didn't realize you were *the* Celestra until . . . well, until we met with Himerak the first night I brought you to my home. It all clicked when he saw your past, and I knew then. I knew that was why those Halabarians were coming for you in the forest."

I almost laugh out loud. I can't decide if I want to vomit, laugh, cry . . . reach out and punch him in the face.

"So, while we were in the cave that last night, while I was losing my mind trying to put all the pieces of myself together, trying to determine how I ended up at that palace, if I was related to them, you . . . you knew. You *knew* I was his daughter. You had every piece of the puzzle. You had every answer right there in your hands, and you didn't tell me?"

"I'm sorry. I did it because–"

"Sorry isn't good enough, Tarak. You lied to me."

"I messed up. I messed it up completely." He stands once more to pace the floor before rushing forward. He's so quick, he's at my face before I can form the next thought.

I don't even have a second to move before his hands are flanking either side of my head, his face mere inches from mine. His voice is barely a whisper.

"Do you have any idea what it's like to grow up with no choice in who you are and where your loyalties lie?" He heaves a breath. "Do you have any idea what it's like to have every moment of your existence mapped out in perfect clarity?"

My palms begin to heat.

"Do you know I was supposed to *hate you?*"

Small tickling tingles inch their way up my arm.

"I was supposed to *kill you.*" The words come as a punch to my gut. "I can't even tell you how many training missions we went on over the years in preparation for *you.* Our task was to capture you in order to force Koreed's hand." He closes his eyes, and I startle at the loud crack, the accompanying vibrations as his fist slams into the wall inches from my face.

A roar of silence fills my ears as his words sink in.

"I imagined your death a thousand different ways before I ever even saw your face."

There is a swirling torrent rising within me. I hold steady to the locks within my mind, trying to force it back down.

"I was going to kill you," he whispers against my lips, and I hold my breath, hoping to dull my senses, to drown out the heat which continues to ebb and flow through my body.

But nothing helps.

The pain-filled pleasure only grows.

I force my hands against the cold concrete wall, hoping to ease the pain now centered there as his words continue to replay again and again through my head.

I was supposed to hate you. I was supposed to kill you.

Hate you. Kill you.

Hate you. Kill you.

Hate you. Kill you.

The echo of those four words consumes me. It becomes too much to bear, and I whimper in both agony and relief when light splinters in my periphery and the ground shakes beneath my feet. My hand reaches out to brace my shaking form on the cool wall.

"Nera?" he questions in earnest. "Nera?" My name is a quiet query. But when I finally look up to meet his gaze, there is fear laced within his sapphire stare.

"Why didn't you do it?" The question barely passes through the air. "I was *right there*. I knew nothing. I trusted you completely. You could have killed me at any time." My voice deepens. "You could have ended this all and not put me through this agony." More heat surges through my chest, filling me with pain and anger and heartache.

"Nera? What are you doing?" he asks as his fearful eyes trail my body.

"I was weak and confused then. And I didn't know who I was, what I was." His body tenses in confusion. "But I do now. You should have killed me then. Now you've lost your chance." I feel a wicked smile rise with each word I speak, feel a new sense of victory as his face contorts.

"Nera," he whispers my name, and I watch his hand tentatively reach out to touch my arm. "Calm down," he pleads, but his words mean nothing to me.

And when his hand finally makes contact with my arm, it is the final fracture in my already fraying resolve. The chains I had meticulously placed around myself, the chains which held in whatever evil hides within me, fall away. There's nothing left to hold me back.

An unfamiliar cold creeps up my arm as heat races through my veins. The room seems to glow as if bathed in orange sunlight. Even the shadows seem to wither away in fear of what I've become. My eyes shift to Tarak, and though I can see his lips moving and his head shaking, I hear nothing but the roar of unreleased fury bubbling up from within. The piercing heat rises to a fever pitch as I reach out and push against his chest. He stumbles backward.

The initial movement breaks through the fire growing within.

No! No, no, no. This is not you!

I hear an echo screech across the expanse of my mind, but my body pays no attention to the weakness which once ruled me.

Stop!

It calls out to me as I step forward to reach his shaking form.

"Nera! What are you doing?!" Tarak backs out of reach, tripping over the leg of the table as he moves. "Calm down."

I feign a laugh at his plea.

This isn't who you are, the familiar feminine voice calls to me and my movement stops as if a cold brick wall has been laid directly in my path. But my eyes never leave Tarak's.

"I hate you." The words seep out as my vision blurs and white smoke wisps into the air. Tarak reaches forward once more, but my hands meet his chest, grasping onto his shirt before he can latch onto my arm again. "I hate you," I snarl as the white hot flame bursts from my chest and his body is hurled backward.

Just as he falls upon the threadbare blanket and cot, my vision clears, and the reality of what I've done settles within.

"Tarak?" I fall forward in exhaustion, my knees scraping against the rocky floor.

He cradles his chest, eyes trained on his now smoldering shirt, and I gasp as the heat of anger slowly dissipates. It retreats within me as if pulled by an invisible tether.

"I . . . I didn't . . . I don't . . ." Words leave me as weariness seeps in.

He barely even flinches as he peels the now tattered cloth away and over his head. As he assesses his skin, I feel tears begin to rim my eyes.

"You didn't hurt me. It just got the shirt. I'm fine. You didn't hurt me," he repeats, trying to calm me.

"What if I wanted to?" I whisper as we lock eyes, my body still as stone on the cold floor.

"I wouldn't blame you," he concedes as he kneels off the cot and crawls the few feet over to where I remain.

"I don't know what that was." My shallow breaths come in rapid succession. "I want to hate you." My voice cracks with the admission as tears fall down my cheeks. A wisp of steam rising from the ground each time that splash down onto the waiting stone. "I want to hate you so damn much, but . . . " And then all I can think of is his mission. The mission he was given. The mission to kill me.

"I don't want you to hate me," he retorts as tears well in his eyes. I watch as they start to fall.

"Why not do it now?" I question quietly; so quietly, I'm not sure he actually hears me. "You could easily kill me right now and end all of this."

His fingers reach up, tentatively wiping away a lone tear as it reaches my lips. He closes his eyes and heaves a deep breath, letting it tickle my skin.

"I don't understand it. You somehow got past every defense I have ever put in place. You started to mean more to me than the one thing I have centered my entire life around. I truthfully don't know how to grapple with that notion. You mean more to me than anything else."

His words hit me like a slap across the face. My anger still lingers, but it's buried so deep in exhaustion, I can't quite seem to care.

"I don't know how, or why, or when exactly. Maybe it was in that tree when you were so scared after that first attack, or watching you train. It could have been the way you helped my mother with the garden, or the way you comforted that child after the Haze, or when we watched the sunset. Maybe it was there all along, settled deep within me waiting to snap into place. I couldn't tell you the precise moment it happened, even if you held a knife to my heart."

He reaches out his hand to grasp mine, bringing it flat against his chest, and I relax as the warmth of his body seeps into me. I feel his rapid heartbeat—the one thing I thought I would never hear or feel again—and the rest of my resolve shatters into a thousand tiny fragments.

"At some point, you wove yourself deep within me. I fell in love with you." I violently shake my head at his confession. "I couldn't help it." The admission hits like another blow. And though he says it with so much certainty, there is a wavering note of falsehood hidden within the words.

"Tarak–" I try to cut in, but he's too quick.

"And I couldn't tell anyone, because by the time I knew—by the time I accepted that fate—Himerak had already devised a plan. And when he found out you were indeed Nera—*the* Nera Thesand—that plan . . . " He takes a deep breath. "That plan became more than I ever imagined."

IX

My body all but recoils at his admission, but I catch onto his last words.

"What plan?" I ask, hoping the question doesn't sound as pathetic as I feel.

He hesitates, but just as I'm about to ask again, he speaks.

"I was supposed to win your trust and determine what your gifts were. You and I would collect the stones, and then, depending on how everything played out, maybe I would kill you."

"Would you have killed me?" I shuffle backward, still not wanting to give in to the closeness I know my body still craves.

"No." His voice is sure and confident, and the lingering note of falsehood I heard earlier is nowhere to be found. "But that was my mission," he admits as his eyes shift back to mine. "*You* became my mission. In more ways than one."

"Why me? Why do I need to find the stones? Why not you?"

"Himerak believes that you have . . . " He pauses, and I wonder if he's trying to find the right words, or if he's the same as Riann and has something to hide from me. "He believes your abilities are far greater than any of the current Celestras'. He thinks you're different from us."

I swallow, knowing exactly what he's referring to. I'm the fifth centra, whatever the hell that means. But I wonder if he truly knows or if he's just going along with a plan.

"How am I different?"

"I'm not sure. But it's not my job to question my sovereign."

"This was never about helping me find out who I was or getting answers to all the questions I had—*still* have—about my life, was it? You already had them. You knew everything there was to know about me the entire time."

His eyes cut away as embarrassment at what he's done sinks in. "I went along with it because I didn't want to hurt you."

I stare at the wall behind him, unable to look at him, unable to see and accept the man who has caused me such pain. "News flash, Tarak. You *did* hurt me."

He squints his eyes in confusion at my words. "I didn't mean to. I was so confused. You have to understand. From the moment I found out about you as a child, I hated you. No–" He stops himself, and I can see a hint of realization flash across his somber face. "No. I was trained to hate the *idea* of you, the idea which had been planted in my head for all those years. The one which said you were evil, and a killer, and were bred just to assassinate my people."

He takes a deep shuddering breath, and I know he's reliving memories I can't even imagine.

"But, then you were actually there, right in front of me, and I . . . I *didn't hate* you anymore. I didn't even dislike you. Elders, I wanted to. I tried to hate you so many times those first few days after I found you, but I–" He looks at me again, tears still falling, his words trembling on his lips. "I fell in love with you instead."

"Stop saying that." The pained whisper leaves my lips.

"Why? It's the truth. I love you."

His plea threatens to break through the swirling cloud of agony, the walls I've built.

"Stop!" I scream, further recoiling backward, hoping—praying the distance will lessen the turmoil surging through my veins.

"Nera–" He starts to make his way toward me, closing the space I desperately made.

"No. No. No." My hands raise up, stopping him. "You don't *deceive* the person you love. You don't capture them and drug them and haul them off into a pit. You don't murder their family. You don't *threaten to kill* the people they love. You don't attack their home."

"You don't understand."

"What is there to understand!" I scream out in frustration as the exhaustion slips away, allowing that deeply buried fury to rise yet again. "Why continue on with the ruse? Why the attack on the palace? Is it all just a part of your scheme?" He opens his mouth, but I don't let him speak. "Tell me this. Are we going to sneak out of here? What about Riann and Alesia? Will they die because of your inability to have even a shred of honor inside of you?"

He scoffs, but I continue.

"What about all those innocents at the palace? What about Mina? *You killed Mina.*"

"I'm sorry. I . . . " He falters and, and for the first time, I can see true and utter agony playing across his features. At least *this* is real. "I never meant to do that."

His words come as a whisper. "I didn't realize who she was. I would have *never* done it had I known. All I knew was someone was running toward you with a knife. I was trying to *save* you. When Alesia told me who she was, I . . . I never meant to hurt you."

"But you did. You hurt me. You promised not to hurt me, and that's exactly what you did."

"I know."

"You promised not to lie to me." It's barely a whisper.

"I know." He hangs his head in shame.

Then, after a moment of agonizing silence, he lifts his eyes to meet mine, and I think back to how he told me he feels physical pain whenever he willingly lies. The curse of his gift. "How much pain did those lies cause you?"

"More than you can ever imagine." His chest expands as he sucks in a ragged breath. Tears trail down his face.

Part of me wants to believe him. To rush forward into his arms. To let him take all this pain away. But I can't just forget everything.

Not after all the lies.

Not after all the death.

Not after his betrayal.

"Somehow, I doubt that." My chin trembles with the emotion threatening to burst through, and I know he can see it. I shift my gaze away from him, unwilling to look upon the face which has caused so much destruction—both physical and mental.

"I know. I don't know how to fix it other than to say I will. Just trust that I will."

"That's the problem, Tarak. I don't *trust* you. I don't trust you or any of the men and women stationed out there who want me dead. I don't trust any of this!"

He stands to walk my way. "I know."

I inch further backward. "I don't think you do."

"I'm going to fix it," he promises, and I laugh through my tears at the absurdity of it all.

"How? We just walk out there and say, 'Hey, sorry for earlier, but Nera isn't actually a threat.' Somehow, I don't see that going over well for any of us."

He shakes his head in agreement. "No. It wouldn't."

"Then, what? Huh? What's your plan?" I implore, my arms crossed over my chest.

"I need you to agree to find the stones."

He must have lost his damn mind.

"What? *Himerak's* plan? After everything you just admitted. After knowing he wanted you to kill me. You still want me to go along with it?"

Of course, finding the stones is already my plan. I made that decision in the pit. But he doesn't need to know that. Finding those stones and harnessing my power through my Committence is the one way I can right all of this. But I won't be doing it for him or Himerak or even Koreed or Riann. I will find those stones for *me*.

"Agree to help us search for the stones, and–"

"Stones you will use to harness power and knowledge, and then use against Halabar and their people—*my* people?"

I wait for his rebuttal, but he just stares at me as if my knowledge on the subject is surprising. I don't bring up the heartstone in the trees or my other newfound knowledge. I'm not sure I want him to be aware of the fact that I know all this.

"I already told you. I'm not a piece in your game, and I will not be played as such," I grind out, glaring at him.

"I won't use the power against anyone. I'm not evil. My hope is you and I together can use the stones to bring peace to this world. We can find out what's causing the Haze, the Drench, the Ashclaw, and all the other horrible things this world has conjured up, and then we can defeat them."

I shake my head in disbelief. Is he truly this obtuse? "It won't work. Your crew wants me dead."

He stares at me for a moment, as if all this information is finally coming together for him. As if he finally understands that we can't do this without his crew's cooperation.

"Fine." He tosses his hands in the air in exasperation.

"Fine, what?" I counter.

"Then let's go tell them."

"Tell them *what* exactly?" My voice is now much stronger with the implication of what he could mean.

"Tell them the truth. I will tell them *everything*. I'll tell them about you and me, and Himerak. And you can tell them about what you found out while in Halabar. We can do this together. We can convince them," he swears with too much confidence and certainty.

"That's going against Himerak. Against your sovereign. You already said his word is law."

"I told you, Nera. I'm done with their plans. I'm tired of being a piece in his game, too. From here on out, I play this the way I want . . . the way *we* want." The truth within the assertion hits me full force. But no matter what I feel, I know I can't yet trust him or anyone else here for that matter.

"They will kill me. They might even kill you."

He shakes his head.

"I am their commander. The only person who outranks me is a fragile old man who isn't even here." He then reaches forward, silently begging me to join him, but I can't. When my arm doesn't meet his, he slowly pulls back in defeat.

"If I go out there, I go of my own free will. I won't be led anywhere else. Do you understand? I am in control of myself."

"I understand," he says with an immediate nod as he turns, heading toward the door. "If you don't want to come with me, I understand that, too. You can wait here, or go back to Riann." His voice falters slightly as he forms the name, as if the thought causes him physical pain. "But if you choose to come, I promise to protect you. And I will tell the truth."

And then he's off.

I square my shoulders, ready to finally be able to face this head on, even if it means continuing to work with him. Once again, I have to put my faith in this man, and that thought fills me with dread. In just a few short strides, I am out of the door and meeting his pace as we make our way through the maze of darkened hallways into the unknown.

For just a split second, I catch sight of the path leading to the pit and tense at the idea of being placed back inside. That might just be the outcome if this plan doesn't work the way we hope. He turns to face me as we pass the opening, a somber expression etched across his features.

"I won't be stuck in that pit again," I declare as I walk beside him. The edge of his lips turn up in a sad smile, but in less than a moment his face returns to neutral and he gives me a nod.

"I'm getting them out, I promise. I didn't want them to be dragged into all this. I'm sorry they were. And don't worry, you aren't going back in there. Ever. At least, not without me being thrown in as well." His smirk somehow calms my nerves, and I allow myself to feel the slightest buzz of hope beginning to stir in me.

It's only a few more bends around darkened pathways before I hear the muffled sounds of celebrating soldiers. A celebration which, I wager, is in part due to my capture. My ears catch a few words through the slurred speech of those closest to the doors.

" . . . queen no more . . . "

"Wicked sigot beast."

My breath picks up as I contemplate what will happen once they see me unbound, walking freely with Tarak at my side.

Which is an entire other concept I still can't wrap my brain around. The pulsing in my veins is screaming at me to run; run far away from this man, this place, and all it embodies. But now I have a mission of my own. A mist of hope.

I'm no longer trailing behind someone else. I may let Tarak and whoever else think I'm still that meek and mild girl they found in the forest, but she left my body the moment he plunged the syringe into my arm.

I am now leading the way. I will be strong. I will be powerful.

And I push away the tingling which surges through my fingertips at the thought of all that I am about to face.

Between Tarak's people and the Halabarians, I have quite a mess to clean up. And that doesn't even begin to touch the surface of all the things Tarak just mentioned. Though I barely know what the Haze is, I have even less knowledge of the Ashclaw and the Drench.

A subtle warning runs through me. The same I felt on my first walk to meet Himerak.

This change in events, this path I'm now on, is not something the inner demon buried deep inside me would ever willingly take part in. It's a warning that I am, once again, walking to my death.

My entire form shivers as the room comes into view. If the motion surprises Tarak, he makes no sign of it, and we continue walking side by side into the dimly lit expanse.

I feel the dagger nick the side of my throat just as we step across the threshold.

Tarak's stunned eyes quickly assess both me and those around as he pulls out his own weapon and opens his mouth.

But his would-be words are interrupted by a familiar voice.

"Less than an hour. You owe me thirty dibs."

Unable to turn my head without the stinging pierce of the blade, my eyes shift to the table.

Ranya is there, sipping on what I can only guess is a foul-smelling concoction by the looks of it. Her eyes move to Kies as he tosses a few coins her way. The rattle of each rounded edge banging against the other is the only sound I hear, save for my rapid heartbeat hammering through my ears.

"Fifty-two minutes, if we're being exact," the soldier behind me calls out as he presses the edge of the dagger further into my skin. I feel a slight wetness seeping its way down to my collarbone.

"Don't," Tarak orders as his eyes catch sight of my position. His own dagger, now poised and ready to strike its target, is gleaming in the dim light of the lanterns hanging above.

"Tarak?" Kies questions, his voice too smooth and precise. But Tarak's eyes don't leave mine. "Here is where you choose, brother. Your family or your *whore*." We may be feet apart, but I can feel Tarak stiffen at the words.

Tarak's voice is low but direct—visceral in a sense, which comes across as more of a growl than true words. "I am your command–"

Kies quickly cuts him off, "Yes. Lest you forget you are not yet our sovereign, and your word is not yet law. As your ally *and* friend, I implore you to think carefully on the matter and answer wisely."

I watch, heart pounding in my chest and blood slowly soaking the upper rim of my tattered dress, as Tarak's eyes move between me and the room around us. Each soldier is now standing with a weapon in their hands.

"She is not what Himerak says she is," Tarak loudly proclaims to anyone who will listen, and he inches himself closer to me. But he stops when my breath hitches, the soldier now pressing the dagger farther into my skin.

And then the crowd erupts.

"*Traitor!*" one man screams.

"*Bitch!*" another yells from just behind me.

"*Whore!*"

More continue to chime in, each with their own choice of insults to hurl at Tarak or myself.

"*Killer!*"

"*Murderer!*"

"*Beast!*"

It goes on and on. A neverending slew of curses thrown into the air. Then an unexpected whistle pierces the room.

"I don't know about the rest of you," Ranya states as she downs the contents of her glass, stands, and stalks toward me, "but I, for one, would like to see the bitch squirm. Let's see what she can really do." She positions herself between me and Tarak as a clamor of cheers rings out into the air. Tarak reaches in her direction as a number of blades are drawn on him.

But he either doesn't notice or doesn't care. I assume he'll attempt to wound or disarm her in some way, but instead his palm finds home on her shoulder. With it Ranya takes a deep, shuddering breath.

My eyes crease at the movement. Nothing about it screams friend or foe. The movement just was, and I marvel as what appears to be a transparent, shimmering haze washing over Ranya at his touch. For just a fleeting moment, a strange emotion washes through me, and I can't quite tell if it's a stab of jealousy that his touch has this effect on her, or if it's something else nagging at me from the back of my mind.

"I'll knock you all out if needed. But that's not what I want. Neither is that what Nera wants. No one here is a traitor," Tarak calmly proclaims to the group. His eyes dart to over a dozen members who flank him. I wait for Ranya's rebuttal, but nothing comes. Her glassy stare stays planted on me. "But there has been a grave misunderstanding. One I plan to reconcile this–" His words are cut short as a sword cuts down through the air from behind.

The swish of the blade is the only warning Tarak is afforded before a sword comes crashing down from behind into his outstretched arm. A ting of metal hidden under his shirt sounds off into the air just as the unknown man yielding the weapon screams, "Traitor!"

Precisely as the word leaves his lips, the unknown soldier sucks in a breath of shock at the realization of his grave mistake. The room stands still as if any movement, even the simple act of breathing would cause the entire structure to implode.

Calmly, Tarak flexes his fingers as he lets go of Ranya. He pulls up his sleeve to reveal a thin layer of golden armor hidden beneath, most likely still in place from their infiltration into Halabar and the palace. The armor moves with ease but is impenetrable and I can only assume it too is made from the heartstone found within the trees.

It takes a mere second from the time the thought is formed to when the act is completed, and Tarak's dagger is rammed through the man's throat and yanked out. A gurgling sound emits from the soldier's lips as a few gasp in surprise.

Hushed whispers and cries of outrage ring out, but Tarak pays no mind to the noise. He latches a hand firmly around the throat of the man now gasping for air. Tarak's stare is unyielding and rigid as blood pours onto his hand, down his arm and drips onto the dirt covered floor.

"It's a sad realization that those will be your last words," Tarak seethes, and I startle as he pushes forward into the wound, pulling back and yanking out the man's trachea with ease.

The crimson spray splatters on anything within reach—including the outer layers of my gown—as the man's lifeless body crashes to the floor. The warm blood oozes into the holes of my torn shoes.

My heart stammers as the room stands in silence. Every pair of eyes now trained on me as I remain still, the dagger still placed at my throat. I wait for the uncontrollable heat to begin its movement through my body—for it to lash out like tendrils in the wind, reaching and grasping for the death it yearns to obtain...but nothing comes. My gaze flits downward to my cold, shaking hands just as one soldier, another, and then the rest descend on Tarak.

The room explodes into chaos.

X

The sudden movement causes the man at my back to falter, giving me just enough time to spin out of his grasp and away from his blade. And though I am no match for any of them in hand-to-hand combat, I have enough knowledge of male anatomy to incapacitate the unsuspecting soldier. I drive my knee straight into his crotch as he doubles over in pain and his dagger becomes mine when it plunges to the ground.

There is just enough time to recover and stand again when Ranya begins stalking toward me, twisting and turning her blade between each finger as if I am a ragdoll she can't wait to rip apart. Her sinister smile slowly shifts upward with every step she takes. My heart upticks, knowing I'll never be able to take her on, and I gulp down my last few breaths of life. I'll still fight—no matter how inevitable my demise.

Out of the corner of my eye, Tarak's movements are quick and efficient as he blocks almost every punch, swing, and dagger which heads his way. But there is no amount of fighting which will safely remove us from this situation. And, more than that, these are Tarak's own crew. His friends. His family. Despite how much I hate him at this moment, the last thing I want is for him to feel the pain of having their deaths on his hands.

And this match is not, by any stretch of the imagination, even. It's eighteen against two. We are outnumbered, but that doesn't mean I won't try.

I stand with trembling hands, prepared to go down with a fight as Ranya steps within swinging distance. The rest of the pack that had previously started my way seems to part with the knowledge that I'm hers to kill.

Her hand lifts, poised and ready to drive her dagger deep within my heart. I have just enough time to twist and shield my body as the blade leaves her hand. But the piercing pain never registers. Instead, I look up to find Micel standing over me, having caught the hilt of the twisting blade in his hands mid flight. Ranya's shock at the intrusion causes her to falter, giving Tarak enough time to reach me before the group encircles us once more.

Unsure whether he is friend or foe, but willing to take the chance, I have just a split second to reach out for Micel before it happens.

I feel the familiar heat overpower me before the shimmering haze floods my vision. The angered cries of the soldiers surrounding us are drowned out, muffled as if underwater.

When I open my eyes once more, I look up to find Tarak's arms encompassing me, his piercing sapphire gaze meeting mine. A sheepish smile plays on his lips.

"Thanks," he says as the smile grows wider, and his stupid dimple pops into place. I almost return the smile on instinct. Almost lean further into him, that damn heat drawing me in, even as the chaos around us continues to unfold.

But then I remember how much I hate him. How much he hurt me. And, at the last second, I steel my face into a visage of neutrality and step out of his reach. His shoulders drop at my response.

The room around us has darkened as if the candles and lanterns have dimmed, and the only true light shining against the contorted faces of my enemies comes from what I have created.

"What is this?" Micel questions from my right, and he tentatively reaches out to graze his fingers along the edge of the shimmering dome we are encased within. His fingers make contact, a jolt hits them, and he pulls back from the barrier. The movement reminds me of when I first touched the window of my palace bedroom. "What is this?" he questions more urgently, his eyes shifting down to meet mine.

"I don't know. I made it once, before . . . " My mind falters on what to say; *before the attack, before you all betrayed me, before I found out the truth*. I don't want to open that vessel of deceit, so I settle on. "I made it once before by accident. I don't know how I did it then either. It just happened."

I shift my eyes back to the room and the awestruck guards standing around. Each seems to be warily inspecting the flickering dome I have created.

"How do you take it down?" Micel quietly asks, immense intrigue swimming in his eyes.

"I– I don't know." I shake my head, and feel an overwhelming sense of incompetence surge through me. "I truly don't know how any of this works. It just happens, and I can't control–"

A spike of electricity bursts through the room. Light floods the area and sparks shoot off in every direction. When the sparks meet their targets, there are audible gasps of surprise, but the gasps quickly turn into tortured screams.

Kies barrels backward as if he's being pulled by an invisible string through the mass of confused soldiers. The room stills as his scream halts, and the only sounds, outside of gasps of awe, shock, and fear, are the eerie noises of shattering bone as his body flattens against the far wall. Blood oozes from every orifice of the corpse as the deep gray stone he's plastered against turns an ominous shade of crimson. A spiderweb of death seeps out and splinters into the natural grooves of the surrounding wall. His once beige skin pales even further.

My breathing increases as I remember the words of the maid from my first day back on this planet.

It's only supposed to interact with those trying to get in from the outside.

The memory shocks me. And then the pieces connect.

It's a defense mechanism, one I created myself. Which means *I* killed Kies.

Another death at my hands.

Another life I have taken.

I look down to find my hands shaking uncontrollably. The dirt and blood covering my nails and embedded within the creases of my palms are easily noticeable. But what no one can see is the layers upon layers of blood which will slicken them forever.

The blood of so many innocents.

I fall to the ground, and just as my knees slam against the cold stone below, the shimmering dome cascades with me, leaving only a smoldering ring of heat around us.

I half expect the group of soldiers to continue their attack. And, if they do, I wholly anticipate being dead within minutes. The surge of weakness currently racing through my muscles has rendered me unable to defend myself.

"She can *shield*?" Ranya quietly questions, breaking the silence as she slides her dagger back into its home. When my head finally raises, feeling as heavy as the world itself, I find those around her following suit. Each slowly and cautiously sheaths their own weapon as their eyes remain focused on me.

But one lone soldier, Casin—the vulgar man from the pier—barrels through the crowd with a curved dagger aimed directly for me. Surprise flickers through my eyes as Ranya is the one to impede him.

"She can shield!" she proclaims, and it feels as if those three words are my salvation.

"That *shield* killed Kies!" he counters angrily as he attempts to shove past her to get to me. His eyes widen in confusion when he looks around to find not a single soul joining in his quest.

"I didn't mean to." My voice cracks as I plead to those around me for forgiveness, not knowing how to bear the thought of another death at my hands. Tarak quickly finds my face, hurriedly surveying my body for wounds of any kind.

"You murdering *bitch*!" Casin screams, causing Tarak to shift his focus from me to the man who now wants nothing more than my blood on his hands. "I will gut you from cunt to clavicle!" Casin growls with unyielding promise as he inches toward me. With great effort, he finally makes it past Ranya, but he doesn't make good on his promise.

Kneeling down beside me, Micel levels a murderous glare at anyone who so much as considers moving closer, and Tarak stands to scrutinize the soldier, quickly positioning himself between us.

"I truly never liked you, Casin." There is a calm, collected air to Tarak's voice. In a breath, his face morphs from bored stoicism to bursting excitement. "But I do believe I am going to love killing you." He chuckles. A shudder runs down my spine.

Before Casin can form a response, Tarak effortlessly relieves him of his weapon and moves to his back. With a swift kick behind the legs and a grasp around his throat, Tarak deftly lifts the man by his neck and slams him into the ground. A thunderous crack of bone echoes through the room along with a scream of pain as Casin lands. While not forceful enough to immediately kill, it's definitely hard enough to shock the soldier, hard enough to break something. A few somethings. A foul stench stings my nose as urine seeps from his clothing and spreads out into a river winding between our feet.

Tarak maintains his tight grip around Casin's throat, not letting his eyes leave the man now so close to death as he addresses the group who remain silent in their shock. "Before anyone else makes the decision to die today, we have a few things to discuss. I suggest you all keep your weapons holstered and your mouths shut. Or, should you choose another option, you will find yourself placed in your very own pit. Except the one I dig will be filled back in, with you chained to the bottom." He pauses as he looks around, his eyes finding their mark on Ranya. "Is that clear?" He enunciates every venom-laced word.

"Crystal," she replies, and the rest of the soldiers nod their agreement.

When Tarak finally lets go, Casin gasps, reaching up to cradle his sore neck, and lets out a blood-curdling scream in the process. "I want him in the pit, and Riann and Alesia out. Bring them here now," he orders to no one in particular, and I hear the hushed whispers throughout the room.

Not a single soldier moves at Tarak's command. I brace myself as he tenses. His face appears hungry for violence, and with more power than I have ever heard him exude, he screams, "I don't believe I misspoke! Casin in the pit. Riann and Alesia in here. *Now!*"

I flinch, almost covering my ears at the intensity of his outburst.

Immediately and without objection, the group breaks into efficient move-ments, three soldiers lifting a still-screaming Casin, and another three heading to the pit to retrieve Alesia and Riann. I can only pray the retrieval goes smoothly.

I keep my head down so as to avoid the grotesque sight of Kies's remains being peeled from the wall. But, by the sounds emitted when his broken bones dislodge from the crevice he made on impact, my mind paints enough of an image of what's happening mere footsteps from where I crouch. When I'm certain they've finished dragging his remains from the room, I look up to find a trail of blood weaving its way through the various tables and chairs filling the space.

With all the tension amongst the rowdy crew when we walked in, I am only now getting the chance to take in the space. The room is large and fits a number of tables, chairs, and what look to be cots. I wager this is the base which Tarak referenced earlier to Jaxon.

At the thought of Jaxon, my head twists around, my eyes searching for him. He's sitting alone, staring contemplatively at me. For just a second, my eyes watch the hint of a smile cross his face as a nod of acceptance is sent my way. The sight causes that deep rift, the loss of his friendship, to slowly mend just a bit, and I turn away, refocusing on the room itself.

A dark, curved ceiling is far above, and lanterns holding round, flickering flames are scattered about, bringing an ominous light to the room. This is nothing like the tree canopy settlement I admired those first few weeks. This room and everything in it seems to be made from something entirely different. And from the intricate designs and remains of paint falling from the sparse furniture, I can tell it's all Halabarian.

Once the movement around the room calms, a few soldiers begin going back to the spots they vacated when we first entered. I don't move, still gathering my energy as Ranya stalks toward me. My body involuntarily starts to tense, but quickly relaxes as she reaches her arm out to help me stand.

"We have a lot to discuss." She looks my square in the eye as I finally stand on shaking legs. I give a silent nod in reply, unsure of where this new alliance may lead.

XI

I find myself sitting with Ranya as a cold drink is set before me. But I don't dare take a sip, still unsure if I'm on the same side as these soldiers. Micel, who I wager has never really been my enemy, slides into a seat beside me and drapes a muscular arm across the back of my chair as if ready to pounce on any unfortunate individual who so much as dares to come my way.

My eyes meet his, and I note the stark contrast of feelings from the first time we met, sitting at a table much like this one. That first encounter left me seething with fury and angst toward a man I barely knew—a man I assumed was sent to torment and embarrass me. But now I sense a kindness I wish to one day embody. It seems that old phrase might still ring true: you should never judge a book by its cover.

I expect Tarak to take the vacant seat beside me, but it appears he's just as much the leader I assumed he was when I first met him.

He stands tall and poised at the head of the room, hands in his pockets, quietly pacing and waiting for each member of his crew to return from trading Casin for Alesia and Riann.

I can't describe the amount of relief which floods through me when I catch sight of the two being brought in and placed at a table not far from my own. A shift in the tension may have occurred, but from the number of men standing guard around them, I wager we all still have some trust to build.

What's even more confusing is Micel's reaction to their entrance. I hear his sharp inhalation of breath as the only other Halabarian citizens are marched in. He lets out a shuddering exhale as he relaxes.

When I chance a glance in his direction, my gaze imploring, he doesn't acknowledge me, but keeps his sight focused on the far off table, and the only two other people I have come close to trusting.

"I would like to tell you all a story," Tarak starts as the last of the crew finds a chair. The mood in the room hovers between earnest suspicion and hesitant optimism.

"A number of weeks ago, I met a woman who didn't know who she was." His eyes find mine. "She didn't even know her last name. And she decided to trust me and allow me, under false pretenses of my own"—his features tense in regret—"to bring her into our home. She had no idea what we had planned, or the deception we were hiding. She had no idea about the stones, her gifts, or any of the things we have let consume our entire existence up until this point."

He steals another glance my way.

"It's true that she and I formed a bond over those days together. At first, yes, I foolishly believed it was with the intention, on my part, to make her useful to our cause—a cause we have so blindly followed since the day we were cast into the trees. I would be lying if I said it didn't become more. However, that's not why we're here." He pauses to look each one of his crew in the eyes before refocusing on me. "Nera, I don't want there to be any more secrets between us or our people." The use of the word *our* stalls me. But he pays no attention to my confused features and promptly reaches out a hand, beckoning me forward. I delay only for a second, unsure of where he's taking this. But, almost without my own volition, my feet begin to move. I stand on shaking legs as Micel escorts me front and center, directly within the sights of those who I still fear want nothing more than my death.

"I believe you have a story to tell." He nods in my direction.

And I do.

I'm not sure if they will believe me. I'm not sure if they are my friends or my foes. But I'm no longer in the business of feeble minded acceptance. Maybe they'll see reason and we can use my knowledge, along with their own, to fix this broken world I've come to know and love. Maybe together we can find the stones and, along the journey, come to some understanding of what is right, what to do with them.

And if not, then maybe Riann and Alesia will forgive me for this twist in our path. Maybe in the end they will at least know this decision to ally with Tarak and those from the settlement was made in effort to help free them and in turn this planet from the despair it has plunged into.

I have never been one for public speaking, at least not that I can remember. But maybe there was a time when I once led people just as Tarak is doing right now. Because, for some reason, the words start gliding off my tongue with no hesitation whatsoever.

I retell the story Koreed explained to me the last night I was with him. The night we sat at dinner and he took me within the depths of the palace to see what the stones can really do. I tell them about using the stone to see a vision of the past. I tell them everything I have learned about Himerak. I reveal everything except my newfound knowledge of exactly what I am to this world. I let my words paint an honest picture of deceit and lies, love and heartbreak. And I hope they see the truth in my tale.

There's a moment, after I finish, when I close my eyes and wait for the attack, when I wait for the onslaught of hateful rhetoric to be spewed in my direction.

But the room is silent. No one moves. They barely even breathe.

I jerk my eyes open once I feel the firm grasp of Micel's hand escorting me back to the table, and I get the sense my words were like a molten knife stuck straight into his heart.

Tarak begins again before I make it back to my chair. "I believe, have believed for a rather long time—long before Nera arrived—that we have been, at least in part, deceived by Himerak."

A flurry of hushed cries and protests filters through the air, and I hold my breath, waiting for another attack, another fight, another death. With just a tentative look from Tarak, the room returns to silence once more.

I contemplate turning toward Micel, not knowing what he may make of the accusation. Not knowing how he will react to the knowledge that his lover, his friend, his husband may be the cause for all this strife. When I watch Ranya's sad expression flit toward him, I do the same. I expect to find anger hidden behind his deep mahogany gaze. Instead, all I find is an unwavering sadness filled with truth.

For a moment, a flickering thought races through me. I wonder if Micel already knew. I wonder if he was once deceived as well. If this strong and powerful man beside me once let his heart guide him despite the evil that, deep down, he knew was taking over Himerak.

My hand reaches out to find his under the table, and without betraying a hint of emotion in his expression, he squeezes tightly in return, lacing his fingers through mine and holding on for dear life.

"Nera isn't what we were led to believe," Tarak proclaims as he paces the small space, winding his way between tables and soldiers as he continues, "I'm hopeful that our other two *newcomers*"—he turns to face Alesia and Riann, stammering on the word as if trying not to say *captives*—"will provide us with some information as to why she has lost her memory. I also do not yet know all of what transpired during her time in Halabar, but I hope she will freely give us that knowledge so we can piece this rather complicated story together and come to a unified end."

His eyes find me once more. His hand raises to his heart, two fingers spread out over his chest, and he looks to his people. "You are not my enemy. I am not your enemy." I steady my breathing as our eyes meet. "She is not your enemy," he taps twice then reaches out, pointing in my direction while scanning the room of soldiers. "They are not your enemies," he turns his gaze to Alesia and Riann.

I feel the room tense as all eyes shift to the lone table in the far back of the room.

"We were once all members of a great nation, and it was my assumption that our goal was to bind what is broken back into one. If that is your goal as well, I ask you to put away your anger, rancor, and weapons, and help Nera and I figure out the truth behind the stones. Let us find a way to bind our world back into the prosperous land we know it can become."

He pauses, as if waiting for the words and ideas to take hold. Heartstopping moments pass without a sound from anyone in the room. I close my eyes, sending up a silent prayer that his words will ring true.

Just as I am about to lose hope, I hear it.

"Ebeli Mushari!" A woman pounds her fist on the table before her.

"Ebeli Mushari!" a deep voice screams out from the crowd as the man's mug slams into the solid wood with a clatter, sending ale splashing out onto the table.

I hold my breath, unsure of what's happening, but then recall Rhea's words. Sweet, kind Rhea said the same to me in our final moments together as she clasped my hands within her own. I look up at Tarak to find his grin growing with the ringing of voices.

"Ebeli Mushari!"

"Ebeli Mushari!"

"Ebeli Mushari!"

The room fills with a thunderous noise as soldier after soldier begins pounding on their tables and screaming out their battle cry.

XII

The cheers slowly die down, a rather ominous silence coating the air as the remaining soldiers look back and forth between the three outsiders in the room—on us. I avert my gaze, not wanting to stare into the eyes of those who might still view me as a foe. The only face I find I can bear is that of Micel. I meet his soft, warm smile with my own.

But the comfort is short-lived as Tarak signals Micel to escort me out of the room, allowing those around us to continue assessing me—their newly proposed ally—as I walk across the floor in front of them. Tarak doesn't let me get far before I feel him step in line beside us.

As I pass the table where Riann and Alesia still sit surrounded by their own entourage of guards, I see their looks of disgust and outrage. Alesia's face is filled with more sadness than strife, and my heart breaks slightly at the sight. But Riann . . . Oh, God, Riann. If looks could kill, I would be dead on the spot.

His piercing glare gives me pause.

Even during those first few days back in Halabar, when he destroyed the room next to mine, he never let me see his pain. He hid it so very well, going off to let his frustrations out where I couldn't see, then coming back to me with such kindness and love in his eyes. But now there is no hiding the disdain he feels for me, and I shudder at the waves of pain which seem to physically ripple through me.

Tarak and I only make it a few footsteps away from the room and down a dimly lit hallway before I hear Riann's balks and protestations at the shackles being once again placed on his wrists. I immediately stall my movements.

"You said they weren't your enemy, correct?" I urgently question Tarak as the heated anger bubbles upward.

"They aren't," he quickly agrees. "But they may not know that yet."

"Where are you taking them?"

"To a safe room while we figure all of this out."

I shake my head. This doesn't feel right. I can't let Riann walk right past me and not explain.

He only knows one side of the equation. Granted, it seems to be the right side at this point, but even so, he deserves to hear it from me.

"I need to talk to him," I plead to Tarak, who visibly weighs my request. As Riann's footsteps draw nearer and it doesn't seem like Tarak will allow me to have time with him, my mouth opens to protest, but Tarak waves a hand in the air, stopping their escort to allow me my moment. But this isn't enough.

"Alone. I need to speak with him alone."

"Absolutely not." Tarak's eyes crease in confusion as I try to rein in the frustration barreling through me.

"You don't get a say in this." My voice is strong and unwavering.

He halts as the realization of my demand hits, and a sigh of vexation starts to erupt. But he relents as I hold his stare, and he turns to open a door a few steps away, signaling Riann's guards to usher him inside.

Alesia is escorted past, and I almost reach out, imploring her to come with us, but she won't make eye contact with me, and my shoulders sag in defeat and sadness, knowing I have most likely alienated the two people who I should be standing with.

I don't think there is anything I can say or do at this moment to change her mind, to make her hate me any less. I know what she feels, because I felt it after seeing her back in Halabar. I held such hatred and resentment for her, knowing she could have told me the truth at any moment on Earth and chose not to. She chose to keep me in the dark, even when she saw the hell I was withdrawing into.

And now I am doing the same to her. I have turned my back on her, and have chosen to have someone else stand at my side. That someone just so happens to be her enemy.

I hope Riann will be more understanding. I may have let my frustration and anger out on him in the pit but I can't say he didn't deserve it.

I can only pray he still holds a small amount of love for me which will allow him to be more open to what I have to say. But even that thought makes me feel like a bad person, because I would be using his love to my advantage, and nothing about that seems right.

I look back as I cross the threshold and find Tarak standing vigilant in the hallway. When my eyes shift to the room where Riann waits, I take a deep breath, willing myself to stay strong.

Tarak fades from view as the door shuts between us, and I realize this may be the first time he hasn't held complete and total power over me since arriving that first day in the forest. It's the first time we've been together in which I get to make the call. It's the first time someone else may have more power and control than he does, and I think that scares him.

Tarak once made it clear he doesn't want all the responsibility being the Celestra embodies, yet he's still so easily reaping the benefits of his status. It doesn't seem like he has reconciled what giving up that position would truly mean, and that's what scares me most of all.

It's too similar to Himerak's story, and even though thoughts of Tarak still burn with hate, the one thing I don't want for him is the inability to walk away from such power. I don't want him to become enthralled in the power's grasp.

I push all thoughts of Tarak into the back of my mind as my feet silently make their way to a lone chair opposite Riann, and I wait for whatever will occur. I sit still, silently preparing for the onslaught of questions—and likely hatred—he's about to throw my way.

But he doesn't say a word as he stares right through me.

At first, I try to think of something that might bring him some sort of comfort in this moment. I think of how to phrase what's happened in a way which won't further break his heart. When nothing comes, I silently beg him to speak, to save me from my agony. I would even settle for a screaming rant if it meant he would do or say something. That would be easier to accept. But this silence . . . this empty, all-consuming silence spreads through the room, taking over every ounce of my being.

It's too much.

It's too painful.

It's not Riann.

For just a moment, I wish Alesia came in with us. Maybe she could have been the middle ground we so desperately need. I wish she didn't walk away as if the idea of speaking with me was the most traitorous thing one could do. But that's just my selfishness coming through.

Mostly, I find myself wishing we weren't alone. Because being alone with Riann is the cruelest kind of torture. The kind where my mind screams for me to take away the pain rippling from his body, but my heart screams for me to run in the other direction.

In his eyes, I've possibly sided with the ones responsible for killing Mina. I've sided with the people dead set on destroying our home, our people, our way of life. I've sided with the *enemy*.

So, instead of saying anything, I wait. Because I realize there may be nothing I can say which will be able to reconcile what I have done.

I wait.

And I wait.

I wait in agony as I allow the waves of pain rolling off him and the silence surrounding us to drown out everything.

Then, just as I'm about to burst, just as the lingering resolve is about to falter, the heat comes.

Out of nowhere, the room begins to close in around me as an all-too-familiar fire strokes my skin. But this is different from when my gifts first ignited, and it comes over me far too suddenly. The room seems to darken as an obsidian shadow trails the walls and the light in the hanging lanterns falters as if something is taking away the blaze.

I blink at the sight, trying to clear my muddled vision. But when I look back to Riann he's still staring directly through me as if nothing has changed.

The warm shadow weaves itself in and around the chairs we sit in and spreads out to encompass the room. A fear like none I've felt threatens to erupt at the sight. The scream is just about to release when an unfamiliar rage joins the heat, overwhelming me with the desire for vengeance, and I'm not exactly sure who may become my victim.

It rises up from the depths of my soul with an all-consuming intensity I have yet to experience, but for some reason feels as though it's always been a part of me. The excruciating intensity burns as it snakes its way through my body, but I will it back down. I push it back within that long-forgotten vault buried far within myself. The one filled with the pain and agony of my past as well as everything else I don't yet have the courage to face.

But it fights me for every inch, and before long, I can no longer hold it back. It bursts through every defense I have as a pulsing ache careens straight through my bones. I fall forward out of my chair, knowing I'll have to let it out, knowing I cannot hold it back any longer, and I release a tortured sob. Not from the pain, though the intensity of it is enough to bring anyone to their knees, but from the idea of what is truly swirling through me.

What I once was.

And, most likely, who I truly am still buried somewhere deep inside. Except, now that I have a taste of her, I'm not sure I ever want to meet her again. I'm not sure I would survive it. Or maybe, I don't want to let her go. It's as if I've somehow opened the chest of unknowns I worked so hard to keep sealed for far too long.

And though I continue to fight, I fail at my mission as it overtakes me. I surrender to the heat and wait for my hands to spark to life, as they did in the palace garden. I wait for the death which will surely come flowing from this hatred surging through my body.

And for the first time, a sinister feeling occurs. I find I want that death. But I can't move a muscle as the enthralling heat holds my body in place, keeping my gaze planted below. Then it finally occurs, and the weight of all I don't have the courage to accept is made known. The small tendrils of constant light inch their way across my skin, wrapping me from head to foot in a red and golden tattoo-like design.

No! The voice I heard so long ago breaks through the heat.

Don't let go. Don't give in, she begs.

"Let me go," I plead, not sure to whom I'm speaking, or if I even speak the words out loud.

No! You must fight.

The voice wraps around me, a cold blanket of ice to smother the heat, and I feel the dread of what I was about to do sink in.

With the little effort I can manage, I dig my fingers into the cold, solid floor beneath me, watching it crumble beneath my grip, hoping to fizzle out anything that may come. Just as the heat starts to recede, I hear a small sneer from somewhere far off in the distance. Somewhere I can't yet reach.

As quickly as the sensation arrived, it dissipates, leaving me on my hands and knees, cold, panting, and confused. I collapse further as I watch the golden tendrils which decorate the ground retreat within me, and I let the cool stone of the floor calm the raging heat still lingering on my skin.

It takes a few moments for me to regain my bearings, and when I lift my eyes, I find Riann's bored expression staring back at me. My mind can't make sense of it. Have I truly hurt him so deeply he won't even help me?

Maybe it was all in my head. Maybe all he saw was a broken girl finally breaking down with the weight of everything that has happened—with the weight of everything she has done.

I expect him to say—to *do*—something. To reach for me or to check to see if I'm okay. That's what the Riann I've come to know would do. But that Riann may no longer exist. That Riann may now realize the one woman he truly loves doesn't, and will never, reciprocate the feeling again.

So, when our eyes finally meet, instead of finding what I hoped I would, all I find looking back at me is a man completely devoid of emotion.

But then, as I'm laying there wrapped up in the engrossing exhaustion which rakes through my body, he finally speaks.

"When you were about eight, you found this small little fowl."

My brows crease. Still unable to fully remove myself from the floor, I lie still as he speaks over me.

"It had a broken wing, and we spent weeks nursing it back to health."

I swallow as he continues, and slowly force my body to move, managing to lean back against the legs of the chair.

"Then, at about ten, there was a gulup. It'd been nicked by a trimming blade when one of the gardeners was clearing out some debris from a storm. We patched it up, but the injury was too severe, and he ended up dying a few days later. You cried for a week." He begins flexing his fingers, stretching each, and then popping his knuckles as he speaks. "Then, when we were twelve, you started volunteering at the sickbay. It was all I could do to get you to worry about training instead of helping those poor, injured and dying souls."

His eyes finally meet mine, but all I see now are obsidian orbs of anger and hate staring back at me.

"By the time you were eighteen, you'd become the most stubborn woman I knew." His face is downright menacing. "You've always had a penchant for delving into matters that don't concern you." I feel the tears begin to fall as the exhaustion creeps in. "You were always worrying about everyone else—the citizens, the world, the crude beasts on the Bend." I can swear there's a slight shift in his tone, moving from anger to contempt. "It was my biggest frustration. I knew you would one day get yourself hurt—or worse—while trying to care for another."

He pauses, taking a shuddering breath.

"We had a fight that last night. You were . . . *are* so damn stubborn. You wanted to do everything your own way, and you wouldn't listen to reason. If you had just *stayed put* like I told you to, none of this would have happened. The plan would have succeeded. You selfishly trekked off in search of answers to all your questions on how to fix this. It was ridiculous. *You* were ridiculous. I was so mad. But I didn't get to you in time. The consequence of that was not seeing you for the next three years."

I gasp at his admission.

This is the first time anyone has alluded to why I went missing. I open my mouth as I try to force the questions to come, but the exhaustion is still all consuming.

"You fix things, Nera. That's what you do. You are stubborn, and unyielding, and you gravitate toward hurting or dying things, no matter to what end. It's one of the things I love about you. One of the things I'll always love about you." Dread settles in my stomach.

"Riann–"

"You can't fix him," he quickly cuts me off. "And you can't fix this world by yourself. You need people who know you—who have always known you. You need people who love you for who you are—not just because of a few silly lines on your wrist." He takes another deep breath, letting the weight of all that has transpired settle on his shoulders. "I don't want our mission to be upended just because you're, once again, drawn to something broken and hurting."

I slowly lift my body, and slide back into the chair, hoping I'll be able to stay upright and not fall completely over from the exhaustion and emotions.

"Riann, wait–"

"There is nothing you can say or do. You have made your choice to join a side which is not ours and never will be. It seems I was right all along." He shakes his head in further frustration, and then out of nowhere, a menacing smile plays upon his lips. "I want peace, and I will get it. No matter the cost. So there's no need for some grand speech for you to worry yourself through."

I feel a tear trailing down my cheek just as Tarak opens the door, and without another word, Riann stands and walks out of the room.

XIII

"**A**re you okay?" Tarak questions as we make our way through the tunnels of the underground system.

I sigh, my shoulders sagging in defeat. "No."

When Tarak came into the room after Riann walked out and found me barely able to sit up, I think he assumed I was overcome by grief, or maybe confusion.

I didn't correct him.

I didn't let him know what had truly occurred in that room only minutes prior. Not because I wanted to keep it a secret. If anything, I want to do everything I can to figure out what keeps happening to me. But I don't think I can handle diving into the truth behind what it was I felt back there. I don't think I'm ready to meet *that* version of myself. Especially since I have no idea where she came from.

And from the way Riann acted, I'm not even sure he fully witnessed or was aware of what was happening to me. He seemed too distant and aloof as I entered into that infernal abyss which resides in my soul.

Maybe it was all in my head? Maybe I have truly gone mad?

"Nera?" Tarak implores.

Without warning, my words spill forth, a river bursting through its dam.

"I don't remember him at all. I don't remember him, just as I don't remember anything else from before. I don't remember him!" I all but yell in the quiet corridor. "I don't remember my father or the palace or the stones or my abilities. But it still hurts to know I'm breaking some part of him. I am not an evil person."

"You're not evil." Tarak's hand trails the length of my arm, and he clasps my hand in his, giving it a gentle squeeze before releasing me.

"It doesn't feel like it right now." I think back to the feelings which have only just recently surfaced within me and look down at my hand, a shadow of his touch lingering on my skin, the warmth which was there now forgotten. I once might've felt the need to keep them clasped in order to hold onto something real. But now? If he didn't let go on his own, I would've pulled away from his touch, wondering if I'll ever know if any of it was real.

"What do you need from me?" His words are quiet, gentle. "I don't want to push you away."

"I don't trust you," I admit and watch as his face falls. "But we do need to talk about Himerak and Koreed. I need to know everything there is to know. I will no longer be kept in the dark."

He nods his head in agreement. And then, for some reason, the idea that Koreed . . . the idea that *my father* may no longer be alive hits me. My only living blood relative may now be gone. I feel the familiar tears of heartache as they rim my eyes and blur the figure in front of me.

"He's alive," Tarak interjects when he recognizes the emotions starting to erupt.

"What?" I blink my eyes and snap my head up in shock.

"In case you were worried." His fingers reach out to wipe away a lone tear, and I allow the contact. I don't have the energy right now to turn away. "I just wanted you to know he's still alive and well. In the midst of planning his own siege on us in order to get you back." The comforting warmth of his touch almost makes me miss the pain in his voice.

"How do you know?" I tilt my head in question.

"We have a host of spies in Halabar." He laughs a little to himself, but then his face falls as he swallows. "I know almost everything that happened while you were there."

"What?" I don't know how, but the revelation shocks me.

I look around this void of a hallway and, though no one's around to hear us, I still bristle at the thought of others bearing witness to this conversation.

"I know you and Alesia were on rocky terms, to say the least," he explains with a half smile. "I know you despised your two personal guards and caused plenty of trouble for them." His smile grows to fill his face, causing those dimples to reappear. "I know Koreed took you down beneath the palace and into the Soul Circle. Though I don't know all the details of what happened once you were on the other side of that door." He raises his eyebrows, indicating he most definitely wants to hear about that later. "And I know Riann barely left your side. That the one and only time in which you left the palace was when he took you to the atheneum." He runs a hand through his hair, visibly frustrated. "We don't have them out here. We barely have enough books for what was the small school."

My heart clenches as I recall the children running through the trees of the settlement.

"From what I heard, that trip made you happy. Devin, our spy who works there, said you looked truly at ease the day you went. You were smiling and even laughing as you walked up and down the aisles."

My brows crease as the meaning behind what he's telling me starts to sink in. "You've been watching me? This whole time?"

"We've been watching Koreed for years. We didn't get access to the palace until the last few weeks. So, before you ask your next question . . . No, I don't have an abundance of knowledge about you from before. I just knew you existed and your basic physical features."

"But now you have spies inside?" I cross my arms over my chest as I try to decide what good may come of that information.

"Yes. Well, inside is more a metaphorical term now. A good bit of the palace was destroyed when we came for you. The lower levels are still intact, and of course we assume the Soul Circle is as well, though there's no longer a Celestra onsite to go and determine if it survived."

I reach out and grab his hand, hoping the gesture conveys how desperate I am. "Tarak, if we are going to do this, there are things which need to change right now. I will only be a part of this mission if I am no longer the mission itself. Do you understand me?"

"Completely." He nods his head in agreement.

"I need to know everything. *Everything.* I can't be blindsided by something again. I can't deal with that."

"I know. But that trust goes both ways. I need to know *everything* you saw. I need to know what happened in that room."

I nearly cringe at his knowledge of my deception on the matter. But then again, I owe him nothing. With the exception of my name on that first day we met, I never lied to him. I never once attempted to deceive him.

He must sense my overwhelming frustration because he quickly adds. "Nera, I promise to be truthful from here on out. My love is unconditional."

"Stop." I shake my head, not wanting to travel down that path again.

"I'm sorry," Tarak pleads. "I just want to start over. And I promise things are different from here on out. I promise to do whatever you need me to do in order to right this," he adds as his gaze falls to the ground.

"Sometimes I feel like I haven't taken a single breath since I woke that first day." I attempt to wipe the exhaustion off my face.

"I know."

"What do we do next?" I look up to find him staring off into the distance of the underground corridor.

"How about we get you some new clothes and something to eat before we get started?" He looks back and motions toward my torn, dust-covered gown which, at this point, holds more holes than actual fabric.

"Déjà vu," I say under my breath as I start to laugh a little to myself to hide the swelling of tears which are trying to break free.

"What?" His brows crease in confusion.

My head shakes as if on instinct as I try to drown out the sensation. "Have you never heard of that phrase?"

"No. Are you calling me another one of your Earth names which doesn't mean something very nice? I wouldn't blame you if you were," he teases.

"No." I shake my head with a smile as I tentatively pull my fingers back and wrap my hand around my middle. "It's just a way of saying 'I feel like this has happened before.'"

I feel the heat encroaching within the small room before I hear the sizzle of evaporating water.

"What is that?" I question with a furrowed brow as I test my movement in the brown leather pants and green shirt Tarak provided me.

He was kind enough to step away as I changed, giving me my first true moment of peace since I woke. And I may have taken a little longer than necessary to fully dress, if only to stretch the moment out for as long as I could.

He keeps smiling at me like the last hour is going to erase everything else. But nothing will erase the memories of his betrayal from my mind.

"I'm not sure," Tarak admits as he turns away from me to grab the door frame and peer out into the darkness.

He takes a deep breath before chancing a glance my way. As soon as our eyes meet, I see a deep remorse gathered in his gaze. It's only a momentary glance, and for a second, I watch the push and pull of all he is forced to be.

I wish things could've been different. I wish he hadn't killed Mina, and I wish he wasn't a Celestra but just some random person that helped me along the way. Maybe then we wouldn't be so stuck within these roles chosen for us.

But unfortunately, things are not different. He did kill Mina, and he is a Celestra. But most unfortunately, so am I.

He shakes his head before quickly turning back to the corridor, and I take the few steps forward to meet him where he stands.

"There are streams which flow above some of the paths under here. It could be–"

His words cut off and his body tenses, the taut muscles across his back threaten to shred through his shirt with any movement.

"Get out!" he screams as he turns and reaches for my arm. I freeze in shock at his quick change in demeanor. "We have to get out!" he shouts, violently pushing me forward, out of the room and back down the hall in the direction we came from only moments earlier.

His feet pound against the dirt floor as he moves. We are running so fast. Too fast. And I nearly trip over myself as I try to gain my bearings. His grip on my arm is the only thing that keeps me upright as we plunge forward into the darkness.

I turn back only once in search of whatever assailant has found us. For a moment, I wonder if it could be Koreed or his men. But instead of a uniform, I catch a quick glimpse of misty air swirling through the expanse. It follows the path, inching its way into the room we just vacated. Then, before I have the chance to realize what's coming for us, I feel a prickling sensation travel down my spine.

A blatant warning as to what is to come.

The heat from before moves within me, and I try to push it back down. But my efforts are fruitless, and I feel it rush forth.

A heinous scream of frustration at the heated battle deep within me is ripped from my lungs, and I wince as the unfamiliar noise reverberates through the empty corridor. Just before I turn back forward, that prowling mist stalls. It pulls back out of the room and, though there is no face and no eyes, I swear it sees what races away from it.

And then it lurches forward.

Its movement is too quick, almost sentient in nature, its tendrils racing and coiling through the hallway and wrapping within and around everything it comes into contact with. The low light of the lantern-lit space causes it to fade in and out of view as it edges closer toward us, stretching along the walls, ceiling, and floor. The path begins to warm. A bead of sweat rolls down my brow. And even now, even knowing what this malicious thing is, I still have to ask. And hope beyond hope that I'm wrong.

"Is that–?" My words are desperate and breathy as I gulp down air.

"The Haze," he immediately answers before I can finish and I swallow hard in anticipation.

Fear and shock roar through me, begging my tired and weary legs to move faster. I wish I hadn't asked. Maybe then I could continue telling myself it was something else. I could continue with the lie in my head, which would keep my feet from shaking and my hands from trembling in fear. Now that I know the truth, I can't hide from the adrenaline spreading through every inch of my body.

Faster, faster, faster!

I internally scream, hoping my weary legs and feet will somehow understand the message.

As if Tarak can hear my silent thoughts, he reaches down to clasp my hand and pulls me forward. A silent plea to increase my speed.

My mind tumbles through the myriad of questions I want to scream but can't.

How did it make it all the way through the forest?

How did it make it underground?

Why is it hell bent on coming after us? After me?

But one question surfaces, seemingly without my notice.

"What about everyone else?" I force out the words through gulps of air, worried as to what fate the others hidden within these tunnels may face. What about Riann and Alesia? What about Jaxon and Ranya and Micel? What about all the others who I have yet to know?

"Elders!" he calls out in frustration as realization hits him as well.

I have seen this manner of death before. I remember Jensin. I would not wish such agony upon anyone. Not even my worst enemy.

"We are the furthest back," he says as our feet continue to pound against the ground, but then he startles as if the idea has just now come to him. He reaches around his neck and yanks forward the silver circle-like pendant I first noticed on our journey into this hellscape, places it to his lips and blows. The sound it omits almost causes me to halt. A piercing shrill, a screaming warning, a plea for them to escape.

That's what it is, a communication device.

Within seconds, I catch sight of a few lone souls peering out from sparsely placed rooms as we pass by. Each grabbing their own pendant as they blow out a scream into the void.

My chest heaves and I want nothing more than to stop and catch my breath but I have a feeling that would only end in my certain death. Every few feet I can't help but twist back and check, but each time it's still there. Sometimes closer, sometimes farther back. But, it's still there.

We don't lose it until we shift directions and twist around a bend.

Then relief hits. I start to feel the cool breeze rush in and I know we must be close to the entrance. But then the heat overtakes us as the Haze slashes across an upcoming corridor and slams into the wall to my right. I try to stop but with my forward movement, I go careering into two others also trying to save themselves.

One grabs my arm, thrusting me upwards onto my shaking legs and before I can even mouth a thank you and take off once again, the misty Haze wraps around the man. His body turns to fire as his skin erupts. Blisters spread out, then burst and a pungent liquid spreads out at my feet. Flakes of ash fall to the ground. Smoke fills my vision as terror consumes my mind.

"Holy shit!" I scream out, my feet paralyzed in my shock.

"Nera!" Tarak yanks my hand, and without my control, my feet start moving.

The next few moments are a blind chaotic mess. I have no idea how I can even control my body, let alone keep up with everyone else. It seems that just when we think we've escaped the reaches of death, it comes barreling toward us once more.

Jaxon joins us just around the next curve, but I barely even meet his panic-stricken face before the hiss of steam and heat close in.

It comes from the front, surging toward all three of us. A bellowing of high-pitched amusement rings through the expanse as if this were just a game and we are the unfortunate players.

We run. Faster and faster and faster. But still it gains on us.

It lurches forward, tendrils scattering across the ground and nipping at our heels as it moves. Tears stream down my face, and I can't tell if they're from fear of what's to come or the pain rippling through my chest with every breath of air I heave. My body slams against a wall at the next turn. Jagged rocks slice through the exposed skin of my arm and I scream out with the blinding pain.

But my attention turns as a burst of noise comes from behind.

The air ignites as sparks fly toward us, singeing whatever they land on. The ground quakes, hinting at an even more violent force hiding far within its reaches. And then agony like nothing I have ever known wraps around my ankle, snaring me within its hold as it burns me from the inside out.

A scream shreds my throat as I fall to the ground, unable to move another inch, and gasping for air as the throbbing torment snakes its way upward and through my leg. The burning sensation comes in waves as it pulsates through me, and I lose both my breath and sight in excruciation.

The pain overtakes me. It suffocates me from within. It covers me like a dark blanket filled with all the horrors of my past, desperate to smother me. But I try to dig myself back to life as I mentally claw upward and away from the pain, and toward the one sound piercing through the darkness.

XIV

"Look up, Nera. *Look up!*" he urges. I feel his arms wrap around me and his face come to rest against my forehead, and for just a moment the pain dissipates.

The clouded darkness I'm ensnared within starts to dissolve as the world begins to once again open back up before me. It takes all my effort to force open my eyes, my body still shaking from the torment which is banging against the doors of my mind, threatening re-entry. When I finally get the strength to shift my gaze to the ceiling, I find the shimmering dome of my shield surrounding us.

It encompasses us like a mound cast from light. The Haze swirls around the shield, sentient tendrils searching out into the air like fingers in the mists, trying to gain access into our momentary shelter. But each time an obsidian wisp hits the dome, a sizzling crackles through the air and a cascade of sparks flies through the tendrils, illuminating the darkened paths beyond. It recoils back as if it can feel pain, as if it is a living thing with its own path, mission, and destiny.

But it doesn't relent. Over and over again, its tendrils reach out, trying to burst open the shelter I have created. Each time, the pathway explodes into light as the dome defends us. But with each pass, the Haze grows more and more angry that it can't get to us, to me, and I find my already weakened state further deteriorating to the point, I fear there will be nothing left.

There is a muttering of words between the two men at my sides that I can't quite catch. The pain, still rolling over me in waves, seems to drown out most of my senses, but I keep my gaze steady and upward.

My focus remains on the dome, not knowing if it needs my attention to stay up. Maybe not? I did somehow make it without even realizing it. Maybe it just appears when I need it? Maybe it, too, has a mind of its own?

"Can you move it?"

I startle as Tarak's words settle in my mind at the same time a zap of lightning hits near my ear, removing me from the trance I've found myself in.

"What?" I answer through gritted teeth. The effort to speak even one word through the pain threatens to wreck me.

"Can you manipulate it? Can we keep running with the shield moving with us?"

"I . . . I'm not . . . " I concede to the waves of agony that undulate through me. I want to scream at my seemingly innate inability to answer, to help, to do *anything* of use.

He grabs my face in his hands and looks me dead in the eye.

"Just concentrate. I promise you, we will get out of here, and when we do, I'll make sure you never need to use this again. I'll take care of you. Okay? We are going to get out of here. I just need you to move it with us."

My head bobs in acceptance and he leans back as he pulls me up to stand. But without the warmth of his constant touch, I quickly collapse back to the ground as the pain in my leg surges once more.

A scream is ripped from my throat as I catch sight of the burn for the first time. The mangled and grotesque sight stalls me. Seeing it on someone else is one thing. Seeing it on myself is a completely different experience.

The red, inflamed skin surrounding the area has swollen, now resembling an angry, rancid monster filled with a poisonous liquid. With any movement on my part, the liquid sloshes within me, causing my vision to blur and the little food I consumed earlier to threaten a reappearance.

Looking at the surrounding skin makes me cringe, but it's the sight of the burn itself which finally causes the vomit to force its way out. It splashes onto the dirt-covered floor, but Tarak doesn't even seem to notice. He is too concerned with my face as he holds it in his hands. He is too focused on me. On my pain, on my foot, on the agony I hold within.

The flesh—or what was once flesh, now charred and broken—begins to flake away as the skin changes color right before my eyes. I catch sight of a long ligament which is now visible within my ankle as the surrounding meat falls to the floor.

And then I hear Tarak's sharp inhalation of breath as the fluid-filled bubble bursts, causing a rancid odor to permeate the air. My vision splinters, and my body goes limp.

"Holy Elders," Jaxon looks from Tarak to me and then stands to survey the chaos still raging around us. "We have to get out of here," he urges and I see Tarak nod in agreement.

When he starts talking again, the words are mumbled and the sounds all mesh together. He shakes my face as he silently screams at me, but the shadows have already started to creep in. I gladly sink somewhere deep within the darkness as the pain overtakes me.

I run my hands along the spines of the books as I wait for Alesia to meet me. It's a habit I've somehow picked up when the store is empty and there is no one left to smile for. When I finally get to the front row, there is a golden streak of light coming through the window.

The sunset for today is almost over. The last bit of light surges through one of the stones glued to the window and bounces off the row of books in front of me. The brilliance of its beauty consumes me. It calls me forward. And without thought, I take another step, and then another, abandoning my mindless habit and locking my eyes on the radiant stone with flecks of gold swirling inside.

It's a new addition. Mary just added it this afternoon. The glue she uses to adhere it to the window still has some drying to do, and I start to laugh. It should've dried by now, but she must have used three times what was needed. I swipe a tissue from a nearby box and try to wipe off as much excess as I can. On the final pass, the stone falls from the window and lands between my feet.

I quickly pick up the trinket and search for glue, only to find the bottle completely empty. I chuckle once more, rolling the stone around in my hand.

"I'll have to fix you tomorrow, before she comes in and sees what I've done," I whisper to the object in my hands as if it were a long forgotten friend.

Then cringe at the idea that I can barely say two words to an actual person, but here I am talking to a damn rock.

But maybe it's not so bad if it's one of Mary's. She calls them her wishing rocks. At least that's what Taylor says she signs to her. Maybe that's why Mary and I get along so well. Neither of us are able to fully communicate with outsiders. We instead tend to bask in the quiet nothingness.

"So you're a wishing rock, huh?" I tease toward the inanimate object as I raise the stone up into the air, catching the last rays of light in it.

The bell chimes and Alesia quickly steps through, shivering and shaking off the flecks of snow from her worn winter jacket. She catches my gaze as she starts to smile. Her mouth opens as if she's about to say something, but then she freezes. The odd look quickly turns to fear and she reaches for me as one wish circles through my mind.

I want to go home.

"Nera! *Stay awake!* You have to stay awake!" Tarak screams as he runs his hands across my face, my arms, my legs, my foot, and I am all but thrown back into consciousness only to have the waves of pain threaten to pull me back.

In and out I go. Again and again. Muddling somewhere between the here and now and what once was.

What should be a deafening shout, but is now barely a whisper above the roaring in my ears, is calling me back to him like a lifeboat just out of reach. But I don't want to stay with him. I want to go somewhere else. I want to go back to the bookstore. I want to go back to Mary and Taylor.

I want to go home.

"Find me." The noise is muffled, almost as if it's under water.

"Save me." It mellows out as if being carried away on an ebbing tide by the soft melody being screamed from above.

"Become me." The words linger in the air as if fighting to remain.

A silent pull within the darkness is calling me somewhere familiar, calling me back to where I belong. I start to edge toward it.

I want to go home.

There is a light so far within the depths of the darkness and it starts to spread. My body tingles with need to reach it.

I want to go home.

It spreads out as muffled cries ring in from above, begging for me to return. But they're too far away.

And I want to go home.

The light beckons me forward and I stand only to find the two men once beside me nowhere to be seen. Instead of a hidden tunnel buried within the ground, I find a darkened cave. Cold emptiness surrounds me and water pools at my feet.

I wrap my arms around myself as the previous pain that once soared through me is smothered by something familiar and cold.

"Hello?" I call out into the darkness just as the light starts to recede, and with it my chance to go. "No!" The sound reverberates on the surrounding rock as my feet race across the expanse. Water splashes at my heels as the light dims. "No! Please. No!"

The whimper is caught in my throat just as the light fizzles out.

The heat fueled by anger which I barely succeed at keeping hidden beneath the surface threatens to rise and for once I don't care. I almost welcome it.

I drop to my knees in acceptance, letting the cold water soak my clothes. It does nothing but turn to steam as it washes over my skin. My fist drives into the obsidian sea as I scream out in desperation.

"Do something!" I hurl the plea into the unknown. "Kill me! Take me! I don't care anymore!"

The last words fade out with no reply in sight. Sobs rack my body as I kneel frozen in time. I scream and fight and send out a slew of curses at the thought of being trapped somewhere I don't belong.

The heat continues to rise.

"I want to go home." The whispered cry seeps past my lips as tears fall down my cheeks and into the shallow water below. Ripples from my thrashing move in waves. Again and again they move, and then slow as my body calms and all that's left are the rivers of regret and longing pouring out from me. And then they stop all together. The ripples hold still as a slow flickering movement of white catches my attention.

The snowflake drops from the heavens and lands on my heated arm. It fizzles into nothing as the unrelenting fire from my anger melts it away. Before the water droplet can fall from my skin, another lands. And then another. And then one more. And soon there are fifty, one hundred, ten thousand landing upon me.

The first hundred or so instantly melt away, but then the burn lessens and heat retreats. Before I realize what's happening, my body and the surrounding water are covered by beautiful powdery snow. I skim my fingers along the top and watch as an indention forms.

"You're almost here," he says.

I look up to find nothing but falling crystals above me.

"Come back to me," he beckons, and I stand letting the snowflakes fall away.

"I don't know how," I admit, and a warm tendril caresses my chin.

"Come back to me."

My mind remains still, balanced so precisely as if I'm on a tightrope being tugged from one end of consciousness to the next. The push and pull of the surrounding air and light is the only thing keeping me from falling off the edge to my total demise as the waves of pain return, surge, and then lessen. Surge and lessen.

Even so, his voice becomes my anchor, tethering me to the here and now as my body fights to reach it. The walls cave in. The ceiling falls toward me. The ground crumbles beneath my feet.

And then I hear a voice. Tarak is talking and talking and talking. He uses a strong and steady tone, asking me question after question which I can't quite comprehend as I feel his arms lifting me from the ground below. I try to reach out to him in the darkness, reach out to that small speck of light where the noise seeps in, but he is still so far away. So very far away.

I want to sink into his warmth, but the air around is too sticky and hot, and I feel our bodies fight to merge against one another as the sweat starts to roll from our skin. My sight comes and goes as waves of pain rock through my body and mind.

At one moment, the darkness is all I can see, hear, and feel. An empty pit of nothingness. It calls my name in languid waves like a siren's song intended just for me.

In the next moment, I catch sight of his face as it flickers into view for the first time. His mouth moves with such force that the curled tendrils of his blonde hair swing with the movement, yet the words don't quite reach my ears.

In the moments I can manage to keep my gaze focused, I search for the shattered walls and ceiling and floor. Instead I find the underground tunnel to be a perfectly intact structure, the dome's shimmering glow surrounding us and moving as we escape. It weaves in and out of sight as the darkness threatens to pull me back under. But my anchor is unrelenting.

I hold steady, letting him guide me, hold me, save me. A calm reprieve seems to settle in me as I bask in the warmth of his arms and the waves of pain begin to dull. But the moment is stolen, and I flinch when I hear the hiss from the haze striking the shield, sending a flash as bright as lightning arcing up over the dome. It spreads and fizzles out as it passes through the pathway behind us.

The brightness further blinds me, and I shrink back into the darkness. Into the pain. But still, that voice somehow makes its way to me.

Finally, I feel my body being pulled upward as a new light begins to splinter in.

And then there are new voices. Too many voices as people shuffle around my form. It's loud, and it's chaotic, and it's messy. And I just want it all to go away.

But I pry my eyes open, and then pull back as the light from the sun threatens to blind me. When I feel Tarak start to lay me down on the soft bed of grass below, I hold steady, not allowing his arms to leave me. He brushes a hand against my forehead, then my arms, stomach, and finally my legs and feet, and the lingering pain slowly dissipates to a tolerable throb. The world fades back into view, as if all the fractured pieces around me are slowly sliding into place.

"She needs the salve. *Who has it?*" Micel's scream is the first noise I can make sense of in the surrounding chaos. "Elders be *damned!*" he bellows when no one rushes toward us.

I search his gaze to find his eyes are focused on a group a few feet over. It takes far too much effort, but I turn, trying to make out what he now sees. Instead, I hear the pleas of agony take hold.

"We can't save her! Don't waste it!" Micel yells out to someone in the distance, and I twist just slightly as his features come into view.

They can't save her?

They can't save me?

Confusion slams through me at the thought.

No. No, that isn't right. This isn't right. I'm no longer sinking into the depths of my agony, I'm here! I'm here!

I force my lips to move, but the dryness of my mouth and the heat which still courses through my body don't allow any sounds to come forth.

A whimper pierces the air, and it's only when the few standing, sitting, crouching around my form turn to face me that I realize the noise came from my lips.

I'm not dying.

I'm not.

I'm alive! I want to scream out, but when I open my mouth, I can't force the words to come.

Why can't they save me?

I sob at the thought, wondering if this is truly the end as various people run from here to there and fuss with my mostly paralyzed form. I should have stayed in the darkness.

Then I feel the sensation of something cold and wet brushing against my leg and I hear a whine of relief cut through the noise.

"I'm not dead." It finally comes out as a whisper only Tarak can hear, and I catch sight of a lone tear as it falls down his cheek.

"No. You're not," he confirms with a smile, but confusion still lingers within me.

I shift my gaze to find Riann and Alesia, but I'm too tired and the brightness all around causes me to squint my eyes. I try to speak their names, to call out to them, but once again the words die in my throat.

And then I hear the screams.

Horrifying, nightmarish screams come from not too far away. I move to sit. I have to see what horror has come for us now, but Tarak moves to shift me against a rock, helping me lean back. The change in position allows just enough visibility for me to see where the noise comes from.

In the blur of my own swimming consciousness, I find a woman lying limp and lifeless on the ground not too far from where I sit. I want to reach out to her and I feel my fingertips begin to stretch toward her form. She just needs to hold on.

Hold on and wait. Wait for the darkness to dissipate and for the light to filter back in.

Then I watch as the screaming man falls to the ground and panic overtakes him. He empties his stomach before quickly falling back to his side, his breaths coming in pants, and then a scream so loud it rattles my bones erupts from his singed and bleeding lips.

"Calm him down!" Micel urges, and I look up to find him not staring toward the screaming man, but with eyes planted on Tarak. "I don't have time to deal with this," Micel adds as he further works on my burned and rotting leg. I look down to the wound, expecting to feel the pain, but find Tarak grasping the skin directly above and rubbing it with a soothing touch. He looks back and forth from me to the screaming man as he weighs what he should do.

Then I shift just enough to catch sight of what's causing the man's screams. It's the woman I saw only moments earlier. Or . . . maybe it's not? She's lying in the same place, but she doesn't look the same anymore. A gasp leaves my lips. With my sight now clearing, I'm able to see what I couldn't before. Her skin is all but gone. It falls from her body, leaving a pile of bones which disintegrates into ash as the moments pass by.

The man screams for her over and over, his pleas filling the air, and it finally hits me. I assumed his cries were for his own pain. Pain from an injury I couldn't see. Part of that is true. I can now see that he cries not for himself, but for her. From the invisible pain of losing something . . . someone.

With a quick kiss to my forehead, I watch as Tarak lets go of me and stands. Without the soothing heat of his touch, the pain returns and I have to bite back the cry that now fights to escape. And while it's still incredibly horrific, it's nowhere near as bad as it was before.

"I'll be right back. It will only last a second," he calls back as he moves.

Within two strides, he's at the man's side, crouching down and placing a gentle hand on his shoulder. I watch in confusion. I know heartache. And I know there is nothing Tarak can say or do in this moment to ease the knife currently being twisted into that man's soul.

But I'm wrong. As if a switch has been flipped, the man quiets and deflates at Tarak's touch. It's not immediate. It takes a few moments—almost a full minute for it all to happen. An almost drugged expression crosses the man's face as his previously erratic breathing levels out. His shoulders droop, and a relief-filled sigh seeps from his formerly pursed lips.

And then Tarak slowly steps back.

And no one even bats an eye at what just occurred.

A needle I know all too well is jammed into the barely moving man's arm, and I watch as he slumps further and seems to drift off into a slumber.

Within a moment, Tarak is back at my side, holding onto my legs and rubbing in the warmth of his touch.

"What did you just do?" I hear Alesia question, and I breathe a sigh of relief, knowing at least she is okay. When I shift to face her, I find Riann standing nearby. Both have an equally shocked look upon their faces.

"What did you just do?" Alesia asks again, more pointedly now, as what's left of the woman's body is picked up in pieces and moved away from the site.

"He calmed him," Jaxon answers, as if that's something one might do every day.

"How?" Alesia quickly questions as she takes a step forward but is quickly halted by a few men and women who surround.

"Soothsayer," Riann's whisper is the answer. Utter disdain oozes from his lips as he tentatively moves closer, placing his body as close to mine as the others will allow. The few soldiers surrounding him draw their weapons, ready to attack.

"I just calmed him. It's not . . . " Tarak fists his curls as his eyes shift between Riann and Alesia, and finally to me. He squeezes my leg as he speaks, "I can't change how things will end, or the decisions someone makes based on their emotions. Free will always triumphs." He takes a deep breath as if preparing for something. "But I can make someone feel better about what is happening in the moment."

"What . . ." My voice finally obeys me, though my brain wavers on which question to ask first. *What is a soothsayer? How does it work? Why do I not know about this?*

Thankfully, it's Alesia who reiterates her same question from earlier. Then one I don't know how to state.

"How did you do it?" Each word comes out with a punch.

Tarak doesn't answer as he takes a deep breath, and I chance a look at the previously panic-stricken man. He is quiet and still as he slows his breathing and lays against a nearby tree base, drifting in and out of consciousness. His eyes don't fully make contact as they slowly cross my plane of view, but I can tell a thousand thoughts are running through his mind.

I know because I have felt that. I have been there. And it's not because of whatever was in that needle.

XV

I stare at Tarak, my glare all but screaming at him to provide an answer. His gaze meets mine head on, but he stays silent and unmoving. And then, for just a moment, his facade falls, allowing a remorseful expression to fill his face. But still, no words are spoken, and with each second of silence, my heart fractures just that much more.

I count the breaths between us as the realization of what has been exposed hits me harder than a bullet, causing new waves of pain to ripple through my tattered heart.

He used this on me.

He used his gift on me.

"You've done that to me before." Though my voice quivers with the words, it is much stronger now with the weight of all that this means.

"Yes," Tarak admits, and I use what little energy I have left to recoil against the rock I'm leaning against. The sudden movement causes him to pause, quickly throwing his hands in the air in surrender, and the pain hits me once more. "But not– not fully," he quickly adds, trying to appease me, a guilty expression crossing his face. "I just barely used it on you. I calmed you. There is this . . . " he pauses as he gathers the words, "wall between us which won't let it all through. I promise. I promise, all I did was calm you."

"Calmed me enough to make me lean right into you?"

"No," he quickly denies with a shake of his head, and my stomach fills with lead. "Enough to make you not afraid. Enough to make you not feel the pain."

His throat bobs with an audible swallow as he reaches forward to once again grab my leg. I swiftly, and painfully, pull back out of his reach.

"But I couldn't take it all away. I tried to stop. I tried so many times. I wanted to tell you. It didn't feel right doing that to you. But I couldn't stand to see you so worried and afraid and . . . " He trails off as he buries his face in his hands. "I just didn't want you to be afraid. I promise I was just helping. I wasn't lying." His final sentence is barely audible, and angry tendrils of ice scatter along my skin.

"And yet that's exactly what you did," I seethe with anger.

The thought that he has somehow altered how I felt, altered how I saw this world, how I saw *him*, causes the lingering pain from my leg to feel as though it is nothing but a small throb in the wake of the true agony.

I don't care that he tried to help me. I don't care what his reasons are. He has once again lied to me; tricked me. He did something to me without my knowledge.

My eyes shift between the various men and women still standing within earshot; a lucky few have walked off, perhaps in search of food or weapons, leaving only a few to watch as my world falls apart. My eyes flit between those who remain: Jaxon, Alesia, Riann, Ranya, Micel, the pained man still relishing in the euphoric state Tarak has induced, and a few others I can't yet name. My heart thrums in my chest as the surrounding air becomes thick and fragile. It settles as a weight as it enters my lungs, and I quickly look away from the prying eyes.

These people out here—his soldiers, his friends, his family—they all know what he can do. This isn't a surprise to them. *But me?* I knew nothing. I've continued to be kept in the dark.

"If I hadn't used it, we would have been found," Tarak pleads. His voice breaks though the silence, and I want so much to withdraw within, to hide away from the wave of regret which is sure to follow.

"That first day in the tree?" I snicker, immediately knowing what he is referring to. "It seems that might have been a better alternative." Maybe I would have been saved from all this.

"An alternative which would have ended with one or both of us dead." His voice is now raised and tense.

"How often?" I finally bring myself to make eye contact as I ask the question, but instantly wish I hadn't.

I want him to look as horrible as I feel. I want him to feel the pain he has given me. I want him to hurt. That's what I want.

No matter how many times I have steeled myself against exactly this moment, no matter how much I said I didn't care, when our eyes meet and I find exactly what I'm looking for, the grief coming from him, washing over me like a thick blanket, suffocating and expanding itself into every inch of my being . . . it all but consumes me.

My voice breaks as I continue on, pushing through the poison-laced words.

"How many times did you alter my emotions and feelings without my consent? How many times did you make me see this place in a way which fit whatever narrative you were working toward?" I scream out, and he pauses slightly before closing his eyes and letting the words fall out.

"It wasn't like that," he counters through gritted teeth.

"How. Many. Times."

He swallows, and when he looks back to me, I find his eyes rimmed with unshed tears of defeat. "Only when needed."

"How. Many. Times?!" The words come out as a dagger, ready and aimed for its mark. "And do not *dare* lie to me. Tell me every instance." I feel the anger continuing to swell inside me.

He looks to the ground, and with a shuddering breath, he finally speaks. "The tree that first day, my home, the waterfall, training, Jensin, the dome, the sunset, the battle at the palace . . . just now."

An audible choke fills the air and it takes a moment for my mind to register that it's *me* making the noise. *No. No. No. No.*

NO!

"The morning in the cave?" It's barely a whisper.

"No. Not then. I may have my own demons, but I'm not a monster. I wouldn't do *that* to you." That leaden ball buried deep within my core thickens as unwanted cold races down my legs. His feet inch forward once more, but he quickly freezes in place at my words.

"But you *did*." A tear falls down my face and I turn away, unwilling to look at him again. "All those times you made me feel safe and whole around you . . . That was just a facade which built and built until I could no longer fight against it. I was scared and weak, and I fell right into your plan. You used your gifts and made me *fall in love* with you."

Suddenly it makes sense as to why I seemed so uncaring and aloof when I was with him. It was as if I had been drugged with happiness and certainty. It was why I didn't spend those days and nights searching and questioning everything before me. It's why I never questioned him.

The surrounding jungle is silent as those around us look between Tarak and myself, no one having a clue what to do or say. No one wanting to test the thin vines holding my frayed mind together.

But then the silence ends as Riann's whispered voice weaves through the agony.

"A sourcer and a soothsayer. It all makes perfect sense." He lets out a low chuckle and my head shoots upward, enraged at the sound. How can he laugh when my entire world is crashing down around me?

"What are you–" Alesia starts.

"You don't see it?" Riann quickly cuts her off as he straightens and looks between us all. "You truly don't know, do you?" His voice is barely more than a whisper as he turns to me, his eyes filled with surprise, almost as if he can't believe my naiveté.

"Know what?" My words are a little more brazen than I intend.

"Your gifts," he all but pleads. "His gifts." Riann sweeps a hand in Tarak's direction. "It all makes perfect sense."

"I think you're going to need to provide more explanation," I implore.

"You are a sourcer," Riann breathes life into the word as if it will answer every question I have about myself. But I have no idea what that word even means. And now I know why I never had the wherewithal to even ask.

"I think we have all figured that out," Tarak spits toward Riann before I can respond. "Tell us something new or keep your mouth shut."

My head whips back to Tarak and those rose-colored glasses which only allowed me to see what he wanted me to see are gone, stomped into a pile of dust and · shattered fragments so that all I see is the horrible reality in front of me.

For the first time, I see him as a cruel and cunning Celestra. A perfect prodigy trained by Himerak. One with a myriad of secrets hidden within.

It takes unrelenting effort to push the rage at his betrayal deep inside before it has a chance to devour me whole. And for once, I am thankful for the enigma that is the Haze. If it hadn't just come, I wouldn't be depleted of energy, and I'm positive the surrounding forest would have been reduced to a blazing river of anger and regret by my fingertips.

But I don't get to lash out as I wish.

"A sourcer is someone who, when needed, can derive their power from other sources. You can take whatever you need at any given moment from your surroundings, whether it be from people or nature."

"We know what a sourcer is," Tarak angrily retorts.

And those words are what finally bring Riann to a halt. It's as if every taut string holding the rage and anger at bay finally snaps and, with it, Riann's restraint. He lunges at Tarak, only held back by Alesia's hold on his arm and Micel stepping in to block his path. A handful of weapons are now trained in his direction. He fists and pulls at his once immaculate black hair, now covered in dust and ash, as a grunt of frustration seeps out.

"*Elders be damned!*" Riann finally bursts. "Would you just be quiet for one moment and let me explain? *She* obviously doesn't know or remember, and I'm trying to help *her!*" I almost want to laugh at the stunned look crossing Tarak's face.

Riann quickly turns back to me.

"A sourcer can also utilize the gifts of other Celestras around them. You would have to be trained to do so, and sometimes the stones are needed in order to fully unlock all the aspects, but at its base, it means you can take on others' gifts at will."

My brows furrow. "I can use other people's gifts? I can use Tarak's gifts?" I would say the revelation is shocking, but at this point—with everything that has happened in the last few weeks, it's not.

"Yes. It's amazing," Riann answers with unabashed exhilaration while the rest of us remain frozen in confused silence. "We figured it out when you were a child. Mina figured it out and . . . well, it was quite an exciting time."

"What does that have to do with anything?" Tarak cuts in, but Riann pays him no heed.

"Tarak is a soothsayer," Riann adds.

I didn't realize his abilities had a title. It seems I didn't realize quite a lot about him.

"He *says* he loves you, and he has spent time altering how you felt about this world, what you've encountered . . . *him*." The words seem almost pained as they leave Riann's lips.

"What's your point?" Jaxon intercedes, and from his tone, I can tell he's getting more and more aggravated with this conversation as each second ticks by.

"Tarak can influence how people feel around him. He can take away their pain or frustration, or alter their emotions in any way he pleases. And Nera can take on what others give. Right now, she's unknowingly taking on what Tarak feels, what he's giving her, and she has no ability to control it. She has no idea how to shield her mind from those kinds of influences. It's a perfectly chaotic mess of emotions which would cause even the strongest of soldiers to drop to their knees, but . . . it's not real." My eyes crease in confusion at his words. *"It's not real,"* he repeats more firmly as he pointedly looks between Tarak and me.

"It's not real?" I whisper, not sure whether the words come out filled with grateful relief or gut-wrenching remorse.

"You're feeling what he is feeling because of the connection between your gifts. Whether he knows it or not, he is projecting his desires onto you. And you're doing what you do and taking in what others give. That pull you feel toward him isn't real. It's just a projection."

His words take a moment to sink in. I'm not sure what's worse. The idea that this was all some ruse, or the weight which lifts with the realization.

"No," Tarak quickly interjects. "I didn't make her feel anything but calm. I didn't do anything but take the pain away."

"I'm not saying you even know you're doing it," Riann replies, and for once, his words toward Tarak aren't laced with anger and hostility, but with a surprising note of sincere sympathy.

"Are you sure?" I quickly ask, looking toward Riann with pleading eyes.

"Yes," he implores. "It makes complete sense."

I turn to the man I once thought I loved and watch as his world shatters around him. He glances between the others, looking for an answer, before his eyes finally find me once more.

When he starts to once again step my way, I hold up my hand, repulsed at the very idea of him even coming an inch closer to where I still sit. I'm not yet sure what all of this means. I don't yet know if any of what I feel . . . what I *felt,* is real and true, or if it was just a pretty illusion which was used to draw me in. But I know I won't be able to find out as long as he's near me. As long as I feel this pull toward him, or feel the warmth of his skin, I won't be able to think this through clearly.

"Don't." This time, it isn't a whisper, but a blatant command.

Tarak drops to his knees. "Nera, just let me explain."

"Explain? That's all this ever was and will ever be. I don't care about your explanations anymore. Just leave me alone."

I quickly turn to Micel, hoping he may provide the way forward.

"I don't know what my part is in all of this," my voice is far more confident than I feel. "But I want the fighting to end. I want to right any wrong I may have done in the past."

"I know, and we are grateful for that," Micel says in a soothing manner, and I nod my head before turning back to the man who has shattered my new world.

Riann swiftly steps forward, but he must see something in my face because, just as quickly, he shifts his movement closer to Tarak and peers at his once rival. I watch as Tarak's defeated face stills and straightens. An invisible mask converges on the features which once gave me hope.

Then the pulsing pain which has dulled to a slow ache begins to grow. It starts as a slight ripple but gains speed as it moves. The veil of ease shifts away, a blanket being pulled right off of me. Then the torment hits. It slices through skin, bone, and muscle. A tortured gasp leaves my lips as every ligament in my wound, in my body, feels as if it is being physically twisted and manipulated from the inside out. I involuntarily reach down and grasp the spot, swearing I can feel the insides moving.

My eyes lift to the sky as the waves of agony undulate through me. Nowhere near as bad as when it first hit, but still so, so much worse than the last few minutes. The lingering throb which was once a smoldering ember has turned back into a raging flame. I fight for words as I push the pain away. I want to scream. I think I might even open my mouth in preparation for the vile noise to spill forth.

"Tarak–" Micel warns, but I barely hear the words.

"I haven't stopped," he states in confusion as the pain further soars.

"Tarak. She's hurting," Micel counters. "Don't do this out of anger," he adds as he smothers my ankle in more salve.

"I'm not! I swear, I haven't stopped!"

But I know he's just lying again. And I know I can no longer trust a single word which comes from his lips. Tarak has stopped using his abilities on me, allowing the excruciating pain to return.

"No. No!" Tarak reaches out, and this time I have no energy left to pull away. He lays a hand on my leg as his face contorts into deep concentration. But nothing changes. The pain intensifies and the panic which I somehow managed to bury so deep within me begins to rise to the surface.

I taste bile as my heart pounds against my chest. My hands become slick with sweat and the rapid beat now filling my ears drowns out all other noise.

I hear his frantic voice call out and, for no longer than the time it takes to blink away the tear trailing down my cheek, I feel quiet relief before the misery takes hold once more.

The two sensations are fighting within me. One side pulling me to a tortuous death and the other fighting for reprieve.

My breathing rushes in and out. Without warning, the pain twists and shifts. It moves from the physical to something else as it coils deep within. I fall sideways, and as my face meets the ground, I feel the familiar sting of a needle and the world turns to a blur.

All I now know is the pain has lessened, the darkness has retreated, and I want to go home.

XVI

"Rivers of blood and frantic prey.
Fire and ice, and shattered clay."

My mind hovers between the here and now as a soothing melody plays on repeat. With every step and shift, it teeters between the muddled conversations of those around me and the deep thoughts and visions which swirl through my fragmented mind. Visions which are new and so far away. Visions which I have seen before. Visions I can't quite seem to push away.

"Scar-filled skin and golden eyes.
Broken crystals and steam-filled skies."

A sinister rhyme plays in my ear. It grates along my skin and forces its way inside as I toss and turn, willing it to end.

"Sinking water and growing crests.
Never allowing a moment's rest."

But as the hours pass on and the drugs wear down, the continuous song finally ceases and the real world seeps back into view.

"A song of agony circling through your head.
A recurrent loop of impending dread."

At some point, I finally wake enough to realize Jaxon is carrying me. His arms are strong and steady. Though I have moved in and out of consciousness as he walks, I can tell the journey takes days on foot. In the moments I can feel his strength is faltering, I'm gently handed over to Micel. But never Tarak. Never once Tarak. As I teeter within the darkness, I count the crew around and breathe a sigh of relief each time I find the sad eyes of Riann and Alesia hovering somewhere behind.

When able, I slowly down a slice of bread or handful of berries, and I don't fight when Ranya slowly tips cool water into my mouth.

Though the pain lessens with each passing moment, there are still seconds, minutes, hours in which I grit my teeth and pray for a quick end to what's happening.

The crew moves at a rapid pace, but the trek is silent. Only stopping long enough for nourishment and sleep, it's five days of noiseless torment as we progress through a mountain pass and into the unknown. And though I would never have guessed this outcome, I find that each time I need to relieve myself or wash off the muck which has gathered from the journey, it's Ranya's kind hands which help me with the most menial of tasks. I never thank her. I don't even look her in the eye. There are too many warring emotions there to understand what motives she may have in this.

But each jolt of movement causes a new wave of pain to burst through and ripple across my skin. Each time I am shuffled from one person to the next, I have to stifle the scream threatening to erupt. And every time I catch sight of *him,* I all but fall apart.

As much as possible, I focus on what I can see in order to stave off the lingering pain, both physical and emotional. Studying my surroundings, I can tell I was sorely mistaken when I thought the roots and limbs were large on my first venture into the Mulara Forest all those weeks ago.

These trees now, in the depths of the unknown, tower so far into the sky I can barely see their tops. The mountain peaks soar even further upward and perforate the clouds, hinting at another world hiding within the misty view. No one has told me where we are, and truthfully, I don't have the strength to voice the question. But I do wonder if these trees are the same ones the centras are fighting over. Are they alive in a magical way? Do they have heartstone at their centers? Is this what I'm fighting for?

The questions continue to pile up, and I promise myself that once I'm somewhere I deem safe, with someone who doesn't hold any amount of animosity toward me, I will give life to those questions.

Until then, I let the days drag on. Micel keeps my ankle covered in his salve and wrapped tightly. And slowly, as the minutes turn to hours, and days pass, the pain lessens to a bearable throbbing.

By the time we reach the water's edge somewhere far from where we began, the throbbing has turned to a barely noticeable dull ache, and at times, I almost forget the injury in its entirety. I marvel when Micel unwraps the bandage for the last time, finding new pink skin where there was once a gaping wound.

"How?" My voice, the first true noise outside of the surrounding nature in the last few days, is rough and coarse. I watch as those around me promptly shift their attention toward me at the unexpected sound.

"The salve helps with regrowth. It's a wonder, is it not?" Micel quietly explains with a smile as he tests the skin and movement.

"How do you make it?" I nod my head in the direction of the silver canister which has been my saving grace. I think I know the answer before he even voices the words.

"It comes from the sap inside the trees near the settlement." His words are infused with regret and sadness, but what he doesn't know is those words also give me more insight to what all this means.

"Thank you," I reply with a smile, not letting him see the turnings of my mind as I revel in new information.

He reaches out his hands to pull me into a standing position for the first time in days.

"Take a few steps. See if you can walk."

I timidly shift my weight, allowing just the lightest pressure, and breathe a sigh of relief when no pain registers. The soles of my feet feel nothing but the cold, wet soil seeping between my toes. It's a welcome sensation. There was a moment in time when I first laid eyes on the gruesome injury, in which I was certain I would no longer walk on this foot again—or even be able to keep the foot at all. A grateful sigh seeps past my trembling lips when the notion that I'm fine—physically at least—settles within.

"It doesn't hurt at all." I catch his eyes with a smile of my own and begin walking in a circle before he reaches out to stop me.

"Go slow. I don't want you to reinjure it. The skin is new; it could tear." He hands over my shoes and I slip them on with ease before he adds, "I'm happy the worst is over. It may take a few days to get full use back, but at least now you're mobile." I smile. His display of concern is in such stark contrast to what I'd assumed of his intentions after our first meeting.

Once again, my ability to judge people is proven to be flawed.

"Is there a boat?" I inquire of no one particular as we set forth once more along the path which winds just out of reach of the rippling water's edge.

"Why would we need a boat?" Ranya counters, almost laughing as she lengthens her strides to fall into step beside me.

I look out to the water and then back toward the forest. It's the direction in which we're headed, but . . . something seems off. The water seems off. "Where are we going?"

"The caverns," *he* answers, and my head snaps forward to find Tarak's piercing gaze trained on me.

I open my mouth to speak, but I can't fathom even a surface level conversation with this farce of a man who allowed me to suffer so much pain. I wanted to believe him when he said he wasn't doing it, when he said he was still using his abilities to shield me from the torment of the gaping wound. But I no longer trust him to any degree.

I turn back toward Ranya before I continue, and watch with relief as *he* walks off to join the group at the head.

"I saw the map. The caverns are across an ocean." *That is, unless we've already crossed it.* I swallow at the thought. I still don't know how long I was kept unconscious after the Haze, and falter at the reminder.

"It's across water. But that doesn't necessarily mean it's an ocean," she clarifies with a smile, and this time, there's no teasing, or hate, or even so much as anger in her words.

"What is it? A river? A lake?" I stop and turn to more fully face her.

"It's a flat," Jaxon answers from behind me.

"A flat?" My attention shifts to him.

He nods his head as he explains, "Technically, yes, it's covered in water, but for the most part it's only a few inches deep. It may get up to a foot or two in some parts, but nothing more than that."

"You've been there?" I look between them both, wondering how they know so much about the place when *he* once said they've never left the forest.

"No. But Himerak has. It's how he first traveled to the caverns for his Committence."

I nod in understanding.

"Tar–" The name almost passes my lips. Both Ranya and Jaxon steal a glance in my direction. My absolute avoidance of *him* has been more than obvious. "*He* said your people have never left the Mulara Forest."

My eyes find him studying a map with some unknown soldier I have yet to meet. As if sensing my attention on him, his head shifts and his gaze finds mine. My heartbeat races as we stand frozen in time.

Oh, how quickly the world changes.

"We haven't." Ranya's words pull me from the trance. "But our education on the entirety of Ithesin was very thorough. We know what is needed."

I nod in acknowledgement of her words, wondering if that education was as one-sided as their leaders seem to be. A tight knot forms in my throat, not allowing me to voice any further thoughts.

We walk for a few more hours, and when the sun starts to set in that beautiful canvas of colors, a sight which once mesmerized me, I shift my focus downward to count the pebbles which fill the spaces between those strange seaweed-like plants growing where we walk at the water's edge, refusing to acknowledge anything which reminds me of the facade I once lived in.

"We're going to camp here tonight. Rest up and ready yourselves for tomorrow," Micel announces as he unpacks one of the few bags we managed to salvage after the Haze.

I barely sleep. It's one of the first nights I don't have drugs coursing through my system to dull the pain and, for just a moment, I yearn for the pin prick in my shoulder, the promise of deep sleep. The ground is too cold and the air is too warm. The conflicting sensations cause my skin to feel feverish and my mind to tumble through a myriad of emotions and visions I'm not yet ready to explore.

I catch Riann's eye more than once. He's no longer shackled, but has also mostly avoided me. Though, I don't think it's of his own accord. The three guards placed by his side at all times seem to be a deciding factor in his choice not to get too close, but I can tell the decision not to act out is the most horrendous test of restraint he has ever encountered. And Alesia still can't seem to decide whether I am friend or foe. At times, she looks at me with such sadness filling her features, and other times, I swear she would end me in a matter of minutes should we be left unguarded.

"Find me."

I wake with a start before the rest, the camp a slumbering mix of people I do not truly know. With steady feet, I quietly make my way to the water's edge only to find Jaxon sitting on a lone log a few strides away. His contemplative stare is filled with much more than words could ever say.

"Hi," I whisper as I find a spot beside him.

"Hello," he says without looking in my direction. Though he carried me most of the distance, we haven't spoken to each other since the Haze.

We sit in silence as the sun slowly rises over the mountain peaks in the distance. It isn't as beautiful as the sunset I watched with *him,* but it still takes my breath away. The river of colors—flowing from indigo to sapphire to gold to emerald—appears to have been dutifully painted by the most precise hands. I shift my gaze to the water, hoping to drown out the view. It doesn't help. Before I allow the gathering tears to fall, I wipe my eyes and quickly turn away from what I now see as a reminder of a once-cherished memory. One I hope to soon forget.

I scan the camp, hoping for a distraction, and watch as the few people I can see stir in their packs and begin to wake. I only recognize half of them, if that, and yet I have a feeling I'm about to venture into something quite ominous—and possibly deadly—in order to help them all.

"Who are they?" My voice seems an unwelcome intrusion in the quiet serenity he's found.

"Who?" Jaxon's eyes crease in confusion when he finally looks my way.

"The people here with us. I only really know you, *him,* Ranya, and Micel. I think I should probably know the others if I'm going to be on their side."

He turns to face the sleeping forms, and after a contemplative breath, begins pointing out the various people and telling me who they are.

He first gestures to a sleeping form with tight curls the color of the damp soil, and says she is Noxen, a woman about my age who lost both parents in the recent Halabarian attacks. Her little brother and sister are stationed in a safe house with the rest of the surviving members of the settlement. He doesn't divulge where that safe house is located. And why should he? I may still be the enemy.

Next, he gestures to Kitz, a girl whose smooth, copper features are befitting of someone barely old enough to be considered an adult. Having been orphaned when her mother died in childbirth, she was raised by the settlement as a whole, just like Ranya. Forrel, a foreboding man who looks closer to Micel in age and has similar scars covering his body, is scowling off to the side. He doesn't appear particularly welcoming, but I've recently learned I'm not the best at character judgment, so I let his demeanor and the cold looks he directs my way slide, hoping he'll soon reveal himself to be someone I can trust. Lysa, is a woman old enough to be my mother and has a permanent grimace which never seems to soften. She and Forrel would be a perfect match.

I laugh at the thought, and Jaxon pauses his explanations, giving me a quizzical stare.

Beginning again, he gestures to Vexsa, a woman with thick sepia hair with streaks of citrine running throughout, and who, I assume, is still in some stage of training, gauging by the way the rest of the crew treat her. Then there's Coren, the man I recognize as the one who broke down at the loss of his loved one earlier, and I have to hold back the emotion at the thought of what he must be going through. Philipa, the youngest of the crew, follows Ranya around as if she is her greatest hero. Lenry, an older man, who I believe has yet to utter a single word during the entire time I've been here, neatly folds his sleeping bag without making a sound. Branon, a younger man, who rarely directs his hazel gaze toward me and stays close to Tarak. Ryker, a handsome man whose resemblance is far too close to Jaxon, is smiling at something another in his group must have said. And Masyn, an abnormally tall man with freckles covering most of his body which hide the scars underneath, is stretching his arms into the sky, causing his already mountainous stature to appear even larger.

"They all seem rather normal," I observe as I turn back to the view of the river before us.

Jaxon laughs. "What did you expect, Nera? We may be trained killers, but that doesn't mean we're bad people."

I immediately want to hide under a rock at my horrid use of language. "I'm sorry. That wasn't my intent."

"I think we all need to take some time to deconstruct our preconceived notions about each other," he says, eyes glued on the still water before us.

With the sun now sitting higher in the sky, and the river of colors diminished to a pale palette, I turn back with him and ponder my new crew.

"Can I ask another question?"

He cuts his eyes over and looks me up and down before tipping his head forward and indicating for me to continue.

"I'm sorry. I don't want to intrude. You were alone, maybe trying to get away from us for a while, and I just–"

"Nera, stop blabbering and ask me the question," he cuts me off, a tentative but apprehensive smile on his lips, and I pause for just a moment.

"Is no one going to acknowledge how hard this has to be on Micel?" I ask when the silence becomes too much.

"I know what I signed up for," Micel's voice comes from behind, and I go still in surprise as he walks into view.

"I didn't know you were standing there." My face grows warm as a blush stains my cheeks.

He takes a shuddering breath. "I appreciate the concern, but as I said, I knew what I was signing up for all those years ago when I started a life with him and, in some respect, I think I had an idea as to where this was going to go when I chose to come find you."

I nod my head in silent agreement, not knowing how to respond, but a heavy weight sinks into my chest.

"Where is he? Did he survive the attack from Halabar?"

"He's in a safe house a little further north. He's out of danger for the time being."

I'm not sure how to feel about that. I guess I always knew he survived. There would be more concern and push for Tarak to take his position if Himerak wasn't still alive.

"We'll be heading out shortly. The walk should take a few hours." Micel skillfully changes the subject. "I want you to promise me you'll let someone know if that ankle needs a break," he admonishes as fully aware of how hard-headed I can be. I give him a sly smile, and he shakes his head, turning his gaze to Jaxon.

"Keep an eye on her. If she starts to limp or show any discomfort, let me know." Jaxon nods his agreement without a word, and Micel quietly walks back to the waiting crew.

XVII

"Where exactly are we headed?" I pick up a pebble, tossing it into the air as I speak. *He* already told me about the caverns, but that answer was too vague. And I'm done accepting half answers.

Instead of replying, Jaxon swings his hand out in front of us, indicating the fog-covered water ahead.

"We're crossing the water? Here?" It's far too wide. I can't even see the other end of this flat. We would be walking for days.

"It's not a long walk," he quickly corrects my thoughts.

"I can't see any land," I counter.

"It's covered by smoke and fog. Trust me, it's there."

"And this land we're headed toward, it's where the caverns are?"

"Yes."

I nod my head in acceptance, waiting for him to move, stand, and rejoin our group to start packing for the day. When he doesn't so much as budge, I use my recently garnered boldness to keep him talking. He may be one of the few people I might be able to trust.

"Why were you mean to me on the boat?"

He swallows and then turns to fully face me, taking a moment to study my face before he answers.

"Nera, this entire situation is confusing even at the best of times. Tarak waivered back and forth so much, feigning hate for you and then obviously being unable to hold in his feelings . . . " He sighs. "I wasn't sure what the plan was. He's supposed to be our leader. I'm supposed to follow him when Himerak isn't here, and yet I couldn't trust him to guide us. I didn't know what was real or fake, and I took out my frustrations on you when it should have been him."

I blink at the sudden and unexpected honesty in his response. "Thank you for that." I give him a sad smile just before he turns back to the water.

"I never really thought you were the enemy." The admission is nearly too quiet for my ears. "I just didn't know how to reconcile what I knew to be true with what I'd been taught for so long."

"Life sucks sometimes," I observe and he bursts out into a fit of laughter. I don't look back, but I sense many pairs of eyes turned in our direction now.

"That is the most honest thing I've heard recently." He reaches over and squeezes my hand. I squeeze back.

"Can I ask you another question?"

"I don't think you will ever stop asking questions." He shakes his head and lets out another sigh in feigned annoyance.

"Micel. I think I've figured out he's good. Like you."

Jaxon smiles at my assertion.

"But what's he going to do when all this is over? I can't imagine him going back to that. Back to Himerak. And at the same time, I know it will be so hard for him to start over and leave the man he thought he loved. It has to be terrible for him, knowing how this is going to end."

Jaxon shakes his head at my words. "You don't need to worry about that happening."

"What do you mean?"

"You won't have to imagine it because it's not going to happen."

I almost startle at the absurdity of what he is suggesting.

"Yes, it will." At first, my voice comes out an octave too high, but I quickly clear my throat, gaining a semblance of restraint at the idea. With the exception of the few remarks made my way, Micel is a man simply going through the motions in order to survive. I know because I have felt the same way many times over the past three years. "Have you not seen how depressed and despondent he's become? He won't stay with Himerak. He can't. Not after everything we've found out. Not after that speech Tarak gave." I cringe as I realize that in my rush to talk I said *his* name. "Micel would be a fool if he did that." I wonder how divorce works here. Or is that even a thing?

"I don't think he really has a choice in the matter. At least not where it counts."

"Yes, he does." Then the thought slams into me. "Wait."

I twist, making sure no one is around to hear, but even still lower my voice to where only Jaxon can understand me.

"Is Himerak controlling him? Mind to mind? Did Himerak make Micel fall in love with him?" Jaxon looks at me with a furrowed brow, and I can't tell if that look is confirmation or not. "Since you aren't giving me a direct answer, I will deduce that, if he's controlling Micel in some way, then once Himerak loses more of his abilities, he won't be able to control him any longer. He won't be able to–"

"Nera," Jaxon quickly cuts me off as he shifts to finally face me. "You aren't listening to me. Unless one of them dies in battle, I'm certain they'll remain together. No matter if what you speak of is involved or not. It would be too mentally and physically painful for Micel to live in this world knowing Himerak was still out there but not with him."

"Why? Is divorce not a thing here?" I inquire.

His eyebrows raise in question. "That's one of those words I don't know."

"Like a separation. Breaking up," I clarify.

He nods his head in understanding. "Ah. Yes. People here can do a divorce."

I have to hold in the giggle that threatens to erupt at his incorrect grammar.

"At least, they can in Halabar. But in Halabar they call it a severance. I haven't ever known it to occur out here, within the trees. We have to stick together for survival in the settlement."

"Hmm. Well then, they can get a *severance*. That is, if Himerak survives." I flinch when I realize that a very real part of me desires the opposite outcome. What kind of person does that make me?

"They won't," he says with a little exasperation.

"Why not?"

Jaxon looks around, giving any who glance our way a death glare, and quickly enough, each busies themselves with something in another direction.

"Did Tarak never explain the rules of becoming a Celestra? Specifically the idea that marriage is not allowed until you have served your time?"

"Somewhat. He said Himerak gave up sovereignty early for Micel." I try to rack my brain for everything I have learned since arriving here.

"Yes. He did. He and Micel weren't supposed to meet when they did. It was an absolute fluke, and what Micel calls a 'change in the stars.'" Jaxon laughs lightly.

"What does that mean?"

"They don't really talk about it. I don't even know if anyone else knows, to be honest. Tarak may not even know," he admits as he stares off into the glistening water.

"Know what?" I urgently whisper as I nudge his side, imploring him to continue, desperate for the diversion this conversation provides from the rising panic at my own current situation.

"Micel is . . . " his lips tighten as he swallows. "Micel is too good for Centra I." The words sound painful, forced when they come out.

My head jerks upward in question.

"Micel is good," he urges.

"I've gathered that," I add with a roll of my eyes. It's obvious Micel isn't exactly who I thought he was in the beginning.

Jaxon shakes his head as if I'm not quite grasping the entire picture he is trying to paint. "He is too good for *Centra I*."

"You already said that."

He rolls his eyes back at me. "There are four centras."

I nod in agreement as the frustration rolls off me in waves. "I know." My eyes bulge hoping he understands I'm not as incompetent as he once may have believed.

"He is too good for *Centra I*."

I grunt. "Jaxon, you–" and then I pause as the phrasing snaps into place. "Micel isn't from here?" I quickly and quietly question, but Jaxon doesn't answer.

"Two years ago, I was out on a mission with Micel and things got rough. We lost a lot of soldiers." He closes his eyes as if recalling the moment is almost too much to bear. "The Ashclaw. It came out of nowhere. There were too many bodies to carry back. That night, after we buried our dead, we all drank ourselves into oblivion."

"You're not making any sense," I whisper-yell, annoyed that he's making me chase the answers. "Is Micel not from here? Tarak said there was no movement between the centras."

"I don't really like the taste of mountain ale. I wasn't as drunk as the rest of them."

"Jaxon?" I nudge him once more and hear the quick inhale of breath.

"Being drunk somewhat takes away one's inhibition. Makes it harder for . . . certain aspects of your mind to stay in control. That's why Himerak doesn't really approve of its use." He reaches down to pick up a leaf and casually twists it between his fingers as he quickly surveys the area for any listening ears. "I think being a little drunk allows you to . . . spill secrets your body would normally never let out."

My body prickles with the idea of what he's *not* saying

"What are you trying to tell me?"

"Secret relationships are hard to hide."

My brows furrow. I feel as though I'm a small child being told a riddle I can't piece together. I need all the details he can give.

"When you're the sovereign, *that* is supposed to be your entire world. Celestras don't have spouses, or relationships, or children. If they choose to move forward with the Committence and the sovereignty, then they must agree that nothing will take them away from the task at hand. That is what was decreed years ago, and no one has veered from the rules, ever."

"Koreed was married to my mother and had me, and he is the current sovereign," I counter.

"As you stated yourself, Koreed isn't a Celestra. The rules don't apply to him in that way."

I nod. Of course he's right. It's just that, for some reason, I keep forgetting these small facts. My brain has been inundated with an abundance of new information over the last few days.

"But what does that have to do with mountain ale, and the Ashclaw, and sovereigns getting married, and Micel? What does that have to do with Micel?"

"Himerak and Micel are bonded."

"Married?" I question, wondering if that means the same thing. Tarak referred to Micel as Himerak's husband, so marriage seems like the appropriate word.

"Yes. He gave up his title and power for Micel. But as we now know, he didn't really. It seems Himerak couldn't let go of it after all."

"Did he have a choice in the matter? Did Micel have a choice? Did Himerak somehow use his mind control over Micel?"

I wonder how this truly works. If Micel can't wilfully walk away, then it seems there is no choice in the matter at all.

"Free will always triumphs."

"If you are trying to explain something to me, you are failing miserably at it. I'm more confused now than when I sat down."

Jaxon stares off into the distance for just a moment. "Nera . . . " He swallows and then turns to fully face me. "I think you are good." My brows crease as I try to follow this shift in the conversation. "I think you are sent by the Elders to aid in finding the stones and stop the warring between the nations. I believe in the prophecy. I think you are the key to fixing this world."

My eyes widen at his phrasing, and I wonder what all he may know. "You're jumping all over the place."

"I don't think it's right to keep information from you. I don't see what good could come from that. But I am bound by law and," he struggles with his next breath, as if a pain has lanced through him, "from the way it hurts when I even try to speak the words, I'm sure I am also bound by other means."

"You're not making sense."

"Himerak's abilities are failing him. We all know this. But . . . " He stalls again as his lips tighten, and I watch the muscles across his shoulders ripple and damn near tear with the tension. "There are things I can't say."

I narrow my eyes in understanding. His previous words flood through me as their meaning suddenly hits. "A part of you is being controlled by Himerak." He doesn't answer, but continues his forward stare. "There is something you want to tell me, but your body physically won't allow it because of the control he has over you." The rush of words comes out as a faint whisper, and I turn my head to make sure no one heard what I said.

The nod he gives is barely perceptible, and were I not waiting for it, I might have missed it all together.

"You're trying to tell me something about Micel. Micel and Himerak?"

He blinks his eyes as he stares out to the water ahead, and I run through every encounter I have ever had with Micel.

"Micel is too good for Centra I," he repeats once more.

"Micel isn't from here," I add, hoping this is what he could mean.

"Please remember, no matter what you may think of Himerak, no matter what horrible atrocities he has committed in the name of Ithesin, Micel was a mostly innocent bystander in that. Micel was, and in some ways still is, unable to fight the hold Himerak has on all of us."

"Do they love each other?"

"Yes. Fiercely so."

"Did Himerak trick Micel into falling into love with him?"

"No. Their bond is true." He takes another breath, as if trying to work out how best to continue on. "Sometimes, Celestras have a more intense heart bond than others."

I tilt my head in confusion as my eyes narrow in on him.

"We all fall in love and marry, we have children and live wonderful lives with those we choose to be with, but there is an ancient bond which can only be found between Celestras. It is binding like no other."

"Micel and Himerak have that bond?"

He looks straight ahead again, and I wonder if that's his way of confirming what I have spoken.

"Why is it different?"

"It's not necessarily different. Just– Just stronger. More intense. Life altering. Bonded Celestras are almost like a mirror of the other's soul. They feel the same feelings, crave the same things, sometimes, even their gifts mirror each other in intensity. Two Celestras together is a force unlike any other. It rarely happens."

The truth in his words washes over me.

"And only Celestras have this . . . this bond?"

He nods in answer, again, a barely perceptible movement, and I shift my head to find Micel standing off in the distance, arms crossed and peering down at a map. His face is turned away, but I can easily make out the network of scars traveling across the expanse of his deep brown skin. His back, legs, and arms are covered in a map of their own making. A gift left from something I hope to never encounter. Each jagged line is filled with gold ink, as if he wants to display what evils he's traveled through and what horrors he's witnessed.

He twists slightly as he raises his hand, a simple movement as he rubs the back of his neck, deep in thought. But then I see the gold flakes marring his skin form a pattern, barely discernible as it melts into the surrounding lines with ease.

My head snaps forward as I clap my hand across my mouth. The words tumble out in awe. "Micel is a Celestra?"

Jaxon's smile is confirmation enough.

XVIII

I turn back and stare at the water ahead, hoping the tranquil movements and ripples will somehow pull me back from this shock.

Micel is a Celestra.

I wonder if all these people know, or if it's hidden from them as well. Jaxon alluded to the fact that he was likely one of the few who'd heard it from Micel's ale-loosened tongue. But maybe they all know? How could they not? It's right there on his wrist.

"Is it well known?"

"I think that when our people fled Halabar, right at the height of everything with Himerak and Koreed," he looks over, gauging whether or not that name has caused me any pain, "a lot of facts about our world were conveniently forgotten with regards to celestial gifts."

I feel the rising anger once again. This world is nothing but a melting pot of lies and deceit.

"How much of this do you think Tarak knows?" My whispered question has no bite.

He closes his eyes as if trying to find an answer without submitting to the pain of Himerak's curse.

"Even though they're slowly fading, Himerak's gifts are still strong. Sometimes it's hard to see things that are right in front of you when you have been indoctrinated to see something else your entire life." He turns back to me then, a sad smile playing on his face. "It's abnormal for Celestras to be able to use their power on other Celestras. It is said the connection is dulled unless the bond is present. That's why Himerak doesn't try to see Tarak's past, the same way Tarak can't truly discern whether or not Himerak is lying."

"But he saw my past?"

"I have a theory about that." Jaxon smiles and I cock my head, imploring him to continue. "You didn't have any gifts while on Earth did you?"

"Not that I can remember. I never caught anything on fire; though that skill would have been nice during the cold winter months. Alesia and I used to trek through the city streets, trying to find an open store that sold firewood." I stifle a laugh at the memory, and the feeling is still so foreign. I haven't truly laughed in far too long.

"I think you lost use of your gifts when you were there, and I think it is perhaps taking time for them to all come back. Like maybe your body had to slowly reacclimate to being home."

Home.

I cringe at the words, knowing I feel farther from home than I ever have before. "Maybe?"

I reach over and pluck the leaf out of his hands and begin twisting it on my own. He rolls his eyes and smiles. But then the thought hits me. Tarak used his gifts on me. Consistently. I felt the heat of his touch, I felt him calm me. He was able to discern each and every lie I told.

"What about Tarak? He used his gifts on me all the time and we are both Celestras."

Jaxon shakes his head, another sad smile meeting my gaze. "He didn't. Not fully at least."

"What does that mean?"

"Yes, he calmed you, but he was truthful when he said he didn't fully use it on you. He couldn't even if he had wanted to. What he gave you was only a fraction of what his true gifts can do." I swallow as bile burns my throat. "Did you see the way Coren looked when Tarak touched his shoulder after his wife died from the Haze? It's like a drug to most people." I nod. How could I forget? Her body was a gruesome sight as it all but melted right in front of us. "What you got was barely an ounce of the power he has."

"And his ability to detect lies?"

Jaxon laughs and turns once more to make sure we are still unbothered by prying eyes or ears. "Tarak is my best friend. We have been close since we were still crawling along the canopy. But, Tarak was raised as a Celestra. He was raised for this world in a way I was not. We have different experiences, and due to that, we have different viewpoints on many things. Tarak is used to getting what he wants. I think, even without knowing it, he has become very good at masking and manipulating things in his favor. He is a good person with a heart of gold, but he has been molded into what Himerak wants in a successor. I think Tarak wants you almost more than he wants the stones, and because of that, he hid the truth and made you believe he could use his full gifts toward you. That way you would be truthful with him, and he could get what he wants in the end."

I push down the bile that begins to rise at the honesty in his words.

"And what is that?"

"A life full of love and happiness, no matter the means of acquisition, and with a dash of revenge for what was taken by Koreed."

"Koreed didn't take anything. That was Himerak."

Jaxon shrugs as if that small fact is barely an inconvenience.

That heavy feeling settles deep within my stomach at the thought of how easily I was deceived and how hastily I welcomed that lie.

"You're his best friend. Why are you telling me this?"

"Because, at the end of the day, I would rather do what's right than what's popular. I love him . . . but I love my people more."

"He can't tell when I'm being untruthful? Not at all?"

"I'm sure there is something there when you lie, but again, it's most likely so dulled that he can barely, if ever, discern it. At first, I thought he could. I thought the connection between you two was enhancing it all. Now I realize it may have been a facade."

"What do you mean by a 'connection between us?'"

He throws a rock into the water, and we watch as it bounces from one spot to the next before coming to rest on the floor of a shallow pool. The surface of the obsidian stone gleams upward. They were right. This water is barely inches deep.

"That's not the exact question you mean to ask, is it?"

I furrow my brow. "What?"

"Nera." Jaxon shakes his head as the hint of a smirk appears. "You do not have a poker face. I have no gifts or powers, but I can pretty much read every thought that crosses your mind."

I swallow. The air is thick with my unspoken words. It takes more than a moment to figure out exactly what it is I do want to ask. And yet, a part of me is desperate not to.

"Is Tarak bonded to someone?" I ring out my hands as I speak the words.

"I thought he was."

There is barely a pause before I voice the question. "Is it me?"

He shakes his head, and the breath of relief I let out is palpable.

"I don't believe so. Being bonded to someone is very intense. I think he believes he has, but I think he's confused. Though, in all truth, only you two will know in the end."

I don't even know what to say. Sitting here on this log has led to unraveling much more information than I initially intended.

"I think Himerak was so determined to keep you two from forming a friendship because he was concerned for the same. He didn't want it to snap into place. He didn't want Tarak to abandon the cause as he had done all those years ago."

Confusion spreads out.

"But . . . but I feel something between us. I have from the first time he touched me. It's more than anything else I have ever felt. What if that is–"

"Nera, I'm no expert on the matter. I'm no Celestra. But I think things would have happened differently if you were. I don't think he would have been able to treat you in such a way as he has the last few days if you were. What you need to figure out is if that pull you feel toward Tarak is really a pull because he is bonded to you, or if it's just a fabricated string built from the intermingling of your gifts."

XIX

The water is surprisingly soothing as it splashes on my mostly healed leg. I tried to help carry some of the supplies for various other members of the party, but none would allow me to carry more than a small canteen of water. Except for the bow and quiver strapped across my back, the now empty canteen and the shoes which were once on my feet are the only things I hold.

We make our way in a single file line across the vast expanse of shimmering water, a glistening mirror embedded in the ground. I fear looking down into it, worried it may show me some truths I'm not yet ready to face.

It isn't until we've walked for well over an hour that I finally turn to look behind me. The green and purple jungle I spent the last few days in has all but disappeared. In its place, I find nothing but a gentle mist of air and cloud-filled horizons.

Those same low-hanging clouds appear to thicken the further we walk, obscuring the view ahead. Before long, each member of our quiet single-file line begins gripping the pack of the person in front of them, making sure to hold on tight in fear of being left behind.

Though I can barely see her, my grip on Ranya never falters, and Micel stays steady at my back. I marvel at the fact that, after everything that has happened, it now seems that two of the people I swore would end me are the ones brave enough to stand by my side. I try not to look at the hand placed on my shoulder, knowing there is a mark hidden within the golden strips tattooed along Micel's skin.

My view to either side is obscured by the incoming fog, but the alternative—staring at Ranya's backside for however long this trek will take—is enough to keep my movement unwavering. I pass the time, mulling over everything Jaxon has brought to light as I replay our conversation over and over again in my mind, trying to make sense of it all.

Micel is a Celestra.

Celestras can bond to one another.

Celestrial bonds are intense and all consuming.

Tarak and I are most likely *not* bonded.

Himerak is still, in some aspects, controlling these people who surround me.

I want to laugh at the absurdity hidden within those words, but seal my lips so the sound can't emerge. The entire concept seems like a fabricated illusion only found in stories. I scoff at the idea. But then again, with just one look around at this vast new world, I realize that I am now in the center of one of those stories. I have been for some time now, and it still doesn't feel real.

It's only at the point when I realize my mind is about to spiral through a thousand more unanswered questions that I break the all-consuming silence and speak.

"Tell me what I need to know of the stones," I ask out loud, not exactly sure who I'm speaking to, and hoping someone will be kind enough to provide an answer.

There is a momentary pause where I think the words will be taken off into the wind and the deafening silence will continue. But then I hear *him* speak.

Him.

Of all the people around, it had to be him . . .

"There are eight stones in all. It is said they were made by the Elders." His voice, once a welcome melody, is now a grating noise in my ear. "Himerak currently holds the Seerer Stone. It helps to enhance his ability to see one's past. It was made by Elder Haziah." He takes a breath, then his feet stop moving forward, and I all but slam into Ranya as she, too, stalls. "There is a second stone in Halabar, currently held by your father."

I barely breathe as he speaks, and I run through every memory of that night and the golden stone Koreed held.

"He showed it to you during your dinner," Tarak adds, and I gasp. Tarak only knows about this because of his spies within the palace walls. Now I wonder what else he may know but is hiding. I don't know if this man has an honest bone in his body. If I were to take a guess, my guess would be that he holds more lies and secrets than truths. "It's called the Omni Stone and is used to travel between worlds and times. It was made by Elder Safar."

I look up at the same time he turns around, and our gazes meet through the misty fog. I half expect him to continue speaking, but it seems he is too frozen at the sight of me.

Jaxon clears his throat.

"We believe there is a third stone currently hidden in Centra I," Tarak finally continues. "I was hunting for it the day I found you."

"How do you know there's another one?" Jaxon cuts in, a sudden quizzical look etched across his face.

Tarak ignores his question and moves on, "It's called the Patho Stone and was also created by Elder Haziah. It enhances the ability to see the future."

I look between the two men and then to the entire group, waiting for someone else to speak. But no one does.

"What about the other five stones? Where are they? What do they do? What about the Elders?" I inquire, the questions barreling out of me.

"It is a widely held belief that the stones are hidden within the Caverns. When you complete your Committence, you are given the stone which correlates with your abilities. You can use it to enhance them should the need arise."

It surprises me when a previously silent crew member speaks.

"Unless, of course, they have been stolen by other Celestras," Lenry adds.

"Other Celestras?" My eyes widen in shock at the phrase. "I thought we were the last ones." I look toward *him*, and then I can't help but cut my eyes to Micel.

"We are." Tarak nods without hesitation, and for some reason, I know he verily believes we are the last two. "Here in Centra I, we are the only Celestras left. But there may be others still living in the other centras."

Ah. Another twisting of the truth. Another little white lie. To his credit, he has the decency to look ashamed.

"So there are other Celestras in other centras?"

He nods in answer.

"And the Elders?"

"They are no longer with us," Ranya answers.

But that doesn't make sense. Tarak told me there were rumors they lived within the caverns. And I have met them. I met them in Halabar. They were the three men and one woman who brought me that awful concoction that night, trying to force my memories to return.

"Wait." I look toward Tarak just as he opens his mouth to speak. "No. That doesn't make any sense. You said something in the cave." My heart tightens as the memories of that night come forth, but I push them back and away. "You said there were legends that the Elders lived in the caverns."

This time, it's Ranya and Micel who look confused.

"Why would you tell her that?" Micel chides as he furrows his brow.

"I– I–" Tarak stumbles over his words. "I needed to get her to the caverns. I needed us to complete the trials and find the stones."

"You needed me to believe they were there and could help me get my memory back."

He pauses for just a moment before I watch his chest fill with air and his shoulders sag in defeat.

"Yes."

"You are a horrible person." It's the only thing I can think to say as the corners of my eyes blur with unshed pain.

The water splashes below his feet as he moves to step near me. I recoil into Micel, but Tarak doesn't stop moving until he is inches from my face, Jaxon has a hand wrapping around Tarak's arm, halting his movement.

"No matter what you think, I promise you that my entire plan, my every intention was to help you."

I scoff and he shakes his head.

"This world is just a pretty facade that hides an ugly truth. I have to find that truth, and I had hoped you would find it with me." He closes his eyes as his breathing deepens. "Yes, I lied. Yes, I had multiple motives, but at no time was I ever in the business of harming you. My lies, my secrets were meant to help you—help everyone." Apprehensive, he assesses the others around us. "Don't make me out to be the villain here. Don't you dare do that."

He is all but heaving, sucking in breaths of frustration as he finishes. But I don't back down. I won't let him see me falter now.

"You are just a product of your upbringing." I take a step closer, letting our breaths mingle as I stare into those sapphire eyes. "You are just another Himerak in disguise."

He jerks backward as if I have physically pushed him.

"Stop!" Jaxon and Micel state in unison as we are pulled further away from each other.

And then I feel a familiar grip on my arm pulling me backward and into a warm chest. *Riann.*

I look up to find a gaze of fury he's failing to conceal behind a well-trained smile. He isn't fooling me. I almost lean into him. I almost accept the momentary gift of comfort he is offering me. But then I remember.

"The Elders?" I ask as I push away from him. "I met them . . . "

I'm not sure if that's a statement of fact or a question, and as soon as the words leave my mouth, I watch as Riann's face twists into something I haven't yet seen. It's only a fleeting moment. A half-second where he lets the veil fall. But I see it. I see the unyielding anger he's hiding beneath as it comes bubbling upward.

"That's not possible," Jaxon counters.

But I keep my eyes focused on Riann.

"That first night back in Halabar after I woke up. Three men and one woman came and made me drink that horrible concoction in order to retrieve my memories. You all said they were Elders."

I look between Riann and Alesia as I speak and wait for an answer to my unasked question.

This time, it's Alesia who has the gall to look ashamed. "They *are* elders," she quickly states, and I hear the scoff of dissent from those around. "But, not the kind we were just speaking of," she clarifies, and my eyes are like daggers as I wait for her to continue. "They are men and women of Halabar who have studied the works and words of the Elders and who practice as such now."

Micel bursts into maniacal laughter. "You think some mortal can study the words of the Elders and suddenly possess all the powers thereof? What madness is this?" He turns now to look at Riann with an unleashed fury seeping from his gaze. "You are smarter than that." The words are seething.

"We were trying to help," Alesia quickly clarifies as she comes to stand near me. "We have the sacred text, Drunia, and we were using some of the–"

"You have Drunia?" Tarak asks excitedly as he moves closer, Jaxon's hand still tightly wrapped around his arm.

Alesia sucks in a breath as she quickly seals her lips, and I realize this was a piece of information they were not meant to share.

"You have Drunia?" Tarak questions again, this time with more urgency.

It's Riann who finally answers.

"Yes. We have Drunia." His statement is almost despondent in nature. "We have many wonderful books of the past kept safe within the Soul Circle." His words are filled with pride and, for a moment, I wonder how he knows what wonders the Soul Circle holds.

"We need that," Tarak states as he tries to shuffle toward Riann.

"It's not yours to possess."

Tarak recoils, his face filled with utter confusion. "I am a Celestra. It most certainly *is* mine."

I see the others react to his words and I realize they believe this is the first time Riann and Alesia may be hearing of exactly what Tarak is.

"It belongs to the Celestras of Halabar, which you are not," Riann counters as he looks at me. "No one else."

"It doesn't matter," Ranya interjects. "Drunia is hundreds of miles away in Halabar, and we"—her arms sweep out toward our path just as the fog begins to part—"are here." It's as if her movement was a signal for the world to finally open up.

"Holy Elders." The quiet whisper comes from someone closer to the front of the line as we all stare up in wonder at the sight.

A mammoth mountain, taller than any I have ever seen, lies before us. Wisps of gray smoke billow from the barren top, and there is no greenery at its base. Giant, dark, fragmented stones litter the ground and steam lifts from the heated rocks as water reaches their edge. Slowly moving rivers of molten lava seep from cracks throughout the structure, and deep rumbles that promise something more sinister hidden below cause the ground at my feet to shudder. It's only now that I realize how warm the water lapping against my feet has become. We are only yards from a torturous, molten death.

I clear my throat as a chill runs down my spine at the sight before us, and I know something ominous lurks in the mist that now surrounds our feet. My thoughts are consumed with a deep-rooted desire to *run* just as I feel Micel's steady hand grasp my shoulder.

"The Caverns," he whispers as he steps up next to me.

Act II

- The Truths -

XX

My heart beats fiercely against my chest as the water grows more menacingly hot with every forward step we take. The mountain looming ahead soars far into the sky, and my gaze follows the paths of lava as they spread out like greedy fingers meeting the water's edge, forming a thick steam which billows off and into the unknown.

I have to admit, I had no idea, no picture in my mind whatsoever as to what exactly I would be walking into. And until this moment, even with all the frustration and confusion which have made a mockery of me, I had no regrets. Somewhere deep inside of me, somewhere buried within my bones, I knew this was the right path. I could feel this place calling to me—bringing me here. Now that we've arrived, I want nothing more than to turn and run as fast as I can. I want to run away from the literal hell I know we are about to descend into.

"You'll be fine," Jaxon whispers as he places a comforting hand on my shoulder, and I suck in a deep breath.

I try to smile. "Please tell me you've somehow gained the ability to see the future and that statement is a fact," I plead as I curl my arms around my middle.

He laughs at my horrible attempt at a joke. "Not quite."

His hand squeezes my shoulder, and then, just before he walks away, he turns back to face me, leaning in close enough that no one else can hear what he says. "I don't know what'll happen in there. Life is a balance. There will always be a trade. I hesitate to think of what we'll be trading for the knowledge and stone." His eyes close as a fearful sigh inches past his lips. "But I do feel like I know you quite well at this point. I have faith in you. We all have faith in you." He looks around to the others, and by the contemplative looks on their faces, it's clear I'm not as certain as he is of their faithfulness.

"But, should you find yourself in a situation in which you need assistance, those who matter will always be at your back, ready and able to tackle whatever it is you might need. Have faith, Nera. You are far more capable than you realize."

He doesn't allow me a moment to reply, for me to say thank you or offer up my own words of comfort, before he steps forward to rejoin the group, ready to face what lies ahead.

Now I must make a choice. A choice to set aside whatever lies between Tarak and me. To set aside my selfish urge to search for my own past. This mission is more significant than the both of us, and I know that, to succeed, we must find a way to work together.

As a team.

Everyone keeps hinting that finding these stones is paramount to joining the fractured pieces of this world, of Ithesin, back together. They're the key to stopping the Haze. From the sounds of it, the Ashclaw, as well. They're the answer to, at long last, ending the wars between nations. To once again uniting the people.

Maybe once that union occurs, I'll be able to focus on me and the questions I have.

I square my shoulders and say a prayer that my churning stomach will settle. Even with the heat bellowing forth from that hauntingly beautiful behemoth rising before us, a chill of uncertainty runs down my spine.

I should have a vast knowledge of that mountain. And yet I know nothing. I know nothing more than what little I've been told. Small fragments of barely useful information carried down from one Celestra to the next.

If I remember correctly, Tarak told me only Celestras can enter the depths below. Which means I'll have no choice but to rely on *him* once we're inside. My life will depend on trusting Tarak, and what a frightening realization that is. I catch sight of him only a few yards away as fear settles in me, and try not to cringe when his eyes lift to meet mine.

This would be so much easier if he didn't look so damn heartbroken. Maybe we *are* bonded? Maybe that heat I felt—feel—from his touch isn't just the mingling of our gifts. Maybe it's something more.

More . . .

This is more.

That's what Tarak said that night in the cave. *I* was more. Is that what he meant? Was he trying to tell me I meant more to him than anything else? Was he trying to explain that we're bonded? Or was it all just another well-woven lie meant to ensnare me?

I startle when I notice his form only a few inches away from where I stand. He doesn't waste time or mince words.

"It will be just the two of us going in once we cross through the Scheol. Only

Celestras can venture into the depths. I'm not sure what exactly we'll find. But I'm hoping–"

"To find the stones," I finish for him.

"Yes," he acquiesces.

I find my arms crossed in front of my chest and a raging anger rising within me. The last thing I want is to traipse off onto some adventure with the one person I know I can't trust. "And what happens if they're *not* there?"

"They will be."

I roll my eyes. "What if they're not?"

The frustration at my lack of blind obedience gets the better of him. "Then we go back to Halabar and we go into the Soul Circle to find out what we can," he replies matter-of-factly as his arms cross, mirroring my own.

"What if the Soul Circle's no longer there? What if your bombs destroyed it?"

Tension builds in his chest. I don't think he's used to someone battling his every thought. "It withstood the attack." His words are direct.

"Ahhh." My brows furrow, hands flexing at my sides. "The spies. Are they still feeding you information from within?" Unrestrained anger laces each word.

"No. I have no contact with them at the moment. All the knowledge I have concerns the people you see before you and the surviving members of my settlement."

I scoff. "*Your* settlement?"

"Why are you being this way?"

"What way?"

"Why are you questioning every word that comes out of my mouth? Why are you fighting me at every turn?"

I glare at him as the anger within threatens to lash out. "Because you earned it."

"Nera–" My name is a weary plea as his feet inch forward.

"No." My command is absolute, unyielding. "I have some ground rules for going in there."

He raises his brows in surprise at my words.

"You are not, under any circumstances, allowed to touch me."

"What?" He jolts as if shocked by my words.

Surely he's not so deluded.

"I can't trust you. I *don't* trust you."

His lips form a tight line. "What else?"

"I won't blindly follow everything you say just because you're supposedly *their* leader."

His jaw flexes as I watch his fists open and close, a sign of frustration I've come to recognize.

"Is this entire journey going to be you and I at each other's throats?"

"No," I concede. I just promised myself to put all of this behind us, and in the very next encounter with him, I aim to tear him down. I count out a deep, centering inhale. One. Two. Three. Release. I try to calm myself, even while refusing to back down, refusing to cower. "But there is no 'you and I' on this journey," I add, my tone bitter, cold despite my efforts.

"We were once a team," he implores.

I struggle to restrain the fire I can feel building as I pray to the skies for serenity.

A team.

I flex my fingers, feeling the sparks of anger settle in their tips.

Rein it in, Nera.

"We were never a team, Tarak." The bitterness is gone. There's no bite left. Just cool, aloof truths. "It was you and all your knowledge against the world. I just happened to be an unfortunate bystander who fielded all the ricochet from your weapons."

He shakes his head. "Don't say that."

"It's the truth. I could have been anyone in the world and the same outcome would have happened."

His jaw tightens and his stance is rigid. "You are *not* just anyone," he says through gritted teeth. His gaze focuses so strongly on my own it feels like he's trying to force truth into the words by pure stubbornness alone.

"Then what am I?" I ask, silently begging for him to answer.

I want him to say it out loud. I want him to admit to what it is between us, or at least what he believes. I still need to figure out what's swirling within me. That unknown warmth which started as burning embers has, for some reason, intensified with each step toward this hellish landscape and I can't quite reconcile what that may mean.

Maybe having him voice life to the ideas that have lived rent free in my mind the last few hours would help bring forth some clarity.

Unfortunately, I've never been that lucky.

"It's time to go," he says, turning to walk back toward the group.

The first step onto the volcano-like structure takes my breath away. The ground is formed from a mixture of solidified lava and jagged rocks which would greedily accept as many victims as they could lure to their deaths.

It's a slow and tedious trek up and along the side to what I can only guess is a triangular-shaped opening a hundred or so yards away. The closer we get, the hotter the air becomes, and I find I want nothing more than to stop before it's too late.

Every few feet, I have to shift and move sideways in order to narrowly avoid the paths of lava streaming out from between the cracks. I breathe a sigh of relief once the entire group makes it across the last of the molten rivers. Though, not many of the others seemed to care whether I maintained solid footing or fell to a torturous death below.

I can see the hateful confusion in a few pairs of eyes. It's a stark contrast to the looks they gave me following their war chant in the underground bunker. But I don't have time to fret about what sinister feelings and motives are hiding beneath their sneers. Only a few seem to tolerate my presence. Truthfully, some seem more frightened of me than anything else, and I feel my hands sliding up within the sleeves of my shirt, trying to hide them from view as they stare at what I'm sure they believe should be clothbound skin. I turn my head back to the murky stone ahead, barely lit by the flickering lantern in Tarak's hands.

In seconds, we enter a dark cave. A void of nothingness. Except this void isn't some figment of my imagination to keep me safe and protected. This is pure and total hell, its monstrous nature so unlike the beautiful world I've grown accustomed to on the mainland. A flicker of recognition flits through me as I stare up at the entrance to the mountain. Trepidation quickly follows.

It's as if this place is familiar in a way I don't want it to be. As if I know what lies beneath. As if this place is where I *belong*.

No one says a word as the dark stone of the passage tightens in, threatening to swallow us whole. As the light from the outside slowly dims, color fades until nothing remains but an enclosure of rough deep onyx all around. The only sounds are those of heated water trickling from cracks in the surface, bellows of steam from somewhere in the distance, and quiet splashing as our feet continue to move forward.

Shadows dance along the walls as we advance. My head tilts to the side as I watch them move, their mesmerizing dance drawing me in, and I tentatively reach out, letting my fingertips skirt along the edge of the heated stone. Instead of finding my own shadow at their tips, the silhouette pulls back as if unsure whether or not it belongs to me. Then, without warning, it crawls back and slips upward along the palm of my hand. A cold tendril of caution winds through me as my skin becomes alive.

My entire body tenses when the weight of confusion settles within my bones, and I think I hear grunts of frustration from the man and woman behind me as they stumble into my stalled form. But I can't move.

I yank backward, trying to force my arm free from the icy grip of the shadow. But it holds steady, utterly unyielding as I fight back against the force. Without warning, the cold stone surface turns fluid and my hand begins sinking into the unknown. My stomach becomes leaden as the fire within grows and my brow moistens with sweat. An eerie sensation runs along my fingertips, begging for entry. I try to ball my fists, but the force is too strong. The shadow doesn't relent.

It slithers up my arm until my body is all but flush against the rock as it draws me in.

"Who–" It abruptly stalls, as if unsure of what it has ensnared. *"What are you?"* The feminine voice, old and icy, slithers against my skin. With each word, the tug on my hand intensifies. Each sound is a grinding melody which tears at my ears. *"What are you?"* it calls out in urgency, and I feel tendrils of frost dance along my bones. *"No words for the one that made you?"* It starts to chuckle. *"Tsk tsk tsk. Such a sad ending to a tragic beginning. Willingly walking toward one's own death?"*

"Let me go!" I scream back at the wall, unsure of what or who is causing this. But the stone further liquifies, as if a rippled onyx mirror now stands before me. I turn to my side, begging for help, but no one's there. I'm alone. I'm alone in the darkness.

"Come to me. Drown out your memories. Succumb to what lies beneath," the withered voice calls out, each syllable dripping with grating delight at the promise of my impending demise.

My mouth opens and closes as if the words I'm trying to push out are blocked behind a wall of ice so thick nothing can pass through. My chest meets the glassy surface of the stone, but I hold steady, not allowing another inch of movement forward, and my body turns glacial as the cold wraps around me, encasing me within a spiraling, shadowy cocoon of regret and misery.

"Become me." The voice slithers into my ear as the hold of the shadow tightens and my body begins to melt into the heated rock.

I try to reach out, a flame of anger barreling from my body in a desperate attempt to fracture the icy coat now covering me. Then, in an instant, the voice changes. Gone is the withered old woman who beckoned me forward, and in her place is a soothing song I find, somehow, familiar.

"Come my dear.
We are but one.
Come my dear.
It's almost done."

The comforting tune relaxes me as it brushes gently, lovingly along my hair. A scent filled with cinnamon and lilac lingers in my nose as my reflection fills the rippled space. I look at myself, but it's wrong. So very wrong. My eyes are too small and my nose doesn't fit. The soft smile across my too-pale face hints at secrets hidden in the depths of my soul. There are no freckles. No curls. And then I watch in horror as the pale skin and blue eyes that aren't quite my own shift and are consumed in flames. I cannot turn away as the me in the onyx mirror screams out in agony, her skin flaking away like burning embers carried on the wind.

"Come see what you did," the unknown voice booms as I gawk at the few remaining pieces of her burned face.

The words are filled with anger. Hate. So much misery and despair blast through me that my hold almost falters.

Then, just as quickly as it came, the burning stops. The flames slow their sway. The air all but freezes in place. It stalls, a movie paused right in the middle of a frame.

"Come see how you killed me!"

The piercing cry barrels into me as I feel a familiar sense of cold inch its way inward. I don't fight this time. I let it take hold. Maybe the exhaustion of what just happened has left me unable to fight further. Or maybe this cold is familiar in a way I crave.

My fingers flex as the tendrils of light within slowly turn from fiery death to icy calm.

"Please," I call out, not yet sure who I'm reaching for.

But then Tarak's heated grip latches onto my arm and the icy coat on my skin bursts away, sending tiny shards in every direction as the shadow sinks back into the rock.

I stand stunned and unmoving as I stare at my hand resting against the solid stone of the cave wall. Solid, not liquid. Not rippling. Rough and jagged. Not mirrored. Not surrounding me with a distorted reflection being burned alive. No waves of pain inching up my arm.

I fall to my knees, trying once more to slow the raging drum of my heart.

Breathe in. Breathe out.

Breathe in, one, two, breathe out.

Breathe in.

My fingers spark against the cold black stone of the cave floor, and I can see out of my periphery when a few of the crew stumble back in fear, unsure what I may do.

Breathe out.

But the breaths I force in and out are not enough, and my body grows tense with a rage I don't understand.

I hear him calling to me. I hear Tarak's muffled voice in the void, in my mind, asking if I am okay, questioning what has happened. But even though I know he's there, even though I can still feel his touch, he can't reach me, and I flinch as he extends his hand out to brush back a sweat-soaked curl from my face.

And then, without warning, I feel something urging me to close my eyes. As if a gentle hand is reaching out to stroke my face. A tingling sensation curls around my chin and licks my lips, and when I open my eyes once again, I see a snowy path. Instead of the cave, I find a vast glistening valley filled with animal tracks and people all around.

I stand, unsure what's real and what isn't. Have I truly gone completely mad? I try to reach out to touch a passing woman, but there's no movement. I can't control this body. I extend my arm once more but this time my body moves forward on strange legs, walking along a path I don't recognize.

Can you hear me? I attempt to scream out, but no sound emerges.

"No. They can't hear you." The soothing voice comes from above, below, to my sides, and all around.

"What is this?"

"You're almost here, Nera. I'm waiting for you. I've been waiting for you. I can't get to you yet. Keep going. You're almost here." His words soothe my beating heart as I search this winter wonderland, trying to find the source of the voice.

"Where are you?"

"You're almost here. Try to remain calm. Don't let it overtake you. Fight it off. You're so strong. Breathe. Don't stop. Don't tell them what you see. Follow the path . . . " The voice fades out and, when I blink again, I find my body still hunkering down on the ground, my hands and knees like ice against the cold stone floor of the darkened cave, Tarak and Jaxon at my sides.

"What in the name of the Elders was that?" Jaxon questions as I find him with his knife out, poised to attack whatever foe he finds. I shift my head, making sure this isn't also some imaginary vision I can't unsee. I hear the readying of weapons all around, and stiffen. My fingers tremble.

A plethora of questions and hurried statements calling for my demise ring out from every direction.

"What was that?"

"Get her away from here!"

"Is she okay?"

"What in the Elders–?"

"Is she–?"

"Leave her behind!"

But Tarak's gaze never strays from mine.

"Are you okay?" His question is urgent, his hands sliding up to cup my face. And though I can barely function or think clearly enough to form an answer, my body knows to instantly avoid the traitorous touch.

He immediately drops his hand as if he's been burned.

"Did you hear that? Did you see it?" My voice shakes as I watch every set of eyes in the group narrow in confusion.

"Hear what?" Ranya's head shifts to keep a steady view of each of the walls that surround, waiting for the next attack.

"It . . . I think it spoke to me. I think it's *been* speaking to me."

"What spoke to you?" Tarak questions.

"I don't know." I shake my head as I rub my temples. "It was a whisper. It said, 'Become me.'" I look up, hoping someone will have an answer. "What does that mean?"

"The only noise we heard was your gut-wrenching screams," Micel says with creased eyes.

"My screams?" My brows furrow in confusion.

I wasn't screaming. I was freezing. The cold air was so tightly wrapped around me that I couldn't move or scream, even if my life depended on it.

"Yes. You were hysterical," Ranya explains. "You reached out to touch the wall before, out of nowhere, you just began screaming." My head shakes as she speaks. "Then you fell to the ground and you stopped screaming, but it was like you weren't even here. Like you were off inside your mind and somewhere far away."

"Tell me everything," Tarak cuts in, placing the lantern on jagged rock, then hastily searching my body for any sign of something untoward.

His hand reaches out to brush my hair back as he carefully assesses each and every inch of me. I know he's only trying to find the source of pain . . . of my supposed screams, but I would rather die than allow him to touch my skin and once again alter how I feel.

"Don't touch me!" I call out and lurch backward out of his reach.

"Nera, I'm just–"

"No!" I command, and for a moment, an impression of pain flits across his face.

"Nera?" Jaxon's tone is calm, an attempt to soothe. "It's okay."

"But it's not," I counter. "I swear I heard it. The rock . . . " I look up one more time for good measure to make sure it is, in fact, still solid. "It turned into a mirror, and then I saw myself . . . but it wasn't me." My voice shakes as I tumble through everything I can remember, trying to speak it as fast as possible so I don't have to dwell long on the experience. "I was different, I think. And it spoke . . . *I* spoke. I heard it back at the camp, too. But that time it wasn't my voice I heard."

"You've been hearing voices?" Tarak crosses his arms as if my rambling has finally confirmed for him how crazy I've become.

"No. No. Not like . . . " I trail off as I close my eyes with the realization it is exactly like that. "I know what I heard. It was real."

"This is absolute nonsense," a man bathed in shadows says from up ahead. His voice is dripping with contempt.

"I'm not making it up. It was real. I felt it. I saw it. I heard it," I all but plead toward the group. I hold back the vision of the snow-covered valley, though I'm not sure why. "Ask me about it. You would know if I lied. Ask me!" But then I remember he wouldn't. Because we are Celestras who are most likely not bonded, and our gifts are dulled against each other.

Tarak looks among those around, taking in everything each might be thinking, before his eyes slide to me.

"If it happens again, let me know immediately." There's an undercurrent in his tone that I can't quite discern, but I know he doesn't fully believe me. I can feel it in my bones. He thinks I'm lying.

"You don't believe me?" Pure shock fills each word. "But I sw–"

I don't get to finish the thought. In an instant, the ground begins to rumble, and the slow trickle of water inching down the raw onyx walls turns into a gushing torrent.

XXI

W ithin a moment, the water is rushing around our legs, knocking some of us to the ground.

"It's coming from deeper within the cave!" Micel bellows out as the crew grabs hold of both the jagged rock and each other, trying desperately not to be flushed away. The water quickly inches toward our hips.

And then, as I'm trying to figure out how not to drown, they start to scream.

One by one, each member of the crew—save myself, Tarak, Riann, and Micel—begins a gruesome torrent of shrieking in pain as the water rises against their form.

"What's happening?!" Jaxon calls back, agony clear in each word.

As the rising flood reaches my chest, Tarak reaches out to grab my arm and pull me to him. "Whatever you do, stay with me. Don't let go!" he urges over barreling waters. White foam and steam pulse upward to invade my nostrils, and my vision blurs.

But my arm reaches up in search of a spot in the solid wall to grasp onto. As I pull up, my head lifts higher up above the current. The hurt in his eyes is true, but I remain unmoved.

"I believe you!" he lies, as if he somehow thinks the words will calm my raging heart. But, in actuality, they would just as soon be able to calm this raging river inching its way up my throat. Because, with certainty, I know he doesn't believe me. I can see it in his eyes. I can hear it in his voice.

But before I can open my mouth to respond, a spindly hand grabs onto my ankle and yanks me down beneath the water's surface.

I am lost to the swirling current as it pushes me into and against the walls. Clothes are torn, and I feel every little nick and slice as my body becomes a canvas of destruction. I scream out, the noise a garbled underwater melody, as my head slams into something hard and the taste of iron coats my mouth.

It's me versus the cave, the shadows, the hell within. And if I had to bet, I would wager my foes will come out victorious in this battle.

I fight for every grip along the edge as I'm moved and thrown, but it's impossible to find a good hold. My chest burns as my body fights for air that isn't there.

A second hand grasps at my arms. I try to shift myself to see who or what has a hold of me, but the water is too dark, and the fading light from the lanterns at the surface seems to be miles away, far out of reach. I can't even see the dangling feet of the rest of the crew, and I wonder if I've somehow been pulled through the floor and into my own personal hell by some sinister force.

My screams of pain are drowned out, and I feel a fleeting moment of panic that I'm drowning before I drop, my soaked body landing feet below on the hard stone ground. I spend far too much time regaining my senses, coughing up all the water I just consumed and heaving in the much-needed oxygen I was deprived of.

"What the hell?" I whisper between ragged breaths, then jerk my eyes upward when I hear another figure coughing and sputtering a few feet behind me.

"Now would be a good time to nock that arrow," Ranya calls out. I twist just enough to see her in the faint wavering light from the gleaming water above. "We should've tested your ability to shoot in the dark," she adds, her voice barely teasing as she slowly moves onto all fours, sucking in breath after breath, and readies her own knife to turn and stare straight above.

It's so dark I can barely see, but from the little I can make out, it's her skin that catches my attention most of all. Black and blue with new burn marks snaking around every inch of exposed skin. Bruised in a manner more one would expect after an hours-long fight for her life than a few moments twisting within a torrent.

"Are you okay?" I call out, nodding toward her legs, and she surveys the damage.

Instead of voicing a reply, she only returns the nod and stands, ready to fight whatever else we may encounter.

My eyes follow hers. Gravity seems to be of no issue here, and neither of us can seem to take our gaze off of what lies directly above our heads.

The black torrent we were flung through looms over us, maybe fifteen feet from where we were before to where we stand now.

"Are we in some kind of air pocket?" I ask as I study the flow above us, trying to discern how the water is defying gravity, but the only answer I receive is the shake of her head. "Not to sound insane," I sputter through lingering coughs, "but this isn't supposed to be possible, right?"

The rippling water overhead shimmers and dances against the surrounding stone high above.

"I've read about this," she quietly confirms, barely moving, and I know we are both thinking the same thing. Both scared to death that any sudden movements or ricocheting noise will cause all the water to crash over us. "Himerak said it was just a myth."

I scoff.

"I don't think I'd trust a word that came out of that man's mouth."

Ranya's shoulders fall. A barely discernible move. She may not have even registered it herself. But I can see the lingering pain that rattles through her body as she thinks of the man who was once her father figure. The ruler whom she once looked up to, fought for.

"I'm starting to believe the same," she admits as her eyes cut over to mine, and I can't tell if it's the lingering water still falling from each of us or if a tear is skirting down her cheek.

"Where are the others?" I ask, tentatively taking a moment to look around and hoping to shift away from her personal turmoil. The cave is dark with only a small amount of light casting down from the water. But there's a tunnel off to the side. It's even darker than where we currently stand, but I think it may be our only way out. I scan the area, hoping to see something of note, and then, just as I'm about to turn back to Ranya, I notice a scattering of white dust trailing the edge of the path.

My heart stutters, knowing exactly what that white dusting is.

It was real . . .

What I saw and felt and heard. It has to have been real. And yet I can't help but worry that maybe the white dusting is exactly where we should *not* venture. Maybe it leads to the evil hiding within this place, trying to draw me in. But something was different in that scene . . . that vision. There was a sense of calm, of peace, of home that danced around me. And the voice. Silky and smooth. It could make the beautiful melodies sung by the birds at Koreed's palace falter in its wake.

"Your guess is as good as mine," Ranya replies, and for a moment, I struggle to remember what it was that I asked her. "They could be anywhere. I saw you get snatched under, so I dove and grabbed onto you just before we landed here."

I nod, realizing now that she was the second hand I felt. "Thanks for not letting me go alone." I give her a small smirk.

She rolls her eyes in mock dismay as she makes her way over to where I stand. "I may have chosen differently had I known where you were going." She lowers her weapon as she reaches me and catches my gaze. For the first time, I think I might sense something akin to friendship in the way she looks at me.

"We should start moving. That"—I point to the small darkened pathway with the dusting of white—"might be our only chance out of here."

She looks between me, the pathway, and then back to her soaked and shattered lantern at her side. "We have no light. Without the light coming from above," she nods upward to the now still water, "we may not be able to see a thing. What if we wait for a while and see–"

A gurgling noise bounces off the walls and the water above ripples at the sound. The dim light seems to brighten as lava seeps from cracks in the walls, illuminating the room in a reddish glow as it flows toward the center of the circular room. I cut Ranya a glance, letting her know it's now or never, and in mere seconds we're both darting for the only exit we see.

The sweat rolls down my brow and drips off my fingertips as we move. Though I can't see it, I know what's causing the tendrils of light to follow behind us as we run. The heat builds and the path becomes increasingly visible with the flowing lava. We run in any direction we can as we follow the open trail. But then the fiery river stalls its advance, the glowing heat dims, and the pathway darkens, as a chill wraps around us.

"Do you feel that?" I question, stopping abruptly now that we can barely see the way ahead.

"I don't feel a thing," she answers, reaching out to grab my arm and pull me forward into the darkness.

"*Find me.*" The words echo through the cavern, bouncing off the onyx walls and slamming into me with such force I swear my body actually moves with the impact.

At first, we barely move, unable to see exactly where we're headed. But then, after one turn and then another, a light flourishes at the end of the path. We chance a quick glance at the other before taking off toward what we hope to be the keys to our escape.

I pull back just as we enter a cavernous room large enough to fit a row of Halabarian buildings within.

"*Find me.*"

"Did you hear that?"

Her breathing picks up as she forces in the needed air and we both stare at what lies ahead. "I didn't hear anything." Her voice is too high, and I think this may be the first time I've ever heard a note of terror in her words.

Her head shifts from side to side as we both search the expanse for a place to hide.

The massive cavern must be fifty feet high with rocks and hidden pathways littered around.

I turn to the right, hoping my guess in direction pays off, when a flash of gold catches my periphery. Two small lights gleam to life from behind a rock and we begin to shuffle backward. The sudden flicker of a lantern down below causes us to halt our movements. Then I freeze. Those beautiful flickering gold flecks blink out momentarily and then reappear, moving to the side as a tall man with long, dark hair shifts into the light.

The stranger's gaze finds mine, and I feel trepidation coursing through my veins even as a pulse, a pull, travels between us. A sudden stirring so deep within me I have to stop myself from curling forward to grasp my stomach. The sudden flurry of emotions causes a tendril of heat to spark at my fingertips. But this isn't the fiery death I've grown used to. The hot spark which flies from my hand is white, a new sort of flame.

I ball up my hands into fists, unwilling to reveal my gifts to this stranger. But the longer we stand transfixed, the more I find a familiarity hidden in his golden eyes.

"Nera."

My whispered name, icy and menacing, reverberates through my head, and I snap my gaze from the man to search the cavern for whoever is calling out to me. The grating noise echoes my name as it bounces from one surface to the next. My eyes are a shifting beam in the darkness as I survey the area, moving from one spot to the next, listening for the fading echo.

"Nera."

My head snaps to Ranya in question as the sound chimes through my mind. But Ranya is too focused on the man standing in front of us. I look between them, realizing no one's said a word. Not me, not Ranya, and not this stranger. And, though the hollowed cavern is now silent as the night, each of us is poised and ready for whatever may come next. For whatever the other may bring.

"Nera."

The silky feminine voice permeates the air as if brought in on a frigid wind, as if breaking through a thousand invisible walls and peering into my soul. It wraps around me, bringing forth an emotion I've never before encountered. Dread bubbles up from within me, filling my veins with an icy hatred, and I can't stifle the now fiery, red sparks which fly off from my fingertips.

"Who are you?" Ranya's question brings me back.

"Arryn," the stranger quickly answers, and for some reason, I know he speaks true. "And you're Ranya, correct?" The hint of a cunning smile creeps along Arryn's face.

Ranya doesn't answer. Instead, she stands silent and pensive, as if trying to decide what goal this Arryn could have.

But I can't take my eyes away from him. It's like there's an invisible electrified tendril keeping me still and focused. My skin prickles, and a wave of alarm envelops me.

"Did you cause that?" Ranya pointedly questions, nodding her head back in the direction we just came from as she pushes forward, placing herself between our new acquaintance and me. "The water? The lava? Did you do that?"

"No." He shakes his head. "I did not. I have, however, been counting down the seconds for this moment to arrive."

"Why?" Ranya counters. The air in the room becomes charged with the tension.

"You have something I need," Arryn replies as casually as possible, while calmly securing his satchel and the items inside, as if he's readying to walk out of here.

"And what's that?" I ask.

"You." He nods his head toward me as he steps forward, and I start in surprise.

"She isn't up for trades," Tarak sneers. My eyes shift to watch his soaked form come into view from a secondary path. The others follow closely behind.

Arryn shrugs. "That suits me just fine. I don't plan to give you anything in return, anyway." He unsheathes a sword as he speaks, and I feel the heat spark as it coils in my palms.

Ranya tenses with every movement he makes. I, however, can't seem to keep my eyes from scanning over every inch of him. His golden tanned skin seems to glow in the light from the fire now blazing at my fingertips. His long, wavy mahogany hair reaches just past his shoulders, and though his winter coat is well-lined, I can tell there's a muscled physique hidden underneath.

A bead of sweat rolls off his brow, and I wonder why he's hiding out in this hot cave in that attire. None of this seems to add up, so I keep my eyes trained on him, prepared to unleash the power waiting beneath the surface should he make the wrong choice.

But Arryn doesn't seem to take mind of the utter stillness he's caused. He deftly moves between the sparsely-placed boulders surrounding the circular space, slowly inching his way toward us while tossing a glowing stone into the air and catching it with each step. My breath halts as I catch sight of the rock he twists between his fingers. It looks just like Gram's stone. Just like the one I used in the Soul Circle. And, though it's at least ten feet away, I watch as a vibrant shimmering river flows through its core. He catches my stare and looks down to his hand, angling the rock toward me.

"Looking for this?"

"Where did you get that?" I ask, unsure if what I'm seeing is the truth or some new vision ensnaring me.

"Koreed is too trusting. Something, I have long waged, he passed on to you." He smiles in my direction, and I find nothing but sincerity in his words.

"You stole Gram's stone from my father?"

Arryn's brows crease. "Gram?" He peers down at the stone as if he's seeing it for the first time, and then his eyes dart over to the corner. I follow his gaze to find every member of our crew now poised and ready to attack. All but Tarak, Micel, and Riann are covered in the same bruising and licks of burns which now cover Ranya.

Arryn is unbothered by their presence and quickly turns back to me. "I don't know who Gram is. Unless, of course, you're speaking of Mina?" His question is genuine.

"How do you know Mina?"

"Nera, I will tell you all of this . . . " He stalls as he shifts to assess my crew, and without warning his cool and perfectly collected features falter.

I turn just enough to keep him in view while also looking to see what's caused his change in demeanor.

"Riann Dolion. You're still alive?" The question is more rhetorical in nature than anything else, but by the way the words are forced off Arryn's tongue, I can tell this man and Riann are the furthest from friends. "I was sure you would be long dead once Tarak retrieved her from the palace. But it's always the worst roaches which survive the greatest blasts."

"Who is this?" Tarak asks, his eyes darting between the two.

I wait for Riann's reply, staring at him, imploring him to respond, but no words come forth.

"Who is this?" Tarak demands of anyone who will answer as he inches closer to me.

Still, Riann remains silent. Almost all eyes are focused on him.

"I didn't take those within the settlement as sympathizers for the Abolition, but then again, nothing surprises me these days." Arryn laughs as he speaks. "Bold of them not to have your entire body draped in heartstone." His words are calculated and precise, and there are notes of both amusement and terror.

"Who *is* this!" Tarak screams out to Riann, and the caverns tremble with the force of his frustration.

"I was his worst enemy," Arryn replies when no one answers, and I stumble back, noticing that, in all the confusion and my focus on Riann, Arryn has moved to stand only a foot from me, his eyes still leveled at Tarak. "And now I'm about to become yours."

Aryyn's hand latches onto mine, and my body's enveloped in wind and all-consuming darkness.

XXII

I lurch forward, vomit spilling from my lips. Gentle, trembling hands pull back my hair, barely caressing my cheek with the movement. My head spins and my body feels as if it's being pulled in a thousand different directions. There was no up or down, there was only my weightless body floating through a vast expanse. But now it is far too heavy and cumbersome.

I keep my eyes closed, too tired and disoriented to even force them open, and then momentarily tense as the cold sensation covers my body, knowing that the voices, the visions, the hell within my own mind is about to come forth. But then, once the nausea and dizziness subside, my hair is released and a warm jacket is draped across my back.

"Elder's, Nera." His tone is filled with exasperation. "You can't fight me that hard in the shift. I could've sent us to Elders know where . . . "

I draw back at his words, damn near falling on my ass as I feel his hands reach down to grab a section of the coat he placed over me. My hands thrust out and my feet kick in fear as I shuffle away. My hair, still soaked from the rush of waters within the cavern, clings to my face. I blink, but my vision is slightly blurred from whatever the hell he just did to me.

"Please don't fight me." It's a sorrowful plea. "You're soaking wet."

I balk as he states the obvious. And yet I can't understand the way his concern wraps around my heart, as if it could warm my very soul.

"You need to get dry. Let me get you home." I hear the crunch of his footsteps as he comes closer and tucks the fur-lined coat tighter around me, securing it with a knot in the sash around my middle. I would force his hands away again, but my body is frozen in an excess of sensations I can't quite make sense of.

Tilting my chin up, I find his golden eyes and tan skin standing before me. The heavy jacket he was wearing in the cave is now covering my shivering body, and the cold I was so fearful of is actually just snow at my fingertips.

Recognition dawns.

"It was *you*?"

"What was me?" he tentatively asks as he crouches down, his eyes now inches from me as he surveys my entire form. For some reason, this time I don't pull back.

"In the cave. You told me to close my eyes and then I saw this." My hand lifts up, a clump of snow in my palm, and then sweeps out before me to gesture at the winter wonderland. "Albeit, this is a little less lively and a lot more desolate than what I saw in that vision." I furrow my brows as he nods his head in confirmation.

"I showed you a memory from the past and a dream I have of the future. Not a vision of what it is now." There is such grief in his voice.

Neither of us move as we look the other over, and I gauge how in the hell I am going to get out of this. He is quite tall and broad, and with the way he's crouched, leaning forward and arms resting on his thighs, his flexed biceps are making themselves very well known. His dark brown hair is half pulled up in a bun at the back of his head, and I catch a peek at the maze of golden tattoos, similar to Micel's ink-filled scars, sneaking out the left side of his collar. He's wearing thick pants, boots, and his own jacket. That must be why he was sweating in the caverns. He was wearing two coats, the one he currently has on and the one he placed over me.

This was planned. His plan was to retrieve me.

"Who are you?" My voice is steady, and for once I actually feel as strong as the woman I'm trying to portray.

He flinches at the question, his hand tentatively reaching out to me, but the movement stops just before his hand grazes my face. An insurmountable sorrow skirts along his features.

"My name is Arryn." I don't miss the amount of effort it takes for him to tell me. I find him familiar in an odd sense, but still can't seem to place him in my mind.

"You already said that." I manage to stand, my frustration rising at once again being at the mercy of a stranger, of a man who has decided he knows what is best for me. The heat settles in my palms and my fury seems to increase with every breath I take.

For a fleeting moment, I consider throwing the thick coat to the ground, not wanting to have anything connected with this man on me, but it is absolutely freezing, and I'm not that foolish. My legs are still soaked, and I can barely feel my feet. If I remain out here much longer, I'll surely turn to ice.

"Why did you take me? Who *are* you?" My words are seething as I try to hide the chattering in my voice, and my head shifts in every direction, trying to discern how to get back to the caverns and my crew—how to get back to somewhere *warm*.

"Nera." His voice is so calming; my name sounds like a song in the wind as he speaks. "I can tell you, but I'm not sure yet if you have the ability to believe me." My brows furrow at his odd wording, but he continues on before I even open my mouth to question it. "But I can show you if you just let me." His hand reaches out to me, but I don't want to see anything else. I don't care what he can show me. I want to go back.

This time, I don't hesitate to shuffle away from him. "Where are we?" I pointedly demand. Anger continues to rise within me, and I know if I don't find answers soon, I won't need this coat. I will burn down this *entire* desolate forest with my rage.

"We're in the city of Bandele in Centra III."

"What!?" *Centra III?* That was not the answer I was expecting.

I rack my brain as the image of the map comes together. Centra I, where Halabar is located, is the largest of all the centras and located in the southeast. Centra II, is also quite large and lies to the west. Centra III, smallest of all the lands, is a barren, icy wasteland that is no longer inhabited. I look up to him as the picture forms in my mind.

"Why?! How?!"

The rage that I have tried so hard to keep hidden is only seconds from bursting and taking us both with it.

"This is where I'm from. We live not far from here. We've been using it as a base," he answers honestly, taking a small step backward as if he can see what's bubbling within me.

"Who is 'we?'" I tilt my head to the side, imploring him to answer more fully as I focus my strength on holding my power at bay. It fights back with every breath. Every ounce of restraint I have is coiled into one small tether. But the edges are fraying with every second that passes by.

He takes a deep breath, readying himself. "Before you were taken, it was you and I, and a few others."

My breath catches.

Before . . .

"The group has dwindled over the last year. Some people lost faith. Some didn't. Dina's still here. She's taken on some of your duties over the last few months. Though, I have to admit, recent events in Halabar have caused our progress to stall." He starts to smile, but then immediately freezes when he sees my face. "Nera?"

"Where is *my* crew? Where is Ranya, and Jaxon, and–"

"They're fine. They're still in the Caverns exactly where we left them. There is an open passage from that specific location, and they'll be able to get out and back to land easily. But they are *not* your crew."

I decide to ignore that last little jab. If I open my mind to the fight that would ensue, this would be over in moments, and I would have no way back to where I'm needed most. "How long have I been unconscious?"

He furrows his brow. "You were never *unconscious*."

I scoff. "I've seen the map. We're all the way on the other side of the damn planet!" I let a little of the power show as my veins become illuminated. "How *long* was I *unconscious?!* How long has it been?" From my calculations, days, if not weeks, have to have gone by in order for us to reach this far away. And from what I've seen so far, the Caverns are not a forgiving place. Between the lava, and the water, and whatever was within the stone . . . they could've been dead within a matter of seconds. A shiver runs down my spine as the thoughts flow through me.

"We left the caverns only moments ago. They're probably still inside that hollow, trying to figure out where we went."

I swallow, once again thoroughly perplexed at how I just *know* he's not lying.

He takes a step toward me. I take a step backward.

"Please don't," he begs. "I'm not here to hurt you." This is probably the most comforting thing he's said because, for some reason I cannot comprehend, I know he's being honest with me. But how *do* I know it?

Still, I balk at his words.

"Let me guess. You're here to save me?" My tone is loaded with sarcasm. Alesia, Tarak, Riann, Koreed, everyone I have met seems to have one job in mind. Rescue poor, unknowing, incapable Nera from her own undoing.

Arryn almost laughs at my question.

"Save you?" He shakes his head as his smile grows. Another small laugh plays on his lips and my heart tumbles in my chest at the sight. "Nera, I couldn't save you if my life depended on it. You, however, have saved me more times than I can count."

I close my eyes, willing my power to simmer. My mind is a bumbling mess of confusion. This man just took me from my crew. He stole me away. I should hate him with every fiber of my being, and yet my chest swells with *comfort* every time my eyes meet his. It's as if there's an internal war raging within. My mind screams a warning of the end, but my soul sings the hope of my beginning.

"Why did you take me? Why bring me– *How* did you bring me here?" I am through being kept in the dark like some incompetent fool. I need to know everything this man knows. I set my jaw, hoping he can read just how seriously he should take me.

"I told you, we shifted. It's one of my gifts. You possess it, too."

My breathing picks up, and though it's bitterly cold in this winter wasteland and I can feel the weight of icicles forming on my lashes and hair, I note the sparks which flare at my fingertips with his words. Arryn does as well.

"Can you control it yet?" He nods in the direction of my hands.

"Yes." A tightness coils in my stomach, a small stabbing pain inching along my spine. A slight gasp of surprise leaves my lips.

He shakes his head. "This world is built on balance. With great abilities comes great pain."

I swallow as the truth in his words hits me. I have a new ability. Just like Tarak, I can discern the truth, but I also can't lie. Well, I can. But lying now causes me physical pain.

"Nera, I think we can both see you have the ability of discernment. Every word I've spoken is the truth. I have never and will never speak an untruth to you." A calm washes over me as he speaks.

My lips tremble. Not in fear or pain, but in all consuming frustration and anger. I don't want another gift. I don't want another piece to be added to this already unimaginable puzzle. I want to get to the caverns and get the stones. I want to defeat the Haze and the Ashclaw, and I want this all to end so I can go somewhere far away from these people and live some semblance of a normal life. Preferably somewhere really boring where nothing overly exciting ever happens and people don't just get whisked away on the regular. I sigh, knowing better than to expect that luck, and decide I have nothing to lose by at least trying to learn what I can from Arryn.

"I possess that ability, too? The one where I can tell if someone is lying or not?" This time, my tone is one of curiosity instead of anger.

"Yes." Cool serenity runs along my bones. His voice, smooth and soft, wraps around me.

"And *you* have abilities?" The burning anger within slowly dissipates.

"Yes." A note of peace settles within my stomach as I watch the swirls of breath seep past his lips.

"That means you're a Celestra?" My shoulders drop in defeat. Not the kind where one has given up, but the kind where one has finally found peace at the end of a long war.

"Yes." My heart calms, and when I once again open my fist, I find the lingering sparks now nothing but smoldering embers. A tendril of light drops from my hand and falls into the snow below.

"And you're acting like we knew each other from before my time on Earth."

"We did. We do," he amends. Then he swallows. "And I can show you."

He reaches out his hand, beckoning me forward while he tugs up the sleeve of his jacket, and I see the outer edge of the mark on his wrist. I also catch a quick glimpse of those golden tattoos inching their way down his arm and into his palm, just skirting around the mark.

As I stare at his outstretched hand, I wonder if he somehow possesses the same abilities as Himerak. "If I grab your hand, will I see my past? Because, if so, I can tell you I've already done that with someone, and I didn't see you at all." The words are almost a whisper as they leave my lips, and I resign myself to seeing what exactly this man has to offer me.

He shakes his head and surprises me when he uses the name I purposefully left out. "Himerak's ability only allows him to see what you know of your past. Mine's different. I can't show you your past, but I can show you my memories. Memories of you."

I cross my arms over my chest as I pore over what those words mean. "How do you know about Himerak?"

"Himerak was once a great and powerful Celestra. If I didn't know about all of the Celestras, yourself included, I wouldn't be doing my job."

His words give me pause.

"And what *is* your job?" My teeth start to chatter with the cold air.

"Up until twenty minutes ago, my job was to find you. Now that you're here and safe, my only job is to help you make sense of all that has happened. My job is to take you home."

"Home?" My eyebrows peak and, though I try not to make it too obvious, I slowly wrap my arms around my body, trying to hold in as much heat as possible. "My home is Halabar. I lived in the palace."

He shrugs. "You did. At least for most of your life," he agrees. "But the year before you left was spent mostly out here, with me."

"I lived with you?"

"Yes. Before you left, we were a team. We lived not far from here. We were working together to eradicate the Abolition and bring an end to the horrors of the land."

"And . . . " I take a moment to think over what he's already said. He has the ability to shift between places, but also can somehow show me memories. "And you have two abilities? You can shift between places and you can share memories with me?" My teeth begin to chatter with the cold.

He shakes his head back and forth in contemplation. "The short answer to that is yes. But it's very complicated. I can explain it all in better detail once we get in front of a fire and warm up."

He reaches his hand back out to me.

"How does the memory thing work?" I know I should be running for my life right now, but my feet are so cold, and my body is starting to hurt. I just need to get somewhere I can warm up and defrost, and then I can run. But the idea of seeing his memories of me seems to outweigh every other option.

"Now that we're out of The Caverns, I need to physically touch you to transfer the memory."

"How did you show me the snow earlier?"

"Our abilities are . . . " he takes a moment to contemplate his next words " . . . enhanced when we're inside the Caverns. I showed you that memory through the stone. But ours, yours and mine, are also connected in a sense. It's easier to share."

"Did you also show me myself in the mirror? Was that you telling me to find you, to become you?"

He freezes, and this time it's not from the cold. "No." His eyes find the snow-covered ground as he steadies his breathing. "You heard it call to you?"

"What was it?"

His head snaps up. "It's called the Shadow. It's one of the four penances. It lives within the Caverns." He quickly runs a hand through the few strands of hair that have burst free. "Nera, if you do nothing else at this very moment, I ask that you trust me. I need to shift us directly home, but if you need me to show you a memory from before to convince you of who I am, I can do that as well."

"I don't trust you." My stomach coils in pain. This time I do a slightly better job at hiding it. "I don't want you to take me anywhere else. I don't want to shift anywhere else but back to the caverns."

He reaches his hand out once more. "Let me show you a memory of us. After that, if you still want to go back, I will take you. That is a promise."

I watch the swirls of breath leave his lips with his words, and contemplate my next move.

"I would see myself from *your* point of view? I would see memories of me from before?"

"Yes. You'd be inside my head. You would see what I see, feel what I feel, think what I think."

I almost want to refuse. The idea that there is another gift I have yet to learn about feels far too overwhelming. But, at this point, I have a feeling there are a lot of things I have yet to learn—or maybe remember—about this place. "That seems rather intrusive."

A smirk tugs at his lips as he pulls his hand back and matches my stance. "You've done it countless times before. I don't mind it in the least."

"Is it painful?" I don't know what pushes me to ask. Maybe I'm just stalling. Hoping to buy time until something happens or someone shows up to help. But then I realize no one's showing up. I know he's being truthful, and we're thousands of miles away from where we left the others.

"No pain." He's certain. "It'll be similar to what happened with Himerak, but instead of seeing the view from outside, you'll be right in the middle of it. Seeing it as I saw it. No matter how long it takes for you to go through the memory, it'll only take a second from this end." He rubs his hands together and blows hot air into his palms trying to stave off the bitter frost that's settled there.

His hand reaches out once more. I take another step back.

"If we stay out here much longer, we'll both freeze to death," he pleads.

"I don't trust you." Another ache lurches down my back, and I know he sees it on my face.

"I understand that no matter how adamant your body is at trying to convince you I'm not your enemy, it will still take time for you to fully believe that for yourself. I'm okay with that. I've made peace with it, and I will work every day to show you who I am and who you were. Just know that I will not harm you. I will not lie to you. I will be your constant. I will be here for whatever you may need."

For just the briefest of moments, my body is no longer cold. I am warm, and calm, and at peace. I revel in the feeling, and then a coil of leaden anger springs forward.

"Are you calming me down? Altering my emotions? Do you have that ability as well?"

"No. You just feel warm and calm because your body's telling you that I'm being truthful. I don't possess any abilities from Elder Balen."

My brows furrow once more as I tuck that name away.

"Will you take a leap of faith and trust me?" he quietly implores, and I stare at his outstretched arm.

"It feels like all I've been doing lately is taking leaps of faith, and so far, nothing has led me where I want to be."

"Right now, you're where you *need* to be. And that's what matters."

I debate throwing some type of sneering comment at him, but instead I just nod, accepting what's happening, and my hand slowly reaches out to grasp his.

I brace myself for what's to come, but nothing happens. When I peer back at him, I find him quizzically looking between our clasped hands and my face.

"Are you ready?" He raises a brow.

"If anything happens other than exactly what you stated, I promise I will burn you to ash."

He chuckles. "I would expect nothing else."

And then the world goes black.

XXIII

Arryn

I've always hated the way this room smells. When I was a young boy, my father would bring me here during training. He would make me stay in the cell for three days at a time with no food or water and only a pot to piss in. In his words, he was 'toughening me up for the inevitable.' For a future where I would find myself stuck in this situation. Except then it would be somewhere far from home.

Little did he know, I would willingly place myself here every single day for the rest of my life if it meant making sure she was okay.

The cold never really bothered me. I could do without food, and with minimal water; harsh nights on the Bend conditioned my body well. But I never quite got past the smell. Even now, eighteen years in, it still makes my skin crawl.

The mixture of blood and shit and death crowd the room, filling my nostrils. I would almost prefer the frozen world above to this hellscape. But I have to stay here. I have to protect her. I'm not yet their sovereign, and at least until that has changed, I have to abide by their laws. So I'll skirt the rules and bend those I can in order to ensure she is safe. I'll hide us until the right moment, until I'm sure the plan will succeed.

I tighten the cloak around my shoulders and take the steps three at a time, hoping to get back to her as quickly as possible. The only reason I even left was to find something lined with thicker fur. I need to keep her warm during this frigid winter night, and she is definitely not dressed for it. I almost didn't bring her here. But she was unconscious with a nasty bump across her temple, and I never did well in my medical studies. It was my one shortcoming, and Father just couldn't seem to get over it. I'm most skilled at ripping bodies apart, not piecing them back together.

My best bet was to bring her somewhere I could seek out help in case she was more injured than I believed her to be. Elders, I pray she'll soon wake. The faster I get to see those vibrant eyes, the faster my heartbeat will return to a normal rhythm, my mind will stop circling through the whirlpool of what ifs, and we can return to safety, to where we need to be. Return to the one place I've seen her thrive.

Truthfully, I've been watching her for close to a year now. Of course, she has absolutely no idea. I've almost made myself known on more than one occasion. Patience has never been a virtue of mine. But watching her on her quests, seeing her frustration and then excitement at unlocking something new, it brings me far too much joy.

But today I wholly regret the decision to keep myself hidden. That wretched choice is what got her into this position, and I will forever hate myself for allowing my selfish nature to cause her harm.

When I shifted into the Caverns late last night, I had planned to make myself known. I had planned to finally reveal who I was and what my motives were.

I was too late.

It took a moment for the scene playing out before me to register in my mind. Vyser had her wrapped up and bound within the heartstone cloths. And from the looks of it, she had been there a while.

Nera was helpless as one of my own people stood over her.

I didn't think through my next moves. There should've been a moment of hesitation, maybe an internal conflict at what I was about to do. At one time, Vyser had been a member of my unit. She'd had my back on more than one occasion, and I knew, should I need it in the future, she would willingly stand by my side again.

So my next move didn't make any rational sense.

In one moment, I was standing twenty yards away, and in the next, I had Vyser's neck in my hands, feeling the life bleed out of her, breath by breath. Her body slumped forward, and I wasn't even sad or disturbed at what I had done. I felt no remorse for ending her. It was a move that, for some reason, my body deemed necessary, even if my mind was a bit baffled.

I thought that was enough excitement to last me at least a few days. Yet here I am, less than twelve hours later, waiting for Nera to wake, watching a far too similar scene playing out as I turn the corner and the cell where I hid her comes into view.

My body and mind wage war against each other. My muscles itch to exact the same punishment dealt to Vyser. My mind races through a list of reasons as to why that wouldn't be an acceptable response. None seem to do the trick.

"What are you doing, Marcus?" My voice is too calm. It's become rather easy to mask my emotions over the last few years. If I reveal even a miniscule amount of the anger and fear pulsing through me, Marcus could end her before I get the chance to reach them. He thrives on the very idea of torturing others, especially me. Elders, I

hate that my gifts are useless down here.

I take another step and the slowly swinging lantern in my hand barely allows me to see, but it's enough. Enough to see what he's really doing.

The rational sliver in my mind that keeps the anger at bay starts to chip away.

"Found something pretty. Just having a little fun." His voice is slurred. Drink must have gotten the better of him tonight. He laughs at something . . . maybe her, maybe me, maybe nothing, and my jaw clenched as his hand skirts the top of her bodice. Her face isn't visible from this position, but from her rapid breathing and shifting of her feet, I know she's awake . . . even if only partially.

"Get your fucking hands off her." This time, I can't hide my wrath as I slowly inch myself closer to the cell.

Only . . . I test the cell door and it doesn't budge. It's locked? He locked himself in with her? He must be more inebriated than I realized.

And an inebriated Marcus is the last thing Nera needs.

"Calm down, Arryn," Marcus slurs with a dismissive wave and another grating laugh. Nera whimpers as his hand snakes around her throat.

The last of my self control snaps.

It's far below freezing in this underground dungeon, but I can feel my ears heat with rage, and I won't take on any guilt for what I'm about to do.

I curse under my breath as I fight the hold keeping my gifts at bay. An invisible barrier pushes back and pain lances its way up my fingertips. Accepting my inability to call my birthright to the surface, my hands wrestle instead with the keys at my side, and I try to open the door. If my gifts weren't veiled in the in between, hidden within the realm of the Elders, I would have already shifted into the cell.

"Touch her again and you will die." My words are barely audible, almost indiscernible through my gritted teeth.

"What?" Marcus counters in disbelief before twisting his body and unsheathing his sword in my direction. "Kill me? You would kill me? Over a whore?" Marcus's maniacal laughter reaches my ears. He doesn't even know he has stamped the seal on his own death order.

I drop the keys just before getting to the last, and watch the frigid air escape my lips as I curse under my breath, grabbing for them.

"Arryn, Arryn, Arryn, be reasonable." Marcus shakes his head as he reaches back toward the one woman I, for some baffling, frustrating, and unimaginable reason, hold in higher regard than any other. He rips the fabric of her shift.

The hot rage which initially rose to life spreads out, inching its way through every vein in my body. I frantically try the keys once more. None work.

By sheer strength—and probably a whole lot of adrenaline—I yank the rusted bars away from the wall and pull my sword free of its sheath.

Marcus doesn't seem to notice the noise, or maybe he doesn't even care. "You will be a pretty treat for the night. I might even come back tomorrow if I desire more use for–"

It's always fascinated me the way a body stalls for just a moment when relieved of its head. It's as if the legs and torso and arms don't know what to do without the commands being constantly sent their way from the brain. They don't even know to give in to gravity. It reminds me of the Centra I soldiers. I have found most to be mindless bodies following a set of commands. Marcus is now the same. What was once a great man turned perverted imbecile is now nothing but a mindless sack of skin and bone.

I should feel bad about slaying him. But I've watched far too many die gruesome deaths for it to be shocking. The only reason I stumble as he falls now is because he goes forward and not back, his bloody stump of a neck landing right on Nera.

"Fuck!" I scream as I haul him off her.

She was awake only moments ago, but now she's out again. I can only hope she won't remember these last few moments as I frantically wipe away the blood from her freckled, olive skin.

I move to lift her into my arms. I try to stand, but my movements are met with resistance, and I realize she's chained to the table. I would never have chained her up, which means Marcus must have.

My eyes meet the lifeless gray sac of the dead next to me, and I momentarily wish I'd caused him more suffering before ending it. His death was too merciful.

Thankfully, one of my keys works this time, and in moments, she is freed. I only brought her down here to hide her while I assessed her injuries and obtained medical supplies. Elders know it wouldn't be safe for her to be found, even if by a member of my own family. It was sheer luck that Marcus was as drunk as he was. That inability to problem solve most likely helped my cause. If he was more sober, he might have thought to question why a Celestra was lying unconscious on the floor of otherwise unused dungeons.

It seems there may truly be a silver lining in everything.

I kick his limp form into a corner, hoping he'll go unnoticed for as long as possible. Maybe, when the morning light comes and the men start to sober, they'll assume he died at the hands of a drunken comrade. It wouldn't be the first time my men tried to blow off steam with physical violence, and it sadly wouldn't be the first time one of those sessions ended in an unneeded death. I'm sure my father, leader of the Restoration, will spend the next week torturing my fellow men as he tries to learn the truth of what happened. I should feel bad about their impending pain. But I don't. I don't because their pain is a necessary sacrifice for her life.

And I will always choose her.

Even in the midst of sleep, she sinks into my touch, and I revel in the feeling of her so close to me. She's something rare and beautiful. Despite the Halabarians remaining *ignorant to her true power, I believe we all know she's someone most people would kill for—that I have now killed for.*

Stalling before the stairwell, I weigh the options. Which direction should I take her? The dungeons are now obviously not safe. The guards, on leave from the Bend, tend to gather a few rooms away in the old taverns once their wives have gone to sleep, and I don't feel like taking another life. Two in less than twelve hours isn't unheard of for someone like me—someone used to the kill—but it does something different to the soul when you aren't on a battlefield. When your targets are your own men.

The stairs heading further down will only lead to more unfortunate guards, most likely too inebriated to help themselves. And the further I go, the less I'll be able to use my gifts.

I need to go upward to the surface. But getting to the surface means going through the communes, through the maze that is my city and home. I barely made it through that chaos earlier. How will I be able to now?

But if I can just get past the inquisitive faces, who will wonder why their final Celestra is carrying an unconscious woman, and make it to the surface, then my gifts will work. I only have to make it up two levels and I'll be able to shift us back into the Caverns, hopefully before she fully wakes.

Her restful face catches my gaze and I slowly brush away the matted curls resting across her forehead. The small bump seems to have leveled out, and I breathe a sigh of relief, knowing she'll most likely be okay.

Her flushed cheeks stand out in the cold of the night, and it takes a great amount of restraint to keep myself from brushing my fingers over them.

With a deep breath, I hide what I can of her under my heavy coat and head toward the surface. She takes a quick breath as I move and further nuzzles her face into the crook of my neck. I momentarily freeze at the movement. Everything about this woman draws me in. Everything. *I turn my head to bury my face into her curls and breathe in the soft scent of jasmine as we move. It calms me. It covers me, and I feel an immense heat travel across my skin. That can only mean one of two things, and from what information I have gathered, there's only one possible outcome.*

My head shakes at the thought, pushing the notion of the heat to the furthest portion of my mind, refocusing on what needs to happen right now.

I only pass two half-drunken guards as I make my way up, and neither seems to notice—or, better yet, care about—the woman in my arms. I guess they both assume she's my nightly entertainment. The thought sickens me.

While our centra has shown some growth over time, some of our men still have plenty of room left for progress. They spend weeks at a time out on the Bend, then come home only to spend moments with their loved ones before galavanting off to find their next acquisition. Thoughts of the change I'll bring once I finally complete my own Committence ring through my mind as I catch sight of the white dusting up ahead.

As soon as my feet touch familiar ground, I suck in a breath and let the winds take us far away from here.

She wakes the moment we land.

In truth, wakes *is probably a terrible term for what's happening. This is only the second time I've ever shifted her, and the first time, she was too unconscious to notice. This time, the motion causes her to fully awaken, and I hold her hair back as she vomits up every bit of the food she last ate before her entire world shifted hours ago.*

She looks up into my eyes, a fleeting image of sheer terror, maybe even surprise there, and then I fall backward in shock and pain as she delivers a swift—and very direct—punch to the center of my face.

Stars cloud my vision before the world fades in and out of view. I keel forward, blood dripping from my face as I catch glimpses of her in the darkness, running away.

It takes a moment to regain my bearings. I was expecting a slap, or maybe even a kick to the groin due to the position we were in. But damn, this girl can punch like no other. I should recruit her for the fighting rings. She would take out more men and bring in more dibs than I could ever dream of. I almost smile.

With a quick shake of my head, I catch a glimpse of her feet as they weave between the vines hanging low from the trees, and I feel my lips smirk in surprise when she shifts little more than a hundred feet at a time. It's more than the previous time I watched her take on the act, but still far less than what I can do.

I can't wait to teach her how far her gifts can truly take her.

It's only a second and I feel the winds brush past me as I catch her in my arms before she can take off once more.

Her eyes widen in surprise and her body tenses under mine.

"You have a head wound," I inform her, then add teasingly, "And apparently, now so do I." I use my free arm to wipe away the blood still trickling from my nose, the other holding her close to me.

I wait for her to say something, anything. Maybe she'll even attempt to get another swing in. I almost revel in the idea of her reaching out to touch me. My arms, as if of their own volition, tighten their hold on her as my fingers brush away the curls swinging freely in front of her eyes. I pray the touch will somehow dismantle any frustration she may still have brewing underneath that beautiful face, but she winces at the motion.

"What's wrong?" My voice shifts from excitement to concern.

She gulps down her swallow, and it's only then that I feel the warmth on my arm. It's too warm to be just the radiating heat from her body. I loosen my grip, taking a step back, and look down to find red staining the sleeve of my tunic.

I suck in a breath as the realization hits. "You're injured!"

The second I let her go, she starts to run, but I easily catch her.

"Stop! You'll only make it worse!" Though I want to scream at her in frustration, the words come out calm and collected. She winces once more, but again pulls away. "Nera, stop moving. Let me check this!"

She blanches at the sound of her name, and I watch as she takes a tentative step backward.

"Let me see it," I plead, searching her eyes. She doesn't move. "How bad is the pain? When did it happen? How did it happen?" She still doesn't say a word, and now it's me who is filled with mounting frustration. "Elder's, Nera. Say something. Scream if you must. I don't care." Again, she doesn't make a sound. One would think this would cause that bubbling anger within me to rise to the surface. Yet, all I feel is a sudden intense wash of self loathing for what I've done. She's woken up in an unknown place with a stranger, and apparently, a new wound. I don't fault her for not trusting me. So I use the only weapon I can.

"Have you suddenly lost your voice? What happened to all those beautiful melodies you like to sing on your missions to save the world?" I cock an eyebrow, my voice now coming out smooth and sincere.

"How do you know who I am?"

I ignore her question, filled with relief the injury isn't bad enough to steal away her ability to speak. "How did you get injured?" I counter.

"How do you know who I am?" Her eyes are bright with fury. "And where in Elders name are we?" Her head shifts from side to side as she takes in her surroundings, and I see her feet inch away as if she plans to shift from me once more.

"Don't try it. I'll catch you again, and you'll lose more blood in the process."

She crosses her arms over her torso, and I can't tell if it's from pain or annoyance. Maybe a little of both.

"How do you know who I am?" she demands, and I can tell this is the last time she plans to repeat the question before she lets her actions speak instead. If I'm being honest, I really don't want another punch in the face.

"I've been watching you."

"Watching me?" Her head tilts to the side in unmistakable annoyance. "Where? For how long?"

The moment I rescued her from Vyser, I promised myself not to hide any detail from her in the future.

"The Caverns. I've been going back and forth from them to my centra for the last few years. I stumbled upon you last fall."

"Last fall!" She huffs, exasperated. "That was over nine months ago. You've been watching me for nine months?"

"If I was better at my job, it would've been longer. You're a Celestra." She bristles at my words, her hand tugging at the sleeve covering her wrist. "Don't worry. I'm not going to turn you in." I lift my own wrist to show her my matching mark. "I'm a Celestra as well. There are a few of us working together now." This time, she does shuffle backward, as if my words were a physical blow to her chest.

Her eyebrows pinch, and I know she's mulling over something puzzling. "How many other Celestras have you met?"

"Counting you . . . hmm . . . I think six. Although, Kerssak is about to no longer count." I start to laugh at my own inside joke. She doesn't.

"Six!" Her wide-eyed expression is almost comical.

"Yes. Nera, listen to me. There's a lot of information I need to share with you in a very short amount of time. Your centra is not all that you've been taught to believe. You're not the only Celestra left."

"Obviously." She rolls her eyes as she quickly looks down to my wrist.

I match her stance as best I can, hoping she understands she won't win this fight. "Let me help you." The faster we get you healed, the faster we can get to work.

"Why do you want to help me?"

"Because we're the same. You and me. We're both fighting for something, and to be honest, I'm tired of fighting alone. It'd be nice to have someone on my side for once."

"How do you know what side I'm on?"

"Like I said, I've been watching you." My hands spread out as if the answer's obvious. "Who do you think left Drunia for you to find?" I hear her breath catch in surprise. "You can't honestly believe someone just accidentally left it there?"

There's a tense moment where I can tell she weighs her options. She looks around once more, and then, as I see a pulsing of pain race through her eyes, she finally relents and lets her arms fall to her side.

It's my opening.

I take a tentative step forward, waiting for her to recoil, but she stands still and unmoving. I'm surprised to find my fingertips slightly shaking as I reach out to touch the skin on her abdomen and slowly lift the torn fabric of her tunic to the side. I tell myself it's from my recent head injury along with the constant change in climate as I shift. But, in reality, I know all too well it's because I am terrified of what I'm about to find. The idea of her being injured, or suffering any amount of pain is probably the most excruciating thing I can fathom.

My breath hitches as my eyes finally land on the injury.

"Fuck." I murmur the word as dread coils inside.

My gaze meets hers, for the first time, she lets the mask of strength fall as pain fills her features. I catch her just before her knees hit the ground.

"How did it happen?" The question rushes out as I try to recall when this could've occurred.

"The Haze."

That wasn't really an answer to my question. I identified the cause of the injury from the presentation, but I haven't seen the Haze this far out yet. Every sense I have is now on high alert.

"It already burst," I observe, not sure if more for my comfort or hers. It's not very deep, and it looks like she's already covered it in salve. As shallow as the wound is, it should be back to normal in hours. It still makes me want to scream. I rein in that frustration and calmly continue, "The worst should be over. Has the pain lessened?"

She nods her head in answer, and I grunt at my obvious incompetence. I had her for twelve hours, twelve fucking *hours, and never even noticed the injury.*

"I think I slept through most of it," she quickly adds with an almost laugh, and I wonder if her comment was intended for my benefit. I can feel the self-loathing written all over my face.

"I'm sorry. I didn't even know it was there. If I had I would have–"

"Who are you?" Her question shocks me.

"Arryn. Ari for short." I don't know why I give her the nickname. Mother is the only one who has ever called me by that name, but for some reason, the idea of hearing it said by her lips causes a deep stirring within me.

"Ah–ren?" She tests the name, and I laugh.

"Yes, but you can call me–"

"Ari?" she cuts me off with the whisper and my heart literally flutters at the sound. I haven't yet put thoughts to what I feel between us. In reality, I know. But the very concept is still too overwhelming to consider.

My head nods in affirmation.

"Why am I with you?"

"What's the last thing you remember?"

Her answer is immediate. "I was too deep within the caverns, and then the Haze was there. I started to run. My shields weren't holding, and the next thing I know, I was bound and blindfolded."

Ahhh, Vyser . . .

"Vyser found you. She was a guard from my centra. She's been out on missions recently, but she wasn't supposed to be at the Caverns." I run my fingers through my hair as I speak.

"That doesn't explain how I got here"—she swings out her hands— "with you."

"Vyser had you bound, and I was . . . not okay with that. You were unconscious.

You have a bump just"—she doesn't pull away when I reach out and gently brush my fingers over the bruised area at her temple, and I smile—"here. I assumed it was what caused you to pass out, but now I have a feeling it's more so due to the pain you're experiencing from this wound." My fingers move to rest just outside the injury on her stomach.

I take a pause to gauge how well she's processing all I'm revealing to her, but if anything, she seems more frustrated that I've stopped talking.

"After I . . . took care of Vyser," I decide not to go into the intricacies of how exactly I took care of her, "I brought you back to my centra. I had only planned to stay for a few hours. I wanted to be near our medic should that bump turn out to be more serious than I could handle. Turns out, taking you back there wasn't the best idea."

"And that's where we are now? In your centra?" she inquires as she leans forward to sit on the ground. I quickly reach out to help her when I hear the sharp gasp of pain.

"No." I shake my head and take a spot directly in front of her. "We're in the outskirts of Boreas, the capital of Centra II."

"I know what the capital of Centra II is," she grumbles with slight annoyance. "Why am I here?"

"Because I needed to bring you somewhere else. Somewhere safe. And no one resides in this area. We'll be left alone to rest until you're ready to head back to your home."

She takes in everything with such quiet calmness that it's almost unnerving. I don't know why I expected anything different. Nera's a problem solver. She's a Celestra. She was born to find her way out of troubling situations. Still, I want her to keep asking me questions. I ache to hear her voice and know that it's only for my ears. But I take the hint and remain quiet as she sits.

When she was in the Caverns, I would sometimes hear her sing to the emptiness. Sometimes she sang for hours as she worked through maps and books. Those were my favorite excursions. Every single lash I received when I arrived home with no new information was worth the time I spent focusing on her.

For some reason, the sight of her, the smell of jasmine, and the sound of her voice brought me more peace than I could have ever hoped. I spent most of my childhood surrounded by death and famine, with every day clouded in fear that it would be my last at the hands of the Abolition. But with her, there was just peace. She was peace. For once in my life, there was a stillness I had never known.

"It doesn't hurt," she relieves me of my mindless ramblings and concern as she looks up at me with a tentative smile. "As long as I'm not really moving," she clarifies.

My expression matches hers.

"Well then, it seems like we'll be staying right here until that changes. I have some burn cream." I reach into my pocket to grab the small container. It's not really meant

to be used on injuries caused by the Haze; that's where the salve comes into play. But maybe it'll be able to help dull the sensation enough to provide her some amount of relief.

She tentatively reaches out to grasp it, and her fingers brush over mine. "Thank you, Ari."

XXIV

I gasp as the air forces its way back into my lungs. My eyes refuse to focus on any one spot as I try to make sense of everything I've just seen, heard, and felt. The sensation of being inside another's mind, watching a scene play out while I was on the other end, but unable to control any motions or decisions, is one I don't think I will ever forget.

Being in the Soul Circle was vastly different. In that valley with those two men, I was physically there. I could even in a minimal way, interact with the world around me. I was able to reach down and feel the wildflowers. I was able to grab their attention, if only for a moment. Even watching my own past flash through my mind with Himerak wasn't as shocking. At least then I was an outside observer just watching the scenes play out as a movie in front of me. But this time, here with Ari, I couldn't do anything but exist.

"What the hell was that?" My voice is weak, and my body is shaking as I force the words out. "What in the hell was that?!"

"Nera," he starts, his voice filled to the brim with concern. "I told you. It's just a memory. It's my memory of the first time we met." His need to calm me is evident in his tone, his expression. The set of those golden eyes are imploring me to believe him.

"How did you do it?"

"I gave it to you."

"How?!" I try to scream as my weakened knees slam into the soft, powdery snow below. He attempts to walk toward me, but stalls as he sees the stems that glare within my eyes.

Arryn throws his hands up in the air in mock surrender, letting me know there's no cause for concern. I wish my mind would agree.

"It's just a gift I have. To be completely honest, I have no idea about the intricacies of the matter."

"I really do know you?" My voice is barely more than a whisper. It almost comes out as cry, but I hold back the swell of emotions, unwilling to let this man see me break. I am a mix of wanting to know everything he knows while also wanting to shut it all out.

He smiles and the sight threatens to shatter my heart into a thousand tiny pieces.

"Yes." It's barely a word. It's more like a breath of relief being let free.

With far too much effort, I force myself back on shaking legs. I can tell he wants to reach out and help me. His body is practically humming with the need. I take a tentative step backward, and then toward him, and then I stop moving altogether, not sure exactly where to go or what to do. My heart hammers in an erratic beat within my chest as my mind tries to wrap around everything.

"Are we friends or enemies?"

He chuckles slightly at my words. I don't know why I asked. It was such a stupid question. I'm sure he wouldn't answer honestly if the correct response was the latter.

"That depends on where you want the story to start. We have been a little of both over the last few years."

The last few years? We have known each other for years. But nobody—not Koreed, not Riann, not Alesia, or anyone else—hinted at having any knowledge of this man standing before me.

"When was that memory from?"

"A few years ago," he replies and I give him a look that I hope shows just how much I don't want to have to beg for something more. He smirks before speaking again, "If we are being exact, then . . . five years, three months, and seven days." His voice drops off in a melancholy tone, and I can't understand why my chest · feels as though it will collapse in on itself at the sound.

"When was the last time we saw each other?"

He shakes his head as if my question doesn't make complete sense.

"That's a complicated answer. Do you want the last time I saw you as you are now, or the last time I saw you from before you left?"

My head tilts in confusion. "I don't understand."

"Do you remember when you first escaped the palace a few weeks ago? You were hiding in an abandoned house on the outskirts of Halabar." I nod. "There was a Halabarian soldier who helped you escape after you came out of the vent. You hid behind a tree while he directed the others to another location and away from you."

I again nod my head, confirming his words, and then suck in a breath when realization hits.

"That was you?" My voice is far too incredulous.

"Yes."

"Why?"

"Because you and I are one in the same. If you're fighting, so am I. If you're running, so am I." He chuckles. "Only, you ran too far too fast. And it was dark. I used every gift at my disposal, but I couldn't find you in time."

"You're a Halabarian soldier?" Dread creeps into my bones and solidifies in my stomach.

"No. No, no, no!" He throws up his hands in horror at my assumption. "I swear to you I am no such thing. I infiltrated their ground troops when I heard from my spies that you had returned. I was trying to find you—I did find you—but then I lost you. Again." His voice breaks on that last word, and with it, my heart.

"What did you mean about seeing me before? You mean before I went to Earth?"

He takes a deep breath before looking at me once more.

"Did Riann explain how you shifted to another planet?"

"No." My answer is immediate.

He tilts his head in confusion. "Did Alesia?"

I shake my head.

"Did you ask?" There's a note of frustration, and maybe a bit of disbelief, in each word.

"I . . . " I stumble, realizing I haven't been asking the questions I should've been focusing on all along. But now I know why. It was because of the false sense of calm Tarak forced on me.

"Nera?" He runs an exasperated hand through the long, silky hair that has now almost completely fallen free of his bun. "I realize three years have passed, but you're still *you*. You're still in there. You didn't think to ask your companions how you ended up on another *planet?*" He is nearly yelling at this point, but I can tell it's more in desperation than in anger. He then sinks back against a waiting tree and rubs his temples. I realize he has no idea how Tarak has used his gifts on me. "I guess it wouldn't matter if you had asked or not. Riann would have had to lie. And he probably avoided the topic altogether, knowing he couldn't lie very well to you."

"I asked Tarak, but he didn't know."

Arryn laughs. "Why would he? He wasn't there."

"You were?"

"Yes, I was there. So were Riann and Alesia, though I will admit that I don't think Alesia was an active participant in any of it."

"Tell me," I implore. "Tell me everything."

"Can I show you instead?" he asks, and immediately I nod. Any fear of what is currently happening drifts away as the gift he offers me comes into view.

"Please!" I want to fall to my knees in relief at the thought of finally receiving the answers I've waited so long to hear.

He looks around and then takes a tentative step forward before brushing a growing mound of snow from my shoulder and flicking a slowly solidifying strand of hair back.

"Can I show you after I get us somewhere warm? I have a change of clothes and a hot meal waiting."

XXV

I run my fingers through the thick, fur-lined coat he placed over my shoulders only moments ago and wonder if it's similar to the one he had gone to retrieve for me in that memory. Maybe it's the exact same one.

As I stand at the door to a tiny, old, wooden cottage, a sudden feeling begins to overwhelm me. The aromas of oak, pine, and an odd note of citrus pull me in. But my feet remain steady on the ice-covered ledge.

That memory he just showed me felt so real . . . so true. Yet there's still a moment of hesitation as I again wonder how I got here. Hours earlier, I was preparing to enter a hellscape in order to help people I barely knew. Now, I find myself once again thrust into uncertainty as my entire world has shifted on its axis.

"You can come in," Arryn beckons from inside as he slowly removes his coat. "There are very few that even know about this place. You'll be safe."

I almost scoff at the idea. *Safe*? This sounds like the exact opposite of safe? Us being here, where no one else knows our location, is exactly the reason I shouldn't enter.

But if I'm being honest with myself, I do trust him. I don't know if it's the fact that I can feel his honesty in my bones. But if I didn't trust him, I wouldn't have let him shift us here in the first place.

"Before I go any further, I need to know exactly what you can and can't do. What are your gifts?" I stand rigid before the threshold of the small cabin as I wait for his answer.

"I can move between locations and between times."

Moving between locations is now obvious, since we've done it twice. But the other . . .

"You can time travel?"

"Yes. But not for long, and there are caveats to my gifts, just as there are to yours."

"What does that mean?"

"I can travel—shift—between various locations within the same time period. That's how we shifted locations from the Caverns to here. But every time I shift between places, it has to be at the exact same time. It's the opposite with time travel. I can shift between times, but I will always end up in the same place. So right now, I could take us to a year in the past, but when we arrived, we'd be standing in this exact spot." I let his words linger in my mind. "Does that make sense?"

"Yes." I nod in acceptance and rein in the growing awe I feel at all he can do.

"I can also alter the reality of what you see."

My eyes narrow. "You could be altering this reality right now?"

He laughs.

"I could. But I'm not." I have to admit that *knowing* someone's being absolutely truthful is a rather odd sensation. I stare at him for a moment as the sensation wraps around my body, and he continues, "Remember when I showed you the memory of people and the snow when you were still in the cavern?" I nod. "I can alter what you see, but you can't interact with the false reality. Hence, you couldn't interact with the people you saw." He takes a few steps forward, meeting me on the rickety porch, then reaches out and brushes his fingers across my cheek. "Can you feel me touching you? Do you feel the wind? What about the cold snow falling on your face?"

My body is one massive contradiction. I feel the tears start to rim my eyes and look down to the tattered and broken boards of this porch at my feet.

"Trusting strangers is what got me into this mess."

He solemnly nods as he leans back against the door frame.

"I'm not a stranger," he whispers while looking directly into my eyes. I quickly shift my gaze away.

"I can't trust this." My body tenses as the statement comes out more abruptly than I intend, but when I look up, I find understanding in his eyes.

"You mean trust that what I show you in my memories is real? Or that what you're seeing now is real? Or that what I'm saying, and what you're feeling are real?"

I nod, hoping he understands that it's definitely everything he just said, and he laughs.

There's a moment of contemplation before he tilts his head to the side and smiles.

"Can I show you something?" His eyes crease. "Or better yet, remind you."

My brows furrow. "The memory of how I arrived on Earth?"

"Not yet. I want to show you something you cannot only see, but feel. Something that you will know as absolute truth."

That piques my interest. "Will it hurt me?"

He laughs again and for some reason I find the sound both exhilarating and odd.

"Nera, know that nothing I ever do to you will in any way be painful. Though, if you don't do it correctly, I guess you could theoretically hurt *me* in the process."

I look on in confusion, but relent when I find no malice in his words or expression.

"Okay. Show me." I have to look up to meet his eyes. His broad shoulders almost block out all the light of the fire inside the small broken cabin, and with the hazy glow behind his figure, he almost appears god-like. His golden eyes, the feature which first caught my attention in the caverns, seem to glow even more intensely out here under the night sky.

"I have been watching you since you appeared back in Ithesin. First when you returned to Koreed's palace, and then, once I realized Tarak would take you to the Caverns, I made sure to arrive before your group did so I'd be ready to intervene."

"To take me away," I amend his statement, but he shakes his head in response.

"You can call it whatever you want." He leans back against the post of the porch as he crosses his arms.

I roll my eyes. "Rescue me?" I almost grunt in frustration. "It seems that's everyone's job these days."

Then he smiles so broadly I swear the fire grows and the darkness dissipates.

"As I already stated, I could no more save you than I could save myself. And if we're being honest, aside from our first official interactions, you never really needed saving in the first place."

I want to believe him. But there's been too much back and forth in my life.

He shifts his stance once more, and a small wisp of hair falls into his face. I fight the urge to push it back, clasping my fingers so tightly I feel my nails bite into my palm.

"I want you to think about something that makes you happy." His words shake away my wayward thoughts, and it takes a moment to realize what he said.

"What?"

"I want you to think of something that makes you smile. I want you to close your eyes and picture something you love. Picture it and hold onto it in your mind."

I furrow my brows. "Why?"

"Because." He cocks his head to the side and shyly shrugs his shoulders, which draws out a tentative smile from my normally sulking features.

"That's not a real answer."

He quickly counters, "Will you try it . . . for me?"

"I don't know you. Why would I do anything for you?"

He shakes his head, then looks up at me through his ridiculously long lashes that I'm somehow just now noticing.

"Then do it for yourself."

I huff in response, debating whether closing my eyes while standing defenseless in front of this man is the smartest decision.

"No." My emboldened resolve barely hides my chattering teeth.

"Nera." He sighs and runs his fingers through his hair.

I step backward, my foot finding the soft snow.

"Can you shift to Halabar?"

His head barely nods in answer.

"You said you'd show me how I ended up on Earth, and you haven't. So, if you won't show me that or take me back to the caverns, then take me home."

"You *are* home," he pleads. "And I will show you."

My head shakes furiously as I unfasten the coat from my waist. "I'm going to freeze to death out here."

"Then come inside!" He is practically begging as his feet inch their way to where I stand.

"No. Take me home. Take me to Halabar."

"I–" He falters, his chest rising and his features filling with something I can only describe as pure grief.

"Take me home."

He takes a shuddering breath before he reaches out then pauses. "Okay." The pained word seeps past his lips.

"Really?" My shock is evident. I wasn't expecting him to relent. I expected to fight, hoping my stalling this long would somehow rejuvenate my gifts enough to allow me to escape.

"If you want to go back to Halabar, I'll take you there. I want nothing more than for you to trust me. And if that means letting you go, then that's what I'll do."

"Why?"

He scrunches up his face in confusion. "Because you mean everything to me. I would rather continue this fight against the world tortured and alone than to force you into something you don't want."

He reaches out again, this time more sure in his movements. But I can barely process the change. I'm so focused on the waves of cool elation that undulate down my spine.

Still, my fingers itch to meet his, and as my hand rises in the cold air, my heart lurches forward.

I pull back the moment before his fingers brush mine.

"Nera?"

I close my eyes as I try to steady my breathing.

"Nera?"

"Shh!"

"What are you–"

"I can't concentrate if you're talking."

"What are you doing?" he urgently questions, and I give off a whispered grunt of feigned annoyance.

"Trying to think of something that makes me happy. Now–" I peek an eye open to find an incredulous look on his face. "Quiet."

I swear a sigh of relief wisps through the air.

At first, I try to recall anything in the last few weeks which has brought me any amount of happiness or joy, but most of those memories revolve around Tarak. That doesn't seem appropriate at the moment. So, I think instead about the one home I can remember.

I think about Earth.

I think about Taylor and Mary and that stupid cat, Mila. I think about my day-to-day life with them, and all the connections I made in that store. I think about how they made me smile. How they accepted me when no one else would. My cheeks become a tear-stained river as I recall every happy moment. Every time Mary drew me a picture, every time Taylor sat with me as we quietly read just so I wouldn't have to be alone, every time that damn cat fell asleep on my feet and then acted as if the world was ending when I had to stand up. Heat pulses through my veins.

I think about how much I miss them. My fingertips tingle, and my clothes feel too warm.

"That's it," Ari says, and my eyes pop open. He quickly places his hand over my face, blocking out the view. "Keep thinking. Don't look. Just keep thinking, picturing whatever it was you just were."

I square my shoulders as I think of Gram's shop. I picture the patrons, and the way Mila bounced up and down as she chased the beam of light the day Mary found an old flashlight during a storm. My cheeks heat, and I can feel the flush that covers them.

I think about Rhea and how kind she was to me. I think about that small boy, Finn, and the yellow flower he gave me. My body sings in excitement and my skin prickles as if a thousand tiny, harmless spiders are drawing out their webs over every inch of me.

"Open your eyes," Ari calls out, but I can't move. My body is frozen in time. "Nera. Look at me," he says more pointedly, and I force my eyes open.

His form is too bright. Far too bright. I'm normally a fairly rational person, and in my head I know it's night, but he appears as if the sun itself is blazing down on him. I furrow my brow as his expression shifts from surprise to excitement, and then to pure elation.

"Why do you look so happy?" I quickly question.

"Because you are incredible."

XXVI

I look down at my feet and find my entire form glowing too, as if dancing diamonds skirt along my skin. Rivers of white light extend from my fingertips and surge into the surrounding snow. When I move to jolt backward, the broken boards at my feet crystallize with a sweep of my hand.

"Whoa, now." Arryn jerks sideways. "Best not to move too much until you re-learn how to control it."

I steady my breathing as licks of ice run along my spine. But this cold is different from the dread-filled glacial sensations which previously consumed me. This doesn't feel scary or confusing. This feels like *me*.

Our eyes lock, and by the way he matches my expression, I know I exude nothing but awe and confusion.

"It's built from your emotions," he explains. "You can yield every element. Fire, water, air, dirt. You can alter them all. You can bend them to your will." He steps back when I flex my fingers and watches as the crystals inch toward his boot. "You can also kill me or anyone else if you don't rein it in." He smirks.

"How? How am I . . . " The words trail off as pure astonishment fills my veins.

"Anger, frustration, heartache, fear . . . We've found that those tend to bring forth a deadly fire. That one's more unstable—chaotic. But love, joy, happiness . . . those bring the light. We haven't completely figured it all out yet."

"Have I always been able to do this?"

"In a way, yes." His words are lined with sadness, and I wonder at what brought on this sudden change in emotion. "Pull it in. Bathe in the feeling. Bring it home to you."

I stare into his eyes as he speaks, and something inside me opens, as if a key has finally found its lock. The tendrils of white light curl back within my palms, and in seconds, Arryn's form dims back to flickers and shadows, a silhouette against the small fire at his back.

"You can kill me with that. You can strike me down at any moment. You almost have a few times in the past, if I'm being completely honest." He laughs and my entire body seems to lurch forward at the sound, wanting to bathe in it rather than this newfound light. "But I want you to know that no matter what I can do, no matter what gifts I possess, you have infinitely more. Except when it comes to yielding a sword." He smirks, and I find I am desperate to know the source of that inside joke. "I will never, at any moment, make you feel anything other than . . . " He pauses as if looking for the right word. "You will be safe with me. I promise. And, should you ever feel as though you aren't, go ahead and use that on me." He quirks a brow and then steps back over the threshold. "And if you ever want to leave, I'll take you back the moment you ask."

I don't even contemplate the last sentence, knowing I now want nothing more than to discover everything I can about this newfound gift.

"Can you show me a dream of me yielding that, controlling it? Maybe if I can see myself using it, I can learn how to control it now?" Patience was never a virtue of mine, and damn if I suddenly find I don't care about the shivering cold, or the icicles, or the fact that my entire body has practically turned to ice. I want to know what I can do. I want to know how powerful I truly am.

"Of course. But . . . it was a memory. Not a dream. A memory," he quickly corrects me. "What I showed you was no more fictional than the cold you feel biting into your toes right now." As if on instinct, I curl my toes in, trying to retain as much of the heat as I can on this frigid night. "They wouldn't be so cold if you stepped inside." He nods down to the rickety boards between us, and I finally relent.

As soon as my foot's over the threshold, the heat of the room engulfs me, and I close my eyes, savoring the warmth radiating across my skin. Then I all but scream in surprise when I open them once more and find the room changed from a small, barely ten-by-ten-foot cabin to a massive home at least two, maybe three stories tall.

My gaze shifts quickly to him and then back to the room and then back to him once more.

The main living area is absolutely massive and reaches up into the sky with a balcony on the second story looking over the first. Rich mahogany stretches across the expanse with deep navy blue and gold accents all around. A roaring stone fireplace is situated in the middle with an opening on all four sides so its heat can be felt from every direction. The ceiling seems to extend up into the night with wooden beams stretching across the expanse. Various leather couches, chairs, massive rugs, and beautiful paintings fill the room.

I look back to where Ari leans against the door frame, arms crossed over his chest and a satisfied smirk on his face.

"How did you–" I cut myself off as I walk back to the threshold and cross over and onto the snow-dusted porch. The cold engulfs me. When I look back, I find the small cabin exactly as it was before, barely enough room for two people, a tattered mattress, and a tiny fireplace that would only hold two or three logs at a time. I quickly race back into the home and watch it instantly transform into the massive structure again.

My eyes squint in confusion. "What kind of magic is this?" My voice is filled with curious enthusiasm.

"I told you. I can alter the reality of what people see. While I have yet to encounter anyone in these woods, I'm not naive enough to believe someone won't eventually venture here, and when they do, I want them to see a small, barely-held-together shack, not a base for mounting a revolution."

"Is that what we were doing? Mounting a revolution?"

He smiles with a nod. "That's exactly what we *are* doing."

I take a breath as I allow the weight of the revelation to settle in. "We have a lot to discuss."

He nods in agreement as he walks directly past me and heads toward a massive wooden and stone kitchen. By the time I meet him in the room, he's ladling warm soup into two bowls and setting bread and other cooked delicacies onto a plate.

"Do you normally prepare this much food at once?" I quirk an eyebrow his way.

"Only when I know *you* are headed home." He looks over his shoulder with a teasing grin as he plates his own meal. "I'm trying to figure out how to explain all of this to you without overwhelming you," Ari admits as he walks my way. "There's no point keeping you in the dark, but I'm not sure how to explain this in a way that's believable, while also letting you know you can trust me." He places a bowl directly in front of me.

"It's odd that you would just admit that out loud." I lean over the bowl and have to hold in the moan trying to escape at the rich aroma wafting upward.

It's only at this moment that I decide, though I may not fully commit to whatever my life was before, I will hear him out.

"Nera." He says my name as if it's a song. "We have a history of direct and pure honesty with one another. Why would I change that now?"

I immediately accept this truth.

"I don't care if it overwhelms me. I want to know it all. I know I didn't ask anyone before, but that was because . . . " I pause, unsure of how to explain everything that's happened while also deciding if I even want to venture into that tale. "I want to know now. That's all that matters." My words are definite and direct.

He nods, takes a spoonful of the soup I've yet to taste, and places a finger in the air, indicating he'll be right back as he walks into a side room. He's only gone for a few moments, but it's long enough for me to scoot off my small stool and survey the cabin. Or . . . maybe cabin is the wrong term. This place might as well be a lodge just based on size alone.

A massive dining room set near the front of the home boasts a table large enough to seat twenty, or more. The kitchen, though almost medieval in appearance, has a number of gadgets I don't know the use of and a wood stove large enough to fill with food for fifty. Despite the enormous size of the living area, it manages a cozy feel that draws me in. At the far wall, I find an immense bay window with a pile of pillows on one end and a blanket thrown on the other. With no hesitation, my feet hurriedly make their way over. My fingers reach out to graze the soft material as I gaze out at the falling snow in the distance.

"That's your favorite spot."

I jolt backward and almost slam directly into Arryn. He just smiles down at me with what looks to be a rolled up map in one hand.

"My favorite spot?"

"You like to read here. Sometimes you read upstairs, but for the most part, this was your place in the house to tuck yourself away whenever we had a moment of freedom." I look over the cozy cushion and thick blanket once more. I could definitely see this as a place I would frequent.

"This is the third time now that I have ventured into a home and been told a plethora of random facts about myself I don't remember."

"I can't imagine what you're feeling right now." His words are defeated, as if he wants nothing more than to provide the answer to my riddle of a life.

"I don't even know what I'm feeling right now. I don't even know you. You could be my enemy." The words feel foreign as they leave my lips.

"You do know me. You just don't remember me," he corrects me with a smile so at odds with the devastation I see in his eyes. "But I can promise you that we are most definitely not enemies."

"Then what are we?"

He pauses for a moment, opens and closes his mouth multiple times as if he isn't sure what to say, then motions for me to follow him back into the kitchen.

I shimmy out of the massive fur coat then reach down to pluck up the blanket and wrap it around my shoulders. Then I move toward the kitchen, stopping to stand by the bar.

"Can we make a deal?" he questions as he sits on a stool beside me.

"Depends." I take a sip of the soup. I was right. This *is* delicious.

He must see it on my face. "Spices, from Niser. That's in Centra II, if you were wondering."

I nod. At this point, it's pointless to question him when his every word comes out as smooth, honest silk.

"What's the deal?"

"I will openly and honestly answer every single question you have. But if I answer specific ones first, it may skew your view of what's actually happening. Will you trust me to answer them when it makes the most sense? That way you get a full view of what we're working toward, and I'm able to help you make sense of everything without outside intricacies clouding your thoughts."

"I don't know if I like that."

He leans over, placing his elbows on the bar before slowly lifting his gaze to meet mine.

"You never were one to make it easy on me."

"Why start now?" I retort and he bursts out in laughter.

He flexes his jaw and I catch the moment he masks the emotion threatening to spill out. For some reason, the view causes me to relent.

"I'll let that one question slip, but no more. Okay?"

"Okay." He smiles as relief washes over him.

"But I need to know one thing for certain."

"What's that?"

"My crew." He bristles at my words, and I wish I could take back the verbiage. "The people we left back at the caverns," I quickly amend. "I need to know they're okay. I don't fully understand everything that's happening yet, but no matter what, I need you to know that I will not allow harm to come to them. I need to know they're safe."

"Okay," he answers without hesitation. "Will you give me one minute?" He sets down the spoon and I nod.

Before I even finish the movement, a brisk wind slams into me. I shield my eyes, and when I open them again, he's gone.

A few drops of soup splash on the wooden bar. My head shifts from side to side as I try to find him, but I'm alone. I turn back to the front door, but also find it empty. Then I hear the clanging of a spoon against a bowl. When I jerk my head back to the bar, I find him sitting directly beside me, a third bite of soup almost past his lips.

"They're fine. It looks like they're headed back to the mainland. Riann and Alesia are no longer with them. Tarak seems to be smoldering with rage, but all in all, they're fine."

"What– How did–"

"I told you. I can shift. I would take you with me, but that's a long journey, and you probably would've gotten sick again. But, if you want me to physically show you, I can most definitely do that." He places the spoon down with the offer and reaches his hand out.

"I believe you." No bites of pain surge down my spine, and it's the first smile he gives that seems filled with pure elation. "Where are Riann and Alesia?"

"My best guess is that they escaped."

"They couldn't have," I counter.

"Yes they could, and they would."

I let his words linger in the air as I toss the notion of what they mean around my thoughts. It's more than obvious—from his reaction in the caverns and talking about him now—Ari boasts no love for my once betrothed. But right now, I have more important things to worry about than where Riann has run off to. I'm sure he'll make it back to Halabar and Koreed somehow.

"Are you ready?" His words cut through my thoughts.

"I'm ready." And this time, I actually feel the confidence my voice exudes.

He pushes his bowl to the side and rolls out the large, map-like paper in front of us. Only, it's not a map. It resembles instead more of a detailed, hand-painted spreadsheet.

Down the left side are paintings of what I guess are eight different stones. One seems vaguely familiar.

Then, in the columns directly next to each are their names, descriptions, more names, and Celestras that, I assume based on what I've recently learned, possess their corresponding power. There are various names crossed out, and it's easy to see where others have been added over time.

"These are the stones?"

"Yes. I'll tell you about them, where they came from and what they do. If you have any questions, please ask." I nod and he smiles before taking a deep breath. "But first, I need to tell you why *we* are here, and judging by the minimal amount of information you've acquired since your return, this may take a while." His smirk hits me and I have to stop my body from giving in to the urge to lean into him.

And then his story begins.

He tells me of the origins of Ithesin and how the centras were once joined in one large landmass called Centrina. The tale's almost exactly as Tarak told it. But then Ari adds in more details. He speaks of the four Elders—Haziah, Safar, Amary, and Balen—who created this world. Of the peace, love, and unity they strove for. That Ithesin lived in this blissful peace for thousands of years. It prospered and thrived in every way imaginable. The more he speaks, the more I can relate them to Earth's mythologies of gods.

He weaves a story I know to be true about a people filled with acceptance and love, who freely gave to each other and to the land, and how the land gave back to them. He tells me about the heartstone mineral found in the trees of what is now known as Centra I, and how it's used in everything from medicine to food to infrastructure. That it's almost otherworldly or magical in a way he isn't sure how to describe.

But then he details how the people of Centrina became riddled with greed and power. About how they used the heartstone to secure and build weapons, and began killing each other over it. The Elders were distraught over this turn. For hundreds of years, the Elders slowly stopped the land from being able to grow the trees, hoping the people would turn back into grateful, loving beings once more. But they were wrong. The fighting continued. The hatred grew as the trees, and thus the much-desired heartstone that drove their way of life, became rarer. The wars raged on. Hundreds and hundreds of years of wars and death and murder between what we now know as these four nations, all committed for a resource only the trees could provide.

The stones came next. Over another century or so, they were found, years between each, in the centers of the remaining heartstone trees of the Mulara Forest. Some people began burning the trees down in order to find a precious stone while others made it their life's work to protect them.

They were used to yield power as the Elders designed a plan for the wars to end. It was a way for mere citizens of any standing to rise up and take control. To take back the world they once knew. It was supposed to be a means to an end. Either use the stones for good, or destroy the world and end it all.

But the plan didn't play out the way they wanted it to. Most citizens were unable to harness the power, and the few who could didn't know what to do with it, so the stones became relics of sorts as the people held and guarded them in hopes that, one day, a citizen would be able to use them for their intended purpose.

It was then, after countless lives were lost and no end to the slaughter was in sight, that a massive quake occurred and Centrina shifted apart to form what we know now as the four centras. A vast flat of water filled the space between the lands and the greedy thrived.

The scale of the wars slowed, but only because people became too fearful to fight back, and those who took power became more and more destructive.

That's when the first Celestras were born. It took another hundred or so years to figure out exactly what they—what *we* were. It took time to determine and study the gifts and learn how each could be used, how they correlated to the stones, and then what exactly the Celestras were meant for.

We were supposed to be a way to unite and bring peace to the lands. But again, people are selfish. There were good Celestras, well-meaning ones along the way, but too many of those born with the mark got a taste of the Elder's power and wanted to hold onto it. They wanted it all for themselves.

So here we are. Thousands of years later, we remain four continents of people who cannot communicate with or reach each other due to growing atrocities. We are destined for more war and death, with a handful of Celestras who are all unsure of how to bind the continents back together.

He finishes his tale, and for a moment, there is not a sound in the room but the whistling of the outside wind.

"You were right." It's barely a whisper. I lay my head down on the table and close my eyes.

He chuckles lightly. "About which part?"

"It is overwhelming. I feel like the *literal* weight of the world is on my shoulders."

He breathes a heavy sigh. "I haven't even told you the worst parts."

XXVII

The soup does wonders at calming my swaying stomach and mind. Or maybe it isn't the soup. Maybe it's him?

"Alright. Tell me the worst parts." My eyes remain trained on the nourishment in front of me and not on him as I scoop in one spoonful after another. I'm so consumed by the hot meal that I'm on my fourth bite before I realize he hasn't said a word.

I tilt my gaze upward and find him carefully surveying me, looking over every inch he can; though, what he's looking for, I don't know.

"What?"

He shakes his head, then looks down to the table in front of him.

"I have no patience whatsoever." He starts to laugh and then stills before locking eyes with me. "I had this plan for when you came back. For when I found you. I didn't know exactly when that would be, or what it would look like, but I *knew* you were still alive. I knew you would come back, and I imagined every scenario. I tirelessly worked through all the details of exactly how I would tell you this story. Your story . . . Our story. But I didn't factor in one very important piece."

"And what is that?" I slowly place the spoon in the bowl, my attention no longer on my stomach.

He runs a hand through his hair and turns, just enough that I can see the whites of his eyes and the golden halo they hold in each. "How hard it would be to . . . to have you here but not in the way you were. Not be able to hold you."

The world—my world—stops at his confession. The snow stalls and the wind halts its every movement. Even the fire, once roaring with life, seems to die down.

"I'm sorry," he hastily apologizes, as if the weight of those words has truly hit him. "You always said I have no self control when it came to–"

"You and I were . . . *together?*" While I may have only met him a few hours ago, I can't say that the possibility hasn't crossed my mind.

"Yes." I feel the verity of that one word in the depth of my bones.

I wipe my sweating hands along my pants, my gaze dropping to a random pattern on the rug. "For how long?"

He waits a moment, as if trying to decide how best to answer. "That memory I showed you earlier, that night we first met . . . " He trails off, making sure I'm following along, and I nod for him to continue. "You were sixteen. I was eighteen. I showed you that specific memory because it was the most neutral I could think of. We pretty much hated each other for the entirety of that next year as we started working together. I think the only reason you trusted me was because I could best you with a sword on my worst day. Still can." He laughs in nervousness and his eyes meet mine. Golden embers matching ice-blue glaciers. "You were desperate to beat me. But I was too bold, and you were too stubborn. We were a horrible mix, always fighting and screaming at each other. I'm surprised one of us didn't snap and kill the other at some point."

"It doesn't sound like we were a very good match."

He chuckles before taking a breath, looking straight ahead as if he can't bear to see my face when he speaks the next words.

"On one of our outings searching for the stones, about a year after we first met, we found the Drench."

This is only the second time I've heard that mentioned, but no one has told me what it is.

"I goaded you. It was my fault. I made a bet with you that I knew you wouldn't turn down. Your gifts were getting stronger at that point. Though neither of us could dare to even speak the idea of it, I think we both knew you could do more than any other Celestra alive or dead."

I swallow in anticipation. "What happened—with the bet?"

"You drowned." I almost choke at his words. He stalls as if the weight of those words damn near undoes him.

The spoon falls to the table. "I drowned?"

He nods. "The Drench had made its way into the river. We got pulled under with the current, and the next thing I knew, you were yards ahead, being thrown into every boulder in your path. I don't even know how I managed to make it to you, but I think something snapped within me, and the next thing I knew, I was holding you." His voice starts to shake. "I pulled your lifeless body from the water. I had barely enough energy myself, but I dragged you up that riverbank. Your lips were purple, and your skin was so cold."

Insurmountable pain courses through every word and breath he takes, and I can tell it's a struggle for him to continue.

"You had only been under for a minute, maybe two. It felt like a lifetime." He blinks away the unshed tear. "I thought I was going to break your ribs with every compression. But I wasn't going to stop. I knew I would keep your heart beating until mine gave out."

My stupid, stupid heart lurches, and it takes everything in me to reel it back in.

"Then, out of nowhere, you started coughing and coughing, and all I knew was that you were alive and I could breathe again."

But now *I* can't breathe.

"We sat on that riverbank for hours. I held you as your coughs died down and your breathing evened out. The sun set and the moons came out, and still we did not move." He reaches up, caressing the line of his jaw. "It was then that I think we both gave up the fight. We accepted what was and always had been."

I sit in frozen shock as his words register. My heart plays a violent song in my chest as his words sink down and bury themselves within the depths of my soul. Though his story brings forth no memory of the event, it does register as familiar in a way I can't explain. Maybe it's the note of truth I find within every breath he takes. Maybe it's my broken mind latching onto anyone who seems to care? Or maybe it's something more?

My head shoots up as I meet his tear-filled gaze, and there is absolutely no escaping the thought that slams into my mind. I try to brush it away. But there's no denying this pull, as if an invisible golden string has finally solidified. As soon as the notion takes hold, heat spreads throughout my body.

It starts in my chest and weaves its way into every inch of my skin. It calms me in a way Tarak never could. It soothes the ache of every pain I have ever felt, both mental and physical. It makes me feel whole for the first time in my life. And, without question, I know what this feeling means.

"We're bonded Celestras." The words are but a whisper as I stare into his eyes, watching as a single tear falls down that beautiful golden skin.

I'd meant for it to be a question, but even my own body can't deny the certainty in those four words as they ring strong and true.

He doesn't answer, but with a shaky voice, continues on with the story.

"Once it was too dark to truly see, you twisted in my lap to face me. The outlines of your face were barely visible in the lingering moonlight. Your voice was so hoarse when you finally spoke. But it was as if we were truly meeting for the first time. Truly seeing each other for who the other really was."

He sucks in a shuddering breath as the moment overtakes him.

"I opened my mouth to respond. I tried to say it back to you, but no words came out. I just knew you were alive, and that's all I could comprehend. You placed my cheeks in your hands, and you stared back at me for just a moment as if you were making sure it was real. That it was really happening."

I'm standing before I realize I've moved.

I can't bring myself to look at him. I won't allow myself to see him or smell him or hear him. I won't allow myself to see the pain and love that fills his gaze. I do what I'm best at.

I run.

My feet carry me in a rush from the kitchen into the living room, and I find myself standing as close to the fire as possible, staring into the flames as if they can tell me how to breathe around *this*.

I can't look at him, because I know the second I do, it'll all come crashing down. That invisible sheet of ice I have so meticulously built, that wall formed from every heartbreak, every betrayal, every forgotten memory, will shatter.

My gaze stays trained on the dancing flames, but I feel his approach from behind. I close my eyes when he stops just a breath away, willing my trembling hands to still.

"We are bonded." I say each word slowly, letting the truth settle within.

"Yes."

A sound bubbles up from the depths of my throat, and I catch myself on the stone as my knees buckle underneath me. He doesn't reach for me, and I am so thankful for that, because the idea of him touching me right now is too overwhelming. Is this *the* more? Is this what Tarak was speaking of? What he wanted me to wait for? Was he waiting for it to snap into place? Was I?

Because damn if this doesn't feel like the most overwhelming emotion that has ever soared through my body. Every hair feels as if it's standing on end. Every inch of my skin feels alight as if it could, at any moment, burst into flames. My every muscle is both taut and loose, and my heart might as well bust straight out of my body.

I pore over everything Jaxon told me about bonded Celestras. It didn't seem like a confusing concept as I took in his words on that log. But being told something and feeling it crash straight through me are two completely different things.

I push myself back up on shaking legs, refusing to look his way.

"What does that mean?"

He takes a step to the side so that we stand shoulder to shoulder, neither making eye contact. Both staring directly into the flames ahead.

"Whatever we want it to." His answer is so simple, yet holds so much weight.

"What did it mean before?" I finally get the courage to face him, and my vision clears. I study his every feature, committing them to memory. His shoulder-length dark hair, such a deep brown it would appear black if the light from the fire wasn't bringing out the sparsely-placed lighter strands. His nose has the tiniest scar across the ridge, and I wonder how it was formed. His tanned cheeks give off the smallest hint of a blush. His kind eyes search my face, and I find their glistening, golden hue is like nothing I have ever seen. He is enthralling, mesmerizing, captivating . . . as if every inch of him is pulling me in.

"It meant we were one. The Elders chose us, and then we chose each other. There wasn't a thought or decision that went through my mind which you didn't already know. It meant everything."

I nod my head and turn to circle the fireplace. I had hoped to step away from the pull of him. But now, with the raging flames between us, he looks even more devilishly alluring than before. His lips raise up in a crooked grin as he catches my assessment through the flames.

I quickly look away, cursing the heat now pulsing through me that I know full well has nothing to do with the flames we're standing in front of.

"You said we were enemies at one time?"

"Yes. And no." He shakes his head a little as he quietly laughs. "We're just very stubborn. We don't fall into line without some sort of push back."

"We have a problem with authority?" I raise my eyebrows and he laughs a little harder.

When did he and I become we?

"Me, maybe. You, most definitely." The laugh dies out and all that remains is a subtle smile, so kind that every little tether attached to my heart gives a little tug. "So we fought that pull for a very long time."

I nod, accepting his words, not sure where to steer this conversation next. My brain goes into overdrive in an attempt to make this very awkward situation, well . . . not so awkward. Then my stupid mouth does what it always has and blurts out exactly what it shouldn't.

"What about Riann? I was supposed to marry him."

That smile falters for just a moment and a steely view sets in. "I think it might be easier for you to see this as my memory than for me to explain it for what it is—what it was."

"What does that mean?"

"We can get back to this," he points to the kitchen, indicating the paper he laid out on the table, "and us, in a moment. But for right now, I think I need to show you another memory."

"Which one?"

He circles around the stone structure, a predator meeting his prey. "The last one. The one where I lost you."

XXVIII

Arryn

She is over an hour late.

I pace the small distance between the pillars, waiting for her shadow to crawl in from across the way. It never comes.

Something's wrong. Something is very, very wrong. I can feel it in my bones. My stomach tightens in warning, and though my hands continue to shake from the cold I just left, my palms are starting to sweat.

She's never been late. Early . . . yes. Always early. But never late. My heart rate speeds up with every passing moment as I run through each impossible scenario.

Riann could've discovered Drunia. He could've taken her directly to the Abolition. She could be fighting for her life at this very moment. I knew we should've stopped this nonsense, this back and forth, months ago. Damn her stubbornness.

We have almost found the location of where the Abolition meets, and between our securing of Drunia and the Omni stone, we are mere steps away from figuring out how to defeat our enemies and how to overtake the penances of the world. If he has her, it's over. He has the final stone, the one we haven't been able to procure, and once he realizes she's aware of the ruse, there will be no reason for him to keep her alive. I can only hope she–

My mind cuts off the incessant circles of dread and doubt as I watch her shadow slowly approach. Every tightly-coiled muscle in my body relaxes at the sight.

"I'm sorry!" she yells out an apology as soon as she sees me. My arms are crossed. To anyone else, it would likely appear as if I'm seething. But my face shifts to a bright smile the closer she gets, unable to feign anger toward her.

"You, my love, will be the death of me." I open my arms and she launches herself *into them.*

Two years. It has been two years since I first felt her skin against me in that dark underground cell, and the idea that she is mine still manages to overwhelm me.

"You need a bath." She leans back, places my cheeks in her small hands, and gives me a wicked grin before scrunching up her nose.

"We can take care of that once we're home." I lean forward, letting my nose brush against hers. I've always found her nose intriguing. I don't know why. It's such a silly thing to focus on. But the way it fits her face in utter perfection makes me smile. Just the same way her eyes, her mouth, her dimples, her freckles, and her lips drive me wild. I could spend all day spreading kisses across every inch of her face . . . her body.

I know she wants me to kiss her now as she leans up on her toes and tries to reach my lips. We haven't seen each other in a week. One of our longest stretches apart.

"Stop teasing me," she whines as she leans further forward, standing as tall as possible, but I don't let her meet my lips. She may be small, much smaller than I, but she has more fire in her than I could ever hope to harness.

She'll be the death of me.

"I should punish you for all the stress you put me through over the last hour."

Her eyes darken. My cock stiffens.

"Take me home," she purrs, leaning up just enough that–

Crude laughter erupts. The vile noise echoes through the expanse, and we both turn to see where it's coming from.

"While I'm not surprised by your treachery, your choice of companionship is rather unexpected," Riann jeers as he slinks toward us from the opposite side of the vast cavern.

My breathing stalls. I have never met this man in person, but I have, of course, loathed him since all of this began. But not just for reasons one might expect. Yes, he's my bonded's betrothed, though Nera and I both know that's a facade. She'd already figured out the truth of his nature long before she found me. But I can't say I've particularly reveled in the fact that she's had to masquerade that perfect version of love with him for the masses over the last two years. She may have had to dance in his arms and walk by his side at dinners and balls, but I am who she comes home to late at night. I am who she writhes under when the world is still and the moons are high. It is my name on her lips when she screams out in ecstasy. I am the man she leans on when the path ahead seems impossible. I am her strength as she is mine.

So no, I don't hate him for claiming something that was never his. If anything, I find pity in the role she had to play.

I hate him for what he stands for. I hate him for his family, his lineage. I hate him being a member of the Abolition and fighting to end every Celestra on Ithesin.

Himerak's reign of terror at the hands of Koreed was nothing compared to the number of lives the Abolition has taken. Innocents slaughtered and families torn apart, all because of greed and the need for vengeance. All because of a lie.

I can feel the anger rising in me but know I've got to rein in my emotions before I explode. I momentarily think that shifting us back home where we can better prepare for this fight would be best.

Nera has another idea.

"How did you figure it out?" she asks with a murderous glare in her eyes. Her voice is steady and loud, making sure he can hear her clearly from across the distance.

Riann pauses as if unsure what answer to provide.

"I found a heartstone cloth in your room this morning. It was tucked between the boards in the closet."

We both tense as he speaks.

"There are very few reasons why one would possess something of that nature, unless they're attempting to overtake a Celestra. Seeing as you're the only Celestra known to reside in Centra I, I found the idea of you hiding it away rather confusing." He clasps his hands in complete nonchalance, as if this conversation is one we might be having on the street.

"We both know I'm not the only Celestra in Centra I." Her words are scathing.

Riann looks up from under his brow and my stomach curls with dread as his lips twist into a sinister expression.

"How did you figure it out?" he repeats her question from earlier, and she answers with a shrug of her shoulders. "How long have you known?"

"Long enough." She crosses her arms. "Tell me something. How is it that the son of the leader of the Abolition turns out to be a Celestra—the one thing they are sworn to hate?"

He shakes his head and that menacing smile grows.

Nera doesn't falter.

"Better yet. How are you not dead? I would've assumed your father would've killed you the moment you were born. I bet he absolutely loathes *the idea of you."*

Riann's smile dips for only a moment, and I can feel the anger ripple off of him. It's almost a confirmation as to what gifts he possesses.

Recognition dawns, but I try not to show it in my face. This is good. Nera's baiting him into showing us his hand, and I could not be prouder. When he doesn't answer, she continues on.

"You stand for everything they despise. You're the filth of the land that they can't seem to reconcile with."

"You're the same as me," Riann seethes, his tone now matching hers.

"I am nothing like you," Nera counters, each word an arrow coated with toxin aimed directly at its target.

There's only a moment of hesitation before I feel the rumble race through each boulder around us. Before my next breath, Nera explodes. Her shield surrounds us as falling rocks slam down into the dome of light and then ricochet away.

"He can destroy," we whisper in unison as the onslaught wanes.

"I would guess that means he can also create," Nera follows my thoughts as the attack slows and the dust settles around us.

Each Celestra typically has two gifts. More often than not, they go hand in hand, two sides of the same coin. If he can destroy the physical elements around us, that likely means he can create what he needs.

But so can Nera.

"We should go," I whisper urgently, reaching out for her hand.

"Absolutely not. If he leaves this mountain, it's over. We haven't built up enough forces yet, and he–"

"I've always hated this thing." His voice, still projected from the other side of the cavern, is now muffled from the shimmering dome that encases us.

It takes another second, but his form fully comes into view as the dust settles from the previously fallen debris. He hasn't moved an inch, and yet I feel as though his presence is about to overtake us.

"This feels about right." He shakes his head in what can only be disappointment. "I came here to face this head on, and you run and hide behind your gifts. If nothing else, at least you're consistent."

I open my mouth to speak, but I feel her hand grasp mine.

"If I let this shield down, I will destroy you in a second. You know my gifts are greater than yours. You know I could kill you before you take your next breath."

"You won't."

She goes still, the ripples of rage are rolling off her with every breath as her coping mechanisms move into place. She hasn't yet figured out how to smother the rage when it takes over, and I can tell this moment is a fight in the making. I need to find a way to calm her. Her wrath has only exploded beyond her control once before. But the consequences were devastating.

"If you kill me, how will you find the last of the sacred texts?" he quietly counters, his voice soft and coaxing. We both still at his words. "If I'm dead, how will you infiltrate the meetings? How will you get this?" He lifts up a shining stone, twisting it between his fingers. "Isn't that what you're waiting for? You won't have a chance if the Abolition goes underground because their leader's dead."

There are far too many statements to digest. The book. The meeting locations. The stone. Their dead leader . . .

"Your father is nowhere near dead." It's finally my turn to speak.

He laughs. The dread I felt when Nera was late to our meeting spot now triples.

"My father has been dead for years. Twelve to be exact."

"Not possible," I argue.

His maniacal cackle intensifies. "Unfortunately for you, you're wrong." He places his hands behind his back and paces a few steps to the left before turning back to the right. "I assume you're thinking of your secret correspondence with him over the last few years?" He quirks an eyebrow in our direction and I freeze. "I guess now's a good time to let you in on a little secret of my own." He snickers as he turns to face us. "You've been corresponding with me."

I look to Nera, and by the expression filling her face, I know every single word he spoke was the truth. She only just recently conquered that gift and now I fear all we'll uncover.

I try to wrap my mind around this new information. I have spent far too many years infiltrating the centras, and even had a foothold within the Abolition. I have sent their leader—Riann's father—several letters over the last few years. But it seems Mikel never received a single one. Instead, I've been corresponding with my sworn enemy the entire time.

Which means everything we discussed was a lie. I had hope, albeit a small hope, that by the way the letters were reading, Mikel had officially decided to assist us. It was the ultimate win. With Mikel on our team, it meant we hadn't just infiltrated the Abolition, we had acquired their leader, and that would make way for a sure turn of the tide.

But, apparently, nothing is ever as it seems.

My father had been having secret meetings with Mikel for a decade before I was even born. Now that all the details are coming together in my head, I realize exactly why some of the earlier confusion in those meetings occurred. In the beginning, when my father and Mikel met, it seemed to be by sheer luck, or maybe misfortune. Then they started to realize the truth hidden within their hatred and those happenstance meetings became more deliberate in nature.

All because Mikel had a change of heart.

Exactly eighteen years ago, he changed. Instead of menacing words and battles that left many dead, Mikel began to seek information from my father. And before long, their meetings became filled with trust and an unlikely alliance. We now know the reason for the change in his demeanor eighteen years ago wasn't just because of a sudden feeling of humanity from those horrid people. It was because of love. Mikel bore a son with a mark. And for the first time in his life, he loved someone more than he hated something.

Though I wasn't exactly privy to them, those meetings between my father and Mikel carried on for years . . . until they didn't. That last meeting never happened, and in its place, a letter arrived. It was filled with hints of betrayal and things my father couldn't make sense of. Some of the words he couldn't even read.

It was as if Mikel was writing down everything so fast that it became a jumbled mess of incoherence as one word bled into the next. My father had no idea what he *could have meant, but there was silence for the next ten years. Then two years ago, out of the blue, I received a second letter. And though very little made sense at that time, I had hoped we were about to work our way back to where my father had climbed all those years ago.*

"How?" Nera screams, anger rising up as her fists fill with bright orange light.

"Calm down," I urge through gritted teeth. "We're under the shield. You let out that rage while we're in here, and we'll both be reduced to embers."

The light flares and recedes from her fingertips as the war inside her rages at the realization we've been fooled.

Now that the air is clear, both physically and metaphorically, Riann turns and slowly sinks back to the other side of the cavern. While all I can now think of is how to get us back to safety.

"I wonder what your little camp, hidden deep within that cave you savages call home, will think once they know you failed?" he all but yells, a villainous smirk pulled across his face.

Nera recoils. Her entire body then stills as recognition of what he just said hits us.

Just as I look up, shock and disgust covering both our faces, I see him dart through a pathway.

The shield drops and I reach out, desperate to take her home. She quickly steps out of my grasp.

"We have to go," I beg.

"He knows." Her words are a saddened plea.

"Nera."

"He. Knows!" her lips tremble, and I watch in horror as she all but crumbles in front of me. Sheer terror stretches across her features. I'm not sure how she's still standing.

"They're safe," I quickly counter in hopes of calming her down. "He's bluffing." My words bring no comfort. We both know she could tell if he was. "I promise they're all safe. No one knows where they are."

She shakes her head as she takes a step away from me and moves in the direction he went.

"We end this now." Fury spits from her lips. "I'm done with this. I'm done."

"Nera?" My brows crease in frustration. She's acting on emotion, not reason. "This is exactly what he wants. For all we know, he's luring us into a trap. Do not follow him. Let's go home. We'll secure the base. I'll put extra guards out. I'll double, triple the watch for the night. The Bend will hold, and our defenses will not fall. Nothing will happen to them."

My words are useless. She's too far gone. That fire she keeps buried deep inside has fanned to the surface, and nothing I say or do will convince her to stay.

A small bit of hope rises within as her gaze meets mine. It fizzles out the second she speaks.

"I can't let this go on any longer. It could take years to get everything in place. But right now, right this instant . . . he is in the Caverns and he can't shift. It'll take him all day, maybe two to get back to Halabar. We have him. Trap or not, we have him. You and me and the combination of our gifts can take down anything. We can take him down."

"Nera . . . " I shake my head in uncertainty. I'm the planner in this equation. I know that. And rushing off after our sworn enemy with no extra weapons is a fight we don't want to risk.

"If you say no, I'll go home with you." My head snaps up at her words. "If you're certain that we can't take him, I'll head home with you right now." She steps back into my reach and grasps my hand. An open offer to send us home, should I so choose. I stare into her face as it glistens from tears. "But if there is any part of you that feels we're ready, that we might succeed, then I want to end this. I don't want to go another night with that threat hovering over us."

"I would follow you into a blazing fire and you know it." I step forward and pull her to me.

"Is that what this is? A blazing fire?" A mixture of sadness and anger settles across her face.

"Most definitely." I lean in to kiss her, but she pulls back.

"You still stink." She smirks, and I laugh. Her shaking hand pushes against my chest, inching us further away from one another. I clasp it within my own as I meet her tentative smile. "But if we make it home after this, I promise I will kiss every inch of your body until dawn."

My smile doesn't even get the chance to reach my eyes before she wraps her frame around me and the world goes black.

I don't expect the shift to happen so fast. I know she's improving, but I have a lingering feeling her increase in ability has more to do with how far down we are within the caverns and not with some sudden improvement.

The caverns seem to be a beacon for our gifts. It's the location of the Committence and where each Celestra receives their stone. It also enhances what we can do. Outside of this underground realm, Nera can still barely shift more than a few feet in each direction. But here, it's as if every gift buried deep within her has come to life.

We move in and out of every crevice, hole, and pathway we can find with ease as we *search for Riann. He couldn't have gotten far. We shift into one for only a heartbeat before we realize he isn't there, then quickly shift to the next. Deeper and deeper we go. Faster and faster she becomes.*

I hold on tight, letting her lead the way. I can, of course, shift on my own, but if we both shift, there's no promise we'd end up in the same place, and I will not lose her.

We also don't want to drain our power. Unfortunately, we don't have an endless amount to be used whenever we want or need. My mentor, Kerssak, once explained it to me as a well filled with water. We can use and use and use as long as it's there to draw from, but once it dries up, we have to stop, rest, and recover.

I catch sight of Riann just before I feel the pull of Nera shifting us once more. My grip tightens around her arm, our silent signal, and she immediately stalls.

"I'm a little disappointed." *He stands near an underground river we've yet to find in our own explorations.* "That took longer than I expected."

"Where is Asfidel?" *Nera demands, speaking of the third sacred text we know he possesses.*

"You just expect me to hand it over to you?" *He paces the water's edge on the opposite side of the cavern.*

"No, I expect you to make me fight for it."

"I don't want to fight you," *Riann counters, and for the first time he looks tired—despondent.* "I will admit that your death is the inevitable outcome to all of this, but I will not–"

Nera scoffs, cutting him off. "You sound so certain for someone stuck in the depths of the Caverns with two Celestras and no way to shift out."

He locks eyes with Nera just as our entire world shifts.

The rumble begins and Nera's shield immediately rises upward. The cavern we're encased within suddenly changes as the walls, the floor, and the ceiling crack under the weight of Riann's ability. The river which was sitting so far away becomes sucked down into a newly formed crack, and just as the last drop seeps into the opening in the floor, I hear a thundering current come from behind. The wall splits in two and water rushes in through the new opening. It spews from every crevice and crack we can see, and within moments the floor around our perfect shield is covered in an inch deep obsidian abyss. It fizzles and sparks as it splashes against our only reprieve. Boulders fall, the floor around us further splits open, and dust billows up from the impact.

The noise is muffled under the safety of the shield, but it soon becomes ear splitting as what once was a well formed shelter starts to fade away.

With a frustrated grunt, Nera falls to her knees as our shimmering sanctuary fizzles out. Water surges toward our legs. Reaching down to pull her up, I furrow my brow in confusion as we lock eyes. She may be brave, but she isn't an idiot. The last thing we need is a cave-in that causes injuries too great for us to be able to shift out.

"Put it back up, Nera," I whisper through gritted teeth, and her gaze searches the surrounding ground.

She pauses for a moment, her head slowly turning to face me.

"I can't." Her words are a breath of shock.

I watch as her shoulders raise with a new inhale and she tries to force the glimmering dome upward from the water that surrounds us. The sizzling ring of fire takes flight at her feet, but only makes it a few inches into the air before it's overtaken by the rising water and we watch in terror-filled awe as it crashes back down again.

Riann snickers at the sight.

"Asfidel may not have great knowledge of the stones or the trials, but it is full of the intricacies which govern the depths of this realm."

We both shift our gaze from the water below to the man now only separated from us by a large crack in the surface.

"What are you saying?" Nera's ire is palpable. I feel the heat radiating from her.

In answer, the ground at our feet begins to shake intently and a chasm forms between us.

Water starts to recede but then with a loud boom it bursts upward. We lose our footing and are both thrown backward as we blindly reach out for the other. Before I can gain my footing, boulders fall from the ceiling, separating us further and turning my vision into a fog of dust.

My arms blindly search as I call to her and stumble through the thick air, barely missing one spindly rock that plummets from the ceiling to my feet before I have to move out of reach of the next one.

I seek out my gifts as I use every ounce of strength I have again and again, but each time I call to them there's only silence in response. Fear like I've never known settles deep within me.

I can't shift to her, and I can't change what Riann's seeing.

As I hear her coughs and realize she's still alive, I feel a moment of solace. When I fall to my knees in both relief and exhaustion, a burning fills my chest as the debris I'm inhaling halts any further motion.

But then, just as quickly as it started, it ends. The chaotic noise, the deafening rumbling that took over my every sense ceases, and the room turns eerily quiet. The dust settles and the cavern slowly comes back into view. Unfortunately, the view is not what I was expecting.

With the movement of the ground, ceiling and walls, and the now surging river coming from the foundation, I find that Nera and I are tens of yards apart. Easily a hundred feet, if not more, separate us. The water that initially forced us apart is still rushing through the space, but I find it now whorls around the cavern, around the unsteady stretches of floor that each of us is trapped on, and then into a whirlpool in the center.

Riann has isolated us as we each stand still and unable to use our gifts on our very own island of terrors.

"Are you hurt?" I call out as I choke through the dust that coats my tongue.

I barely note her nod as she, too, struggles to fight for clean air.

Now we know with absolute certainty Riann can destroy and create. At least we have one question answered. I just worry at what cost.

As I stare at the scene before me, I am momentarily reminded of the Drench and what it almost took from me once. My skin prickles with rage, dreading the thought that Riann has somehow brought that possibility of death upon us again. But as I quickly scan the obsidian deluge, searching for signs of what exactly this is, I find it is completely different from what I saw that unforgetful day.

This water is almost black in appearance. You can't see more than an inch within. The Drench is different. It is filled with shadows that dance within its grasp. Smoky tendrils snake through its ripples like hands reaching up from the depths of the underworld to ensnare those who enter.

This water may not be the Drench, but I have a sinking feeling it's about to take something from me nonetheless.

When I catch Nera's gaze, she wears the same terrified expression I do. Surely filled with secrets I hope never to discover, this obsidian water inches closer and closer to her as every second passes, making the small island she's found solace on become nothing but a harrowing trap. And with every inch it moves, I feel my heart splinter apart just that much more.

Something in me screams not to get too close—not to let the water win. I think Nera feels it as well, because with every inch the water gains on us, we both move further back.

When I catch sight of Riann, I know my calculation is correct. He is standing in nearly the same spot as before, except each time the water gets within feet of him, he too quickly steps outside of its reach.

"Did you know that the river running through the deepest expanse of the caverns is called Esehtel?" Riann's tone is amused, unconcerned as he rolls his dagger between his fingers.

Neither of us answer. I have never heard the name, and I doubt Nera has either.

"I learned about its existence as a child while reading Asfidel." His words are too calm and collected to fit the current situation. "Did you know that when surrounded by Esehtel's current, your powers become useless, non-existent?"

My eyes cut over to Nera and find her fingers flexing, and then her hands fisting in frustration.

"The only way to override the culling of your powers while the water surges is with

the use of a stone.” He reaches into his pocket and holds up a glistening emerald jewel, studying it as if this were some new discovery he was presenting fondly to a group of schoolchildren. My breath catches in my throat. Nera barely holds in her own gasp of surprise.

Riann has the Genesis Stone. It is the one stone that can manipulate the elements.

He looks around to the water that stays clear of his feet, as if finally acknowledging what it is he's about to do. I catch Nera's eyes once more in warning as I try to decipher a plan that will get us out without the use of our abilities, but none come to mind. She quickly looks down, severing the gaze and letting her eyes find my pocket. I tense with the recognition of what she's saying. Something Riann obviously didn't plan on.

I have the Omni Stone.

I inch my hand ever so slowly into the pocket of my pants and breathe a sigh of relief as my fingers latch around our smooth, golden salvation.

I can't let him know we have it. My shift will have to be quick. Quick and precise. One move to her and then one out. It'll have to take place in less than a second if we want to get away before he can separate us once more.

Our gazes lock as the silent plan takes hold. She stands tall and ready for me to make my move.

“Did you also know that this is called the Lost River?” Riann adds, not paying a moment's attention to where my mind is now focused. “Not because it's been hidden. In fact, it's been very well known.”

With a deep breath, I make a silent plea to the Elders, grasp the stone tightly in my hands, and let the wind envelop me.

My feet land on solid ground just as her body is slung out of reach and a thousand dagger-like stones are hurdled in my direction. I shift to miss one just as another is launched. Over and over again. They push me backward with each attack. With every foot I gain in forward movement, I lose another three in retreat. It is endless. Jagged rocks slice my arms and legs, and a few hit their mark as I am bombarded with the onslaught.

“It's called the Lost River because of what it takes from those who enter.” Riann calls out, paying me no attention as I continue to fight and Nera becomes a dust filled mirage I know I will never reach. “It's because they will inevitably become a lost soul. They will lose themselves in the process as everything they are slowly slips away with the current.”

I fall to the ground just as the last dagger falls before me.

The stone is gripped tightly within my right hand, but it doesn't matter. My power is drained.

“Stop playing games.” I'm not sure how the words even coherently make their way from my lips with the amount of rage and exhaustion that continues to fill every

crevice of my body.

He snickers. The noise grates along my bones. I hate this man with every fiber of my being.

"This was never a game. It has always been war."

The rocks that, only moments earlier, fell from the ceiling to further separate and disorient us now move on his wordless command. Driven by a living force we can't see, they are flung across the expanse and toward me. I have no fight left. Some shatter as they meet my body. Others break my skin as they slam into me.

"Stop!" Nera calls out. Her voice is shaking and her dust-smeared face is now a beautiful river formed from the tears I know are for me. "Stop. I'll do whatever you want. Just stop!" She pleads and my heart breaks.

He never answers her.

And with each moment that passes, the water circling the cavern slowly deepens, working its way up toward our feet. A weaving spider web of liquid death crisscrossing in each direction. A maze I will never work through.

"This is far more enjoyable than I thought it would be," Riann laughs as he watches us become more and more worn down with every passing second.

I must reach her. I fear I only have seconds before something happens, but no matter how hard I try, it is not enough. There is not enough time.

With one last heaving breath, I stand, just missing the most recent rock and weave my body around one boulder just in time for a wall of water to surge past me, blocking me from lessening the distance between us.

She is so close. So, so close. But no matter how fast I am, no matter how quickly I shield each blow, no matter how agile I have become, there is always another barrier between us. It's as if this room is built for the sheer purpose of keeping us apart. Our private torture chamber meant to break us apart. Meant to take her from me.

I make one last-ditch effort, forcing all my energy into my legs as I sprint, hoping to cross a newly opened crevice in the ground. I don't even make it to the jump. The ground seems to roll, as if it knows my next move before I even take it. It rotates and I fall to my knees as I lose my balance. I roll across the smooth surface, my fingers finally finding purchase in a jagged rock as the floor tilts.

A crack runs across the center of the room, further widening the crevice, and I watch in terror as water rushes in, forming an even larger, more ominous pool.

"I wouldn't get too close if I were you," Riann calls out from his spot. "Never know what the current may take from you."

I look to my side and find the water mere inches from my face, and a momentary fear surges within. The water is pouring in from the ceiling now, and I hold on for dear life as my prone form becomes more and more vertical with every tilt. The floor I was once fighting for my life upon becomes a wall I know I can't let go of. If I did, I would fall straight into the water below, and I don't yet know where that decision could end.

I hold fast to the rock, my feet dangling below me, as the water congregates in a whirling pit large enough to swallow our entire home and most of the surrounding fields. My gaze moves to find Nera, and I can't tell if the sound that pours from my lips is relief or agony when I finally see her.

She's in a matching position to myself, the floor having split in two, her thin arms holding on to a jagged edge in what is now the wall, and her feet kicking in search of a ledge to take hold of.

"Now would be a good time to say your goodbyes," Riann croons as he stands from the only solid ground remaining and twists that green stone between his fingers.

I look back to Nera just as one of her hands loses its grip, and she grunts out in frustration. We only have one chance. There's no way to reach her. There is no way to get to her and keep the stone safe at the same time.

I let go of the wall with my right hand; sheer will is now the only thing keeping my left hand steady in the small crevice I found.

I don't give her a chance to counter. If I did, she would do everything in her power to save me as she's done countless times before, and I won't let that happen again. This time, I save her.

"Nera," I call out, hoping my voice isn't shaking as hard as I feel it is. Her gaze finds mine. "I will find you. I promise, I will find you!"

I lift the stone and throw it across the empty space between us. My pleading eyes tell her to jump.

Please jump. Trust me. Catch the stone. It will take you home.

The barest hint of terror is etched across her features at what I've done. She knows I'm sacrificing myself, and I hope that one day, when I find her again, she channels all of that frustration she's feeling right now into the punch she is sure to land on my face. And then I hope she alternates between yelling at and kissing me senseless.

And should I have to break that promise I made to her, if this moment in time becomes my last, then I hope she knows I will enter death and stand at the feet of the Elders filled with happiness and pride that my sacrifice allowed her to live.

She has to live.

She doesn't jump.

She watches as our stone careens through the space between us. My body becomes paralyzed at the idea that this ill-conceived plan won't work.

But I see the moment her decision is made.

At first, I think she's going to let it drop, and maybe we enter into the afterlife together, as one. But then she braces her feet against the wall and prepares to jump. Only, Riann has other plans. Before she forces her body outward and toward the flying stone, the wall she's on crumbles, and her body falls straight down, toward the pit of swirling water below.

I open my mouth to call out to her. But when the echo of her name bounces through the room, it's not my voice that carries the sound.

My head whips sideways just in time to watch a woman I don't know running toward the pit of water. Nera's name is a terrified song on her lips. She doesn't hesitate as she leaps through the air, arms outstretched, and diving head first, destined to grasp onto Nera as she falls.

I don't know the words I say as I watch both of their bodies fly through the hole in the ground toward their swirling end. A moment of confusion crosses Nera's face at the sudden appearance of another person, but then her face shifts and her eyes remain steady and focused.

Their hands collide just before they reach the water, Nera heading feet first with this unknown woman falling from directly above, her left arm latched onto Nera's right. But then, as Nera's feet break the obsidian pool of death, Nera reaches out. Slim fingers find the tiny, golden salvation and she clasps it in her grasp just as her body hits the obsidian torrent. Within a second, before the unknown woman even reaches the surface of the pool after her, both women seem to shift. Only a glimmer and the ripples that suggest someone was once there remain.

XXIX

I t takes a moment for me to reconcile why the room is shaking and my vision is blurred. I blink again and again, finding a cool wetness seeping down my cheeks, and realize I'm crying.

And not just crying. I am sobbing. Damn near wailing. Nothing has ever hurt as bad as this. I thought finally finding out what happened to me would bring some sort of peace. Instead, all it's brought is pain.

More betrayals, more heartache, more broken trust. More of everything I was so desperate to leave behind.

I don't want this. I don't want this chaotic, magical, unbelievable life. I want to go back to the mundane. I want to walk past the same three grocery stores everyday as I make my way to Gram's. I want to spend hours guessing what lives others lead rather than having to lead my own. I want to become frustrated with the amount of smog and beeping horns, and I want to yell at the stupid cat every time she knocks over my lunch and I have to resort to the half-broken vending machine next door.

I want to go back.

"Nera?" Ari's voice, while soft and smooth, comes barreling in through the darkness. It shatters that whirl of emotions I was sinking within and fills in the empty pit I was about to climb inside.

The room finally begins to clear as his blurred form bends down in front of me.

"Nera." He finally comes into focus as I feel his forehead touch mine.

"I want to go back." The words come out in between the sobs.

"Okay," he says, though I'm not even sure if he knows what exactly I'm referring to. Maybe I don't either. All I know is I want to go somewhere where *this* isn't my life.

But then I catch his gaze.

Those golden eyes like burning embers in the night finally clear, and I find comfort within them.

And I don't know why, but I find myself comparing them to the sapphire gems I found hiding within Tarak's eyes. I hate myself for it.

There was a moment in time, not long ago, where I remember thinking I would gladly drown within that sapphire gaze. There was something so alluring and enticing about the look he sent my way. It was as if it were made for me and me alone. I now know it was. It was made for me because it was just a fabrication of what I needed to see at that moment. It was the mingling of our gifts, and the facade he played.

But Ari's eyes are different.

Ari's eyes don't make me want to drown within them. Because drowning within something, no matter how alluring it may be, will never be anything other than a quick, painful death. Which is exactly what Tarak and I were. I did drown within his gaze. And a part of me died when that happened.

I have been drowning this entire time, but it's only now, in this moment, when I can finally see the light, see these beautiful golden flickers standing in my path, ready to guide me back to the surface, that I realize I don't want to drown.

I want to live.

"I want to live," I whisper, and the sobs ebb away just as the water I was once slowly sinking within disappears. And this time I promise myself to never let that happen again.

Ari laughs at my admission. "I'm glad," he holds my still-trembling face in his hands, "because I'm not letting you go anytime soon."

My eyes look down to find my hands quivering, and the chattering noise in my ears is my own teeth as they shake violently against each other.

I try to smile at his words. I *want* to smile at his words. But every time I move my lips, they shake that much more.

"I didn't know." It's more of a croak as I finally force the sound past my lips.

"I know. I'm sorry. I'm so sorry." His breaths tickle my cheeks and somehow bring a warmth back into my freezing form.

"I didn't know," I repeat once again, wanting nothing more than to make everything I am, everything I now know, just disappear.

Ari doesn't reply, and with no hesitation at all, he reaches around to pick me up, cradling me within his strong arms. I don't fight the touch, but instead bury my face into his neck as I try to hold all the pain within.

"Is this okay?" he whispers at my ear, and I nod.

The girl in that memory, fighting for the truth . . . She was so strong. What a contradiction to who I've become over the last few years. I want to be her again. But how can I be strong when I am blind? It was all there in front of me, and I chose not to see it. I was so focused on my own stupid goals and finding out who I was that I couldn't even see the truth behind Riann or Tarak.

When Riann shattered the room beside mine in the palace, I believed that destruction was born out of his rage at the loss of me. Now I know his rage wasn't from the loss of the me he once knew, but because the me he had desperately tried to hide away was found.

I'm the enemy he managed to get rid of, but I've returned.

Ari takes me down a dimly lit hallway, lays me down in a bed fit for royalty, and the tension begins to dissipate as my body sinks into what feels like a thousand cloud-filled pillows. Without a word, he slowly slips a blanket across my still-trembling and crying form, and then instantly seems to evaporate into thin air. Before I can fully process where he's gone, he's back with a glass of cold water.

"Rest," he whispers.

"Did you just . . . "

"Shift," he completes my thought. "I shifted." A sad smile forms on his lips. "I need you to rest," he urges.

"I don't– want to– rest." My words are broken by the lingering silent sobs. "I want answers." The plea is so soft and quiet as exhaustion looms.

"And you will get them." He reaches down to squeeze my hand. "But you just went through two memories in less than an hour. Your body isn't used to that anymore. You need rest. I'll be right here when you wake up. I have so much more to show you."

I move to sit up more fully, trying desperately to show him that I'm not weak, but strong and resilient. That I'm still that girl from his memory. I can be her. I want to be her. But the exhaustion starts to settle within my bones.

He stalls my movement as he cups my cheek, letting his thumb catch the slowly falling tear. "Please. Rest." His plea is urgent but kind. "I will be here when you wake."

"Promise?" I ask as I lay back against the pillows, no longer able to fight.

He smiles as he nods his head. "I promise."

And with his words, I finally give in and watch as his form flickers out of view and the darkness takes hold.

Scorching flames come from every angle. I twist once, twice, three times, trying to locate a break in the inferno all around.

But there is no salvation here.

The rising heat inches closer with every second. Shrieks of pain consume my thoughts as shadows dance on the outskirts of my periphery.

"*Save me*!" The tortured woman cries out. "*Save me.*" Her mangled voice mutates. The previously familiar tone turns to something I can't quite discern. Something darker, more sinister, echoes within.

I fall to my knees as licks of flame reach high above my head and the deep green forest floor at my feet turns to ash.

But my body stills at the sight of my hands. Ribbons of fire surge out from each, feeding the flames. And when it finally skirts along my battered skin, there's no pain or heat or even discomfort found. But still, I know something is very, very wrong.

The scream starts from the deepest corners of my soul, burning me from the inside out as it rises.

"Nera!" My shoulders are lifted from the singed ground, the ash coating my hands fades aways, and . . . "Wake up. You're having a nightmare. Wake up!"

My eyes open, certain I'll find death and destruction all around. Instead, I find worried golden eyes staring back at me. My hands search the surrounding area, expecting to see ash and lingering heat, but my fingers instead find the warmth of thick blankets.

"You're okay," Ari whispers as he pulls me to him and starts to rub my back in soothing circles. "You're shaking." He pulls another blanket around my shoulders and a rush of cedar and pine surrounds me.

I quickly pull back and look around. I'm not sure how long I slept, but right now I feel more awake than I have in weeks. The light's off in this room, but there's a faint glow coming from what I assume is a bathroom, and I hear the crackling from a roaring fire down the hall.

Ari looks down to me, a sad smile playing on his face. "Are you hungry?"

I shake my head.

"Are you ready to talk?"

I nod, and he gives off a small smile. I'm not sure I've fully processed all that I saw within those two memories, but I know for certain that I'm ready to figure it all out. He scoots back so his head leans against the dark wooden footboard.

"I thought we could talk in here instead of out there." He nods to the door, indicating the hallway that leads to the expansive living area as he hands over a steamy cup with the most amazingly sweet scent wafting from its top. "I started making it once I realized you were stirring."

"What is it?" My voice is hoarse, and I go still at the thought that I was most likely stuck in that nightmare and screaming my lungs out for far longer than I care to admit.

"Your favorite. Hot chocolate," he says with a smile, and I lean over the cup, inhaling the steam. It instantly warms me. I take a tentative sip and barely suppress a moan at the taste.

"Thank you." I give him a genuine smile as I try to hold back the tears burning my eyes. "How long did I sleep?"

"Only a few hours. Sun's not up yet." He sips from his own mug, then clears his throat and sets down the glass.

I shift my head to the table to find the lamp, wondering if he plans on flicking it to life. I would normally reach for it, but I'm in the middle of the massive bed, and would have to lean across his feet in order to get to it and, to be completely honest, I'm not ready to be that close to him while fully awake and coherent.

"Do you want to turn on the light?" I ask between sips as I lean back further into the pile of pillows at my back.

He shrugs once more. "You once told me it was easier to talk in the dark." He looks around the room and then back to me. "Actually, I think every life-altering conversation we've had has been in almost complete darkness, whether that be on purpose or not." He gives a quick laugh, disappointment creeps in at the idea that he's referencing something I can't remember.

All I can do is nod my head in acknowledgement. I *do* think it's easier to talk in the dark. It's as if the darkness is somehow a shield against the terrors which hide within my mind.

"Where do we start?" I ask as he adjusts his position opposite me on the bed. From this distance, and with the light from the doorframe now behind him, I can barely make out his features, and I think he knows that. I think he knows that sitting this far away will allow me some semblance of security.

"Where do you want to start?"

I ponder the question while taking a few more much-needed sips from the steaming cup in my hands. I want to know about Riann. I wonder if Tarak was a part of my life before; though, from the way things are looking now, I doubt it. I want to know about my father's and Alesia's roles in all of this. I want to know what the Abolition is, and what he meant in the memory when he said, *Don't worry. I'm not going to turn you in.*

And though I am nowhere near ready to face all that his words and memories have implied, I want to know about us. I want to know about it all. The thoughts become a whorl of confusion within my own mind. I have a feeling this is going to be a very long conversation filled with a hundred different emotions I'm not sure I'm ready to experience yet.

Except one. Because right now, outside of the safety I feel sitting here with Ari, I only feel a cold anger building within me, and decide to let that take hold.

"Riann did this?" I hope he knows the *this* I'm referring to is me. That Riann stole something from me more precious than anything else. He stole my memories, my life. He stole my time.

"Yes."

I wait for the tears to surge forth, but that icy rage keeps them at bay.

"What about my father, Koreed? Did he know? Were they working together?"

"No." His response is immediate, which brings me a rush of relief. "Not directly, at least. He had no idea about Riann."

I nod in acceptance as I close my eyes.

"But Mina knew."

"What?" My breath hitches and my gaze quickly meets his.

"Mina figured it all out long before anyone else did. She was our inside contact in the palace."

I stare silently for a moment longer, making sure I heard him correctly. "Mina? My grandmother?"

He nods. "She was the one who alerted me that you were back. Before you fled. The first time." He clarifies. "I had just made it to the palace when the alarms started blaring and the search party went out. By that point, I knew what the River Esehtel did to those who entered it, but I wasn't sure how quickly you and Alesia had shifted once you grabbed my stone. The longer you're under, the more you lose. You went almost completely under. After far too much research, I reluctantly came to the realization that you would have lost something, if not everything." He clears his throat. "I stayed at a checkpoint we frequented, hoping you would arrive and it would be just as if you'd never left." He takes a deep breath, and I watch as his shoulders drop, his hand cradling his forehead. "But you never came."

A few steadying heartbeats later, he looks up and clears his throat, ready to

begin again. "After a few hours, I joined the search under my alias, and then
. . . Well, you know about us finding you in that abandoned house and what
happened next."

"I ran into the forest."

He nods. "I told you how I tried to shift multiple times to find you, but it was
so dark. I searched for hours, but . . . " he trails off as if the reminder of his failure
is too burdensome a thought to even speak on.

"Did you know I was with Tarak?"

"No."

"What about when I was captured and taken back to the palace after Halabar
attacked Himerak's forest settlement? Did you try to come for me once you knew
I was back?"

He nods. "I did."

"Did I see you?"

He shakes his head, then quickly lifts a hand before I can respond. "Actually,
that's not completely true," he quickly corrects. "I believe you might have looked
at me, but you just saw another guard. And every time you were in public, there
was someone attached to you. Most of the time, it was you latching onto Riann's
arm as if he was the one tether holding you together," his tone turns bitter, and
I know those moments must have been agonizing for him, "but there were also
Alesia and your two guards. It was only then, after watching you at the palace,
that I realized she was the woman that dove for you. But there was no way for
me to get close enough to shift you out of there, without launching the entire
palace—and most of Ithesin—into war. Still, Mina and I did try a few times. Your
walks in the garden were always timed around shift change for the guards, but it
never seemed to work out."

I take a moment to let all he's said sink in. I think the mention of Mina alone
has me frozen with a mix of emotions swirling through me that I can barely think
through.

"In the dre–" He opens his mouth to correct me, and I quickly amend, "In the
memory, you and Riann talked about something called the Abolition." He nods.
"What is that?"

"The Abolition is a rebel group that was formed years ago, shortly after the first
Celestras were born. It started out small, and truthfully, their initial goals had
merit, but over a few hundred years, they grew and grew to the point where they
now have numbers in the thousands across each of the four centras. And they
slowly shifted from good to evil. They have infiltrated most of the higher nobility
and advisors in each centra."

"What's their goal?"

"To kill Celestras."

The words send a shock through my system.

He shifts slightly in his spot. "When we first met—before you left—and I showed you my mark, it was mostly to let you know I wasn't one of them. That's why I said I wouldn't turn you in. There was—*is*—a bounty on the heads of any who carry the mark."

My eyes shift down to my arm and I can just make out the symbol in the dim light. "The Abolition is in Centra I?"

He nods again. "Very much so."

I take a breath as I mull over his words. "That doesn't make sense. The entire palace knew I was a Celestra, and I interacted with hundreds of people between all those dinners and balls, and . . . " I cringe as I recall being paraded around like a trophy for everyone to see.

He shakes his head as if my words or memories aren't correct. "They saw the daughter of a sovereign. They saw a possible heir. An heir they hoped would take over power once the Celestras were abolished and a new system of government was put into place. Koreed hid your truth in order to save you. He may not have done many things as he should have, but he protected you in the way you needed it most."

I stare at him in confusion. There is absolutely no way they didn't know what I am. Luckily, he catches up with my train of thought quickly, and I feel his fingers reach out to grasp my ankle and brush over a scar I didn't know I had.

"I want you to think about something. Other than Koreed, Riann, Alesia, Mina, the small group of soldiers who took you back from the settlement, *your* maid, *your* guards, the people who were allowed around you day in and day out, did anyone else ever see you in short sleeves? Did they ever see you when you weren't wearing some hideously thick bracelet? Did anyone else ever see your wrists? I want you to think about your ball gowns and how you were dressed whenever you were in view of someone who wasn't directly connected to the inside."

The saliva becomes thick in my mouth as I think through every single interaction I had. I assumed they all fawned over me because I was a Celestra. I was so wrong.

"Did you ever wonder why no friends showed up once you came back? Did you really think you had no friends outside of Alesia and Riann?"

"I didn't really get to think that far." My eyes find my lap as I mentally berate myself for being the absolutely worst main character in my own story. I'm the girl I scream at in the pages of the novels I read. But then I remember it was all because of Tarak. I was so deep within that clouded mindset, and then, after I was captured, it was a depression so consuming I couldn't have fought my way out of it if I wanted to. I wonder now if the self hatred I felt in those initial weeks in

Halabar had anything to do with coming off the drug that was that horrible man who deceived me.

Maybe that hell I went through was the withdrawal.

But then I think back to before. Before I first fled. I think back to the first morning I woke up in that bed, and the maid who walked in.

"What about the pictures on the dresser? There were pictures of me with people I don't remember. Were they my friends? Or were those pictures just planted to feed me a false narrative?"

"You had friends . . . once. You became close with them. Too close for Riann's liking." He pauses a moment before continuing, "Your three best friends, Lara, Renee, and Ann, were all found dead by the time you were sixteen. It was shortly after Lara died that you started putting the pieces together."

My heart beats wildly in my chest at the implication.

"Riann is . . . " I trail off when I can't think of a word that fits exactly what I want to say.

"He's a monster, Nera. He is the epitome of evil. He always has been and he always will be."

"What's his story? Riann told me he moved to Halabar when he was a child."

Ari nods. "Riann's father, Mikel, was the leader of the Abolition." I think back to the memory and how Riann let us know he was now the one in charge. The shock that surged through Ari's body at the notion still registers within my own. "From what we learned, Riann came to Halabar as a refugee with his mother when he was about five. At least, that's the story they gave everyone. The lie was that they lived in one of the remote settlements of Centra I, far down on the southern border. There are a few that line the outskirts, not unlike Himerak's, but they're all heavily guarded, and when they came into Halabar stating they were the only surviving members from a recent attack from the Haze, there was no one to dispute their story." I bristle at his words. "They concocted a tale filled with just enoughs truths to be plausible. The palace took them in, I believe so they could extract information from his mother about the attack. The Haze had just started forming around that time, and every centra was on high alert trying to find out how to overtake it. It was during that time that the two of you became friends, and when his mother died only a few months later—supposedly from injuries that never healed—he remained at the palace."

"She wasn't his mother, was she?"

"No." He shakes his head. "Riann isn't even a citizen of Centra I, he's from Centra II. He was born to take over control of the Abolition from his father, Mikel. He was groomed for it. The one thing holding the Abolition back from completely taking over Ithesin is Centra I. Centra I is too large, and there are too many people. Not to mention they have the heartstone trees. If the Abolition tried to destroy the centra, they risked destroying the trees. They needed to infiltrate it, but security's so tight, they knew they'd need to do it from the inside. From somewhere no one expected."

I furrow my brow as I take it all in. "Even as a child, Riann was the inside man for that job?"

"Even at five years old, he knew what his job was. The Abolition was clever. Who would have suspected an injured woman who landed on the shore in a barely-floating boat, asking for help for herself and her young child? We think her death, likely a suicide, was the first step of the Abolition's scheme. She needed to die so the plan could take hold."

"Koreed knows none of this?"

He shakes his head. "Not in its entirety. I think he allowed himself to keep his head in the sand, but maybe something has recently changed. A good number of his crooked advisors, the men and women he refers to as 'elders,' are in on it as well. They've kept him busy, ignorant to almost all of what's really going on out there."

I'm damn near fuming at this point.

"How do the *people* not know? Halabar is a massive city with a large population. And aren't there people in various settlements along the border? How do they not know?"

"Sometimes it's easier to remain blind to the atrocities around you. Easier to go on with life, convinced that keeping things the way they are is better than the alternative of fighting and risking greater loss. Except they had no idea that they may be losing more by remaining blind."

I let out a huff, my frustration ready to boil over. "I don't want to talk about Riann anymore."

Ari laughs softly. "Me either. How about we switch to something lighter? Something exciting."

"Like what?" I'm not sure anything could be classified as exciting right now.

"Your gifts."

I was wrong. The corners of my lips turn up at the thought.

He returns the smile, but then takes a deep breath.

"I've never had to explain this before. Most people learn it over time." He clears his throat. "Celestrial gifts are tied to the stones, the Elders, and the trees. There are four Elders and eight stones. Legend states that each Elder was responsible for infusing a very specific ability into each stone and thus into the chosen Celestra." I absently nod along with his words. This is very similar to what Tarak said as we were making our way to the Caverns. "On average, each Celestra is bestowed with two gifts; though there have been tales of a lucky few who received more, and an unlucky few who only received one."

"And you have two gifts?"

I catch the subtle movement of his golden eyes as he smiles.

"I can alter the reality of what someone sees, thus giving them my memory, and I can shift between times and location." I catch a sense of pride in his voice, and wonder if these gifts are somehow more valuable than the others.

"And Tarak can alter emotions and discern truths?" I question.

"From what I've been told, yes."

"And Riann?" Just saying his name now causes fury to surge through my veins.

Ari clears his throat. "He can destroy and create. Physically, that is."

"And Himerak can see the past."

"Yes, Himerak can see the past, but his gifts diminish as he ages. The stone he carries keeps those lingering abilities available."

That's news. It seems as though each stone carries a mirrored ability within their gifts.

"How is the stone helping him?"

"Think of the stones as an external energy force which increases the user's gift—their specific strength. Himerak's ability to see one's past comes from the Seer Stone. He carries in it his walking staff so it never leaves his side."

I search through every memory I have of that man and realize that I've never seen him without his staff. And I recall the way the light seemed to move within that small, almost opalescent blue stone mounted to the top of the twisted wooden cane.

"Himerak's abilities may have diminished over time, but he's able to draw more power from the actual stone when he touches it to impede the loss."

"Are the stone's powers transferable? Could you use Himerack's abilities if you had access to his stone?"

"Himerak's stone will do nothing for me because his abilities were never meant for me. It's just a rock in my hands. Just as my stone"—he lifts a small golden stone from his pocket—"would do nothing for him."

I nod again. "That makes sense." I sip a little more of the liquid that has started cooling in the mug in my hands. "Can *I* use his stone?"

"Yes."

The idea surprises and excites me. "What? Why? Why am I different?"

"Because you are everything," he answers without hesitation.

I cock my head to the side, imploring him to continue. "What does *that* mean?"

"You are an anomaly." I roll my eyes, and he must notice, because I hear a warm chuckle leave his lips. "I mean that in the most amazing way," he explains before clearing his throat once more. "You don't just have one or two, or even five gifts. You possess all eight, plus some other things we haven't yet figured out."

"All eight of the gifts?" My words are filled with surprise as I try to recall each of the gifts we just discussed.

"Yes. But you've only mastered a few, some . . . " He pauses while he shuffles to find a more comfortable position closer to me. This time I don't shrink away when I feel his leg slightly brushing against my own. "You know the heartstone trees in the Mulara Forest?" I nod. *How could I forget them?* "Right before a tree takes to life and surges from the ground, it takes root. And once those roots have taken hold deep within the dirt, the small sprout can finally burst through the ground. Think of your gifts like that sprout. Right now, you're able to reach down and grasp what that sprout gives, but there is so much more beneath the surface that you have yet to reach. Sometimes, it takes years and years of digging to find all the roots. Though, there are some lucky souls who are able to fully access their gifts after the completion of their Committence."

His words call to mind the trials that were meant to take place soon, and I tense.

"How long ago was the attack on Halabar and the palace?"

"About a week?"

"Are the moons aligned yet?"

His brows peak in surprise. "I'm assuming someone told you about that and it's not you remembering?"

"Koreed told me the night before everything happened. He said I could complete my Committence when the moons aligned."

"Arranging zones," Ari quickly clarifies.

"Yes. He used that term."

"You can complete it then. But you don't have to. Legend has it that if someone completes their Committence during the alignment of the moons, their powers will be exponentially stronger than they would've been had they completed their trials at a different time."

Something in his words strikes me as odd. As if my body is questioning what he's said. My clothes feel too tight and my skin prickles with uncomfortable heat. Suddenly, the meaning of the sensation dawns on me.

"You don't believe that to be true, do you?"

He shakes his head. "I'm not sure. I think our ways have been altered over time, and not always toward the path of truth."

"I want to complete the Committence."

He leans forward as he peers so deeply into my eyes I swear he can see my soul. "Why?"

His question causes me to pause, and I realize I don't have an answer. Maybe I want to because Tarak was so insistent about it. Maybe because I need to get the stones. Maybe because I need full access to my gifts in order to defeat whatever it is that's attacking the city. Maybe because I need to prove that I can.

"I'm . . . supposed to?" My statement turns into more of a question by the end, and I cringe at how ridiculous that response sounds out loud.

"If that's the path you choose, I will stand by your side. However, if that isn't something you wish for, please don't feel coerced into it."

"But isn't that how I become the sovereign? Wouldn't I be able to overtake Himerak if I completed them?

He stills as he looks my way, and I can tell there's a war raging inside his mind over whether or not to let the next words free. Thankfully, he does.

"You will never become a sovereign. You are already so much more."

XXX

"What exactly do you mean?" I hope he broaches the topic of the fifth centra before I have to, because the concept still seems so unbelievable.

"We've always known you were different. That much was certain. But there's something else going on with you that I haven't quite figured out." His gaze never leaves mine as he lets the words, so full of truth and certainty, fill the air. "I've never voiced that thought out loud."

For some reason, my skin starts to tighten, and not in a way that would indicate he's lying. It's almost as if my body is preparing for something it doesn't want to happen. Another truth. Another mystery. Another betrayal.

Quickly tossing the covers off my legs, I stand and walk to the largest window in the room. The sound of shuffling and then the soft padding of footsteps follows, coming to a halt just behind me.

"I think you knew. Before you left. Before the Caverns and Riann and my stone took you away from here. I think you knew, and you didn't tell me because you were scared of what it might mean," he whispers, and I turn to face him.

"What am I?"

"I think you are one of them."

"Them?" Is he implying I'm a member of the Abolition. Am I the enemy?

"I think you are the missing piece," he clarifies.

"The fifth centra?"

His smile is my answer.

I swallow as my hands cover my face, trying to calm myself enough to take all of this in. "You know, every time I decide to fully accept something unimaginable," I peek up at him through the slits in my fingers, "like being something called a

Celestra from a strange planet," he laughs and I reach out to playfully push his ridiculously muscular arm backward, "I accept it and then I barely have a moment to even breathe through the new information before something exponentially more unimaginable gets thrown in my face." I can't tell whether I want to laugh at the unbelievability of it all, or cry because I know that, whether or not what he says is true, he believes it to be true. "What does that even mean? The fifth centra?"

"You're a bridge. Physically and metaphorically." He reaches out to twist a wayward lock of my curly hair. "You're here to return our great world to what it once was, but I believe there's something more. I believe you were sent here on purpose. I believe you weren't just destined by nature or the Elders. I believe you're one of them."

"One of them?"

"I believe your soul's too old for this world. I think you're the missing link between our world and the next. I think you're the tie between us. You're an Elder."

My head shakes vigorously in denial.

"What if I can't do it? What if I don't want to do it? What if I don't want to be a fifth centra or an Elder or anything else?" My voice is strong and certain.

He takes one more step to close the gap between us and wraps his warm hands around my wrists after he slowly lowers them from my face.

"I didn't want to be the sovereign. I never wanted my mark, or the gifts it gave me. The only good thing that ever came out of these wretched lines"—he looks down at his wrist at the same time I look at mine—"was you."

I suck in a breath at his words and pray that weight on my chest lessens. He's looking at me with so much love and adoration, and I don't even know him. I can't remember him. I can't remember us or this or anything. I don't know how to save this world, and yet he's looking at me like I may also be the missing piece to his heart.

"I would do it all again in a moment if it meant I still got to be with you in the end. And I *will* be with you in the end. I don't know exactly what the future holds. But I do know that you are something that no one on this planet has ever seen before." His words are calm and quiet, yet they exude so much emotion and sincerity. "I think you're the last ditch effort to save this planet—this people—from themselves. I think that without you, we all die." My shoulders tense and I hold my breath at the implication. "And I know that's a lot to take on. I know that, even before you left, this was not the life you would've chosen for yourself. But I need you to know that it is the life we have been given. I say 'we' because I plan to be by your side through every moment, every step, every fall, every tear, every drop of blood, and I damn sure plan to be standing by your side when we defeat those who aim to harm us and we right this world for good."

"Ari . . . " My gaze finds the wooden floor as I try to find the words to say.

"Nera, you possess every gift of the Elders plus more. You are the embodiment of all Celestras. You have the power to alter the course of history, and thank the Elders you're on the right side of it. But if you don't want it, then I don't either." My eyes shoot forward to find his. "If you want to go off and live life in whatever capacity you can in some remote place, or even back on Earth," he laughs slightly to himself, and for a moment, I have a picture in my mind of teaching him how to use an elevator, a smartphone, and a microwave, "then I will accept that. You don't have to decide today or tomorrow. For all I care, we can stay here for the next ten years and let the rest of the damn world burn to the ground if it means taking time to make sure you're happy. But I don't think that *would* make you happy. You care too much."

He slowly lowers my hands from their frozen place between us and takes a tentative step back. And it's in this moment right here that I know this man loves me. He loves me in a way Tarak, Koreed, Riann, or Alesia couldn't. I know he loves me because he isn't telling me what I need or what I should do.

He's telling me that I can do anything in this world I want, including heading up a revolution to save humanity as they know it, but also that it is perfectly fine if all I want to do is nothing at all. He would still stand beside me even if I said I wanted to leave and never come back. He wouldn't fault me for being a coward or selfish or a murderer. He would let the entire damn world burn for me, and only me.

And it's that thought which causes my right foot to step forward first and then my left, and then my hands are grasping his cheeks, and I'm not even sure how it happens, but his lips tentatively graze mine and the entire world shifts on its axis.

This.

This is what I have been waiting for, searching for. A surge of heat rushes through me at the contact as a thousand sparks fly off. Every weight of pressure, pain, and sadness that had been so perfectly etched into my bones starts to disintegrate, and for the first time in years I feel at ease. I feel safe. I feel at home.

The idea that this, him—Ari—is what I have been searching for all these years. All that time stuck in a downward spiral of depression and self loathing must have been partly built from the subconscious idea that he was gone, and if he was missing then so was I.

I straighten my entire form as I pull back, not letting my gaze leave his. "I want to fight."

In the dim light, I can just make out the smile that slowly grows to cover his face.

"Then we fight."

XXXI

T he words are barely spoken before his lips come crashing back onto mine. A moan of contentment erupts from my soul. He hungrily devours the sound as he fights for every inch I give him, and I don't recall a time I have ever been kissed like this.

The previously dark room explodes into light as white sparks explode off my body, leaving sizzling burn marks in the carpet at our feet. Neither of us seems to care or even notice.

I'm too worried with letting my fingers slip back toward his neck and tangle within the locks of hair that have broken free. He lets out a strangled sound of desire as I tug him further into me.

We melt into one another as his skin lights a fire against my own.

The sensation surges through my veins and deep within my core as I let every pull toward him overtake me and I relinquish the restraint I didn't know I was fighting.

He lifts me up, and I wrap my legs around his waist as hot desire pools in my core.

I rock against him, searching for relief, and when he grabs my ass to intensify the friction, I moan out as light explodes into the room.

I jolt backward with the deafening sound, and watch as the curtains, now covered in flames, fall to the ground at our feet.

I stand frozen in fear and shock as Ari rushes to toss the fabric into the waiting tub.

Holy shit. Holy shit. Holy shit.

I just caused a fire . . . again. He barely touched me, while we were fully clothed, and I caused a fire! I can't imagine what will happen when we–

His quick return to the room halts the incessant thoughts, but he doesn't stop moving until he's standing directly in front of me. Barely an inch from my face, our breaths mingle as he looks over every part of me he can see in the dim light.

"I'm sorry. I didn't mean to. I didn't even–"

"I missed you, Nera." He cuts off my rambling apology as a tear trails down his face before it falls, landing on my arm. "I don't know if I could've gone much longer without you back with me." He doesn't pay any attention to the fact that I just damn near burned down the house.

"Ari–"

"I'm sorry. I know you need time." He shakes his head. "I know you don't remember me or us. But *I* remember us. I–" His voice cracks as his body shakes, and I quickly reach around him to crash his body into mine. I hold steady as he lets the waves of pain and then relief wash over him.

My face turns so my lips line up directly with his ear as I whisper, "I may not remember the details, but I could never forget the way this feels." I tighten my hold around him. "You never left." Then, I lean back just slightly and place his hand over my heart. "Not from here, at least. I know it's not much, but even on Earth, I think I knew you were out there. I had dreams about this place. I constantly dreamt of snow and ice and . . . " I trail off, not sure exactly how to explain it in a way that feels right. How do I explain those golden eyes that filled my dreams? "These lines on my wrist aren't the only mark I carry. You have always been burned within me. I'm just sorry it took so long to get back to you."

"You're here now, and that's all that matters." Tears are streaming down his face and there is an urgency within me to take away every pain he's ever felt.

When I finally let go, my feet inch backward and my fingertips graze over my now swollen lips. The urgency at which I gave into every desire pulsing through me causes waves of confusion to rise. It was so raw and real. It was everything I ever wanted.

There was a time on Earth when I did the same. All those nights I spent craving and searching for something I never found . . . not until now at least. But then that brings the thought of those nights to the front of my mind.

I was with Ari then. I was with Ari, and yet I eagerly climbed into the arms of so many others trying to drown out the misery in my own mind. Regret settles within me, and I turn away in shame wondering how I will confess that to him.

"You're right. I need time." I stare off into the empty room before turning back to face the person I will undoubtedly hurt. "Give me time," I ask, and he immediately nods. "I'm here. I'm back, and I believe you. I believe every word you've said. I know them to be true. But I need time. If you just give me time, maybe I can one day be that girl you remember. One day, I can be her again."

Maybe, I can make you forgive me for what I did; for leaving, for cheating, for taking so long to find my way back to you . . .

"Nera, I don't care if it takes our entire lives, I'll still be here in the end."

My heart shatters at his kindness. I don't deserve him.

He deserves someone so much better than me. He deserves someone strong and sure. He deserves someone he can trust and not someone who so easily dove within the depths of depression only to let random strangers give her unfilled moments of reprieve. He deserves better than me.

He clears his throat and quickly wipes the wetness from his cheeks with an embarrassed laugh before finding my gaze once more. "And for the record, you don't need to be her, either. I love you just the way you are now."

I freeze, a hold within me keeps my reply—those words—from spilling free, but Ari doesn't seem to mind. He lifts a finger, indicating for me to wait a moment, and then he's gone and I'm no longer staring at his beautiful golden eyes but the empty, darkened room.

I audibly gasp when he suddenly reappears before me, a new steaming cup of warmed chocolate and a plate of delicacies in his hands.

"We need a warning for that." I awkwardly laugh, trying to push away all those lingering thoughts of regret.

"Truthfully, I never used to shift this often, but seeing your reaction to it is one of my new favorite things." He places the cup and plate on the nightstand.

I clear my throat. "You have to teach me how to do it. I used to, right?" I pray the quiver in my voice comes off as something other than the immense self-loathing I feel growing within me.

He smiles and takes my arm as he guides us back to the bed, and within a moment, we're both huddled back under the blankets just as we were only minutes ago before I found out exactly what I am.

He picks up where we left off.

"Just like Himerak, you can see the past and alter the minds of those around you." I sigh in relief as he seems none the wiser to my moment and continues on with the previous conversation. "Though this has been one of the gifts you were struggling with mastering before you . . . before you left." His eyes meet mine. "Just like me, you can shift between various times and locations, and you can change the reality of what people see. You were getting quite good with that one." His voice is filled with pride as he speaks.

"I have a feeling that may have had something to do with who was training me?"

It's the first moment I let a little life enter my voice. It seems to cause him to pause, unsure of what to do or how to react.

"You had an excellent trainer, if I do say so myself." Through the dim light, I can just make out the hint of a smirk on his face before he hides it behind the glass in his hands. Then he continues, "Just like Riann, you can destroy and create physical elements." His free hand lifts up and completes a sweeping motion. "Who do you think built this home for us?"

I turn from side to side, taking in everything I can see.

"I made this?" My voice is incredulous.

"Yes. You built this. Took you a few days, and once it was complete, you slept for damn near a week after. It completely drained you. But you used your gift and you built us a home, and a base."

I sit up a little straighter. I can't see much in the light, but what I can see brings a smile to my face.

Before I can dive too far into trying to piece together how exactly I did this, his voice cuts through my thoughts.

"And just like Tarak, you can discern whether or not a person is being truthful and you can alter a person's emotions. Though, you rarely used the latter."

"The truth telling thing didn't come back to me until I was in the Caverns yesterday." I quickly look up to find his gaze. "Wait, was that only yesterday?" It feels as if every moment is blurring together, and I can't tell which way is up and which way is down.

"Yes, that was yesterday." He reaches forward and drapes a blanket across his legs. "I think it was because you entered the Caverns. The location is sacred, and it was the home to the Elders." Our eyes meet at the last word. "I'm sure it helped to awaken your gifts."

The thought somewhat scares me. What else will make itself known over the next few days? And will I be able to use and control what gifts I have, or will they overwhelm me?

"What about the fire I can create? And the dome? What are those?"

I hear the audible gulp and then watch as he reaches forward to place his cup down on a tray in the center of the bed.

"They're not tied to any stones. At least, not from the research we've completed. The fire is questionable. Dina thinks it's a manifestation of the physical manipulation gift. Like what Riann has. But I'm not so sure. You see, for Riann, in order to physically manipulate something, it needs to be in his presence. He can't just conjure things from thin air. From what we know of those who had that gift before him, the same holds true. But *you* can make fire when there is no fire around for you to draw from. We do know that the dome is a defensive gift, a shield of sorts. It protects you. And you can manifest the shield in a physical sense as well as in a mental sense."

My eyes quickly shift from the glass in my hands to his face. "What do you mean, 'in a mental sense?'"

"Physically, the shield protects you from the elements or other physical threats.

Mentally, it can shield you from other Celestras who might try to enter your mind," he explains. "When you mentally shield, you can keep someone like Himerak from seeing your past or controlling what you do. Or you can keep someone like Tarak from altering your emotions and determining whether or not you're being truthful. You can also transfer those abilities to someone else. For instance, if we're in close enough proximity, you can cause the dome to shield us both, or you can shield my mind from letting others in."

It's so much information to take in, but for some reason he makes it all sound so simple.

"Is that why they called me a Sourcer?"

He laughs lightly while shaking his head. "Usually, it's difficult for Celestras to use their gifts on or for each other. We can, but it ends up being a muted or dulled out version of what we can fully do to a non-gifted person. Celestras are not supposed to be at war with one another. Celestras are meant to be a team. But a Sourcer . . . " He takes a deep breath, as if the mere word is laced with immeasurable potential. "Well, Sourcers are . . . There's a passage in the sacred text which speaks on Sourcers and what exactly they are. Except there it's all legend, because there's never been one before. At least, not one that was recorded." He stills and places his hands in his lap. "Sourcers are supposedly the most deadly beings there are. But I think it's something more, and I don't think anyone else truly realized it. I think that being a Sourcer is the physical manifestation of the Elders."

I laugh at the absurdity of his statement.

"The whole fifth centra thing?" I raise my eyebrows and then shake my head before he can answer what I already know to be true. "I don't feel deadly or unimaginably powerful. I feel weak and tired." I let my head fall back to rest on the headboard for emphasis.

He smiles, a slight chuckle seeping past his lips. "Sometimes your body can lie to you. But I promise you are deadly, and magnificent, and . . . " He pauses as if realizing he's about to say something he shouldn't. "You're amazing. But it's not because of your gifts. It's just because of who you are. You don't need those gifts to be you."

"And who exactly am I?" I set the empty cup on the bedside table as I speak.

"Whoever you want to be."

I swallow at his words. There's so much truth and love and kindness buried within them. And that's terrifying. For the first time in what I can remember as my life, I actually feel safe. And not because someone else is telling me I'm safe. I feel safe because I'm learning who I am. Who I can become.

One's past is a funny thing. Some people say that their past can determine their future, but I don't think that's true. I think the past is just that. The past.

Sure, they can learn from their mistakes and change the direction in which they're headed, but it doesn't make them who they are. Which means I've been looking for the answers in the wrong place all along. I keep thinking I'll find myself in the past, but I'm not her anymore. I'm no longer that teenager who left this world and crash landed into a new one. I'm a woman who has come to take her place and make her own path.

My eyes lift to meet golden embers staring back at me. The last few weeks have been such a whirlwind of chaos, but somehow, sitting here in the middle of the unknown with him feels more serene and manageable than every other moment before.

Less than a day ago, I was prepared to enter the depths of hell to take on something I wasn't even sure I understood. Now, I finally feel as though that understanding has taken hold.

And I know it's because of Ari.

There's a tidal wave of emotions toward this man which are desperate to be unleashed. I have known him for just hours, and yet there's a sense of belonging and familiarity that tells me our paths have been intertwined for much, much longer. And though I know he would wait years for me to reach out and grasp what we once were, I know there's a part of him wasting away with every moment I keep that barrier intact.

"I am the bridge between the centras?" I mimic his words from earlier. The same words that have been playing on repeat in my head.

"Yes."

"And I'm this all-powerful being?"

He smiles as he reaches forward, letting his hand brush against my leg. "Yes."

"What if I'm not? What if they picked the wrong person?" I shrug and he shakes his head before leaning forward.

"You have a lot to take in." His thumb rubs lightly against my ankle. "It was an almost unimaginable task even when you fully understood the risks and benefits. I understand if it all seems like too much now when it's all so new." I scoff at the obviousness of his words. "You've been back home for less than a day. We don't have to figure this all out tonight. Or this week. Or this month."

"The Committence is in–"

"Don't worry about that. If you really want to go through with it then you can complete it when you feel ready, but don't do it just because someone told you to." I swallow at the honesty in his words. "I already alerted Reeves and the others that you were home. They know and are patiently waiting for your return . . . on your own time. And only when you're ready."

I eye him knowingly.

"While I appreciate that, I'm not planning on just rolling over and going back to sleep while all this chaos occurs out in the world. I want to learn as much as I can now," I urgently state and he laughs.

"So impatient," he coos and he slowly tightens the hold on my leg. "Okay. We can stay up and discuss every detail," he concedes and I smile.

He returns the looks before sadness covers his features. He tries to hide it under the steaming mug as he sips, but I catch the change and immediately want nothing more than to take away his sadness.

"You said you could never save me. But you did save me." I peek up through my lashes.

He furrows his brow at the sudden turn in conversation.

"If you hadn't tossed me that stone, I would have ended up in his hands."

His shoulders drop as if he isn't quite ready to discuss this part of our story.

He quickly counters, "I should've figured something else out. I should've gotten to you sooner. I should have insisted we leave. I should–"

"You did great," I quickly cut him off. "I'm sitting here with you right now because you chose my life over yours. You saved me. Thank you."

I watch as another wave of unshed tears wells up in his eyes and he quickly blinks them away.

"I was worried you would hate me for what I did," Ari confesses.

"I don't think I could ever hate you," I whisper the words, not even sure if he can hear them. Then my voice grows louder. "So . . . " I take a deep breath. "He used that river to steal away my memories?"

"Yes." Ari gulps and then removes the blanket from his legs, gets up, and walks around the massive bed to sit beside me.

"How?"

"I have spent far too many hours poring over information on the Esehtel River these last three years, and from what I've learned, it was created to be a way to start anew for someone who had been through unspeakable tragedies. Some walked willingly into the river and came out oblivious to the pain of their past."

Realization dawns.

"Riann wasn't trying to kill me, then. He was just trying to make me forget about all of this. About us, and about what I was fighting for."

Ari nods. "At first, he was meant to kill you. But then he found out what you could do. He wanted you for their side . . . For the Abolition. He knew that having you, who he believed to be a Sourcer, as an enemy was a death sentence. That the only way to turn you toward his cause was to make you forget your past . . . and let *him* become your future."

A wave of nausea covers me at the thought.

"And the stone you tossed to me? That stone sent me and Alesia to Earth?"

"Yes." He scoots just a bit closer and takes my hand, turning over my palm and running his fingers across the lines of my mark. A familiar warmth seeps deep into my bones. My body stills at the thought. "You were getting pretty good at shifting between places and times. You couldn't go too far yet. You still had a lot to learn. I think you went under just before you caught the stone. I think you lost your memories at the exact time you shifted the two of you, and in the chaos of it all, you ended up somewhere you hadn't intended."

I turn my wrist back over to interlace my fingers with his. "Is Alesia in on it. Is she with Riann?"

He quickly shakes his head. "I have no confirmation, but I do believe she is somewhat knowledgeable about who Riann actually is."

I nod my head in acceptance, because what else can I really do? "Okay."

"Okay?" he asks incredulously, as if he isn't quite sure how I am taking this all in with such calm.

"That all makes sense. But . . . " I take a deep breath. "I won't allow myself to blindly follow what I've been told any longer. I refuse to rely on someone else. For all I know, I could have been drugged, and all of this could be a dream."

He smiles. "But it would be a dream, right?"

My brows furrow. "What?"

"Being here, right now, with me. It would be a dream and not a nightmare, right?"

I huff out a laugh. "Definitely a dream."

XXXII

The next few hours are spent in a variation of the same pattern. Sleep, eat, ask questions, listen to Ari provide answers which lead to more questions, receive more answers, eat more food, and so on and so forth.

By the time the sun officially sets at the end of the following day, I feel as if my brain has just imploded. I wrap the thick blanket around my shoulders and stare out into the falling snow, thinking back on all that I've learned.

Most everything Ari described about Centra I and Halabar is information I've already learned from experiencing it firsthand. The terrain is arguably the most agreeable of all four centras, and thus was immensely desired during the Great War. Outside of the city of Halabar and the Mulara Forest, there seems to be just more of the same with a mixture of grasslands and mountains scattered throughout. Beyond the settlement where I stayed with Tarak, there are a few other settlements which linger near Halabar that are filled with various people, but their numbers and motives are not yet completely known.

We chat about the way the people dress, the gold lined streets, and the massive balls and dinners Koreed hosts at the palace. And about the sheer absurdity of it all. But Ari lets me in on a little secret. The city is *dying*. What is hidden behind that beautiful facade was just a failing system rooted in evil and destruction. It seems Centra I likes to flaunt a picture of wealth to its citizens while hiding the depths of despair anywhere they can. Ari says it's so the people won't defect.

I try to hold in the anticipation when he tells me that if they knew the truth of Ithesin, the Haze, the Ashclaw, the Gloom, and the Drench that have descended on the forest in search of the trees, then they would willingly leave in a heartbeat to seek shelter as far from the caverns as they could. I don't interrupt as he speaks, but on the inside my nerves are alive in terror as to what all those words may mean.

He explains that in order for Halabarian officials to keep things as they should be, the heads and advisors paint a picture of wealth and desire, all while entertaining the idea that every other centra is made from nothing but dirty scraps. Little do they know that the other parts of the world are thriving in a sense they could only dream of.

Ari tells me of his knowledge of the Soul Circle I entered within the underground portion of the palace not so long ago. My eyebrows peak when he informs me that there is a variation of one located on each centra.

When he starts speaking of what the room looks like, I nod in confirmation and then tell him the tale of my recent encounter inside.

He then explains that I was previously able to come and go from the Soul Circle as I pleased, a fact that was in complete contrast to what both Koreed and Tarak had alluded to.

"I thought I couldn't enter until recently?"

He laughs. "Is that what Koreed told you?"

I nod.

"Well, at least we know he never did find out about your ventures there." He gives me a sad smile. "It's how you were able to travel here so frequently. It's how we spent so much time together."

"What do you mean?"

"The Soul Circle is similar to the Caverns. Our gifts are enhanced when we are inside them. You used this stone," he lifts up the shiny gold contraption in his hand, "and you traveled to me."

I start to laugh. "I guess that's the Ithesin version of sneaking out of your house to meet up with your boyfriend."

He furrows his brow in confusion.

"I'll explain later." I quickly dismiss the notion and thankfully he accepts it without question.

"You hid the sacred text, Asfidel, in there for quite a while before you gave it to Reeves."

That makes three sacred texts I'm now aware of. Tarak has Elithium in his pack, and if the memory that Ari showed me still holds true, then Riann is now in possession of Drunia.

I almost ask Ari to tell me more about them, but he starts talking again, and it's as if his voice just sucks me in. As if it were a melody I have waited years to once again hear, and I know there is absolutely nothing that could make me stop the sound. It's so easy to talk to him. It's as if my body knows he's safe, and nothing else matters.

He has the most knowledge of Centra III, which makes sense, as it's where our base is. I recall what Tarak once told me about this place. He described it as *a frozen tundra reliant on the goods sent over by other centras.* Tarak thought this place was a barren wasteland. He was so wrong. Though it is sounding more and more like Tarak was, or rather *is,* a lot of things I don't wish to entertain any longer.

Ari tells me of the hard times that befell his centra during the Great War. There was some truth, albeit minor, to the idea that this centra was reliant on the goods being sent back and forth, but the main thing Tarak had incorrect was the past tense phrasing he used. It seems most in the settlement, or maybe even Halabar for that matter, believe all four centras to be mostly cut off from one another. From what Ari tells me, that is far from the truth. It turns out only Centra I and Centra II are cut off from the others. Centra III and IV are completely intertwined.

He continues his tale, slowly letting all the pieces form together as he plates our dinner and sets it before us on the stone hearth. I quickly find that I am fully unprepared for these revelations when he starts talking about Centra II. I now know it's where Riann is from, and where the Abolition originally formed. Where most of our enemies lie. What I don't know is how exactly Micel is connected to all of this.

"... and when Micel came over to–"

"Wait." I cut him off. "Is Micel from Centra II?"

His features freeze, as if he is just now realizing this is a new piece of information for me.

"Yes. He's from Centra II. He was sent over to Centra I on a mission from The Abolition, but then he started a relationship with Himerak, and . . . Well, that mission never came to fruition."

The realization is so jarring, I knock the nicely plated dinner off its spot. "Micel was a part of the Abolition?" I whisper the question so quietly.

Ari furrows his brow. "What do you know about Micel?" he questions.

"I know he isn't from Centra I, and that he and Himerak met when he came over for peace talks from somewhere else." *Somewhere I now know is Centra II.* "Himerak ended up stepping down due to the relationship and their inability to be together while he was still serving as sovereign, but then–"

"Nera." Ari stops me with a warm hand covering mine. "Yes, Micel and Himerak formed a relationship of sorts when they met, but the rest of that story is a tall tale." My brows furrow as he speaks. "Micel was a high-ranking member of the Abolition. He wasn't sent over for peace talks. He was sent over to *kill* Himerak."

"What?"

"Micel and Mikel were twins. Micel is Riann's uncle."

I jolt with such intensity that I trip backward, landing directly on my ass.

"Are you okay?" Ari asks as he quickly reaches down to lift me up.

"What?" I blink, still trying to process what I've heard. "Yes. No. Wait. I mean, yes, I'm fine, but . . . " As soon as I'm upright, I start pacing the heated spot between where Ari now sits and the crackling fireplace, letting all the jagged pieces in my mind slowly slip into place. It suddenly makes complete sense as to why there was such an odd reaction to Micel seeing Riann in that underground base. The next words come out in a rush as the puzzle starts to come into focus. "Mikel is Riann's father. Mikel was the leader of the Abolition. Mikel died twelve years–"

"Fifteen years ago," Ari quickly corrects me.

I shrug off the minor detail. "Fifteen years ago. Mikel and Micel are twins. That makes Micel Riann's uncle. Riann is now leader of the Abolition after his father, but is secretly in disguise in Centra I as a refugee, trying to take over the continent so he can further his cause, which is ultimately the killing of Celestras. But Micel is now married to Himerak, who is also a Celestra. That means that Riann is actively trying to kill his uncles? And Micel has known about all of this from the beginning?"

"I *think* the answer is yes . . . to all of that." Ari laughs a little with each word.

"Wait!" I freeze my frantic movements with my hands in the air and lock eyes with Ari. "Riann is a Celestra as well!"

"Yes." He nods in agreement.

"That doesn't make any sense. The Abolition wants to abolish the Celestras, but why would they do that when their leader is one?"

"That's a complicated question that I may not have the correct answer to." He shuffles slightly then looks back to me. "There are many Celestras within the Abolition. Some are there willingly and some are under duress."

"Are they under some kind of mind control?"

Ari shakes his head. "I don't believe so. Remember, it's very difficult for Celestras to use their gifts on other Celestras they aren't bonded to."

I pace back and forth a few times before finally looking up. "When did Micel and Himerak meet?"

"Ummm . . . " He takes a moment to do the math in his head and then answers, "Twenty-five years ago. I think."

"Micel would have known about Riann before he came over," I say to myself, almost as an afterthought, before turning to start my pacing once more. But then another thought hits me. "Wait!" My eyes shoot to Ari.

His face contorts into a laughable expression before he lifts a finger and says, "Can I just jump in real quick and say that you are adorable when you're piecing things together?"

I roll my eyes even as I try to hide the flush that covers every inch of my skin.

"Please don't try to flatter me while I'm in detective mode," I tease as I cut my eyes back to him and find his expression filled with curious confusion.

"Detective?" he questions with a raised brow.

I bite my lip as I try to find the correct words. "It means someone who's trying to figure out a mystery."

He chuckles as he nods in understanding

"And besides, I'm always adorable," I add, and he laughs.

Then I feel an instant wave of uncertainty at the ease with which that comment came out. I shouldn't feel this comfortable around him. Not yet.

I immediately switch back to the matter at hand, hoping he doesn't notice the rising blush that I'm sure now stains my cheeks.

"Jaxon told me that Micel came to Centra I during the peace talks. But you said that's not true?"

"Right, it isn't. Micel came to infiltrate. His role within the Abolition was to kill Celestras, not to fall in love with one," Ari explains, clearly still recovering from his bout of laughter.

"You can't help who you bond with." I shrug my shoulders and he smiles.

"While that is true. Micel and Himerak don't have a bond, since Micel isn't a Celestra. They are–"

"Micel is a Celestra."

For the first time in the last few hours, it's Ari who has a complete look of shock seared into his features.

"No, he's not," Ari shakes his head, and from the ease that runs through my bones, I know he believes that falsehood to be truth.

"Yes, he is," I retort. "Jaxon told me right before we entered the Caverns. Well, I don't think 'told me' is the right phrase. Himerak is somehow using his gifts to keep them from speaking about it, but Micel is also a Celestra. Jaxon made me play some stupid little guessing game so I would know without him having to actually say it."

XXXIII

There is a long pause, during which I'm not exactly sure what's going on in his head, but then he abruptly stands and rushes over to the large dining room table near the front of the home. There are a few papers scattered there I didn't notice when we first arrived, and I wonder if he spent some of the time I was sleeping working through this mess of a life.

"Ari?" I question, not sure if I want to know what exactly is happening as he frantically reads one paper before switching to the next.

Then he quickly meets my gaze and points to a door on the second level. It is heavily carved with intricate designs that remind me of the entrance to the Soul Circle back in the palace.

"That is . . . our room." He momentarily stalls his chaotic movements as if suddenly realizing anything with the word 'our' in it may take me some getting used to. Then, as if he can't seem to correctly piece together what it is he wants to say, he rapidly states, "If you would rather not go in there yet, I understand." He runs his hand through his hair. "Your closet's there. I need you to dress warm for where we're going, but I can get your things if you–"

"It's okay." I hold up my hand to stop his hurried, and obviously tortured, speech. "I can find my stuff and dress warmly enough."

He nods. "Your closet's through the back . . . I need to grab my pack, but layer up. Make sure you have on boots and a jacket." Then he walks back to where I stand, earnestly peers into my eyes, and I wonder what answer he's searching for.

Then he tenderly leans down, kisses me on the cheek, and says, "The gray, fur-lined coat was always your favorite," before he vanishes into thin air.

I startle at the sudden disappearance. "I don't think I will ever get used to that," I mumble under my breath as I turn to climb the stairs.

My breath hitches as the door opens to a large, dimly lit room.

I can barely see as I make my way to the bedside table, but I notice the same lamp style that I became used to in Halabar and slowly glide my hand over the bulb. A glistening hue appears as a thousand golden flakes dance in intricate waves and turn the once-dark room into a warm retreat.

I recall one day inside the palace reaching out to touch a similar lamp in my room as a flickering light that seemed to be alive with fury danced inside a glass bulb. Alesia was the one who found me standing there, mesmerized by the sight.

"It's a current made from bits of heartstone and embedded with tiny flecks of flames," Alesia explains from where she stands in the doorway. "It's not unlike the electricity we used during our time on Earth, except that once activated, these lights never tire."

I give her a curious look, knowing they dim at night as I've seen them do each time when I crawl into bed.

Noting my confusion, she quickly clarifies, "What I mean is, you don't have to pay for it, and it will never die out. There will always be life inside of it as long as you should require it. Here, let me show you." She walks over and waves her hand across the top of the bulb. I hold in the breath of surprise when the light slowly fades out, leaving us standing in the shadows cast from the sinking sun outside my window. She quickly moves her hand back across the top, and the world opens back up with the glow.

At the time, I remember wanting to ask more, to inquire as to how exactly that worked, but I was still fighting the hatred and resentment I held for the secrets she had been keeping from me for the last three years.

Turning back to the room, my eyes skirt along every curve, line, and inch they can find. The bed that stands before me could easily sleep five, and has thick wool blankets draped over every inch. The walls are a dark mahogany, interrupted by a few doors, and the large window across the way shows a dream-like view of falling snowflakes inside a winter wonderland. My own personal snow globe has come to life.

The first door in the room brings me into a bathroom with a massive natural stone tub in the center. The floors, walls, and ceilings are a glistening white and such a stark contrast to everything else within this home. When I look up, I find the ceiling a beautifully made tangle of branches. Over in a corner, those branches thin out, leaving small openings scattered. By the look of the handle directly below, I have a feeling this shower must be set up in a similar fashion to what they had in the settlement. I smile at the thought of this room turning into its very own rainforest in winter.

Before I can get too lost in the beauty of a simple room, I step back and close the door, but make a promise to come back soon. Right before the next door is a curved archway that leads to a darkened alcove. As soon as I step across the threshold, the ceiling lights with a thousand glistening, golden bulbs that illuminate the expanse. An audible gasp leaves my lips as I survey the thousand or more books. My fingers caress the weathered spines as I circle the room. A smile so big that my cheeks hurt spreads across my face, and I reluctantly step back out of the room, watching as the light dims.

The next door I find opens to a modest closet. With just a quick look, I can tell it has everything one may need, except there's no extravagance here like there was back in the palace.

I rub my fingers across each of the items as I venture further inside. It only takes a moment to guess where Ari's clothes end and mine begin. His side is filled with deep browns and blacks, with just a few randomly-placed items of white and gold. My side leans heavily on deep grays and midnight blues. But as I dig further, I also find a few items of white and gold that mirror his.

I know the coat that was my favorite the moment my eyes land on it. It's a soft gray with white wool lining the hood and white stone-like buttons down the middle. An intricate design of deep blue and gold snakes along the edges. It isn't regal in the least. To be honest, those I mingled with in the palace would balk at its simplicity. But it's beautiful, and perfect, and so very . . . me. I quickly strip off the clothes I've worn for the last day and layer with what I hope are enough items to keep me warm wherever we're going. I smile as I let the soft, gray coat melt against my skin.

As I'm lacing up my shoes, I hear a knock on the door.

"Are you dressed?" he questions.

"Yes?" I state with uncertainty, not sure if this is exactly what he meant when he said *layer up*.

He looks me over with a smile. "Glad to see you back in clothes from home again."

"They're very comfy." I run my hands over the fur-lined pants and thick warm top before wiggling my toes within the cozy boots I found.

"I'm sorry," he says as he walks toward me.

"For what?"

"Shifting." He gives me an apologetic smirk. "As soon as I was at Archer's, I realized I probably scared you again. I'll try to not do it so much."

I shake my head in disagreement. "You didn't scare me. It's just . . . shocking." My shoulders shrug.

"Come on." He reaches out a hand. "Dina damn near took my head off when I told her I had found you."

My interest peaks at the familiar name. "Is she a friend?"

"She is your *best* friend. Besides me, of course." He winks as he tugs me closer, and before I can even laugh or reply or breathe, we're transported out of the bedroom and onto a stairwell in a dimly lit hallway.

"What the . . . " I call out, almost falling when one of my feet hits the air instead of the step below it.

"Sorry." Ari tightens his hold on me. "I didn't want to just shift straight in there." He tilts his head down the stairwell I'm currently still trying to find my footing on, and toward the wooden door with light and music flowing from the other side. "But we also can't have anyone up there"—he turns to look toward the top of the stairwell where there's a faint glow and faded music playing—"knowing you're back yet. We still have a lot to figure out."

I give him a tight smile, unable to hide the nervousness consuming me at the thought of meeting another someone from my past.

He guides us down the stairs, and when he reaches the door, instead of knocking, he slowly pushes it open and pulls me inside.

I shield my eyes from the bright light of the lantern hanging directly above just as a gentle gasp comes from across the room. When my eyes adjust, I find a woman standing not twenty feet from me. She's currently frozen as she takes me in, and as I study her, I find a note of familiarity in her kind eyes. Enough familiarity that I feel a momentary twinge that maybe a memory of her will surface from before. But of course, none do. I watch, unsure of what to do or say or even think, as her shoulders seem to lift and fall in a pattern consistent with someone who has suddenly forgotten how to breathe.

"Is she okay?" I whisper to Ari, and he gives me a sad smile.

"Nera?" the woman whispers as she inches closer and closer. With every step she advances, more of her form comes into view. She's slightly older than me, but not by much. Her long brown hair flows across her shoulders in perfectly formed waves, and for a moment, I wonder if curling irons are a thing on Ithesin or if she's just this beautiful without even trying.

"Hi," I tentatively state as she stops a foot from me.

We stare at each other for a moment longer as she takes in someone I'm sure she thought she would never see again. But then the weight of that fear seems to melt from her shoulders, and I watch as a relieved smile covers her face.

"Hi," she replies back so quietly I'm not even sure if I heard it correctly. Then she softly asks, tears filling her eyes, "Can I hug you?"

I quickly nod, and before I can take my next breath, her arms are wrapped around me, holding me tighter than I could have ever imagined.

"You're real," she whispers into my hair, and again I nod, knowing she can feel the motion. Then the dam breaks, and I hold her as sobs race through her figure, and a torrent of tears so thick they damn near soak through every layer of my clothing straight down to my shoulder.

I'm not sure how long we stand there with her crying into my neck, and me standing stone still, trying to figure out exactly how I'm supposed to respond to this. But I don't move. I won't end this moment for her, even if it means next to nothing to me.

When she pulls back, eyes red, runny nose, and all, she looks me dead in the face, points her finger at me and says, "If you ever tell a soul I cried like that on your shoulder, I swear to the Elders, I will burn every book you own. Especially that stupid, naughty romance one you keep hidden in your bedside drawer."

My cheeks flush as a smile covers my face.

"I have a naughty romance book hidden in a drawer?" I question as my eyes shift to meet Ari.

He quickly lifts both hands in surrender. "I know nothing," he lies while shaking his head, a guilty smile covering his features.

I quickly turn back to Dina, hoping my embarrassment is hidden under all these layers of fur. Her eyes are now bright with laughter and a familiarity I can feel deep in my bones.

"That sounds like something I would do." I shrug, and then, unsure where to take this next, I quickly place my hands back into my pockets.

"I missed you," she says, and then looks over to Ari before letting her gaze slowly track back to me. "This man can be ridiculously annoying to deal with on the regular by myself. I'm mostly glad you're back just so you can wrangle him in when needed."

"Hey!" Ari calls out and we all three laugh. Theirs is more genuine, mine is somewhere in between.

"Come on." Dina loops her arm within mine and pulls me forward as if I had never left. "Ari says you have some intel on Micel that I need to know."

Her statement causes my feet to halt just as I start moving, and the sobering realization of why we're here hits me. I dart a quick glance between the two.

"I don't want anything to happen to him," I state in earnest. As frustrating as my first encounter was with Micel, I have grown to find that he is built from nothing but kindness.

"Neither do we," Ari assures me, and I feel a weight lift.

"What's the plan for him, then?" My eyes shift between the two.

"How much does she know?" Dina questions.

Ari shakes his head. "Not enough. I've spent all day and part of yesterday laying out the basics, but it would take another month to relay *everything* that's happened."

"Just hit me with the main points for now," I cut in, imploring them to say whatever is needed.

"We need Micel," Dina starts.

"He is the only one we feel comfortable with who has a great knowledge of Centra I, Halabar, and Himerak's settlement," Ari adds from behind me. "And while it is dated, he has inside knowledge of the Abolition and their inner workings. If he was on our side, then there's a chance we could take them down from the inside out."

Ari stares at me, an unspoken plea lingering in the air.

"We can trust Dina," he quickly adds. "She's been a part of this since she was a child."

Dina nods her head with Ari's every word.

"Nera," her eyes are soft and kind as they implore me further, "if you know anything about Micel that could help, I'm begging you to tell me. Ari won't say a word to me unless you give him the okay." She looks over to Ari, rolling her eyes, and he shrugs his shoulders as if to say, *What do you expect?* "Micel made a life with a Celestra. Fell in love with a Celestra. The same Celestra he was supposed to kill. He may have come from evil, but with everything that's happened, he may now be sympathetic to our cause. He may be sympathetic to the Celestras and–"

"Micel *is* a Celestra," I cut in before she can utter another word.

"No. He isn't," she abruptly retorts.

"That's what I said," Ari adds with a grin.

But Dina keeps shaking her head in protest. "I know him. There is no way. I would have seen it."

"Himerak's hiding it from his people," I cut in. "He's using what little of his gift he has left to trick their minds into not seeing what's directly in front of them."

Dina frantically looks between the two of us as her mind works overtime to piece all of this together.

"No," she refuses with more certainty than I have ever heard. And I know she believes it because my entire body sings in truth.

"I promise," I plead. And then as an afterthought I add, "How do *you* know Micel?"

"I used to live in the settlement." Her brows furrow and I can tell that, even though she's aware of my memory loss and the fact that I no longer remember anything from before, it's still odd for her to lay out all the information I should know. "I was–"

"Nera," Ari cuts her off while staring directly at me. He opens and closes his mouth multiple times, as if the words themselves are stuck somewhere deep inside him.

"What?" I finally ask in confusion when the silence lingers for far too long.

"Dina is short for Adina," he explains with a tortured look in his eyes.

I quickly shift my gaze between the two, wondering why him telling me her full name is causing so much pain to ripple off him.

"Adina Duvelon," he adds and cuts his eyes over to my new . . . old friend who, thankfully, looks as confused as I do.

"Why are you acting like my name is poison on your lips, Ari?" she asks just as I start to piece it together.

And then the reason she feels so familiar finally hits. It's not because we were once the best of friends. Of course, I still have no memory of that time. She's familiar because she has the same sapphire gaze. The same high cheekbones and the same dimple hiding within her porcelain skin.

Dina is Tarak's dead sister.

"Oh my god!" I shriek as I step out of her grasp. "You are–"

"I'm what?" she cuts me off in question, but my mind is spinning far too fast to comprehend the words. "I'm what?!" she demands again, and I can practically feel the rising frustration and confusion starting to build within her.

"You're Tarak's sister. You're his *dead* sister!" My hand flies up to cover my mouth as the waves of shock continue to rush through me.

"How do you know Tarak?" she spits out as she looks between Ari and myself. "How does she know Tarak?"

"He had her. Tarak was the one who found her within the Mulara Forest that first day. She spent those weeks we couldn't find her hidden within Himerak's settlement."

Her face pales as he speaks.

"You were with Tarak?" she questions with an air of surprise and bewilderment. I quickly nod. "What about my mother? Or my father? Did you meet them, too? Where are they now? Did they make it to one of the safe houses?" Her gaze quickly shifts to Ari. "If they're out of Himerak's reach, we might be able to get to them. It's not too risky. My father would be of great use. Ari please, please!" she begs. "I only need ten—no, five—five guards from the Bend. Five guards and two days, and I could–"

She freezes the moment she sees the tears trailing down my cheeks.

"Nera?" she questions and then recognition dawns. But still, she has to ask. "Where are my parents?" Her voice is calm, her words now all but a whisper on the wind. "Where's my brother?"

My heart breaks, shattering into a million pieces as my silence becomes her answer.

"Nera!" she screams at me as what I'm assuming is her worst fears are confirmed. "Did you see them? My parents?" Her voice breaks. "What about Jaxon or Everett? Cam?" Her lip starts to shake as the reality of my non-answer continues to sink in. "You know where they are?" A tear slides down her face. "Please tell me where they are."

"I'm so sorry. I–"

"No," she stops me, her voice now heavy and strong. "No!" she screams in anguish and Ari reaches out to pull her into his chest.

"I don't know a Cam or Everett," I quickly reply. "I never met them."

She leans back with a glint in her eye and I berate myself at the continued nonanswer that has now given her just the slightest bit of hope. "But you know Jaxon and my parents? My brother?"

I nod. "I met Jaxon. And I met your mom." My heart is beating so fast within my chest I swear it'll surely burst at any moment.

"My father?"

I shake my head as I frantically look between the two people standing in front of me.

"I never met your father." The confession is a barely audible mumble I'm not sure even occurred.

"Why?"

"He–" I close my eyes and then look up to find Ari, hoping he'll help me through this, but it's now that I realize he may not know any of this either. "Tarak told me that your father died a few years back. I don't know how."

She pales even further, and her body seems to shrink within itself. My hand flexes, reaching out, hoping to comfort her, but before I can move further, she takes a deep breath and closes her eyes.

"And my mother?" Her bottom lip quivers with the question, and I know that she already knows the answer.

I hold my breath for just a moment, knowing I am probably about to burst every last hope she's been hanging onto, kept buried within. It's Ari's tentative squeeze on my hand that gives me the courage to speak. "She was killed by Halabarian soldiers the day they attacked the settlement to bring me back to the palace."

The air is sucked from her lungs as reality sinks in and her world crashes before her.

XXXIV

I only have two memories that involve someone breaking down in my presence.

The first was Tarak with the death of Rhea. Holding him that night when he finally let the dam burst will forever be seared within my heart. No amount of the hate or anger, the frustration or confusion that I currently hold for him and what he did could take away my sympathy for what he went through in that moment.

The other memory is different. I recall the way the vases sounded as they shattered against the wall when I thought Riann loved me. When I thought he was grieving the loss of me. The sounds of his cries and grunts of frustration echoed through my ears for days after as I tried to reconcile who I was then with who he wanted me to be . . . with who I once was. I push the false memory away, promising myself not to think of that wretched man any more than I have to, and slowly move to stand beside Dina who has untangled herself from Ari's hold and is standing frozen as a statue in front of the fireplace.

The first few moments after the words slipped out, she was all but paralyzed in shock, but then she crumbled to the floor as bellows of pain and agony burst from her lips. She fought off Ari as he tried to comfort her, but eventually she fell into his arms and let him rock her until the cries slowly ebbed away.

Unsure of my role in all of this, I just stood still, unmoving. I was the one who just provided that horrendous news, and I was sure she wouldn't want me to come near her anytime soon.

It was Ari who helped me see that my line of thought was jaded by my own past. What she needed most was her friend. He silently pleaded with sorrow in his eyes as he looked up to find my gaze, and then there was no question in my mind as to where I was to fit in with all of this.

My feet quickly made their way forward, and then I was standing next to her with my arm draped around her middle, pulling her into me.

She laid her head against my shoulder as she let the soft cries slowly fizzle out.

Which is how we currently find ourselves, leaning against each other and staring into the wisping flames ahead.

"I will kill every last one of those bastards for what they have taken from us." Dina's words hold unyielding promise.

Once we shift back to what Dina calls base and Ari calls home, they leave me alone to shower and change. I've been so consumed with trying to find out everything Ari could tell me I didn't even realize it's been days since the last time I truly washed. I crinkle my nose in disgust as I realize that was probably not my best decision.

This world is so different from Earth, and yet some things are so similar. In one respect, Ithesin feels as though it's a mirror to medieval Earth, with its swords and animals, dresses and customs. But, every now and then, a pop of modern life will jump right out at me. Yet, somehow it doesn't seem out of place in any respect.

This shower seems to be made similarly to the one at Tarak's home in the trees. Holes litter the tangled ceiling above, and when I turn the carved stone knob, a warm waterfall cascades down over me. I didn't realize how much I've missed this.

For the last week, my *baths* were spent fully clothed and quickly washing off the grime in a cold river as we trekked toward the Caverns.

Unlike my accommodations in the settlement, though, there seems to be a form of electricity here just like there was in the city.

But still, it's different from Earth's.

The settlement was full of firelight and oil lamps. But the light here is more similar to what I found in the palace in Halabar, except for the massive fireplace in the center of the living space.

By the time I find myself walking back onto the balcony of the second floor that overlooks the living space, I can hear Ari and Dina's hushed conversation.

"She really doesn't remember a thing?" Dina whispers, still somewhat unbelieving in my memory loss.

A quick pause of silence and then. "Nothing."

"Not even you?"

"Not even me," his voice betrays his pain.

"But you're bonded. Does she at least know that? Can she feel it?" Dina urges, as if the concept of my not feeling this growing thing between us would be unfathomable. And in truth it would be.

"I told her. I think she understands, and she *can* feel it, but . . . " He lets out a small chuckle, and I can tell the sentiment is meant to lessen the sting he feels at the thought, even if only for his own benefit. "But she's going to make me work for it."

"As she should," Dina teases.

Ari takes a ragged breath. "She can feel me. Just as I can feel her. But . . . " He trails off, and Dina quickly moves a chair to the side as she cuts in.

Her voice is muffled as her face is buried against him. "She's back. That's all that matters. She's here, and she's safe. You did it, Ari. You brought her back." She assures him, her voice much more confident now that the conversation has moved from her own grief to his. "What about her gifts? Are they all still the same?"

"We haven't tested them yet. We've somehow kept the world from crumbling without them for the last three years, so I think affording her some time to adjust to all the change is more important than running off to slay monsters."

There is so much relief in those words, knowing that he's giving me the time I need, and I'm so damn thankful for it.

Dina lets out a small laugh just as I make my way down the stairwell and enter the room.

"I would like to slay monsters." I smirk when I notice their smiles of realization that they've been caught stretching across their faces.

"And you will," Ari declares as he stands to offer me his seat.

"What exactly do you know about the war, the land, and the four penances?" Dina asks as she turns her chair to face me while Ari leans back on the table, arms crossed and hair falling into his face. I almost laugh at her directness. She wastes no time. And I think I like her.

But I stall in answer, because as I shift my gaze to Ari I find massive muscular arms directly in my view.

I swallow as I turn my eyes back to Dina and try to forget how damn delicious that view is. It definitely has nothing to do with the bond and everything to do with the fact that rolled up sleeves and muscular arms are a damn near drug when it comes to me. My own brand of poison.

I clear my throat. "I know about the Haze. I saw it. It got me just here." I lift up my leg to show off the wound before remembering what an excellent job Micel did at healing it. You can't even tell it happened.

"It made it to the settlement." Ari's words are more of a despondent realization than a question.

I nod in confirmation.

"But I don't know about the rest. You mentioned a number of things that you all are fighting against, but I don't remember them."

"The Shadow. The Drench. The Haze. The Ashclaw," Dina lists them each distinctly before swallowing in preparation for what she's about to say. "Those are the four penances of the land. Each slowly killing something we hold dear. Each brought into creation as a result of selfish Celestras who dared misuse the stones."

"It's part of the reason the Abolition was formed," Ari chimes in. "The first Celestras didn't have a very good track record. They used the stones without first gaining the knowledge needed. The power, being too great for them, backfired, and the first monstrosities were created from their greed." He unconsciously rubs the mark on his wrist. "The Abolition's aim is to destroy Celestras because they fear we hold too much power, that our abilities will one day destroy this world. But it's the exact opposite. We want to use our abilities to save this world. We aren't our ancestors. The past doesn't have to repeat itself as long as you learn from those mistakes. We aren't seeking power or vengeance. We just want peace." His sincerity washes over me in languid strokes.

"What are they? I've seen the Haze, but I don't fully understand it."

Ari quickly nods and then takes a few steps from the table to the bar where he grabs the map of stones we were initially looking at when we first arrived.

"The Haze, the Drench, and the Shadow were all formed either during or after the Great War. They were kept at bay for so long that they eventually became legend. Stories to tell a stubborn child to keep them in line. But recently, it's as if something has awoken them."

He swallows thickly and I'm unsure if he will be able to tell me this tale. But just when I think he will for some reason break, he starts to speak.

"The Haze, as you've seen, is a gaseous entity. It was formed right here in Centra III . . . by my own ancestors." Guilt coats each word as his jaw flexes in anger. "It was created in order to gain power and now it feeds off the deaths of the souls it ensnares. The burning wisps that lift from the bodies nourishes the Haze, causing it to grow. The more lives it takes, the bigger and stronger it becomes."

My mind instantly races back to Jensin, and then to that dying woman from only days ago. Both smelled of horrid burning flesh, and black smoke seeped from their bones as their body disintegrated before my eyes. I find myself struggling to hold back the vomit that threatens to make an appearance at the memory.

Ari continues as he points to the two drawings that now lie in front of me. "During the Great War, Centra III's Celestra attempted to use the Ruination and Genesis stones to alter the landscape. He didn't have those gifts but had come in possession of the stones thinking he could use them to create and destroy which resulted in immeasurable casualties for the warring armies." Pain laces each word and Dina reaches out a comforting hand that finds purchase on his shoulder. "Fires erupted from the cracks that formed in the land, and the Haze was born from the blackened smoke that billowed from the burning bodies of dying soldiers." Bile rises in my throat with each word. "The Drench was created when the Celestras in Centra II, who possessed the same gifts as I do, attempted to use the Omni and Eso stones to return to a time before the war where they could gain the upper hand. The Drench is a body of water that snakes along the caverns and throughout the lands. It takes the souls of all who enter. The death is prolonged and torturous as the water seeps into the body and slowly disintegrates the bones, flesh, and muscles, all while the victim slowly drowns."

"That sounds horrific." My voice quivers.

"It's nowhere near as bad as the Shadow," Dina cuts in just before Ari can resume his explanation.

"The Shadow is exactly what the name implies . . . a shadow figure which lives within the Caverns. From what I know, it's attached to the stone walls, and there have been no sightings of it within any of the centras. The penances gain their strength from the lives they take. The Shadow cannot reach as many people because it's tied to the Caverns and thus it's taken the least amount of lives, since only Celestras tend to venture inside."

"What does it do?" I tentatively ask, not sure I'm ready for the answer.

"You already know," Ari answers as he reaches forward and interlaces our fingers. "It alters your mind. It makes you see, feel, and hear things that aren't there. And unless you can break free of the hold, it will drive you to insanity."

My breath catches as the realization of what he is saying sinks in.

The Shadow is what attacked me when I first entered the Caverns. It seems it didn't waste a moment on its mission to get to me. I feel chill bumps cover my too-warm skin as I recall the way the voice, so strange and yet oddly familiar, called out to me; how it tried to reel me in, and how the stone wall shifted into murky, shining blackness that showed an unknown version of myself burning from within. Was that me? Was that some sort of vision, or maybe a memory? Or was it–

"Nera?" Ari catches my attention as he lifts my chin toward him, and I realize I was stuck in my own memory, reliving every vile second of that horrible moment.

"That's when you altered my mind. That's why you showed me the snow?"

He nods. "I didn't alter your mind. I wasn't far away. I was just on the other side of where you were. But I couldn't get to you, not with Tarak"—I feel Dina tense as he voices her brother's name—"and Ranya guarding you. I did what I could. I used the Shadow against itself. I used my gift and entered you through it.

That's how I showed you that memory."

"How was it made?"

"Unlike the Drench and the Haze, the Shadow wasn't made long ago. It's a more recent manifestation."

"It was made by Himerak," Dina cuts in, anger and hatred coating each word. "That's one of the actual reasons we fled Halabar in the beginning. But he tricked us. My mother, my father, everyone. He tricked us into thinking we were fleeing to build up an army to fight against the horrors which had been made, but it was so much more."

Ari places a comforting hand on her shoulder. "That's why there are empty houses on the outskirts of town. The Haze moves underground, and with each passing day, week, month, it gets closer and closer to the city. Koreed pulled all the citizens closer to the palace following the most recent attack a few months back."

I nod in understanding. Now all those empty homes make so much more sense.

"The more you talk, the worse these things get. I hesitate to even ask what the Ashclaw is."

Dina's head quickly turns to meet Ari. His features mold to match the worry lines etched across her face.

"The Ashclaw is worse, isn't it?" I guess.

Ari lifts from where he was leaning against the table and slowly pulls out a chair so he is fully facing me.

"Nera, before I tell you this, I want you to understand something."

I tentatively nod, afraid of where this may be going.

"Your abilities aren't like the ones we've seen over the thousands of years of Celestras. There was no way for you to be properly trained in their use, because no one knew what they could do."

I break the link in our gaze, letting my eyes fall to my trembling hands. The breath in my chest feels as though a thousand tiny knives are slicing me from the inside out. I know what he's saying before he even voices it.

"It was me, wasn't it? I made it?" My voice is low and tentative, but filled with hope that, by some chance, the question will sound absurd, and instead of an affirmation, I will receive a quick shake of his head. Unfortunately, that is not what happens.

"It was a complete accident. You were so young, and you had no idea what you were doing."

"How?" My vision blurs as tears spring forth. I knew already that I was a killer, I just wasn't sure how that truth I felt so deep within my bones had come to be.

"I want to preface this with the fact that I'm not speaking from memory, as I wasn't a part of your life when this occurred. So I can't show it to you."

He squeezes my hand, and I nod in understanding.

"I can only relay to you what you once relayed to me."

I once again nod as I look up into his grief-stricken eyes. He opens his mouth just as familiar sounds of screams echo through the forest outside.

Act III

- The Shadows -

XXXV

Before I can fully process the sound, I'm standing with Ari at my side, and Dina has somehow made her way to the large bay window in the back of the living area.

"I can't see a thing!" Dina's call is fraught with frustration as she starts to pace the area, as if moving five feet to the left will afford her a better view out the exact same window. "The snowfall's too dense."

Ari takes a few steps further into the other room to survey the sight himself while still keeping me in view. He halts, taking a deep breath as recognition freezes his features in place. His dread seems to permeate my soul, and without question, I know that what he feared has come to fruition.

"I thought you said no one knew about this place?" Unsettled, I close the gap between us.

"They don't. I'm sure of it." His statement is warm and languid as it rolls across my skin.

I open my mouth, not sure what I plan to say, but am halted by the wretched screams that barrel through the trees. Each pain-filled echo bounces off the walls of the home and straight into me.

"What is that? Is it the Ashclaw?" I question as fear races down my back.

Ari doesn't answer. Instead, he studies the trees a moment longer, before turning back to me.

"We have to hide you." He inches closer to where I stand. "I will *not* lose you again."

"I don't want to hide."

It comes out so effortlessly, but before the sentence can fully escape my lips—before the sounds even have a chance to skirt the air between us—a darkened fog I know all too well seeps through the cracks around the windows and doors, spilling into the room.

There's only a split second for a decision. I barely have time to process what we're doing when my body is wrapped in Ari's arms and he shifts the few feet to Dina—not even taking the extra second to run—before we all three evaporate into thin air.

The moment my feet hit the ground, my body falls forward, and the wretched bile is pouring onto the ground.

"Water!" I hear Dina command someone I can't see.

My vision's too splintered and my head's spinning too fast to focus on anything other than forcing the inhale I need. But then a soft hand brushes my face and the world slowly shifts back into view.

"How long before I get used to that?" I croak out, leaning into his touch as he practically holds my head up.

"I'm hoping sooner rather than later," he whispers with a hint of amusement in his tone.

A cold glass is placed in my hand, and I greedily gulp down the icy water in hopes of smothering the lingering burn and close my eyes as the nausea subsides. "I didn't get sick when we went to find Dina earlier, though."

Ari hums in agreement. "That was to cross only a few miles in Centra III. Very easy to adjust."

My eyes flutter open and closed as I beg the nausea to end and my wobbly legs to function, but I can't even seem to make it off my knees.

"We went much further this time." Ari's chin tips up just as two darkly-tanned bare feet step into my periphery.

I scan the length of the long legs to find a rather beautiful and, by the look on her face, confident woman attached. Her shit-eating grin is damn near blinding, and with her arms crossed over her chest, she appears ready for some type of battle of wills.

Her grin quickly turns from amused to worrisome as her gaze shifts from me to Ari.

"What happened?" Her tone is laced with urgency.

"Our home. The base," he answers.

She takes a deep breath as she lets those four words register, and I take the silent moment to assess exactly what I am up against here.

Her deep mahogany skin is covered in beautiful gold swirls and her black hair is fixed in a way that reminds me of Ranya. The twisted pieces are covered in what look like golden rings. I see now that the light, flowing white gown she wears is really hiding a pair of pants under the open skirt, while golden twirls, similar to what I found on my coat, line the entire outfit. The strapless design shows off her broad shoulders and muscular arms.

"Has it been infiltrated? Traitors? Abolition sympathizers?"

Ari shakes his head. "I know this sounds impossible, but I believe the Shadow has made its way into–"

"That *is* impossible," the woman counters.

"I saw it as well," Dina swiftly adds in defense of Ari. "We left as soon as it–"

"I had to get Nera out." Ari holds out a hand in a way that I know means he's pleading his case. Still leaning on one knee, his other hand reaches back down to run a finger across my cheek as he pushes my hair behind my ear.

The woman's attention shifts back down to me at the mention of my name.

"Welcome back . . . *Vitamor*." She purrs into the warm air. And it is only now that the heat starts to fully settle. I am clothed for a frigid winter night, but this air is warm and muggy.

I stare up into her deep green eyes for a moment too long, my confusion evident in the cast of my features.

She meets my quizzical stare head on before a chuckle erupts.

"Listen, we've gone over this before." She looks me up and down as much as she can with my still slightly crouched position. "You're beautiful, but not really my type."

Suddenly the stifled air thins out and an ease settles amongst the group.

"Stop teasing her," Dina chides, giving a playful shove to the woman's arm.

"What?" she shrugs with a quizzical brow and then turns to Ari, "Now, you . . . You are definitely my type."

Ari rolls his eyes as the woman gives him a wink. I can't suppress the small burst of laughter which erupts. Dina immediately matches the sound. Maybe I will like this woman after all.

"This is Reeves, an old friend of ours," Ari explains as he reaches a hand forward, silently asking if I'm okay to stand. "She's the sovereign of Centra IV."

I let my eyes linger on the woman and say a silent thank you that the nausea has now subsided. For some reason, the idea of vomiting in front of her feels as though it would be extremely embarrassing.

"Hello," I tentatively start as I attempt to reach my full height, but add a quick, "Sir, Ma'am?" when it kicks in exactly what Ari called her.

That causes Reeves to burst out into another round of laughter.

"Does she call you *Sir* as well?" Reeves wiggles her eyebrows at Ari, who shakes his head as he tries to hide the beginnings of a smile. "Damn. You three are so serious," Reeves comments before turning back to me. "If I recall correctly, the first time we met, you punched me in the stomach. Will there be a repeat this time?"

My eyebrows peak.

"At least she's consistent," Ari chuckles from my side, and I instantly blush, the memory where I immediately punched him the first time we met flashing through my mind.

"I'm sorry?" I feign an apology, but from the looks splayed across each of the faces before me, none truly believe it, and after another playful scoff, Reeves gets straight to business.

"I am not a Sir or a Ma'am. That's an outdated tradition from Centra I where the sovereign likes to raise him or herself above their people. Here, we are all the same." The very way she speaks makes it known she's a born leader. Her cool but direct tone offers no room for question. She swallows thickly as she assesses our group. "I must say, while I expected your visit, I did not expect it to occur like this. Not this soon. It seems the Elders have sped up our mission."

"I hope the sudden appearance doesn't thwart any plans?" Dina replies.

Reeves waves her off, shaking her head. "You know you're always welcome here."

Then she turns back to Ari as all amusement leaves her features. "What of the Bend?"

"It still holds." His response is sure and confident.

The breath she was holding is released with a sigh of relief.

"When's the last time you–"

"Last night."

"Have you assessed it since fleeing?"

He shakes his head. "We came straight here."

Reeves addresses a man standing to her right, commanding him to send men out to survey the area.

"I trust my people," Ari argues.

"I know you do," Reeves agrees in an almost dismissive tone. "But one can never be certain when it comes to the penances or the Abolition. We need to make sure it's safe before moving further."

Though he nods in agreement, I can tell there's a war of thoughts going on within him.

She then looks me over once more. But this time there's only sincerity found in her gaze. "Your gifts . . . have they returned?"

While it seems that Reeves is, at a minimum, an ally, I still look to both Dina and Ari for confirmation before letting my secrets out. They each nod.

"They're coming back. I can use some of them, but not all."

"She needs training," Ari cuts in. "I'm sure they'll all come back to her once we start working." He takes a step closer and tentatively places a hand on my back; a welcome gesture of support, confidence. "I had hoped to give her time to adjust before throwing her back into the chaos."

Reeves nods as she further looks me over. At this point, she's been staring at me long enough to see damn near inside my soul. I square my shoulders as she continues on, and she tilts her head a little as she smirks.

"And it's true that you remember nothing from before?"

I swallow the thick saliva. "I remember nothing."

She groans as if, though the answer's not unexpected, she was still holding out hope it would be different.

"You have free reign of anything you might need. Stay as long as you like." Reeves motions to a woman standing off to the side, who I haven't even noticed, before zeroing in on Ari. "If what you saw was truly the Shadow . . . " She pauses, then closes her eyes in contemplation.

"I know." He answers her unspoken words. "I know."

Reeves nods in solidarity before turning away.

"We need to call a council," Dina cuts in before Reeves has even taken one step.

"That was done the second I was alerted to your arrival." She looks back and gives Dina a smirk. "I asked for everyone to arrive in four weeks. That should give you enough time to get her up to date and acclimated." She slowly turns back to survey our trio. "Outside of my direct advisors, I will not alert anyone else of your arrival. I'm having most of the palace emptied as we speak." She claps her hands in front and zeros in on me. "Take the time you need, but don't linger. We need to know what you can do. If the Shadow is truly outside the walls of the caverns, then our timeline for finding the stones has just accelerated . . . immensely."

I raise my eyebrows at her comments, and wonder exactly how she was able to complete that task so quickly when I've been here for less than five minutes.

"Okay." I nod as a wave of uncertainty washes over me.

"You should have full and free use of the east wing, and the staff will be discreet concerning your sudden appearance."

Dina gives Reeves a quick thank you as Ari nods his head in appreciation, and then, without warning, Reeves is leaning forward to place a quick kiss on my cheek. When she pulls back, there's a look of adoration etched across her face.

"You were greatly missed, Nera. I hope you feel at home here." My only response is a shy smile before she takes off down a corridor.

The east wing of the massive structure is nothing I could have imagined. While in no way as opulent as Koreed's palace . . . the size is far more impressive. And by the time we get to our rooms, I feel like I've walked as far as I did on that first day traipsing through the streets of Halabar.

"How big is this place?" I ask as I practically fall into the plush cushions of the couch. Large floor-to-ceiling windows cover one wall with sheer curtains flowing from the open breeze, and there are multiple doors leading to unknowns all around.

"Do you mean Syrsea or the palace?" Dina clarifies as she starts opening and closing every drawer and looking into every door she can find.

"Well, the palace, but I guess– is that– is Syrsea the–"

"Capital," Ari and Dina both clarify in unison, and I nod.

"Syrsea is about twice the size of Halabar." Ari comes to sit across from me. "Most people who reside in Centra IV reside closer to the capital city, but there are vast numbers who live further west and south. Settlements similar to Himerak's, but they're not fighting against their capital, they're united with it." He answers the questions that have been stacking up in my mind before I can even voice them. I then see Dina nod to the woman who followed us. I assume letting her know that we no longer require her assistance.

"What are her gifts?"

They both look at me quizzically.

"Reeves?" I explain.

Dina nods in understanding as Ari speaks. "Same as mine."

"Is that how she alerted the 'counsel' of my arrival before I was even able to fully stand up?" I can't hide the sudden snark in my voice. The idea that we're once again somewhere new that I have no recollection of is starting to tire me.

They both look at the other before testing glances my way.

Ari reaches out to place a comforting hand on my knee as he speaks. "She alerted who she needed to here in Centra IV. Her advisors will make sure the ones who need to know and don't reside here will know before the end of the week."

"We came completely empty handed." Dina cuts in as she continues to survey the room. "No clothes, no supplies, nothing." She leans back into the plush chair with closed eyes, and I just now notice the level of exhaustion in her features.

"Reeves has everything we need and then some." Ari throws a pillow directly at her face and snickers when it hits its intended target.

"Ugh!" Dina groans before giving him a death glare and then looking my way. "Do you see what I've had to put up with *alone* for the last three years! Men!" She then rolls her eyes in amusement. "I swear, they never age past year twelve!"

I can't help the laugh that erupts.

Ari shakes his head as he looks between the two of us.

"What about this palace?" I attempt to get us back on track. "How big is it?"

"Um . . . " Dina tilts her head back and forth, considering. "About how many would you say live inside the city walls, Ari? Two? Three thousand?" He nods in answer. "And the palace itself? Maybe a few hundred?"

Ari nods again.

I think back to my time in Halabar. "That seems like a lot."

"This is where the head of the Restoration is located," Ari says.

"But I thought that was back at your home? In Centra III? You said your father was the head of it."

"*Was* is the operative term there," he notes. I furrow my brows. "He died last year, and while that mantle should've gone to me, I know enough to admit that neither I nor Centra III have the resources required to scale the attacks and level the playing field with the Abolition. Reeves is in a much better location, and has armies and supplies to back her up without having to rely on things coming over from me hundreds of miles away."

"You just gave it to her?"

"I did."

There's a moment of quiet restlessness before I realize I have more questions that need to be answered. I waste no time.

"You think that was the shadow thing from the caverns that got into the cabin?"

"I don't know," he answers. "But I didn't want to find out while you were within its vicinity."

"Why come here? Because of the Restoration?"

He nods. "Yes. There are no Abolition sympathizers within these walls. It's the only other location outside of our home which I trust."

"How long will we stay?"

"As long as we need to."

I look down to my wrist, to the lines there. "As long as it takes me to relearn my gifts?"

Dina stands to walk toward a floor-to-ceiling window as Ari answers.

"Yes."

I stare at Dina's back for just a moment before I look at Ari. By the worry lines etched across his face, I can tell he knows what I'm going to ask before I even voice the words.

"I want you to finish telling me about the Ashclaw." My words are direct, and the moment they leave my lips, the air in the room shifts.

He stalls for just a moment before positioning himself closer to me. Dina turns and then moves so that she's now standing tall and ready. The tension rolling off both of them is palpable.

"You were ten. It was two weeks before your eleventh birthday. Your gifts had started becoming more . . . pronounced. And, from what you told me, it was becoming harder to hide what you were. There were whispers amongst the citizens of Halabar that Koreed was harboring a Celestra, and that wouldn't do. Not with half the palace working for the enemy." The words are spoken with such disdain, I can practically taste it.

Dina quickly picks up where Ari stops as she makes her way back to the chair beside me. "While some still believed in the old ways and the purpose of the Celestras, the Abolition had already deeply infiltrated, and hatred toward the Celestras was growing. The palace in Halabar was the first meeting location of the Abolition outside of their home base in Centra II."

My stomach sinks at the thought. I wonder how many I walked past daily who, if they'd been apprised of exactly who I was, would've outright killed me.

"You'd been taken out of the city for a few weeks, far away from prying eyes. It was supposed to be a time for you to learn and grow, and determine how to control your gifts. But that day, something went wrong. You were upset. You were out in a field with your mother and Mina and a few trusted guards as well."

My body immediately tenses at the mention of my mother.

"You said you entered some kind of trance. That it felt like something else had taken hold of you. Mina had been working with you on breaking through some of your gifts. You see . . . " he fumbles for the right words as he finally makes eye contact, "when our gifts first arise, they tend to take over. They are in control. It takes years of practice to establish dominance and lead the way. To learn not to let the gift lead you."

He pauses and I quickly nod my head in understanding.

"Your fire. It came first. That was one of the main reasons they moved you away from the palace. Then, that morning in the field, with no warning, you just . . . exploded. You erupted into fire and ash, and burned down everything in your path. The entire field burst into flames. There was so much chaos and smoke. They thought you were dead. Mina eventually found you, and the next thing you remembered was her carrying your burned body underground. You slept for the next week. It was just you and her hiding away as the forest burned. You don't remember much of those days. When you woke up again, you were back in Halabar, but . . . "

He instantly freezes and I know whatever comes next will rip me in two.

"What?" I plead as he looks at Dina who decides to add in the final piece to the puzzle.

"Five people went out to the field to help you train that day. Only two came back."

It takes but a moment to recognize what exactly she's implying, and I feel the tears fall down my cheeks as Ari speaks again.

"Nera." His hands find mine. "You were just a child. It wasn't your fault."

"I killed them?" My bottom lip begins to quiver.

"*You* didn't kill anyone. It was an accident," Dina clarifies.

"Three people died. Because of me. Three people died. Who were they?" *Please don't say it. Please don't say it.*

"There was an aide of yours. Her name was Kassi. A guard named Maxu. And . . . " Tears are streaming down her face as the final words stick within her throat.

"My mother."

XXXVI

I once read a quote.

The night is always darkest just before the dawn.

It was hanging on the wall at the entrance to the cancer center connected to the rehab center I stayed in during those first few weeks on Earth.

I always hated that quote.

I hated the mental picture that went along with it, too. It painted an idea that, just when you're in your darkest moment, just when the pain can't possibly get any worse, just when all hell has broken loose and you welcome the inevitable end, the light will appear, and that pain, heartache, nausea from all the chemo pumped into the body—or whatever it is the reader of the quote may be going through—will be over, with only good days ahead.

That is complete and total bullshit.

Night is not darkest just before dawn. It's darkest at midnight. Right in the middle. Right in the middle of the pain and suffering. It's not realistic that good things happen just because you need them to. Most of the time, those good things come from perseverance and struggle, they come from not giving up, from holding on. Those good things inch their way in, little by little, until one day, maybe months or years or decades later, the good finally outweighs the bad—the light starts to overcome the dark.

I thought I found that light along the way. I thought the dawn was within reach. Maybe it still is. Maybe it's just over the mountain of confusion and lies and horrors looming over me. Or maybe after that mountain there'll be another. And then another. And then another, moving into the rolling hills of trials ahead. I guess I won't really know I'm inching toward the light until I'm almost there. But I won't give up.

I may be in the pit of darkness, clawing my way up from the depths of hell, but one day I will walk into that light, and I will find my dawn.

There's a brief moment in which I almost collapse back within the darkness. I almost give in to the grief and the self hatred and everything else that makes me wish all of this would go away. The idea of climbing another mountain just to find out another is in my path almost overtakes me.

I can tell Ari sees it coming. The previous sadness that filled his face is now replaced by a steely view of determination.

"Nera?" he calls to me, begging me to come back to him. But in reality, I never really left. No matter the amount of grief circling within, there is something there now that wasn't before. Something strong and comforting and anchoring me to the here and now. When I look up, I find that it isn't a thing at all . . . It's a someone. It's him.

As I open my mouth, I find my voice is far too confident compared to the way I feel inside. "How do I make sure that never happens again?"

His shoulders drop as if those nine words have somehow taken away all the weight he was preparing to carry.

"We train. Right now. We teach you how to control your gifts once more, so that the next time something comes for you, you won't have to . . . burn down the world, and your soul with it, to defeat the horrors you face. So that next time, you will have the confidence to strike where it matters most without even breaking a sweat."

Training isn't exactly how I pictured it would be. The only reference I have of training is when Tarak, Jaxon, and Ranya took me into that valley. Then, it was swords, knives, and bows.

Now, it's just me.

And this time, my training ground isn't some desert or forest or somewhere with unknown enemies possibly lying in wait. It's a beautiful garden the size of an entire city block encased within the center of Reeves's palace.

"I don't understand. Shouldn't I figure out how to control the shield first?" I search for guidance even after Ari explains the plan.

"That's a defensive weapon. Yes, we'll make sure you know how to control it all, but right now I want to see how well you can attack. You already said you built that shield on multiple occasions since you returned, but the fire has been more elusive, so let's start there."

"I have no idea how the dome or the fire happened."

"What did those situations all have in common?" he muses, and I pause a moment to think.

Every single instance, whether it be the dome or the fire that surged from my fingertips, was a moment filled with terror. Once I piece it together, it's not a hard puzzle to solve.

"I was scared."

Ari nods. "Like I said, pretty much everything you can do is somehow tied to how you feel. When you're frightened and need to protect, the shield makes itself known. When you're frightened and need to attack, the fire erupts. But now, the challenge is taking control of that emotion and making it your own."

"You want me to learn how to not be frightened anymore?" My brow furrows in confusion. That seems like a rather unattainable goal.

He shakes his head. "Absolutely not. Fear is just the manifestation of the unknown . . . of what you can't control. And no matter how good you get, there will always be things outside of your control."

"So . . . I'll always be afraid?"

He smiles at my confusion. "You're a person with a heart, so yes, there are moments in which you'll be frightened. But that's not what I'm referring to. I'm speaking to what you choose to do in those moments. How you choose to react to them."

"I've never been able to control how I feel." I look at my hands, which at the moment feel normal.

He kicks at a few leaves scattered on the ground around us as he ponders my words. The silence stretches on, and for just a moment, I wonder if he, too, is losing faith in what I can do.

"I want you to turn these into nothing but dust."

My brows furrow in confusion. "I don't know how."

He tilts his head to the side as he assesses me. "There are a few ways we can go about this."

"And what would they be?"

"I can make you mad. I can hurt your feelings or make you angry." I swallow at the thought of how much heartbreak that would bring, even if I knew it was purposeful.

"I don't like that."

"Me either," he answers as he steps forward.

"What's the other option?"

"I need to get some kind of response out of you. I need to trigger your emotions so your gifts make themselves known in a way that we can teach you how to control them." He reaches forward as his fingertips graze the exposed skin of my waist and my entire body explodes in shivers at his touch.

"Is that so?" My voice is too tight as I try to not let him see the deep breaths I suck in as an attempt to calm myself down.

"Yes," he whispers. "Is this okay?" His thumb grazes my hip bone.

"Yes." My whispered answer is involuntary. There's no way I could turn him down. The path of goosebumps seems to intensify with every moment his touch lingers on my skin.

He brings his left hand up to my face as he pushes back a wayward curl that's flown free of the bun. "You have the most beautiful eyes." He stares at me intently.

"You're just saying that," I counter knowing full well he speaks the truth, and then gulp as the hand on my waist pulls me in closer to him. Every nerve ending on my body begins to spark.

"I'm not." His finger trails along my eyebrows, down my nose, and across my cheek bones before it barely grazes the outline of my lips. As if he's recommitting the sight to memory after so long apart.

As if on instinct, my tongue peeks out as I attempt to sooth the burn of his touch.

"Just being in your presence is both the most precious gift and the cruelest exercise in restraint," he purrs as the fingers grazing my hip bone slowly dip into the waist of my pants.

"You're holding back from me?" I question.

In answer, he gives me a throaty laugh so deep, I make a mental note of the sound, knowing I will replay it in my head a thousand times. "Very much so."

I raise my hands to find purchase on his strong biceps, hoping he can't tell the move is to help steady my now shaking body.

My fingertips begin to tingle.

"I don't want you to hold back."

My breathing becomes labored as he brings our bodies even closer together. Every inch of skin he touches burns with an intensity I have never known.

"What do you want?" he teases at my ear, and I damn near melt at the sensation of his breath against my skin. My entire body floods with heat. If I wasn't holding onto his arms right now, I know I would be laid out.

I close my eyes as the image of exactly what I want pieces itself together. "You."

Hot white light surges from my hands in a boom so loud the trees shake and the few guards stationed in the upper balcony of the expanse ready themselves as if an attack is imminent.

Startled, I jump back. The flowing waves of light soar upward with my movement, and unfortunately, slice a beautiful tree in half. The sight causes me to freeze, fearful any other sudden move will cause more destruction.

"Hold it," he commands as he inches a few feet out of my deadly reach.

"Ari?" I stare at the light in confusion and fear of the power I now yield.

"Hold it," he commands again. "Don't let it slip back in. Control it." He nods toward the ground at the undulating waves of light now weaving around the fallen tree.

His broad smile's on display, and he can't help but let free a small chuckle at what he made me do.

Recognition hits.

"That's not fair," I call out.

The shock of the sudden white firelight I've created settles, but then the lingering internal frustration hits. Every vein in my body pulses with need as I watch him stare at me with a knowing smirk plastered on his stupid, beautiful face.

"I never promised fairness." He chuckles, and I have the feeling he knows exactly how much restraint it's taking me not to rush toward him. The only thing keeping my feet planted in this spot is the idea that if I move without controlling this fire it could hurt him in the process.

"I hate you," I whisper through gritted teeth, not really meaning it at all.

He bursts out laughing even more. Then wipes his eyes as he says, "No, you don't."

"I do," I counter as I focus on the light before me.

He takes a step forward as he unbuttons his sleeves and skillfully rolls them upward, exposing just enough rugged muscle to cause a plethora of unsaid curses to spring to mind. When our eyes meet, his grin intensifies. He knows exactly what he's doing.

"You're a tease," I whisper-scream at him through gritted teeth as I force the light to stay as still as possible. He wiggles his eyebrows and I grunt in frustration.

"Oh, Nera . . . " He shakes his head. "Some things never change."

The light is heavy and it takes more restraint than I knew I possessed to keep it from lashing out at every object in view, but with each passing moment, the weight lessens.

"What do you want?" he asks again as he crosses his arms over his chest.

When I don't answer, he laughs a little more before running a hand through his long hair.

You have got to be kidding me. If he keeps this up, he might as well strip fully naked and put on a damn porn show for me.

"I asked you a question." He nods his head as he speaks. This time his tone is serious. "What do you want? Are you mad yet? Frustrated?" I groan in response. I'm most definitely frustrated. "Do you want to slice me in two like you did that tree?" He takes another step forward.

Ha! What do I want? What do I want? Ugh . . . it's definitely not slicing him like I did that tree. Maybe climbing him like one . . .

I shake my head as the mental image of that is promptly stored somewhere safe for me to pull from later. "Stop teasing me, and tell me how to make this stop."

"You like when I tease you," he counters, then thankfully takes pity on my newly shaking form.

"Concentrate. The light is a part of you. It's made from you. It only does what you command it to. Breathe. Just breathe, block everything else out and tell the light what to do."

I let his words wash over me and slow my breathing in hopes that my erratic heart will somehow calm. And then I think back to what I've always done.

What do I see? The strings of brilliant white light that flow from my hands, with sparks that fly off in every direction. Small wisps of flames cover the ground around us. It is brilliant and hideous all at once. The light moves in languid waves, as if waiting for a solid command. One I know only I can give.

What do I hear? It gives off no noise. The winding threads are deathly silent as they inch along the ground. Even the disturbed leaves seem to have been warned not to dare rustle in its path.

What do I feel? Power. It feels powerful and heavy. And I know I will have to work hard to learn how to properly wield this massive weight I've been given. But just the same, it feels freeing.

One finger tests the theory as it tentatively pulls in. I suck in an awed breath as the wave of light undulates at my command. When I move two fingers, the same result occurs. Within a moment, I have my entire right hand slowly twisting and turning as I watch the light shift through the garden. I try to avoid each of the plants, but unfortunately, a few are left a bit more than charred.

Then I do the same with my left, finding I have less control on my less dominant hand. *Maybe I should stick with the right for the time being.*

But I take a minute to concentrate on the left, hoping I can rein it in. It takes a moment . . . more than a moment, but as if a switch has suddenly flipped, the light flowing from both my palms coils back inside, and that heaviness that once encompassed my left hand disappears.

"Was that on purpose?" Ari asks and I jerk my head up at the noise, having forgotten he was standing here with me.

"Yes."

"Good." He smiles back at me before turning to smolder the small lingering flames scattered about. "This is built from you. No matter how erratic it seems, it will always do what you say."

I nod in agreement.

"Can it kill someone?" My eyes remain on the sight before me as I speak.

"It can. It's built from fire, after all. But it's more like an electrical current. One that runs through every living being here. Like the currents made from the heartstone of the trees."

I shift to meet his gaze. I'm the fifth centra. That's what they said. But a centra is a piece of land, and I am certainly not that.

"Am I made from the heartstone trees?" Even as I voice the question, it sounds silly and wrong.

I can just make out the shaking of his head in my periphery. "I think you have that backward. I think this world was made from you."

XXXVII

T he next two days are a repeat of the same.

After some more heated touches from Ari which do nothing but cause every nerve ending in my body to fire off, I'm able to produce the white light with complete ease. Each time requires less emotion to build for it to grow. And each time, it takes unbelievable restraint not to say *fuck the training* and crash my body into his.

Unfortunately, neither of us let it go that far, and he never lets those heated touches occur outside of training.

I spend most of the afternoon repeating a quick apology to Reeves concerning which plants I've incinerated, and by sunset on the second day she holds up a hand and rapidly admits with a hushed breath, "I have no idea which plants you're talking about. I couldn't care less if you demolish them all. I would probably sneeze less if you did anyway," before swiftly turning to an aide to ask for more wine.

Each night, after dinner in our rooms, Dina, Ari, and I take a walk down the white and golden stone pathways of the palace, passing by a plethora of people I don't know, who stare at the curious woman who has entered their home. It isn't lost on me that, for the third time in less than three months, I'm living somewhere new with people who just don't understand me. But for the first time, it feels mostly right. It feels more natural and normal than before. And that might be the most terrifying aspect of it all.

Living on Earth was survival in the sense that, at every turn, my mind was fighting me for something I couldn't quite grasp. Then in the settlement with Tarak, and even in the moments where I felt that connection stirring deep within me, I always knew I wasn't one of them. I wasn't necessarily an enemy—although

Ranya did a very good job at making me feel that way more often than not. But with them, I was so close to *me*, but yet not quite there.

Waking up in Koreed's palace for a second time felt like taking three massive steps backward. It was too ornate and all wrong. Everything from the food to the air to the clothes had me drawing further inside and away from what they wanted me to be. Only Mina was able to pull me toward home. But even that didn't last.

There are moments over the two days in which sitting with Ari and Dina feels as natural as breathing. They bicker, we bicker, they provide endless answers to all my mundane questions, and laugh when I try to explain some of the chaos of Earth.

It's only when I'm sitting alone in bed at night that all the doubts and fears seem to make themselves known. I run through every small piece of information about the penances and the people. I try to commit their customs and their way of life to memory, but the sneaky notion that I still don't fully belong never truly leaves me.

Maybe it's too hard to see the good in things when you've been trained for so long to always be wary of what evil is lurking within the shadows. Before, I thought of that notion as being more metaphorical in nature. Now I know there literally are shadows out to get me.

Which is the thought running through my mind on our second night here when Dina walks into my room with two glasses of wine and a plate full of snacks.

"Are you okay?" she asks as her flowy white gown seems to float across the floor.

My mouth opens as I stumble for the correct response. She shakes her head before I find one.

"That was a dumb question," she admits, and we both laugh.

"It's just a lot to take in. Every moment feels as if I'm learning a thousand different things about this world and myself, and yet I still feel completely on the outside of it. As if I'm watching all this happen from the sidelines."

She slides into the bed beside me. "What can I do to make it easier?"

"Switch places with me." The phrase is out before I even think through the words.

She laughs a little as she shakes her head and swallows down her most recent bite. "You don't want my life, I assure you."

"Would you tell me?" I ask, only to find a quizzical look in return. "About you. Will you tell me about you? We are best friends after all."

Her smile grows as she pats my hand. "That we are." She swallows, then braces herself, and an inkling of regret at the question settles in my stomach.

"My story isn't pretty."

"You don't have to tell me," I amend my previous request when I see the pain hidden in her eyes.

"I want to," she counters.

"Are you sure?"

She quickly nods, pops another pastry in her mouth, lies back against the pillows, and closes her eyes.

"I remember that morning like it was yesterday." She gives off a subtle smile and I wonder where this story is beginning. "We were getting low on meat. The settlement wasn't yet built up to what Ari says it has now become. And as my father was one of the most skilled hunters, it tended to be him and his men who brought back the bulk of our food. That day, I went in their place." That subtle smile inches upward as the memory grows. "Tarak was mad. He was always so mad and jealous of others—jealous of me. Due to being a Celestra . . . and a secret, he was under such guard and surveillance, and was never allowed to come. He hated me for it. Told me every time I got to go and he didn't."

"He hates that he said that to you," I cut in, and her eyes pop open. "He told me a little bit of what he remembers. He remembers telling you he hated you the last morning he saw you, and he completely regrets it."

Dina nods in acceptance, and I still can't figure out exactly what she thinks of her now grown-up sibling. "He was always jealous, but I can't say I blame him. He never got to grow up in what I would call normal circumstances. None of us really did." That smile quickly turns down. Then she closes her eyes and continues on. "We had one of the largest kills we had ever gotten. Two full-grown bricken and three brelick. We couldn't even carry it all back. I remember my father trying to figure out what to take first." She turns over to face me. "You have to understand, we barely had anything. There was just enough food to go around, the gardens hadn't even been fully established then. Leaving a fresh kill in the wild to retrieve later was the same as gifting it over to whatever animal was closest. We couldn't afford to lose the meat."

"What happened?"

"He packed up all the kills on the sykkel where I would have sat and perched me high in a tree. Gave me a knife for an emergency, a flask of water, and told me to be silent and still until he returned. I knew he couldn't be gone long. It was just over an hour's trek back home, so I guessed at the longest it would take would be two to three hours. But five hours later, he wasn't yet back. I was worried."

"He left you alone in the woods? You were just a child." My astonishment is apparent.

"A child of the settlement," she adds. The words are heavy. "And at that point the Abolition had no idea about Tarak. They believed him to be a dead baby and me to be the rumored Celestra child."

My fingers intertwine with hers.

"I don't even remember how long I walked. It had to have been at least an hour when they found me—Abolition sympathizers. Of course, they were looking for the settlement. And I couldn't lead them back to where everyone was. So when I realized I was being tracked, I took off in the opposite direction of home and lured them away."

"You saved your people. You saved your family." The words catch in my throat.

"Maybe." She closes her eyes and her face tightens. "I don't remember everything that happened next. They caught me. I tried to use the knife, but it was no use. I was ten and they were grown, trained men. You should have seen those soldiers' faces once they realized who I was. It was like they had found an oasis in the desert." Her chest rises and falls in effort. "They staged my bloodied clothes in that den. Made it look like I died." The words are smooth and direct as if she had told this a million times already. "But then they didn't find the mark."

Her shoulders rise and fall with the weight of the memory.

"I spent a year chained to a wall in an underground bunker in Centra II." My heart rips at the confession. "The Abolition tried to beat the information out of me, but I didn't break." The rims of her eyes shine in the lanterns hanging above. "They tried so hard but I never backed down." There's so much pride in her voice at her strength. She slowly sits and lifts the hem of her shirt, unveiling a patchwork of scars marring her back. "Their preference was the whip. It made a horrendous sound as it soared through the air. But I didn't scream loud enough for their liking."

She replaces her shirt and then turns to face me as she pulls up her long sleeves. A mangled mess of burn marks and engravings cover her arms. There are so many slashes, I can barely make out the freckles hiding underneath. I stare a moment before I realize those slashes aren't random lines, but form letters and words . . . names.

"What . . . "

"They're the names of my people. My family. Everyone they knew about who had defected from Halabar and lived in the settlement. Every time I refused to speak, they carved in another name, stating they would be the next kill. My next kill. I killed them because I wouldn't talk. And every day I had to look down and read the names of those I knew I would most likely never see again."

My eyes fill with unshed tears and my fingers graze her scarred skin.

"Dina." A sob rips out. "I'm so sorry." There are no other comforting words I know to say. She gives me a soft smile.

"I'm not. I wouldn't be where I am had it not happened."

"You were so young. So brave. Dina, you were so brave, I can't even imagine."

"Ari's father and older brother rescued me just before the carvings reached my shoulders." She pulls the neck of her shirt to the side so I can see the pebbled marks. "They rescued over a hundred of us. The Abolition has taken so many innocent lives, and many of us were knocking on death's door. Had they come any later, I don't know if I would have made it." She replaces her long sleeves and pulls the blanket up over us. "It took over six months to heal my skin and set the broken bones. And then another six months before I actually believed I was safe. I didn't speak a word the entire time. I was silent for that entire year."

The thought haunts me. If I have learned anything over these last few days with her, it is that, while I may cause fire to erupt, she burns with it from the inside. She lights up a room with her laughs and her stories without even trying. My mind can't reconcile the woman I now know with the child she once was.

She clears her throat.

"But it was all worth it. Because now I know the truth and I'm on the right side of history. Now, I'm working as a spy for the Restoration." She reaches over to wipe away a tear rolling down my cheek.

My eyes peak in interest. "A spy?"

"The best spy," she corrects me, and smiles with pride.

I laugh a little at her change in demeanor, wanting nothing more than to hear about her amazing adventures after enduring all that torture. "How did you come to meet Ari and become a spy?"

She finally laughs a little, as if relieved to be moving on to the lighter stuff. "I didn't plan it that way. The Restoration had a healer who helped me. I didn't have many friends besides him. He was older, and kind, and he had a son, Cerus, who was in training to become a spy. I trained alongside him. At first, it was just to get me out in the open. I was so depressed and lonely. But then, over the next two years, I started to open up. I poured everything I had into training, and let's just say it worked out really, really well." She gives me a lavish grin. "By the time I turned sixteen, I was one of the most highly-trained members. And I was small enough to sneak in and out of places with ease. I was supposed to travel back to the settlement more than once. I wanted to sneak my family out. But each time I was set to go, there was some form of attack or ambush. More Celestras were being taken, and finally I realized that I could do ten times more good here on the ground, fighting for the Restoration, than hiding in the trees."

"Did you know Himerak's truth? Did you know he was bad?"

"Himerak isn't bad," she quickly counters. "He's just misguided. And now that you've given me the entire picture," she nudges my shoulder with hers, "with Micel being a Celestra," she clarifies, "I think I understand his motives better."

At some point on day three, after two hours of trying to use my other gifts with no luck, Ari notices the frustration lingering in my eyes.

"That's it for now," he commands, pulling me out of my most recent blunder with ease.

"It's not even time for lunch. Why are we stopping?"

Ari practically falls back onto the iron bench beside me. "You're not okay."

I furrow my brow. "I'm fine."

"What's bothering you? Is it the training? Are we spending too much time on this? Do you want to move to something else? Do you want a break?"

I shake my head in answer.

His shoulders sag as he carefully pieces through his next words.

"The meeting's just over three weeks from now."

"I know." I've been counting down each morning since we first arrived.

"We haven't talked much about it. Do you have any questions?"

"I always have questions." I plop down beside him, leaving just a few inches between us and hoping it's enough to keep my body from incinerating from the inside out at the nearness.

He laughs and then reaches out to intertwine our fingers.

So much for the needed space . . .

"There will be various Celestras and other high-ranking members of the Restoration in attendance. They've all been apprised of the conditions of your return, and while most will be sympathetic to what happened, there are a few who will expect more from you than you can be reasonably expected to give at this point."

Our eyes meet as I process the words.

"They're going to be tough with you. When you left, you were the one everyone looked to for advice. You held us together—it's why so many disbanded after your disappearance. But I want you to know that I have your back. Dina, while she has no abilities, I'm sure would also find a way to shred anyone who causes you trouble." I burst out laughing at the picture that forms in my mind. "And, of course, Reeves and her people are behind you."

"I thought you said these people coming to the meeting are our allies. You're making them sound more and more like the enemy."

"They're not the enemy. But from their point of view, you just spent the last three years with no abilities, and then the last two months with the literal enemy. They won't be so freely forgiving."

I balk. "I had no knowledge of any of that." The anger begins to rise. But this time, the tingling on my fingertips never comes. I immediately command it to stop, and as it should, it follows my lead.

"I know. They know it as well. But that doesn't mean they will be immediately open to you."

I turn away, not wanting to follow this conversation further; not ready to face the reality that I will once again have to convince others of my worth.

"I checked on Tarak," He confesses.

My gaze shoots back to his.

"What?"

"Last night, after you went to bed. I shifted to Centra I."

"Why?" I don't voice what I really want to ask. I don't question if Tarak is okay, or how Micel or Jaxon or anyone else is doing. I don't have to.

"Riann and Alesia are still nowhere to be found. My best guess is they've returned to Centra II. The main crew you were with has traveled back to one of the safe houses strung along the edges of the territory where Himerak and the rest of the survivors are safely hidden."

"Why are you telling me this?"

"Tarak is headed back to the Caverns . . . alone. He's going to complete his Committence within the next week when the moons align."

"He's going to be their sovereign."

"Yes," he confirms before finally looking at me. "You know what that means?"

I shake my head in answer.

"My guess is that he will initiate a war with Halabar. It will officially be his rightful place. He'll command the palace—what's left of it—and–"

"What about my father?" I quickly cut him off.

Ari shrugs. "Your father was never the rightful sovereign. Normally, the transition is quite uneventful. But I don't think that will happen this time."

"Because of those within the palace who are actually members of the Abolition?"

"Exactly," Ari agrees. "They will become Tarak's enemy. Which means he will become our ally."

I suck in a breath of fear at the idea of coming face-to-face with him again.

"We will, over the next few weeks after he takes charge, reach out to ascertain if he and his people in the settlement will join our cause. He is not Himerak, and I'm hopeful that once things change hands, we may be able to form an alliance. If he doesn't take us up on the offer, then there will be no question . . . he and all of his people will become our enemies."

My heart beats a fevered song in my chest. The words, questions I need to ask, are lodged within my throat. All that comes out is a pitiful, "Why?"

"I don't want this to turn into something it's not. I have no qualms with him in the same way that I don't with Riann when it comes to you. I know you. I know that at that time when you were within the safety of the settlement, Tarak provided a safe haven for you, and I thank him for giving you that security when you needed it." He swallows hard. "But I am not an idiot. I know there was something between you two."

"Ari–"

"I am not going to turn this into a war between him and I. And even though you and I are bonded, I know that isn't a promise. It may very well turn into a curse. I know that, at any moment, you could choose to move on in this life and not take me with you, and I will accept that." He gulps as if the mere thought is excruciating. "But please know that, at some point, we will need Tarak on our side. If we want to take the Abolition down once and for all, then we need him and his crew. We need to gain their trust. We need them as an ally."

"It wasn't real," I burst out with the phrase I've been avoiding for days, not wanting a reminder that it may actually be true. Even though I know full well that it is.

"What wasn't real?" Confusion laces each word.

"He and I . . . " I pause, not sure exactly what to say or how to phrase it. The words catch in my throat as I try to hold back the warring emotions. "He has the gift of truth telling, but he can also manipulate emotions."

Ari nods as I speak, already well aware of Tarak's gifts.

"When I first arrived back on Ithesin, my gifts were–" I swallow thickly, "they hadn't made themselves known yet and . . . " I pause again, not sure how exactly to explain this in a way Ari will understand, while also not sounding like a blubbering mess.

"Nera?" He twists his body off the bench so that he's leaning down in front of me. One hand caresses my knee as the other cups my cheek.

"He used that ability on me," I confess, blinking back tears. "When I was scared or unsure of what was going on, he used his gift to calm me, and in turn cause me to trust him. He caused me to fall for him outside of my own control."

Rage blazes in Ari's gaze.

"You weren't aware of what he was doing?"

"No." My head shakes with the answer.

Ari stands and begins pacing the few feet between us.

"How often did he do that to you?"

"A lot." I shrug, and Ari crosses his arms as if trying to hold back all the anger he so desperately wants to unleash upon the world. "From what I can tell, it was an almost daily occurrence." He runs a hand through his hair, knuckles whitening with tension. "I have spent some time—more recently, and especially since I've been away from him—thinking about what I felt when I was with him. It doesn't make sense. I have never, at least from what I can recall, been one to so easily fall for someone."

Ari laughs a little at that. "No, you aren't. You most definitely made me work for it." He gives me a sad smile I quickly mirror.

"But it wasn't just him. I was so calm and not myself. I didn't even have any dreams when I was with him. Before him, I used to dream every night. Every single night, it was like a movie in my head. Dreams and nightmares over and over again. But when I was with him it was different. It was as if there was nothing, nothing but him and just feeling calm. I didn't even question the things I should have, I just went along with everything. I now know that it was because of what he was doing to me. Those weeks within the settlement, I wasn't really myself."

"I'm so sorry, Nera." Ari kneels down directly in front of me and once again grasps my hand in his. The fire that ignites within his touch is urgent and true. "He should never have done that."

"I'm sorry." I'm not sure exactly what it is that I'm apologizing for, but at the moment it's the only appropriate response I can form. "I'm so sorry." The tears burst free and the reality of exactly what I need to confess comes forward. "I didn't know about you or us, and I–"

"Nera, it's okay. I–"

"No!" I quickly cut him off. "It's not okay. I am bonded to you and I slept with him." I pull my hand back to cover my face. "And not only him. I slept with so many people on Earth." My heart caves in on itself as I squeeze my eyes shut, desperate not to see the pain I know is rushing through Ari. "I was so desperate, and I just wanted to feel something and I'm sorry. I'm sorry. I'm so so–"

"I don't care." He slowly removes my hands from my face and wipes away the trail of tears.

"What?" My voice cracks on the word as my chest heaves with the effort to breathe through the sobs.

"Nera," he whispers my name as our foreheads touch. "You did nothing wrong."

"You were waiting for me and I betrayed you."

"Stop. You didn't know."

"They didn't mean anything. I promise not a single one meant a damn thing to me," I plead.

"I know. I know." He holds my face.

"And I trusted *him*." I feel the heat of hatred rise once more. This time I don't smother it out. "*He* made me trust him." Orange sparks fly off from my palms.

I feel the nod of Ari's head against me as he places my hands in his. "He shouldn't have done that."

"I hate him," I admit.

"I know."

"He's Dina's brother, and I hate him." The weight of my predicament sits heavy in my stomach. "How does that work? My supposed best friend is the sister of someone I hate. That's not fair."

"There are rules to war," he cuts in as if he can see through to my tortured thoughts. "Don't worry about Dina. She knows that the Tarak we will meet with is most likely not the Tarak she left behind so many years ago. She has accepted that, in the end, they may be on opposite sides of this war. The only thing that matters is that when it's all over, we are on the right side."

"Ari–"

"But now, knowing what he did to you. I don't know . . . " His eyes close as he considers what to say next. When he opens them once more, they are clear. His expression is serious as he starts, "There are rules that we have to abide by as Celestras. Rules he is well aware of." He stares at me urgently. "You were not attacking. You were not a threat. *You were a victim*. What he did is punishable by death."

"Please don't." The words leave my mouth before I even process what they mean. My head vehemently shakes from side to side. "Not everyone there is bad. They are just doing what they have been taught."

He stands and quickly starts to pace once more. "He drugged you. It may not have been with a concoction he brewed, but it is exactly the same in the end. He altered your emotional capacity without your consent." Rage builds with each word.

I make it to him just before he turns back. I reach out to take his hand in mine, hoping to interrupt his line of thinking. While a part of me wants nothing more than to see Tarak feel the same pain that now runs through me, I know he was only doing what he has been taught. And more than anything, I know those who surround him are not evil and don't deserve the death Ari would prescribe.

"Let me help. Let me talk with them. Can we meet up with them? They may listen to me. I might be able to convince them to fight with us, even if Tarak refuses."

"I don't get to make that decision."

"Then who does?"

His fingers flex around my own. "A few years ago, the answer would have been you. That's one of the reasons for the meeting of the Restoration Council. We have to vote on whether or not to reinstate you to your rightful position."

"And what position is that?"

"Leader of the Restoration."

I shake my head in astonishment. "But Reeves already has that title."

"She does. But in truth, if history had traveled a different path, then I would have given it to you, not her. You are the rightful heir."

"I'm not an heir to anything."

"You are the heir to everything."

XXXVIII

By afternoon on day three, and with a full belly from lunch with Dina, I'm back in the gardens with Ari.

"What's brought this on?" He points to my smile.

"Dina just told me some stories about her and I. Apparently we caused a lot of trouble." I raise my eyebrows and he laughs.

"Yes you did." He crosses his arms and my body grows hot at the sight of bare skin.

I clear my throat. "So what's on the schedule for this afternoon? Shielding? Shifting? Turning water into wine?" I tease.

He cocks his head to the side in confusion before his smirk settles into place. "That would be quite useful. But no. Unfortunately, that is not a skill you possess." He quirks an eyebrow in my direction. "Unless you've learned a few new tricks I don't know about?"

I smile, shaking my head. "No. That was just a stupid Earth joke." I explain.

"Ah." He nods. "Well, actually . . ." He pauses as he looks me over. "I did want to try something else. I want to see if you can see my past."

The idea causes my entire body to freeze as knowledge of what he's saying settles. "Not the memory kind, but the Himerak kind . . . right?"

He nods. "You've never done that before, but I figure we could try it."

I take a deep breath before reaching out my hand to his. "Okay. What should I do? Just grab your hand and think about . . . you?"

His laughter surges through the expanse of the open garden. "I like your tenacity." He reaches to clasp my hand before he yanks forward and I all but fall into him. The fingers of my free hand grasp his arm to steady me as our bodies melt together.

When I look up, I find his golden stare fixed on me. There's a moment of quiet appreciation, both of us standing still, transfixed on the other.

"Hi," I state and he smiles.

"Hi."

"Were you trying to make me fall?" I question, still refusing to move my body off of his.

"That depends on your context?" he counters.

"Did you mean to make me fall onto you?"

He laughs. "Onto? No." He smirks. "Not yet at least." My legs tense in anticipation. "Fall for . . . most definitely." He corrects my wording and I have to lower my face to hide the blush that creeps upward.

"You are a horrible flirt," I whisper as I stare at our feet, willing the heat in my cheeks to dissipate.

He wraps his free arms around my waist. "Change of plans."

I jolt my head upward, this time finding heat in his gaze.

"Can I touch you here?" His fingers stroke the exposed skin of my waist.

My answer is a quick and definite smile, and then his arm is wrapping tightly around me.

"We used to do this alot." His eyes seem to see right through to my soul.

"Stand still in the middle of a garden with various guards looming overhead?" I tease, but my voice is too high and I can't quite focus with the way his fingers flex against the bit of exposed skin at my side.

He laughs.

"Dance. We used to dance."

"There isn't any music," I immediately counter. My mouth runs dry in anticipation.

"There is in my head." He starts to hum a beautiful melody that rings true as he pulls my body flush with his. My skin begins to sing as a tingling runs from my head to my toes. Wisps of white light spark from my fingertips all the way up to my shoulders, and no matter how much I will them to simmer, they don't do as I command. Small burn marks begin to pepper the ground.

I tense as I try to move us out of the way of the nearby foliage, not wanting to have to give Reeves another apology.

"It's okay," he whispers as he stops us, and then runs his fingers along the exposed skin on my arm. I gasp in awe as the white sparks make a path in his wake, and soon my arm is covered in swirling designs of his making. I am my very own firelight.

"What is–"

"I don't know," he answers before I can even ask. "But sometimes, when you're really, really happy." His eyes shift from my glowing arm to my awestruck expression. "The sparks expand and cover your skin."

"I'm happy?" I ask, not knowing who exactly is supposed to answer as his hand makes light movements over my right shoulder.

"Are you?"

"I don't know." I swallow as the sparks explode from my neck and I feel light tingles caress my cheeks. "Maybe?" I close my eyes as the comforting waves roll across my skin.

His hand follows the path, and soon he's tracing a maze of light across my neck and down my left arm. The effort to control the feelings I know can only be for him almost overtakes me. In one moment, I want to lean in further, and in the next, I want to pull away.

My gaze follows him where it can, and when he reaches the mark on my left wrist, he pauses before slowly tracing the symbol. Each new stroke of his finger soothes me, and soon it isn't just a subtle discoloration I once thought to be a birthmark, but instead, I find a glowing map of lines and truths.

"Wow." I smile as I shift my eyes from my arm to him.

He pauses all movement as he looks me over, and though I can't tell exactly what he sees, from the glow that's shining against him, I would bet my entire form appears lit from within.

His chest expands with a deep breath and then his smile meets mine.

"Now we can dance," he whispers as he places his hand at my waist and pulls me in.

I slip my hand back onto his shoulder, my thumb just barely grazing the skin of his neck. "But I'm wearing pants."

He chuckles at my awkward admission as he looks down. "I don't care," he whispers with a smile, and then he's moving, first his left foot and then his right. I look down, trying to match his rhythm and movements, but I know none of the steps. Every few seconds, my foot lands on his in an awkward stumble. He doesn't seem to mind or care. But as he tightens his hold, my palms start to sweat.

When I look up, I find his eyes trained on me. A thousand unsaid words lie between us. My heart rate spikes and my breathing quickens. The history we share tugs a little harder, and my body—my heart—yearns for more. Those lingering sparks intensify, flying off with every turn we take to an unheard melody, and the heat that hovered just out of reach settles deep within my core.

"Ari," I whisper his name.

Either on instinct or pure carnal desire, he catches the sound as he leans down to graze his lips across mine. The heat flares to life within my chest as fire erupts in every direction. A thousand sparks dance through the air, and I jolt back when the ground at our feet becomes a mess of smoldering embers.

Clouded images of raging fires and death spring forth in my mind. The last time

I created a true fire, I damn near burned down the settlement. What will keep me from doing that here as well?

He shifts from one spot to the next, stomping out one flame and then another. There's only a moment to think before he stills in front of me. His hand reaches out, but stills the moment he catches my gaze.

"Are you okay?"

I silently nod as a thousand competing answers run through my mind.

"It's okay," he appeases. "That was too much. I understand." His confession is so wrong, and yet I still can't seem to make the small space between us disappear in order to assure him I want nothing more than his hands on me.

"It wasn't," I counter just as he starts to draw back, but I reach out to stop his movement and slowly let my fingers graze across his palm. "It's just–" I swallow, willing the right words to come. "It's just that . . . I'm scared." The truth comes bursting out of me.

"Can I tell you a secret?" His fingers interlock with mine as he tentatively takes a step forward and disintegrates that empty space. "I am too."

I can't tell if the noise that erupts out of me is more of a cry or a laugh. "I don't know if that's reassuring or not." I smile a little at his admission, and he mirrors the action. Then, just as the thought settles, my expression falls. "I don't want to be afraid. I want to be strong, and I want to be . . . I want to be who I used to be."

"You don't have to be her," he says with so much conviction, I almost believe it.

"*She* is who you fell in love with."

He pales at my words, as if that small confession has opened up an entirely new realm of possibilities. His hand reaches upward and his thumb caresses my cheek before it catches the lone tear I didn't even know was there.

"I fell in love with *you*. Yesterday. Today. Tomorrow. It will always be *you*."

Tears spring forth and I cover my mouth as I try to hold back all the emotions that threaten to erupt. He pulls me into his chest and his arms wrap tightly around my back.

There is no concept of time when I am with him. We could stand, my face buried in his soft training leathers, for five minutes or five years, and I would never tire of the feeling.

"What about a memory? It's been a few days, would you like to see another?"

Unable to speak, I quickly nod and feel his chuckle as he puts his hands on my shoulders to separate us.

He licks his lips and looks to the sky, as if considering exactly what it is he wants to show me. The hard lines of his face, built from the weight I know he carries, soften as he lets out a soft chuckle.

"Yeah. I have just the one."

Ari

"*I thought we were a team.*" *Aggravation seeps from my lips as I watch her standing over Drunia, diligently taking in all it has to offer. The dimly lit area and makeshift table formed from falling cavern rocks barely allow either of us proper sight or work space. And the heat billowing up from the underground does nothing but further kindle the rage which burns each time I meet with this woman. Yet, the longer we spend together, I feel that rage slowly turning into something else altogether.*

We are mere feet apart, and the battling forces within me threaten to rip my entire body to shreds. My skin is itching to touch her, and yet something inside is urging me to run away.

She snickers as she tilts her head slightly to the side and those piercing cerulean eyes turn to slits, observing me. "A team . . . and what gave you that impression?" Her words are sharp, full of contempt.

I barely hold in all the rage I desperately want to throw her way. "For starters, the fact that, after I helped you that night when you were injured, you stayed. You. Stayed." I throw the words at her. "You spent the next three hours with me poring over everything . . . meeting locations, names, Celestras." I fist my hair in frustration. "And then we spent even more time dissecting their gifts. You stayed."

"And?" Her arms cross over her chest in boredom.

"You came back. Every week, you came back."

She shrugs as if that small little fact means absolutely nothing.

I throw my hands up in the air in both exasperation and emphasis. "That makes us a team. We are working together."

She rolls her eyes and my frustration grows. "And what did you get from those conversations?"

My brows furrow in confusion. "What?"

Her eyes bore deep holes into me as she slowly repeats herself. "What new information did you glean from those conversations? All those days we met up, what did you get from it?"

Her question gives me pause. I run through the last few encounters with her, piecing together each moment. She never once gave me a hint of knowledge I didn't already possess. She didn't even confirm the things I knew she knew to be true. It was an entirely one-sided effort. I gave. She took.

She nods as the realization hits me, then turns to grab her pack, effortlessly throwing it over her shoulder as she speaks. "Exactly. We are not a team. You had information, I extracted it. Now we are done."

"No, we are not!" Her small wrist feels almost fragile in my grip.

"Don't touch me," Nera seethes as she yanks out of my reach and takes another step away.

I don't let her get far, quickly shifting to stand directly in front of her again. "I just spent the last three weeks teaching you everything I know. I have poured out every secret I spent a lifetime learning and earning with the cost of more death and pain than you have ever seen, and you're just going to up and go off all alone? You would use me like that?" I'm not able to steady the trembling in the words.

"I don't even know you." She looks me up and down in utter disgust. "So, yes, I am using you like that. This is bigger than you or me." She teeters from side to side as if weighing her next words carefully. "It's not my fault you're gullible enough to share everything you know with the enemy."

"I. Am. Not. Your. Enemy," I shout so loudly I swear the cavern wall will come crashing down around us.

She cocks her head to the side as she gives me the most abhorrent smirk.

"I say otherwise." Her words are cold, calculated. "I don't work with members of the Abolition."

"Elders, Nera. I'm not with them." I pace the small space between us before turning to find her stare planted firmly on me. "And you know that," I whisper. "If you truly thought I was one of them you would have already killed me. So what is it? Why not kill me?" She doesn't answer. "You know damn well I only infiltrated the lower ranks to get the information I needed."

"And what if you're infiltrating a friendship with me right now?" I swear she stands just a tad taller as her own anger grows. "What if you're trying to trick me into working with you, and then you turn on me at the last moment?"

I could scream with the amount of frustration this woman evokes. "If you would train with me and develop your abilities more thoroughly, you would know that what I'm telling you is the truth."

She throws her hands in the air, matching my earlier movements. Exasperation rolls off of her in waves. "I don't have the ability of truth telling. I can shift. I can shield. And the only reason you even know about those two is because you tricked me into showing you!"

I walk a little closer, and for the first time in days, her skin touches mine as she reaches forward and pushes against my chest. I don't move.

She grunts in frustration at my strength and turns, separating us by mere feet. When she turns back, I find building anger rising in her stare.

"*My gifts are nothing but a nuisance.*" Hatred seeps from her lips. *This isn't the first time she has insinuated her disgust with her birthright, and I doubt it will be her last.*

"*You sound like one of* them.*" I throw the words out, if only to see how she'll respond.*

"*Don't you ever say that! I am not one of them!*" *This time it's her feet that step closer to mine as her anger grows.* "*I am fighting against them!*" *A spark ignites in her palm, and I draw in a ragged breath at the sight I've been trying to pull from her for days now. She doesn't even notice.* "*I have been for–*"

"*Don't stop now.*" *I lean in just enough to invade her space, hoping to draw out her bluff and make her see reason once and for all.*

Another spark erupts at our closeness, then fizzles out as it splashes into a pool of lingering water at our right. That she notices, and immediately clasps her hands into fists. Her eyes close as she stalls and quickly regroups. When she opens them again, I find cool indifference circling within.

Her voice quiets as she looks from me to the ground. "*I can only shift and create that dome. I can't do anything else,*" *she falsely admits, but even I know it's a lie.*

"*Can't or won't?*"

Finally, my words give her pause and her gaze shoots back to mine. I know there's a story she's holding too closely within. But I also know we're nowhere near close enough to a friendship where she'll let that secret out without some pushing on my part.

"*We both know you can do so much more than that. You're just scared.*"

She visibly recoils as if my words have physically pierced her soul. "*I am* not *scared.*"

"*Yes, you are.*" *I take a step closer.* "*You can put on a tough act. You can pretend that you're out here all alone because you're better than everyone else and you think you can fix this dying world all on your own.*" *The gap between us slowly closes.* "*But you want to know what I think the truth is?*" *Her lips start to tremble.* "*You are scared of what you can do. You are scared of the gifts you've been given and what they mean.*"

"*You have no idea what you're saying,*" *she whispers as she blinks away the tears beginning to gather.*

I don't let her interruption stop me. I step forward once more, allowing just inches between us. Her breath mingles with mine.

"*You are scared to accept what fate has to offer you. You are scared that fully becoming one of us*"—*I lift up my wrist to show the mark*— "*means becoming something wretched and evil.*"

She grew up in Halabar, and I've been inside their ranks long enough to know that hate she's been taught about our kind. About Celestras. At this point, I know her mark is hidden from most, with only a few of the higher-ranking elders and advisors aware. I didn't even know about it during my time spent undercover.

"You have lived inside a world that has taught you to hate yourself for who you were born to be. But that mark"—I twist her wrist upward, pushing back the fabric of her sleeve with the movement—"is a gift. You just have to know how to use it."

"Stop." She looks away as she yanks back her hand, and I know I've hit the root.

My voice calms. "You won't." Her gaze shifts to mine. "You could never do what they're doing. I have faith in you. You just need to have faith in yourself."

She steels her face, wiping away all emotion as if there was never any there to begin with. She squares her shoulders and takes a deep breath.

When she finally speaks, my heart all but shatters.

"Leave me alone. If I find out that you have followed me again, I won't hesitate to kill you."

"You don't want to do this," I plead as she walks away. She only makes it a few feet before I shift and wind up straight behind her once more.

"Is that a threat?" She quickly turns, expecting me to be yards away. Her eyes widen in shock when she realizes how close we are.

"No. It's a warning." I shift out of the Caverns before she can speak another word.

"Why was I so mean to you?" are the first words out of my mouth once the vision clears.

"You had just found out about Riann. You weren't looking to trust anyone or anything yet."

"I shouldn't have acted that way though."

Ari laughs. "Nera." He closes his eyes as he shakes his head. "Your feisty demeanor is one of the reasons I fell in love with you in the first place." He speaks the words with such ease, and for the first time, I don't feel my entire body seize up in fear when he does.

"So what you're saying is I should start being tougher with you?" I tease.

He quickly steps to within inches of where I stand. As tall as he is, I have to tilt my head back to keep eye contact.

"I want nothing more." His fingers reach up to graze the side of my cheek, and without thinking, I lean into the touch.

"Should we get back to training?" My voice is low and breathy.

"As you wish."

The next three days are a mixture of everything and nothing.

While I do surprisingly well with elemental manipulation, truth detection, and even at one point manage to bring the destructive fire, I never once succeed at shifting.

"It's okay," he appeases me when he sees the frustration inching its way across my face. "That was a hard one to begin with. It'll work itself out in time."

"Not before the council meeting," I counter with a sigh.

"Maybe not." He shrugs his shoulders.

I shake my head. "But if I can't show the others what I can do, they'll never trust me."

And if they don't trust me, then I won't be able to lead. I won't be able to make a dent in this war. I won't be able to meet with Tarak and the settlement to plead my case for allyship. I won't be able to make amends for all the wrong I've done.

"They aren't expecting perfection. They're all aware of what happened."

"I've been at this one for days and nothing is happening." The words come out as a guttural groan.

"Because you aren't leading with your heart." He places my hand over my rapidly beating heart. "You're leading with this." He releases his grip only to place a finger against my forehead. "You're letting frustration and emotion take over. You have to find a way to control that."

"How?"

"I can't answer that."

Defeat settles deep within my bones as I sag against a nearby tree.

"Okay." He rubs the back of his neck in thought. "You can summon the dome."

"Barely," I argue, knowing that outside of the few times I did it with Tarak, I have only been able to make it appear once here, and that was practically by accident.

Ari cuts his eyes in my direction, refusing to comment on my frustration. "You can bring forth the white light and the firelight. You can discern if someone is lying. And you can alter elements."

I bark out a laugh.

"I caused the pastry I was holding to turn to crumbs. I don't think that counts."

He laughs. "It counts."

I close my eyes as I run my hand through my hair, then groan when I remember I placed it in a braid and now all the pieces I just tugged free will be flying all in my face.

"Stop it."

My muscles jolt when his voice sounds from directly in front of me and my eyes shoot open to find him barely an inch away. I meet his stare, unwilling to be the first to turn away.

"You have *got* to stop talking down to yourself." His free hand cups my cheek. "All you're doing is making it harder." He steps in closer, his body now flush with mine, and a blush stains my cheeks. "You can do this. You have done this many times before." Our breaths mingle as I shift my gaze, not ready to soak in everything that view has to offer. Not ready to accept how right his words, his touch, his body feel against my own. But then I catch sight of the arm he has extended to lean against the tree above my head. The sleeve is rolled up, revealing a patchwork of scars. Scars which look to have been made from fire.

"Where did you get those?"

He quickly jerks back, but I reach out to grasp his hand.

"Oh, no. Don't start hiding things now. Where did you get those?"

"Does it matter?" His fiery demeanor is now far too cold.

"Yes!" I answer so loudly that even the few guards above on the encircling balcony twist to stare.

"It wasn't you, if that's what you're wondering. You didn't do this to me."

A rush of relief seeps out.

"Then what did?"

He pauses for a moment as if unsure whether or not he wants to answer. But in the end, he knows he can't lie.

"The Ashclaw."

My breath catches in my throat at his answer. "Then it was me."

"No, it wasn't."

"Something I created did that to you!"

"It is not your fault. You weren't even there. It's not your fault." He steps forward, taking my face in his hands. "Listen to me. It was long before I even met you. You had no part in this. *None.*"

"But I made it." I'm barely able to force the words out. "I hurt you."

And it's that thought which finally causes me to break. Out of all the horrible things that could possibly litter my past, the thought of having hurt him—having *scarred* him—causes me the most pain. But the tears don't come. Instead I find a surge of anger rising within me.

"You were a child," he keeps going.

"I'm sorry," I beg.

"Stop." His grip tightens on my cheeks as he tries to pull me in. "Don't go there. Stop apologizing for things outside of your control."

I open my mouth, not sure what will come out, but find the sound lodged deep in my throat. Heat spreads from my chest to my limbs, and then light sparks in my periphery.

"Nera!" his urgent plea barely resonates.

The light spreads out as the man before me blurs into nothing.

"I'm the enemy," I whisper, not knowing if I actually speak the words or if they're only in my head.

"Find me," the withered voice I have prayed would never return caresses my skin.

I shake my head in defiance, but the beckoning is so strong. My eyes close as I unsuccessfully fight off the words.

"Become me," it urges as my body surrenders to the heat. With each passing second, the heaviness and burden of my past I've longed to discard lessens and the far off sounds of frantic screams die out.

"Save me."

I open my eyes to find a woman I don't know standing before me. I blink again and again, but her form never fully comes into view. The blurry world stalls just out of focus.

"Who are you?" I ask.

"Save me," she pleads. Her voice is now soft and yet heavy with remorse. A movement catches, and I think I see her hand reaching out to me.

"Save you from what?"

"You," she states with a chuckle, as if the answer was right there all along.

"Me?" I try to stand on trembling legs, but when I look down I don't see a body or a form at all. I am nothing. Nothing but a void of air and darkness. "What is this?"

"Save me," she pleads, and for the first time I hear actual sorrow in her words.

"I don't . . . " My gaze shifts from one side to the next as I try to make sense of this odd predicament, but there's nothing here. Just her blurred form and vacant obsidian. I can't even reach her. This place could be five feet or five miles wide and I wouldn't be the wiser.

"Save me," she repeats, and I scoff at the notion. Small droplets of water land around, and ripples spread out in all directions.

"I don't understand." The darkness begins to soften and a foggy white light emerges.

"You are the enemy," she accuses, but her voice is distorted.

"I am the enemy?" I question.

" . . . the enemy." Her words are lost in the void as the light expands and she slowly disappears.

"I am the enemy," I whisper as confusion settles, and I look away as the blinding light encompasses the darkness.

The quiet void of nothingness disappears as frantically hushed voices gather around.

"I am the enemy," I confess, knowing her words are true. The blurred world slowly comes back into view, and Ari takes a shuddering breath above me.

"You are *not* my enemy." His voice breaks as he wraps his arms around my crumpled form.

I sleep through most of the afternoon, not waking until well into the night. When the haze of sleep finally clears, I find Ari nestled in a chair at my side, an open book cradled in his lap.

With no hesitation whatsoever, I get up to make my way to his side, peering at the pages he holds.

It's not a book, but a journal. Handwriting and simple drawings cover the pages.

"You okay?" I jump back at the sound of his voice, my chin tilting to find his golden stare fixed on me.

"Yeah . . . " I lie and then groan, shaking my head as I relent, "No. I'm not. I . . . don't think I have been for a while."

"I know." His voice is soft, gentle. "You were trying so hard to be brave, but, Nera, it's okay to not be okay. Especially in front of me. You can fake it to everyone else, but don't with me."

I almost laugh at the notion as I sink back onto the bed. "I don't know what's fake and what's not. I don't know who the real me is."

He places the book back on the nightstand and sits beside me on the bed. "What happened?" he questions as his fingers lace with mine.

There's a moment of confusion where I'm not sure which life altering event he could be referring to. But then the memory surfaces and my body tenses in fear.

"It was a woman."

"A woman?"

"She said, 'Find me, become me, save me.'"

He hangs his head as he runs a hand through his hair.

"What was that? Who is she?"

"The Shadow." He balls his hands into fists before cracking each knuckle. "Did you see her? Did you go to her? Could you–"

"She was blurred. And I wasn't *really* there."

He quickly turns his head to look me over.

"It was like my mind was there, but my body wasn't. I couldn't move. I didn't have legs or arms. There was nothing but emptiness and her blurred form."

His shoulders rise as he contemplates all I've said.

"It's getting stronger." He swallows and I can tell this is a notion he has been trying not to voice for far too long.

"The Shadow?"

He nods then turns back to me.

"It's going to try and come after you again. I thought Centra IV would be safe, but I don't think there's a single location I could hide you away that something wouldn't try to take you again."

"Stop hiding me."

His brows furrow.

"Stop hiding me. It's going to come for me. It *has* been coming for me. So it doesn't matter where I go." I swallow as fear washes over me. "How long before the meeting?"

"Three weeks."

"How long before morning?" I question, knowing I have three weeks to gain as many abilities as possible so I can prove my worth and show whatever this thing is that I will not go down without a fight.

"A few hours."

I stand as I walk to the closet and grab my training clothes. "I need to get started." I pull the door between us when I see him stand and start to make his way toward me. "I have to work harder." I shrug off the gown I hope Dina placed on me and throw on the clothes as fast as possible. "I need to get better—stronger." I inch the door open as I start my braid. "I have to be better than her."

"Who?"

"Me," I answer as my hands drop to my sides. "I have to be better than the *me* from before, because she lost. She lost, and I–"

"Nera." He shakes his head as he lessens the space between us. "Stop. You don't have to be the girl from your past or the girl who you were when you were gone. The you who you are right now is more than enough."

"No," I counter, and feel the stubbornness making itself known. "She wasn't. And I'm not either. I have to be better."

He shakes his head.

"Ari." I take a deep breath as I try to find the words. "I want to fight, but sometimes I don't know what's real and what's not." I shake my head and close my eyes when I see him start to speak. "Is the me standing before you the true version, or is that voice, that girl . . . " My lips start to tremble. "Is the killer who I know is hiding inside . . . Is she the real me?" I confess the question I have been so afraid to voice.

"Can I show you something?"

"I don't want another memory right now." Knowing how the exhaustion seeps in each time I've seen one, I want nothing of the sort. I need to train. I need to get stronger.

"No. I want to take you somewhere."

"Where?"

"Trust me?" he asks and I nod.

When the world comes back into view, I find us standing in the middle of a forest. Ari points into the distance. "This is where you punched me the first time."

I make a sound somewhere between an audible gasp and a laugh. "From the memory?"

He nods and pulls me forward to follow him. "See this tree right here?" He points to what I would call a stump rather than a tree. "We had just started working together, right here." He spreads his arms, gesturing all around us. "The memory of that fight I showed you where you were a tad bit mean to me . . . " He trails off with a knowing smile, and I nod my head in understanding. "This is where we started meeting after that day. You came back. You came back and you acted like that conversation never even happened. You told me to take you somewhere far away. You still didn't trust me, but I had knowledge you needed, and I think . . . " He pauses again as his smirk forms. "I think I'd convinced you to at least try to see what gifts you possessed. After that day, we would meet in the Caverns, and then I would bring us here so you could train."

"What does that have to do with the tree?"

"You destroyed it," he says with a chuckle.

"What?"

"Once you started training, it was weeks—really, days," he clarifies when my eyes widen, "before you started to gain control over your gifts. Not unlike the way your training is going now."

I shrug in confusion.

"You don't know this because you can't remember, but it should've taken years to learn what you were able to master in a matter of days. There were, of course, some gifts that we were still working on when you were taken, but all in all, you took control of your abilities at an incredible pace."

My attention shifts back to the stump at my side. "I still don't get the tree."

He laughs again. "One day, you took me to the ground. We were playing with the elements. Seeing how fast you could manipulate them. Seeing how well you could control your gifts. We knew you could shift, albeit small distances at once, and we knew you could create the dome. So it seemed a fair possibility that you could create other things. The day before, as a complete accident, we'd found out you could manipulate elements. Water, fire, dirt. Same as what we now know Riann to be able to do."

I cringe at the sound of the name.

"We tested the theory. I would shift, and you would try to attack me with an element before I could get out of the way. Sometimes it was a splash of water," he raises an eyebrow, "or dirt."

My eyes widen in shock as he laughs.

"But you couldn't destroy. You'd tried, and nothing happened, so we assumed you didn't have that gift. The next time I shifted into your view, you tried to smother me with a pile of leaves from that very tree. But you were stronger than you realized. Next thing I knew, there was an entire tree trunk hurling through the air, headed right at me. I caught it around the middle as it slammed into me, but with the direct hit and force behind it, I ended up over a hundred feet that way." He points to some far off point to his left.

My hand flies to my mouth and I'm afraid to ask, but that doesn't stop my mouth. "Were you okay?"

"Relatively," he chuckles. "I had a few bruises, a cut . . . " He points to the scar across his nose. "And a dislocated shoulder."

"Oh my god! Ari!"

He smiles at my distress, which I don't find the least bit funny.

"You shifted over to me. It was the farthest you'd been able to go in one shift." There is pride in his tone. "And before I could even make my brain reconcile with the fact that I was trapped under a tree, could barely breathe, and was slowly being crushed to death, it had been reduced to dust."

"How?"

"You. You destroyed it without even thinking. You reached out, and then it was gone, and in its place I saw you. I remember being in pain, but at that point, I'd dealt with far worse injuries from my father. But you were terrified." He shakes his head as the memory settles. "You started blubbering about something as you were setting my shoulder, there were tears running down your face, and nothing I said or did calmed you down. Then, after a lot of prodding and more crying, you realized I was fine. You stopped and wiped your eyes as if nothing had happened. You put on a brave face once more."

"I hurt you. Again." Pain lances through me.

"Nera," he shakes his head, noting the direction my mind is taking this, "up until that moment, you had seen me as an enemy. But when you saw me pinned under the tree, you shifted and you turned it to dust. It was the first time you destroyed anything. And you did it to save someone who you thought was your enemy. Someone who you didn't even trust."

"I don't understand." Tears rim my eyes.

"You are not evil. You are *not* my enemy. You are the greatest gift I have ever been given. And if I have to spend every day of the rest of my life proving that to you, then I will consider it an honor."

XXXIX

T he second week of our arrival brings on a new adventure . . . and one I'm
not sure I'm ready to embark on.

Apparently, Reeves likes to hold massive dinners each night. When Dina first
explained the notion to me, I gagged in response. Up until then, I had what I
thought was a well-designed idea of what Reeves was like.

I have only seen her a few times, which all appear to be random in nature, but
she never gave off the idea that she was one to exude wealth or excess. If anything,
everything she did, wore, and said was understated, with just the smallest hint of
attitude bubbling upward. I like that. I like her.

Even in her astute assessments of me, I never find her eyes to be judgmental or
her tone to be harsh. She is accepting of what I can do, and trusting of what I say.
There's some kind of faith hanging between us that I haven't found with anyone
outside of Ari. It's almost as if she knows me better than even Dina, and she wants
nothing more than to see me shine.

She walks down the hallways with such grace and simplicity that I usually don't
even know she's there unless you pointedly take note of the guards and advisors
who seem to follow her every step. Sometimes, when I let my gaze shift from Ari
to the upper balconies of the palace while we're in the middle of training, I find
her leaning over a railing and acutely studying every inch of me. I always smile or
wave as we lock eyes. She quickly returns the notion.

She isn't one to say much, but when she speaks, the entire room listens. I think
that's what draws me in the most. There's a mysterious notion about her that I
just can't figure out. She lets her actions and her reputation speak for themselves,
knowing there isn't much words can do to overtake what can be seen with the
naked eye.

And in the moments where we do speak, albeit very rarely, I find her to be kind, and straight to the point.

Each article of clothing, while seeming to fit her like a glove, is nothing but a beautiful masterpiece of simplicity. And the only jewelry I ever see are the golden rings entangled within her mahogany braids. I've never even seen her wear shoes.

So as Dina starts describing the delicacies and treats covering the tables each night, my idea of her starts to blur. I had painted a picture of someone who hated the idea of opulence and was the exact opposite to what I saw in Koreed and Riann.

But the thought that each night, prior to my arrival and since, has been spent in copious amounts of food and drink makes me a little nauseous.

"Why would she waste all that food? I thought Ari said people in Centra III were having trouble with–"

"Oh, no!" Dina shakes her head as she laughs. "It's not like that. Normally the palace is filled to the brim with the people. Reeves doesn't keep the food for herself, she freely gives it to anyone who wants or needs it."

"Oh." As she speaks, I somehow recall Ari telling me something similar when we first arrived. "I just . . . wait. Where are all the people now?"

"Reeves emptied the palace for you, remember?" She tilts her head and I nod as the memory surfaces.

"Sorry. I think my head is too full of training and all this other nonsense to keep up with everything you two have told me."

"I bet." She stands to walk behind my chair. "What about an updo? Maybe some braids? Or a–"

"Why are you doing my hair?" I cut her off and she gives me a quizzical stare.

"For dinner?" She crosses her arms and looks on in confusion. "Have you been listening to a word I've said?"

"Um . . . I thought I had been." I shrug my shoulders and she laughs.

"We aren't eating in our rooms tonight. We're going to go down and eat in the dining hall."

"With the people of Centra IV?"

She rolls her eyes. "No. Oh, Nera . . . " She shakes her head as she comes back to sit beside me. "It's just Reeves, you, Ari, me, and a few others who live here. They've all been eating together every night while we stay up here. Ari thought it might be time for us to finally join them."

"Only if you're ready," Ari's deep voice cuts in as he stands in the doorway.

"Should I prepare myself?" I tease and he laughs.

"No. Just some old advisors and a few less-than-impressive guards."

"I like it best when Mavs sneaks in the good wine," Dina interrupts. "It tends to liven things up a little."

Ari shakes his head as he holds back what I know would be a mesmerizing smile. "It's just a normal dinner with people other than us."

It's anything but a normal dinner.

There's too much food. I can barely take time to decide which items I want to pile on my plate before another dish is brought out. Ari helps me choose, and by the time all the empty space on my plate has been filled, I realize I have chosen more desserts and sweets than actual food.

"I don't think I should eat all this." I scrunch my nose up as I wonder what repercussions I'll face tomorrow in the garden if I indulge.

Ari shrugs and reaches over to pluck what looks like a danish off my plate before stuffing it in his mouth. "More for me," he mumbles, and a dash of what I think is powdered sugar lands on his chin.

Without thinking, I reach up and swipe the spot clean before licking the sweet substance off my thumb. I don't even realize what I've done until he stops talking, takes a shuddering breath, and swallows.

He opens and closes his mouth more than once, acting as if the words he wants are just out of reach, when an older gentleman slaps him on the shoulder, and the heated stare we were just frozen within is broken.

"Ari!" the man slurs his name as what must be at least his fourth glass of wine sloshes out of his cup and onto the shiny floor below. "It is so good to have you back. I have missed you dearly, boy." The man chuckles. His white beard and thinning hair seem almost translucent in the shimmering golden orbs which hang from the ceiling.

Confusion flickers across Ari's face before he smiles broadly in response. "Yes. We've missed you as well."

The man chuckles more heartedly before giving Ari another slap on the shoulder and wandering off toward the bar.

"Who was that?"

Ari shakes his head as he starts to laugh. "I have absolutely no idea. One of her nobles, I'm sure." He looks down to me with raised brows. "I'll have to get the inside knowledge from Reeves later."

We laugh as he guides us to the large table where most of the group now sits, chatting and eating away their worries. From the looks around, you would have no idea we were in the midst of planning an upcoming war and a battle to find the stones.

I turn to face Ari as the thought rushes through me.

"What are we doing about the stones?" I ask as I scoop one delicious mouthful in.

The previous laughter seems to melt off his face. "I'm trying to figure that out. There are so many things going on at the moment, it's hard to decide where to turn my attention to."

"Care to explain?" I nudge his shoulder as Dina settles into the chair across from us.

"You two look rather serious?" she teases. "Not enough wine?" Her face pales when neither of us react how she hoped we would. "What's happened?" Her tone turns serious.

"Nothing," Ari answers before taking a bite of a roll. "Just discussing everything and nothing. You know how it is."

"What is the 'everything and nothing' tonight?"

"The stones," I answer, and Ari nods.

"Ah." She immediately settles and starts to dig into her plate. "I don't know why, but this food is so much better when eaten here versus in our rooms."

"Probably because there's actual entertainment," Ari counters, and we all look over and laugh at the same old man now singing to a portrait hanging on the wall.

"Okay. Stones. Let's talk," she mumbles between bites.

"I just asked what we were doing about them, and Ari said there was a lot going on."

He nods. "Between training you and keeping tabs on Tarak," Dina and I immediately lock eyes, "and then keeping up with the Bend, Avandell, and Bandele," he pauses to take a sip of wine, "I haven't been able to do much with the stones."

"Where are those places you mentioned? Avandell? Bandele? The Bend?"

"Avandell in the capital of Centra III. It's where my family's home is, and my people. It's where the palace once stood. My brother is currently holding things down, but I have to shift over and check in every now and then." He gives me a sad smile, and the realization of exactly when he goes hits me.

"When are you going there?" The question is more accusatory than I mean for it to be.

"Mostly at night. I don't want to check in when everyone is awake and bustling around. That would cause too much chaos."

"You go when I'm asleep?"

He nods in answer.

"And that's why you're so tired all the time?" I confront him.

"I don't need much sleep." A heavy weight scrapes down my spine.

"I call bullshit."

Ari recoils at my confusing phrase.

"You what?" Dina asks with a furrowed brow.

"Bullshit. It means that's not true." I shift my gaze from her to him. "You're awake whenever I am. Don't think I haven't noticed you sleeping most nights in that chair in my room," I chastise him, "and most of the time I'm keeping you up with some kind of nightmare or . . . " I pause, looking for the right words " . . . or when I do something stupid like somehow get ensnared by the Shadow."

"Nera–"

"No. You are going to wear yourself thin. You told me yourself we have to keep up our strength and our energy to have full access to our gifts. If you are barely getting any sleep, then what happens when we are attacked, or someone tries to–"

"Okay," he cuts me off. "I get it. And you're right. You're right," he finally appeases, and I can't help the small smile that slips out in triumph of getting that admission from him.

"Tomorrow I want to train with Dina, and I want you to sleep."

"With me?" Dina damn near chokes.

"Yes." I turn to face her. "You are supposedly the best spy the Restoration has ever known."

"Is that what she told you?" Ari starts to laugh, and Dina throws a roll at his face.

"Stop it! You know I'm the best thing that's ever happened to that unit!" she whisper-yells across the table, and I cover my mouth to keep the laughter from erupting. He flicks a bean directly into her face. "Ugh!" she scoffs just as we hear someone clear their throat, and we all turn to find a peculiar look plastered on Reeves face before she turns back to finish whatever conversation she was having.

"Okay. Fine. Fine. You're not too bad," Ari concedes, throwing his hand up in surrender.

"Tell me I'm right," she counters as she crosses her arms over her chest.

"Absolutely not." He shakes his head with a smile.

"Ari!" She goes to throw another roll before Reeves catches her attention once more, and I realize this is probably the most fun I've had in a very long time.

"Oh, don't make him say it," I plead Ari's case to Dina, and she rolls her eyes. "He's already had to concede to me tonight. If he also has to say you're right . . . well then," I look him over and he cocks a brow, "all his pretty muscles might just deflate as his ego shrivels into nothing."

Ari balks, Dina laughs so hard she chokes on her wine, and for the third time tonight we get a curious glance from who I now consider to be the matriarch of our little family.

"I thought you were on my side," he whispers with a grin so large, it's practically blinding.

"I defended you."

He crosses his arms. "Was that defending?" he scoffs, then leans in close to my ear. "But at least now I know you think my muscles are pretty." When he pulls back, he wiggles his eyebrows, and I bury my heated face against his shoulder.

By the time dinner ends, I am full and content, with probably a little too much wine in my system. When Reeves invites us into the adjoining room for some music and dancing, I look at Ari as I recall what it felt like for him to hold me the other day.

And as much as I want his fingers against my skin, I don't want it where everyone can see, and I sure as hell don't want them to watch my entire body start glowing from his touch.

"I think I'll have to say no for tonight. But maybe another time."

Reeves smiles as she nods. "I'm glad you got out of that room and came down here tonight. I hope this will be a more regular occurrence?" She squeezes my hands, and I nod in agreement.

"I promise."

She lingers for just a moment, then nods to both Ari and Dina before disappearing through a doorway.

The walk back to the east wing is quiet. Until, of course, I open my mouth again. "You never finished telling me what the plan was with the stones."

"You're right. I didn't." He intertwines his fingers with mine, and I feel a nudge in my shoulder as Dina notices the motion. I cut her a wide-eyed knowing glance that I can only hope conveys the phrase *shut up*, though I doubt she would know what that means.

"Eight stones. We need them all, and we only know where five are."

"Remind me."

He reaches into his pocket as he pulls out the beautiful golden gem. "We have the Omni stone." He twists it between his fingers, and I pause my walking to stare at the bouncing light swirling inside.

"That was Gram's stone?"

"So you've said." He gives me a knowing glance. I explained Taylor and Mary and her little window of stones yesterday while taking a quick water break during training.

"How did you get it back from Koreed?"

"That was me," Dina chimes in and I turn to face her just as she swipes the stone from Ari's grasp. "I went in after the Halabar palace was destroyed and retrieved it."

"How?" I stare at her incredulously.

She shrugs her shoulders before smirking. "A little infiltration, some low cut dresses," she pushes her chest out, both of us laughing, and Ari rolls his eyes, "and a lot of spiked wine." She hands the stone back to Ari. "Halabarian soldiers aren't the best. Most are recruited unwillingly and would rather be anywhere else, so it's easy to distract them when needed."

"I'll keep that in mind." I nudge her shoulder with my own and Ari groans.

"Please don't get any ideas," he says as his gaze scans me from head to toe. I don't miss the moments when he lingers a little longer on specific parts.

"A little possessive, aren't you?" I tease, and he licks his lips.

"Very." His tone is much deeper than normal.

Dina gags. "Please stop. At least wait till I'm in another centra before you two go at it," she pleads, and heat immediately rushes to my cheeks.

We all three clear our throats at once, hoping to stave off the awkwardness, but nothing can take away the building need I have for this man.

"What about the other stones?" I state far too quickly and see Dina cover her mouth as she tries not to laugh at my embarrassment. I silently promise to get her back for it later.

"Himerak has the Seer stone," Ari answers.

"Which I'm sure Tarak will somehow acquire, even if by force, once he completes the Commitence," Dina adds.

"And if history remains true, then he will gain either the Soothsayer or Affinity stone as well," Ari states.

"Could be both?" Dina questions, and Ari nods.

I tilt my head in thought as all the pieces start to form a more complete picture. "Because of his abilities of discerning if someone is telling the truth and altering emotions?"

They both nod.

"Where are those now?"

"We have no idea," Dina answers.

"Best guess is a Celestra inside the Abolition," Ari replies.

"A Celestra *inside* the Abolition?" My brows furrow in confusion. "How does that work?"

Ari gives me a sad smile. "When you're born into something and grow up thinking it's correct . . . " he pauses as he thinks through his next words. "That training runs deep. Celestras born outside of the Abolition are seen as a threat and are eliminated. Celestras born inside the Abolition and Centra II's walls . . . well, they either conform to what's accepted or they walk straight into a worse fate."

I shake my head, not willing to accept that so blindly. "Why can't they make the choice to flee?"

"Some do," Dina says, and I don't miss the emotion laced in those words.

"But most die trying," Ari cuts back in. "It isn't really a choice. Not in the way you're thinking, at least. Those who stay are typically of two camps. They either stay in order to survive, or keep a close family member or friend who's also a Celestra alive, knowing what they're doing is wrong, and hating themselves for it each and every day. Or they're so indoctrinated into the idea that we—they are the problem, that they hide behind the false narrative so they don't have to face the self-hatred they've been taught."

The memory of Dina's explanation of her time in Centra II surfaces, and I have barely enough strength to hold back the emotion threatening to spill forth. My only option is to swiftly move on to the stones so I don't have to think about the horrors which lie before us.

"Okay. So you mentioned four stones. You have the Omni stone, Himerak has the Seer stone, which will most likely soon be Tarak's if Himerak gives it over." They both nod. "And Tarak will also soon possess either the Soothsayer or the Affinity stone, or both." I swallow at the thought. "What about the others?"

"Reeves has Eso," Dina answers, and I look at her in confusion, but it's Ari who answers my unspoken question.

"Reeves and I have the same gifts. I got Omni, and she got Eso," he quickly explains before Dina chimes in again.

"Riann has Genesis."

"And we have no idea where Ruination and Patho are." Ari says as his shoulders sag in frustration.

"What do those do again?"

"Ruination is the sister to Genesis. Genesis creates, Ruination destroys. And Patho assists with seeing the future as it will currently play out." My eyes widen in shock before he quickly adds. "But that stone has never been found."

Dina chimes in. "And we don't know a single Celestra that has ever had the ability."

I let that knowledge soak in before I finally speak.

"So . . ." I slowly pull my hand from Ari's as I halt our movements. "Each stone is given to the proper Celestra after they complete their Committence?"

"Yes," they answer in unison.

"And typically the stone correlates with the Celestra's gifts?"

"Yes."

I giggle when they again answer in unison. "And I possess all the gifts?"

Neither answers as they look between me and each other.

"I have to complete it." The words tumble out as realization dawns.

"We don't know that you would get them all," Ari clarifies. "I have two gifts, and yet I only got one stone."

I let out a frustrated breath as what he says settles in.

"But we won't know unless we try," I plead. "Unless, I try."

"She's not wrong." Dina looks from me to Ari. "What if she's right? What if she completes the Committence and she acquires them all? We could end it all right then."

He shakes his head. "The likelihood of that happening is very small."

"But it could work!" Dina's voice rises in excitement. "Ari, it could work. We could–"

"And she could also die in the process!" he all but screams as his voice bounces off one wall and then the next in the massive corridor. When his gaze finally finds mine, there is utter terror hidden within his golden stare. "Do you really want to?" he whispers the question as if it's almost too painful to even put into words.

"If it will help. I'll do anything. I'm tired of sitting on the sidelines. I want to be a part of this—a real part."

Ari stares between Dina and I as his fight softens. "You know I will support whatever you choose. But please just wait until you have full access to all your gifts."

"Okay," I surrender as I reach out to shake his hand in promise. Instead, he grabs my hand and pulls me into his arms.

Dina groans. "I'm headed to bed." I hear her shoes begin to move across the stone floor before the noise pauses and she says, "Don't stay up too late. If you're training with me then you'd better be up bright and early." She laughs a little as she starts to move again.

Ari and I stand motionless in the dark corridor for the next few minutes. I wonder if he feels the smile that grows on my face against his chest when I hear him inhale the scent of my hair.

"You are going to drive me mad," he whispers, and I move just enough to look up and catch his gaze.

"Maybe that's what I want?" I give him a wicked smile and he levels his forehead to mine before he takes a deep breath, pulls back, and escorts me back to my room.

When I enter the garden the next morning, I find Dina sitting where Ari normally stands.

"Hi." I wave as I approach.

"Hi," she greets me with a welcome hug.

Arms crossed, I tease, "And what kind of training are you going to provide?"

"The spy kind," she says in a playful rasp as she reaches out to grab my hand and takes off, pulling me through the garden at a racing pace.

"What are we doing?" I ask with a hushed voice as we weave in between various plants and trees. Normally, Ari and I stay within the center opening where there's the most space. I don't think I've even ventured into all the hiding spots of this beautiful oasis.

She turns back to face me, expertly dodging each low lying branch and potted plant with ease. "Getting *into* a location is only half the job. The most important part is getting back out." She stops just before a gate I've never even noticed. I look back to the guards looming above, but none seem to have taken note of where we've run off to on the far side of this massive garden.

"You have five minutes." She yanks out a key and slowly opens the gate before stepping through.

"Five minutes for what?" I go to follow her, but she holds up a hand and shuts the gate between us.

Her gaze shoots around to those unsuspecting guards we've evaded.

"You have been inside this garden training for the last week. You know this place like the back of your hand."

I look down, realizing I don't actually know what the back of my hand looks like. She catches my movement and then rolls her eyes with a laugh.

"Look around," she instructs. "What do you see?"

I twist, surveying the massive expanse. It's a large garden that has to be at least the size of a city block, if not larger. It's filled with trees and flowers, hidden pathways, water fountains, and beautiful gazebos. It's also completely surrounded by the palace. The only people allowed in here are guests, and as of recently, that's only included the three of us.

Looking up, I find the second story wrap-around balcony mostly empty with the exception of a few guards lingering here and there. Ari initially told me they were here for our protection. But what are guards going to do to protect two Celestras and a spy?

"Um . . . Lots of foliage. Some guards. Walls? Windows? A gate?" I say in question, not sure if that's quite the answer she was looking for.

"How would you get out of here?"

"This gate," I reply, grasping the iron bars separating us. The only exit which leads to the outside.

"What if you couldn't use the gate? What if the gate wasn't here, or it was blocked?"

"I don't know." I shrug.

"How would *you* get out?" she urges, and I turn back to once again survey the area.

"Use my gifts?" There's no confidence in the question, but when I turn back, I see her brilliant smile on display.

"You're hidden from the guards. My guess is you have about five minutes to get out and make it to me before they realize you aren't standing by the pretty gazebo and they sound the alarm. If that happens, the entire palace will come to a standstill in search of you."

"I'll just tell them I'm over here." I bore my eyes out in protest.

She rolls her eyes in annoyance. "You're supposed to play along. Now, five minutes to get out of these walls and find Ari and I."

"Find you and Ari?"

She gives me a look. "You know what to do. I want you to focus, think. You have gotten yourself out of a plethora of situations in the past. This one is easy."

I stare blankly at her, wondering if she's somehow forgotten that I lost every bit of that prior training three years ago.

"Meet us at the water's edge."

"What?" I reach out to wrap my fingers around hers. "What water's edge?"

"Use your gifts. Find us."

"Which one? How?" My voice grows frantic. "What if I don't get out? Just wait here till you come back?"

She laughs at my growing confusion.

"Listen to your body.? We'll be waiting on the other side." And then she takes off down a corridor and out of my view.

I have no way to assess the time, but I'm sure I stand there for the better part of three minutes trying to make something happen. The white light forms when I think of how it felt to be held by Ari in the darkened corridor the previous night. It quickly changes to a bright orange at the frustration of seeing him step outside my room once I went to bed. I attempt to create something next. My first thought is to make a bridge of some sort to walk across the wall, but this palace is multiple stories high and I haven't even used this gift yet. I contemplate destroying something, and then realize I would feel bad about destroying something of Reeves's. There's no use for emotional manipulation or seeing the past here, so the only things left are shifting and creating the dome. I try both gifts, but neither make themselves known, and I know for certain I've been at this for longer than five minutes.

It's only when I start to pace the small hidden area I'm standing in that I hear it. The metal on the bottom of my shoe gives off a ding as it hits the metal bars of the drain at my feet. With a slight tug, it loosens with ease.

"Dina, I swear to God, if there are mice down here, I will kill you," I mutter. Reaching down, I fully move the grate away from the hole, only to find a set of steps leading down into the dark unknown.

When my feet hit the bottom, I find inch-deep lingering water that splashes up with each step I take. I twist to find a myriad of pathways, and I can't tell exactly which one will take me in the direction I need to go.

My huff of frustration echoes through the chamber. I am positive my time would be much better spent working on shifting, or elemental manipulation, or even recreating that dome as opposed to traipsing around down here. But I'm the one who put myself in this situation by telling Ari to rest. And if this is what Dina wants, who am I to question her? The main thought that remains constant is how long of a bath I plan to take once I get out of here.

The further I walk, the darker the tunnel grows. Eventually, I can barely see two feet in front of me, let alone determine which direction I should go. And it seems that every sense I have is being slowly overrun by my surroundings.

I miss the garden. It was bright and warm with the massive sun looming above. Down here it's so dark and cold, and my wet feet and legs have me trembling. I'm not sure my nose will ever again be able to enjoy the fragrant aromas of the garden above, now that the smell of moldy food and feces are being burned into my nasal passages. And every few seconds I have to convince myself I don't hear the pitter patter of tiny animal feet, or a distant melody of voices echoing in from some lonely guards I know are stationed all around.

Maybe a hundred feet in, I stop moving. I don't have a plan. I don't even know why I'm doing this. The frustration starts to build.

And then something else comes to mind. Dina wants me to be able to find my way out of here. My guess is this is a trial run for something I'll do in the future. And if that's the case, I won't allow myself to fail.

I made a promise to Ari the other night that, while I may not understand what's happening or why, I would at least give it everything I have for the moment. He of course promised me I had nothing to prove to him or anyone else and that, as he stated before, he would gladly walk away from this mess with me at his side if that was the choice I decided to make. But I think we both know that's not something I could ever do. So as silly—and utterly disgusting—as this task currently feels, I trust that there's a bigger plan in place.

I linger for a moment, trying to decide how to proceed. I could attempt to shift again, but at this point I still need to have a clear picture in my mind of the location I'm trying to reach, and right now that location is blank. I have barely seen anything but the palace grounds and my living and training quarters. I could use the fire to bring about a lighted path. That could work. But what if there's something flammable and I cause the entire structure to collapse? Just as I'm working through the limited options at my disposal, I notice the voices which seemed so muffled and far away before are now clear and precise.

"And then Jean was sick for a week straight," the man says with a laugh.

"Serves him right!" another adds, and by the way their voices carry, I know they're only a few paces away, just around this curve. The glow of the light builds as they come closer. I don't think them finding me would end in anything other than my bruised ego, but still, I want to prove that I can do this. I can escape from a highly protected palace. I can find Ari.

My head snaps up in recognition of what exactly I'm doing down here just as they round the curve.

"What are you–" the first guard starts.

I lay a hand on each of their arms. "I'm safe." Languid smiles move across their faces. I haven't even practiced with this gift yet, and in truth, using it after it was used on me feels wrong, but I need to get past. "I'm safe. Just taking a stroll."

"You're safe," the first guard parrots as he lowers his weapon at the recognition of who he's speaking with.

"You're safe," the second guard repeats. The lazy smile inches up his face.

Now they know I'm safe, but I can't risk them trying to take me back upstairs. I need them to think me being down here is a perfectly normal occurrence.

I think of everything that calms me. The rippling waves of the ocean; the sounds of a waterfall. I picture a rain storm in the middle of the night. Warm, strong arms, golden eyes, and soft touches.

Then I quickly pull back at the thought, not sure if it's somewhere I'm fully ready for my mind to go.

"You're safe," the guard says again as he sits on the ground at my feet, not paying any mind to the water now soaking through the seat of his pants. The second follows his lead. I momentarily wish I knew of this gift during my time at the palace in Halabar. It would have been quite useful with Thing One and Thing Two.

I slowly step around them as they each lean back against the murky wall I hope to somehow avoid touching. They quickly drift off to sleep, and I wonder how exactly I was able to use this gift so fully when I haven't even trained with it once. Before I take off further, I reach down and run my hand under the floating ball of light I have now become used to. It dulled as the men slowly sunk underneath my gifts, but in my grasp it flickers to life, and the darkened tunnel becomes slightly less foreboding.

With the newfound light and my pride at what I just did, I refocus on my next task. I need to find Ari.

Ari.

"Ari," I whisper as I take a few more steps.

The further I go, the colder it becomes. Recalling what I can of the layout of the palace, I take each turn with a silent prayer that this will lead me beyond the palace walls. Then the light begins to flicker. I run my hand over the ball just as all the light disappears.

"No, no, no," I whisper as my world goes black.

There's a moment of pause where I have to calm my racing heart. I let my mind linger on what memories I do have in order to bring me back to center. And even I can't hide from the fact that all those recent memories contain the one person I know I'm holding back from.

"How do I find you?" It's the only possible answer to this riddle they've tasked me with solving. I have to find Ari. I need to feel him. I need to somehow reach down and tug on that small invisible string between us that will lead me home.

Home.

He is my home.

As much as I want to fight the notion, I can't help but accept what was . . . okay, what *is* between us. Maybe if I stop pushing against it so much, this will all come a little easier to me in the end. But it would mean depending on someone else before I depend on myself, and I can't fall into that trap again. I need to be able to trust myself. I need to be able to do this myself. I need to use my gifts.

My hands reach out as I try to summon some form of light from the now empty glass ball in my hands. When minutes pass and nothing comes, I slowly let it rest in the water at my feet. I flex my fingers and concentrate on the light I know resides within me, and a spark of white light emerges. It roars to life for only a second before it quickly fizzles away. I try once more, and though the tingling sensation works its way to the surface, nothing comes.

The only other thing of use down here would be the shift, which I barely know how to do.

I picture the waves, the water, the cool breeze as it flows over my skin. I picture Ari standing at the water's edge waiting for me. But all I see is the water outside of Halabar and the pier I was led down by Tarak.

Those images cloud my vision, mucking up the picture I so desperately try to form.

Next, I picture the walking paths surrounding this palace. I've used them on an almost nightly basis to travel to and from training, and then that dinner on the opposite side of the massive structure. I feel the shift take hold as soon as the complete image comes to mind.

In seconds, I'm wrapped in a cold wind as I push forward, only to stop a few feet ahead. The sudden stop after the jolt of movement causes a loss of balance and I careen forward, slamming against one of the cold, damp walls.

I don't even have time to curse the situation before I hear him, and then the world goes black.

My vision comes and goes as a cold wind wraps around my arm. It slides into my core and through my soul.

I move to stand, but my arm is trapped, buried within the stone wall just like it was within the caverns. The icy stone liquifies, and I watch in terror as my own shape once again reflects back at me.

"*Find me*," it calls out, and adrenaline pumps through my veins, commanding me to run as a charred arm reaches out of the reflection to caress my cheek. Horror washes through me at the contact. This time, the woman is not fully blurred as she was the last time I saw her. She isn't unreachable. And when I feel her icy touch, I recoil as a shudder races through me.

I yank back, forcing all my strength into the pull, knowing I would gladly lose the limb if it meant escape. My heartbeat pounds a furious beat in my ears as I throw my weight backward again and again and again, only to lose the fight. The hold of the stone is too strong.

"*Become me*," it bids.

"Leave me alone!" I shriek in protest as I fight against the unknown. As I fight against what I'm sure is a version of me I never want to know.

The feminine voice that is and is not me cackles, sounding so very far away and yet right at my ear.

"*I can never leave you alone. We are but one,*" she calls out as a lock of my hair is twirled around a bony, blackened finger. I try to slap it away with my left hand, but an invisible force prevents the movement, and when she slowly pulls back, running her finger down the strand and letting the ashen soot linger, I all but vomit.

"*Come home, my dear. Come home to where you belong,*" she begs in a sickeningly sweet voice.

Icy wind wraps around my middle and jerks me forward. I tighten every muscle, trying with all my might to resist the pull. "I will *never* give in to you!"

The cackle distorts into a chilling laugh. "*Oh, dear.*" She shakes her head in earnest. "*You already have.*"

And then the woman, who is at once me and not me, bursts into flames. The inferno engulfs my vision, effectively blinding me to my surroundings. The ends of my hair sizzle in the scorching blast as pieces of my clothes burn away. Still, it continues to pull me in. I fight with everything I have, but my feet begin to slide forward toward my doom.

The laughter bellows out of the flames, the sound clawing at my ear drums.

"*Stop fighting me!*" it howls and then erupts into a maniacal laugh at my futile attempts.

A gulp of fear lurches from my lips. "Ari!" I call out, desperate. Hoping that the bond between us will guide him to me. "Ari!" I scream once more.

But he doesn't come.

No one comes.

The grip on my arm tightens as the liquified stone covers my shoulder, inching its way closer to my throat. Only a matter of moments and I will be forever lost within a hellscape I can't even begin to imagine.

A fire of my own spreads through me as my power barrels forth, breaking through every safeguard I've put in place to hold it at bay.

I feel the chains snap as each tendril of light bursts to life along my veins.

"Save me," I whisper to the power deep within my soul, willing it to assume control.

It answers with cool strokes down my back, urging me downward, urging me to take hold, to take control once and for all. I reach down, down, down into my soul, into that pit of despair I once hid within. The further I go, the warmer I become. But it's a never-ending hollow, and I fear I won't make it back to the surface before I become fully encased in the unknown. Then, just as my faith starts to wane, I feel the cool tingles of water skirt across my fingers. Tiny sparks dance in the ripples as they soar toward my hand. A thousand remnants of light gather all around me. The darkness settles and the light filters in as each tiny orb soaks into my palm. Heat and power like I have never known surges through me. Pain races up my arms, and my chest burns as the heat settles. I scream out as the obsidian expanse I once sought refuge within explodes. The walls of that self-made prison shatter, and the world sparks to life. Flickers of light—golds, blues, greens, yellows and reds—float around me. More and more come with each passing second. They land on my skin in a flutter. A warm and comforting caress, and I crash down into the waiting water at their touch.

And though I can't see or hear them, I know there are now a thousand souls moving within me, urging me forward, grasping my ice-crusted hand and shattering the cloak of fear I've so meticulously wrapped around myself.

I hear them call out to me, not in words but in feelings, asking me for direction.

Protect me, I command.

Just as the words enter my mind, I feel that warmth slowly unfurl. It starts in the pit of my stomach, and ripples outward as every inch of my skin begins to sing with a welcome melody.

My body begins to glow just as it had with Ari in the garden. On instinct, I force the feeling outward, casting forth the dome-like shield to encompass my body.

I relinquish control as it takes my place, fighting against the clutches of what I now realize is the Shadow. The heat and cold wage a war on my skin, sending searing pain barreling up my arm and into my chest.

"You can't have me!" I call out to the woman standing on the other side. Her charred form sizzles as her body is slowly reduced to ash.

Just before she completely disintegrates, her face at last comes into focus. A calm, hopeful smile lingers on her lips as a tear falls down her cheek, curling into a wisp of smoke as her head nods in answer. Then she is ash on a phantom breeze.

"ARI!" I screech out in one last effort as tears of defeat roll down my face.

But then the light explodes into a thousand tiny fragments and the wall turns from liquid to stone before a crack runs through the expanse. The walls cave in, and my vision fades to black.

"Nera!" Ari's words pull me back as pain surges down my spine. I attempt to move, but my body is so heavy and none of my limbs cooperate with the command. My mouth opens and closes but no sound emerges, and when I finally force my eyes to focus, I find terrified gazes standing around.

"She's freezing," Dina calls out as too many hands shove broken stone off my battered form. I groan with each movement made. And whimper in relief when I can finally fully breathe. Voices, some I know and some I don't, call out commands as the chaos ensues. As soon as I'm freed, I feel familiar hands lift me up, arms wrapping me in a warm embrace.

"Something's wrong," Ari calls out as his hand cups my cheek, and I lean into the touch. "Why are you down here?" He whispers as panic races through him.

"I– I was trying to get to you. Dina said to–"

He glares his fury toward Dina, and her eyes go wide, her hands coming up as she clarifies, "I was trying to get her to shift! I didn't expect her to go into the tunnels."

"I didn't know," I confess through the coughs as I will my breathing to steady.

"Shh . . . It's okay." Ari brings my cold cheek to press against the warmth of his.

"I saw myself again. And then–" I falter as the visions of what just happened rush through me. "I don't understand."

"I know." His lips graze the skin just below my chin as he starts to move forward, securing me tighter within his hold.

It's only another moment before darkness engulfs the world, and then he's laying me down somewhere soft. I expect the overwhelming exhaustion and nausea to hit. I have never before exerted myself more than I did in those tunnels. But nothing comes. My body stays solid and strong. I don't vomit, or even feel an ounce of nausea this time. Still, I don't refuse the glass of cold liquid Dina places in my hand.

Ari quickly places his hand over the top as he looks between us.

"Does it contain a tonic?"

"Yes." She nods. "To help the pain."

Ari looks back to me, questions swirling in his gaze. "Do you want this?" He tilts his head toward the cup which seems to be suspended between the three of us. "It contains a tonic to take away the pain, but it may also make you sleep."

I open my mouth to refuse, but even that slight motion causes a surge of agony to race through my bones. I heave a deep breath. "Yes. Please."

He slowly removes his hand and then tips the glass to allow the cold, tasteless water to flow into my mouth. I cringe at every swallow as even that small movement causes ripples of pain to race through me. But soon the pain lessens and I can move more freely.

"Tell me everything," Ari requests, and I do.

Before I give in to the ease of sleep, I sit up and explain how I used the same gift as Tarak to calm the guards who found me. Somewhere in the middle of the explanation, Reeves comes bursting in with a look of terror etched deep in her features. I watch as she leans forward, grasps the back of a chair, and visibly relaxes at the sight of me sitting up and speaking.

I tell them how I was trying to shift or create the dome, really willing any power to come, when I finally moved a few feet forward within the underground tunnel and lost my footing.

I explain the way the cold stone latched onto my skin just as it had back in the caverns. I detail out the feeling of hope and ease as I finally broke free from the chains I had placed around my power. I tell them how good it felt as it rose within me, and how the light rushed through me. How voices of hope rang forth.

And then just as I finish, when I start to feel the edge of sleep drawing near, I hear Ari's soothing voice.

"I'm so proud of you."

XL

When I finally wake, the sun is just starting to rise in the distance. I stretch, noting that my muscles are more stiff than usual, and then I startle when I notice Ari staring down at me from above.

"Hi." He breathes the word into existence as his fingers stroke my cheek.

"Hi." My reply is hoarse and frail. Confusion hits. "Why did I fall asleep? I wasn't tired."

"Dina gave you that tonic to take away the pain." A slight smirk crosses his features. "It worked a bit better than we thought it would."

"Ah." I nod as the memory surfaces, and reach up to wipe away the sleep from my eyes.

His laugh bursts out, deep and soothing. "You okay?"

My brow furrows at his response, and then not a moment later, the rush of memories of what occurred hits me.

I gasp in recognition as I throw the covers off and assess every inch of exposed skin I can find. I gasp again when I notice something not quite right. I expect to find cuts and scars and deep bruises covering every inch. But my smooth olive skin seems to shine in the glow of the incoming sunlight.

"What is this?" My fingers trace over my legs and then my arms. Though I'm fairly positive this wouldn't be considered outright glowing, I'm definitely shimmering. How, I couldn't begin to explain.

"You did it."

"Did what?" I meet his gaze.

"You found your power." Pride beams from every word. "You found the source."

"What does that mean?"

"Shield the room," he tells me.

"What?" My fog-riddled mind can't seem to grasp his words.

"Shield the room. Protect it as if an intruder's about to attack us," he instructs once more, and I feel something deep within me stir to life. He must sense it as well, because before I can even question what it is, he's frantically nodding in answer. "Yes. That's it. Use it."

And I do.

I slowly shift my legs off the mattress, letting my feet dangle to the floor, close my eyes, and reach down into that pit, the one no longer consumed by darkness but overflowing with light.

Protect. I direct it, and in an instant, I feel the heat surge through my veins and spread out in a blast throughout the room.

When I open my eyes again, I find Ari assessing me with the biggest smile etched across his face. We both look upward at the same time to find the shimmering dome encompassing us.

The door to my room swings open, and both Ari and I scream out in protest as Dina almost walks straight into my shield. I pull back on instinct as she freezes in place.

As soon as the room is clear, she takes a heaving breath. "Well. I almost just died, didn't I?"

"Almost is the key word." Ari laughs as he leans down to press a kiss to my forehead.

Dina then rushes over, throwing her arms around me as soon as she's within reach.

"I'm so sorry!" Her eyes lock onto mine. "I didn't mean for you to go down. I thought you would shift. I was just trying to get you to shift."

"It's okay."

"It's not!" she protests. "You almost died because of me!"

"Dina," Ari tries to soothe her frantic mind. "She's fine. She made it out."

"She almost didn't. A moment later, and she would be dead."

"No." I look her full in the face and explain, "I used it. On the wall. I used the shield. I was able to fight it off. I was fine." Dina gives out a huff, and I know my words barely appease her. "And it worked. It may not have been executed in the exact way you expected, but your plan worked! Look!" I grab her hand. Within a moment, and with barely any thought required, I shift us to the opposite of the room.

She catches her breath as we land and slowly looks over to where Ari still stands twenty feet to our right.

"She can shift." Disbelief coats her words.

"She can shift." He's practically radiating pride, his smile reaching every inch of his face. "She can shift and she can shield. And if all else is as it should be, she can do much more than that."

"What else should I do?" I feel unyielding excitement at my newfound gifts.

Ari pulls up a chair, matching my enthusiasm with his own. "You can shift between places, and possibly time as well." He smiles in awe. "You can also tell when someone's lying, and you can impact their emotions." I cringe at the thought of what I did to those guards.

"Are they in trouble?"

Ari laughs at my question, immediately knowing who I'm referring to.

"Not at all."

I breathe a sigh of relief.

"Next, we need to find out if you can manipulate the elements as Riann can. Can you destroy and create?"

"I think she already did," Dina chimes in, and we turn to her in confusion. She stares at us in disbelief as if the answer is right in front of us. "She cracked the walls in the tunnels. She almost brought down that entire structure. How else could the walls have caved in?" she questions, and Ari contemplates her words.

"That would make the most sense," he agrees before turning to me with a grin. "Okay, so you can most likely destroy and create.

I mirror his expression as pride in what I can do swells. "What else?"

"Himerak. Can you see the past? Can you control a person's mind? And like me, can you alter the reality of what people see?"

"Those don't seem like easy feats to conquer."

"No, those are some of the most difficult ones to master, for sure. But you have yet to disappoint me. I doubt you'll start now."

I laugh at his words.

"Want to try?" He gives me a knowing smile.

"Which one?"

"I want you to alter what I see. I want you to give me a memory. Think of it and send it to me as if I was in it." He reaches out and grasps my hand.

"I don't even know what to send you." I laugh at the idea, and then pale as I run through a thousand visions that only show what hell I lived in while on Earth.

"Anything. Show me anything," he pleads, and I finally give in, knowing there's probably not a thing I could ever deny him.

When I close my eyes, I take a moment to let the picture form. I focus on the sounds of Mary's laugh and the vision of the rows of books I used to escape within as the bookstore solidifies in my mind. As soon as the picture is real, I send it straight to Ari. There is a gasp as he takes it in, and not a second later, his eyes frantically open as he bursts into laughter.

"What did you see!?" Dina's tone is filled with excitement.

"Mila?" Ari's brow quirks inquisitively and I start to laugh.

"Yeah. She's a cat. And she hates me."

He bursts out with even more laughter. "I could tell."

He wipes his eyes, and I think of the exact memory I sent him. The one where that damn cat refused to do anything but annoy me for the better part of an hour one morning, causing me to spill and drop everything I touched. I tried to hold in the bouts of cursing for Mary's sake, but even her innocence wasn't worth the frustration that ensued when that animal was involved.

"The little girl. Her name was Mary?"

"Yeah." I feel the tears start to gather. "She was one of my only friends." I smile at her memory.

"Is that where you lived? On Earth?"

"No, it's where I worked."

He looks from me to Dina. "Of everywhere she found to work, it had to be a bookstore."

Dina laughs in response. I attempt to match the noise, but my voice breaks instead.

"Nera?" Ari's expression quickly changes from curious elation to worry. "What's wrong?"

"Nothing. I'm fine." I shake my head and wipe away the lingering wetness. "I just miss them."

He nods, and a quiet settles over the room. It only lasts a moment before I resolve not to wallow in grief I can't control, and my mind shifts to more important matters.

"How long before the counsel meeting?" I blurt out.

"Two weeks," Dina answers as she finds a spot on the sofa to my right.

"I do want to train more with my gifts and make sure I can do all those things, but first I want to do something else."

"Whatever you want," Ari promises.

"I want to see more memories of me. I want to see myself using these gifts."

He smiles and stands, walking my way with an outstretched hand.

"I have a few in mind."

His fingertips graze mine, and then the world goes black.

Ari

I can smell her. She thinks she's being cautious, but she doesn't realize I can smell the expensive soaps she bathes in. No wonder she wasn't able to kill any game the last time she came. Her scent alerted them to her arrival before she even had a chance to take aim. I guess that's what growing up in a palace will do to you.

At first, I was confused as to why she hunted. I knew who she was. I know who all the Celestras are. It's my job to know, after all. And I knew that after her silly little adventures out here on these days and nights when others assumed she was fast asleep, she could just go right back to her gold-embellished table and dine on delicacies from her centra instead of killing and cooking something herself.

It was during those musings when I questioned exactly how it was that she came to find her way so far within the jungle, and away from the pretty prison she was otherwise encased within. I can't say exactly how it is that I can always seem to find her when she comes out this way, but for some reason, the invisible cord threaded between us always pulls us together.

So I stopped questioning the Elders and started my quest to find the truth. If anyone were to ask my father where I go late at night, his answer would be various places within the centras, completing my work and training to infiltrate their ranks. He isn't wrong. But what he doesn't yet know is that most of those nights are spent within the confines of Centra I, on its outskirts or within the Caverns themselves. And all have one thing in common.

Her.

Nera Thesand.

Celestra heir to Centra I.

I keep my secret close to my heart, not even letting my direct superiors know how much information I have gleaned from watching her, learning her.

And in this moment, I am learning that although she's well skilled at bringing down her prey, she needs much more practice when it comes to skinning it.

I have to hide the chuckle that threatens to erupt when she nearly vomits at the sight of the dead animal in her hands. I want to shout at her to leave it be. That I'll take it back to my people who will be glad to feast on what little flesh the small carcass has to offer. But I keep my mouth closed as I watch her work, silently meddling through the question of why.

Then I realize that her hunting isn't about finding nourishment, but the skill. She's practicing. Practicing for a future I haven't yet seen.

But what future is she preparing for?

She obviously doesn't need the practice of the kill. She's far more skilled in archery than anyone else I know. I think perhaps she's preparing herself—her body—for the idea that, at some point in her future, this may be required of her. And that is frightening. More so because Celestras from Centra I tend to be plucked from promise. Plucked from wealth and destiny and privilege. They don't prepare for the worst, because they are the worst. They are our only known enemy outside of the Abolition, and at times, I find it difficult to tell where one group ends and the other begins. In truth, their ranks are so deeply intertwined that even the most loyal Centra I citizens, who otherwise hold fast to the teachings of the Elders, fall to the horrid teachings and propaganda of the Abolition.

So today, as I watch her stalk the small creature with precision, and then skin it with shaking hands, I know she does it keeping in mind something I can't see. And for an entirely different reason, that makes me proud.

I've been watching her for over three months now, and each time, the lurch in my chest pounds more fervently than the last.

I think I know what it could mean. I've heard the stories and tales. But I don't—I can't yet accept it. She could still be my enemy. I don't know her well enough to wager otherwise. Yes, she's a Celestra, but she lives within the one stronghold outside of Centra II we have yet to fully overtake. So I will spend my days preparing for battle, and my nights watching her.

It's not high up on the list of jobs one would expect a would-be sovereign to be given. And many are confused as to why I continue to accept these missions, but I know the truth hidden within the lies. And I hope to one day share that truth with her.

Some unlucky souls looking in from the outside might say I, too, grew up among riches and nobility. How wrong they would be.

Yes, my mother comes from an origin line, a direct line of descendants from the original Celestras, and yes, my family is one of the more wealthy, but wealth means nothing when you live in a frozen tundra where the only true currency is warmth and meat.

I was only a child when the Abolition crossed our borders. I don't know whether they believed our centra to be a deserted, frozen wasteland as the rest of Centra I had been trained to think, or if they knew we had been here all along. I tend to lean mostly to the latter, only due to the reasoning that when they arrived, they came packed with weapons and heartstone cloths. Some still say they had no idea what we were hiding, but I think they always knew.

Ari

Four months and she still can't skin the kill without at least one bout of dry heaving. At this point, it takes all my strength not to rush to her aid. But she is adamant, so I'll stand and watch from the sidelines.

As I hold Drunia in my hands, I wonder at what knowledge we could gain if I were to make myself known and share the intel I've found. I wonder if she would be a willing partner in my quest. Would she join me in ending this centuries-long war? Ending the killings of innocents? Or would she take what I give her back to my enemies and betray the trust I'm already inclined to afford her?

It took over a week to secure the book without anyone becoming aware of what I was doing. And this morning, as I walked out on my mother, it was with hope that her mind would be too blinded by my dedication to the cause to consider the truth about the Celestra I've found. But while I hoped for her not to see, I also wondered if she would approve of the woman who now consumes my every thought.

My body aches to move from the strained position I huddle within. It's been over an hour with barely any muscle movement, on my part or hers. Which means I'll have to make some excuse as to why I have no new information to provide when I return. The only thing of note I would truthfully be able to speak on is how the dim lantern light looks far too appealing against the curve of her neck as she moves over the map.

It was only once she pulled out that map from the hidden hole in the wall on her last trip that I realized she was far deeper within this quest than I had previously believed.

Ari

Elders, this woman is beautiful.

She still hasn't seen me, and I know I'm already ten minutes past our arranged meeting time, but I can't seem to make my body shift from behind this wall. I keep telling myself it's because I need to survey the room. A room deep within the Caverns and which I have yet to venture inside. But even I can't hide behind that lie. I know she can fully trust me, but she isn't aware of that, and I wouldn't put it past her to have brought and hidden someone around here.

I might even relish the idea of some unknowing spider of a guard springing from behind a hidden crevice, thinking they could best me. It would provide some much-needed entertainment.

Being without her these last few days after having finally held her the night I made my presence known . . . It's been the definition of agony.

But in truth, my reason for hanging back now is because watching her is like receiving a hit of a drug I so desperately crave. Like a tease I'm holding onto. I crave the pain.

Ari

"Why are you always where I don't want you to be?" she spits without even looking my way.

I halt what I thought was a silent walk in her direction and cross my arms over my chest.

"I don't know what you're talking about." I feign ignorance.

Though I can't see her face, I can just imagine her eyes rolling at that. Outside of the night we first met, we've actually had very few encounters. Most of those were filled with my spilling forth every secret I ever kept in hopes of gaining her trust. It didn't work.

"Why are you always here?" she asks without moving from the makeshift table in this darkened cave.

"Same reason as you."

"I doubt that," she counters.

I take another step forward. "We're both Celestras."

"That means nothing," she whispers.

"Nera, stop lying to yourself."

Before the utterance fully leaves my lips, she has twisted and shifted the few feet directly in front of me, arrow nocked and tip pointing into my chest.

"Stop it," she growls through gritted teeth.

"Stop what."

"Following me." The tip cuts through the fibers of my shirt and I feel the piercing sting against my skin.

"How do you–"

"Do you think I don't know when you're hiding in the shadows as I work? Do you think I can't feel you?"

"I know you can feel me," I whisper as I inch in just that much closer, not allowing my face to betray the building pain in my chest. Oh, how I wish it was just from the nick of the arrow.

"Stop!" She grunts before she steps away, throwing the arrow to the ground. "Just leave me alone."

"I can't."

"Why? Why do this?" Her voice breaks on the plea, and my resolve starts to *crumble at the sound.*

"Why do you not want to work together? Why are you so against an alliance? Why are you so against me?"

"Just because you found me in trouble once, *and helped me* once, *doesn't mean I owe you anything in return."*

"We don't owe each other anything," I counter. *"But we owe the world everything."*

I gasp as the world shifts back into place.

"You really did watch me?" I look up into sparkling golden eyes.

"I told you I did."

"Did I get any better at skinning animals?"

"Yes." The tortured word rakes against my skin.

"Liar." I smirk and he laughs. Then my tone sobers. "Was I always so mean to you?"

"You weren't mean. You were defensive, and loyal to what you thought was the right path."

Though I don't fully believe everything he says, I know there is truth in his words.

"I need to see more."

There is only a moment of pause before he reaches out and my world once again goes black.

The rest of the afternoon is spent in the past as I watch countless interactions between the two of us.

Sometimes I let him speak and we have decent conversations. Sometimes I outright ignore him. But the moments in which my heart twists in agony are the times in which I am a bitter soul—the times in which I aim to hurt him.

I watch as my resolve slowly ebbs away with each encounter, but the sting of the woman I didn't know I was capable of being is still there.

"I'm sorry," I say for what is probably the tenth time as we take our nightly walk around the palace grounds. Each night after dinner, when everyone else gathers for drinks and music, Ari guides us into the gardens, but this time there is no training.

"I told you to stop apologizing." He twists a blade of grass through his fingers.

"I just–"

"Nera, we've already been through this. You were defending yourself, and at that point you had only recently found out about Riann's deception. Your ability to trust others was so low, you barely even trusted yourself."

I still don't. The words stick on my tongue.

"You weren't mean. You have never been mean. You were just scared. And alone."

"I'm still going to apologize."

He laughs. "I'm sure you are."

The music from the other side of the garden picks up as the faint glow from the open doors spills out into the night. We both stand silently, soaking in the melody.

"You used to dance," he says, as if currently reliving the memory itself.

I twist in his direction. "You already told me that."

"You loved this song."

I close my eyes, focusing on the melody. My body begins to sway as if the song itself is my only direction. A soft hum seeps from my lips, and after a moment, I feel the tug of a forming smile.

When I open my eyes, I find him staring down at me in earnest as he reaches out his hand. This time, there's no hesitation as I interlace my fingers within his.

"I don't remember," I whisper as he wraps a tentative arm around my waist to pull me in.

"It's okay. I'll show you."

But he doesn't move. He stands still as he steadies his breathing, and I watch as a thousand emotions flutter across his face. Longing, pain, desire . . . love.

My heartbeat rages and my palms become sweaty. I jolt backward just as he takes the first step with the beat. His eyes find mine.

"Are you–"

I cut him off, "I'm sorry. I'm tired." My voice is meager, mild as I lie. "I'm going to go to bed."

I turn as the pain lances through me. Before he can utter a word, I head for the nearest stairwell in a rush to escape every mounting emotion.

XLI

We have three days before the council members arrive, and for the first time since we shifted here, I feel ready and almost giddy with excitement to show them all I can now do.

I force the breakfast down as quickly as possible in order to rush out to the training grounds to meet Ari. He still spends every night curled in the chair at my bedside, and leaves shortly after I wake so we can both ready ourselves for the day. I still fuss at him each and every morning when I see the lingering exhaustion he can't quite hide.

The hallways are a blur as I race through them out toward the gardens.

"Hello," Ari says as I pass through an archway, and I jolt back in surprise.

"Hi." I laugh off the embarrassment as I stumble backward and regain my footing.

"Want to come in?" He steps to the side, and I slowly pass him by as I make my way into the previously undiscovered room. It's similar to mine in every way but one. The table in my room is all but empty while this one is covered with various maps, books, and items I don't recognize.

"What is this?" My fingers rim the edges of the largest book on the table.

"That is Asfidel."

I jerk upward as a gasp leaves my lips. "The sacred text?"

He nods. "One of them, yes."

"Tarak has Elithium."

He again nods before adding, "And Riann has Drunia."

"Can I look through it?"

He makes a sound as if the question was unimaginable. I quickly pull my fingers backward before he says, "You don't have to ask."

I give a tentative smile before reaching for it once more. "I looked through Elithium when I was with Tarak." I flip through the tattered pages.

When I look up, I find Ari's eyes filled with surprise.

"What?" My brow furrows.

"He let you read it?"

I shrug my shoulders. "I think it was probably a last ditch effort of sorts to see if anything would jog my memory."

"Did it work?" He sounds hopeful.

I laugh at the absurdity of the question, and he mirrors the noise.

"Can you tell me about them?" I inquire as the noise dies out.

"There are three texts. Drunia, Elithium and Asfidel. They each provide various information on the beginning of our world and the stories of the Elders."

"Where did they come from?"

He begins to circle the table as he speaks. "They were found thousands of years ago, and are said to be a gift from the Elders, a guide as to how this world works." He clears his throat. "Drunia holds knowledge of the Soul Circle hidden within each of the four centras. It also tells about the Committence and the trials a sovereign will face. It warns of corruption and greed—everything bad that has already happened."

"But this isn't Drunia. Riann now has that." I look down to the worn pages in front of me. "This is Asfidel."

He nods. "I've learned all I can from Drunia. Although I do wish Riann wasn't in possession of anything relating to our beginnings, at least it's that one."

"You gave it to me when you found me in the Caverns all those years ago."

He nods. "I did. I placed Drunia in a spot I knew you would travel in hopes of gaining your favor."

"Did it work?" I question as he circles the table once more.

"Hmm. Yes and no. You made me work for it."

I laugh. "You said that before."

"Because it's true." He pauses for a moment before he squints his eyes in concentration. "I want to show you something. Would you like to see another memory?"

I eagerly nod in answer.

Ari

The sword is thrown from her grasp.

"You have to hold steady." My frustration is ready to boil over for what feels like the thousandth time today.

"You have to hold steady," she mocks as she reaches downward, but I clasp her wrist before she takes hold of the weapon at her feet.

"This is not a joke." My jaw is so tight with fury that I can barely grit out the words.

"I never said it was."

"You aren't taking this seriously."

She rolls her eyes and yanks her arm free of my grip. "We should be in Niser searching for–"

I scoff. "And what happens when we're attacked?"

"We use our gifts."

"Nera, you don't yet have control over them. You could end up killing not only yourself, but me and–"

The bright orange and red fire light erupts from her fingers and circles my form.

"What was that?" she counters.

My chest heaves with the effort it takes not to defend myself. "Bring it back in."

She rolls her eyes again. "According to you, I can't. According to you, I don't have control over it." The snake-like protrusions slither upward and back into her waiting palm.

As soon as they're gone, my body shifts to hers, and then we're no longer inside the safety of the cavern but standing in a tropical expanse.

"What in the . . ." Her words are seething as she disentangles herself from my grip. "Why . . ." Her breaths come in pants. "Take us back! Now!"

"Do it," I counter.

"What?"

"Bring forth the light."

She stalls at my words.

"No." Her eyes alight with indignation.

"Do it, Nera. Bring on the light. Attack me."

"No!"

"No?" I cross my arms over my chest as she turns to walk away. "Is that a no because you won't? Or is it a no because you can't?"

Her shoulders twist around to face me. "You know I can. You just saw me do it." Every word is spit out with venom. "This is just a control thing with you. But I won't fall for it. I've been controlled for far too–"

"You can't do it because you're relying on the connection to the Caverns in order to heighten your gifts. You can control them when inside, but out here"—I swing my arms out into the open air—"you can't."

Even from this far away, I watch as her jaw flexes in frustration, and I know I have the answers to the questions I have yet to voice.

"You don't know a thing."

My feet move toward her until we are practically nose to nose. "I know enough. Enough to know that you're relying on something that won't always be there."

"Just stop it!" She pushes against my chest, but I don't move an inch.

"No! I won't allow you to walk into danger with no way to defend yourself."

"Why do you care?!"

"Because you–" My words stall in my throat.

Her brows furrow in confusion. "Because what?" The inquiry is barely audible.

"Because this isn't just about me and you. There are too many lives at risk, and if you don't stop being so damn stubborn, you're going to get all of them killed."

Her anger rises and again she pushes hard against my chest. Still, I remain steady. She pushes me again. I don't move. A soft punch lands in my gut, and then another and another before her resolve falters and she breaks down, screaming and sobbing in an agony I know I'll never fully understand.

She collapses in my arms.

"He lied!" she screams out. I don't take the moment for granted. We have been at this for months, and it's the first time she has volunteered anything.

"Who?" I whisper, unsure if my voice will cause her to replace the barriers between us which have now broken.

"He lied! They all lied! It was all a lie!" The muffled screams reverberate off my shoulder as I tighten my hold.

"I'm sorry. I'm so sorry."

"You're going to lie to me, too."

"Never."

"You will. It's my curse. Everything– Everyone close to me either ends up dead or fighting against me." She falls back to sit and pulls her bent knees up to her chest.

"I'm not fighting against you. I never will." I try to comfort her.

"You don't know that!" She recoils from my touch as she wipes away the tears and snot now covering her face.

"I promise," I vow in hopes she can hear the sincerity in my tone.

She further tightens the hold around her knees, and for once, I don't see the brave and strong woman who has captured my every thought. No, now I see what's hiding underneath—someone broken.

"Do you know?" She sniffles with the question.

I shake my head in confusion. "You're going to have to give me more to go on than that." My body longs to inch back to her, but I respect the space she has placed between us.

"Riann? Koreed? Do you know all the horrible truths of Centra I?"

"I know about your father. I know what happened with Himerak."

"And Riann?" Her eyes flicker to mine and I can tell even stating his name caused her pain.

"Yes. I know about him as well."

"And you know I'm supposed to marry him."

I swallow at the thought, a sudden spear of jealousy barreling through me. "Yes."

"Would you have let that happen?"

"You were never going to marry him." The words come out with more conviction than even I knew I possessed.

"He's a traitor," she bites out. My head bobs ever so slightly.

"Nera?" I softly speak her name and find her gaze lingering on mine. "I want to defeat him. I want to shred the Abolition in two. I want to watch him drown and then I want to burn the leftover pieces."

A hint of a smile teases on her lips. Then, "I loved him."

"Do you now?"

Her head shakes vigorously. "Maybe I never really did. I think . . . I think I loved the idea of him. I think I loved him because I was supposed to. Because it was what I was told was my path."

"What do you want your path to be?"

She looks up into the canopy, as if asking the heavens for the answer. "I don't know. I want to find out as I get there." That tease of a smile lifts just that much more. I mirror the sight.

"Would you allow me to join you on that journey?" I shrug my shoulders and she laughs. A true deep laugh.

"It's your death wish."

"Nera Thesand, I would be honored if you took me to the grave."

She shakes her head as she tries to stifle the building giggles. "You're an odd one."

I smile so broadly my cheeks hurt. "Unfortunately, that's true."

"You really want to work together?" Now her tone is serious.

"I do."

"Because we're both Celestras?" Her head tilts to the side, and curious optimism laces each word.

"Because we're fighting for the same end."

She nods, finally accepting what I've been screaming for months, then stands and walks over to her pack, reaches in, and tosses an old friend my way.

I cradle Drunia in my hands as she makes her way back to me.

"Tell me everything," she pleads.

XLII

T he next two days are spent in history lessons of sorts as I attempt to absorb an overwhelming amount of knowledge from each of the texts. I learn that while Drunia is filled with knowledge of the Committence, and Asfidel speaks of the horrors we now know about in the Caverns, it's Elithium which Ari currently seeks to find. It holds more of the origin story he's so desperate to decipher. I watch as his shoulders sag in utter disappointment when I tell him that many of the pages have been ripped out and lost.

On the final morning before the council members are set to arrive, I wake to find golden eyes peering down into mine, and the two moons that linger outside my bedroom window have finally merged into one.

"It's time," he whispers as he strokes my face.

"Tarak's Committence?" I question, and he nods.

We've been waiting for the alignment for days. The two moons, which would signal the moment when Tarak would officially enter, have seemed to lag in movement.

"Get dressed. Nothing too warm. It'll be hot where we're going." He smirks, and I nod, recalling what it was like inside that horrible place. "We're leaving within the hour."

When I make my way outside the door, I find Ari and Dina standing nervously. She passes over a plate of fruit and bread, and a glass of juice, urging me to eat.

"How long will we be gone?"

Ari shrugs. "Depends on how long it takes."

"Will there be other Celestras there? Do they normally watch?"

"No." He shakes his head. "Not unless Riann suddenly gets the urge to cut Tarak off before we can get to him."

Dina takes the glass away as soon as I down the last of its contents. "Keep her safe," she commands, and Ari laughs. Confusion races through me.

"Are you not coming with?"

"I can't," she answers, and my brows furrow.

"She's not a Celestra," Reeves cuts in from behind me. I didn't even hear her enter. "She can't enter the areas beyond the river."

"What happens if someone who isn't a Celestra enters the river?"

"That depends on how long they're submerged. If it's only for a relatively short time, then they'll most likely survive with only surface injuries. Bruises, cuts, burns. But those who remain in the water for too long usually succumb to their injuries once they get out. If they get out."

As she speaks, my mind instantly thinks back to the first time I entered the Caverns. When the water began to rush in, the rest of the crew—with the exception of Tarak, Micel, Riann, and myself—rang out in bellows of agony. I didn't understand it then, but I do now. I then think back to Ranya and the way she looked when we fell from the water and into that pocket of air. Her body was covered in patches of deep purple bruising.

My heart stutters at the idea of entering that water again.

It takes a moment for my nerves to calm enough to steady my steps. The shift to the Caverns is relatively eventless this time, now that I've come into my powers.

Ari reaches out and loops a finger through mine as we stare at the bubbling rivers of lava which seep from the top. "Nothing will attack us. Not this time. You're safe," he whispers in my ear. Though his voice is filled with so much confidence, I know by the grating feeling rushing down my spine that even he doesn't fully believe the statement.

"Tell me the truth," I plead, my eyes boring into his.

His shoulders sag. "It most likely knows you're here. I'm sure it's waiting for us. We have to be vigilant. Don't let a moment pass without being aware of everything around you," he urges, and my chin bobs in agreement.

"What happens when it comes for me?"

"The second something gives me the smallest hint of a threat, I will shift us home."

I nod, unsure if my voice will betray me.

Home.

That is such an odd concept now. I feel as though it was mostly a slip of the tongue. Because he can't mean Reeves's palace. While beautiful and alluring, it's not home. And the cabin in the woods? Well, we haven't been back to see what damage has occurred there.

Maybe when all of this is over, we'll find somewhere to make a new home.

We enter through a north-facing hollow, opposite of the entrance I used when I last entered. But no matter which location we choose, I have a feeling each and every one would be just as foreboding as the last.

We walk in silence, barely letting even our mingling breaths make a noise. The farther we travel, the darker it becomes, and eventually, Ari pulls out one of the beautiful orbs of light from his bag and swipes a hand over the top, igniting the burning embers inside.

"That's so beautiful," I whisper, in awe of the contraption. He smiles.

After another couple hundred yards through the twists and turns I will never be able to memorize, we come upon a deep obsidian river.

"This is where we enter."

"Do we swim?"

He shakes his head, a small smile playing on his lips as he secures his pack to a nearby jagged rock. "We'll go under, and then once the guides deem us worthy, we–"

"Worthy?"

"Celestras. Once it's known what we are, they will pull us down and through the current."

My entire stomach caves in on itself as I recall the spindly hand which yanked Ranya and I down into the air pocket. Ari stills, noting the panic rising inside me.

"Nera, you've done this countless times before." He runs a finger over my hand in an attempt to calm me, but my hands shake even further. "Nera?"

"I don't know if I can do this."

"You can, and I'll be right with you the entire time. I won't let you go." He grabs my hand. "But if you don't want to go, I can take you back."

I shake my head, and he squeezes my hand.

"You can do this," he promises once more as we step up to the edge of darkness and plunge in.

Time is suspended for a mere moment as we hold our breaths and wait, Ari's arms wrapped tightly around my middle and my head buried into his neck. Then I feel it.

My muffled scream dies out in the murky water as something slithers around my ankle. I can't help but wrestle against the grip, but Ari holds me still and I feel the shake of his head against my own.

My lungs burn in effort to stay under as the creature coils itself up my legs, around my side, and then finds my arms wrapped so tightly around Ari I have almost lost all feeling.

It pauses for a heartbeat, as if contemplating exactly what it has found. And then, just as it tightens its hold around my body, we're forced downward, the rushing current passing at our sides.

Ten, fifteen, twenty seconds pass. I fear I may drown if we're kept under a moment longer. But then the darkness turns to light, and we're moving upward. Up. Up. Up.

I gasp as we break through to the surface, but I don't release my hold on my sanctuary.

"We made it," Ari whispers in my ear just as the creature slowly disentangles itself from my body and slithers away.

There is barely any strength left in my body. Ari swims us up to the bank, and I have to crawl upward as I suck in each breath of air.

"What was that thing?"

"The guard of the Committence."

"I didn't like it."

Ari laughs. "I would be more frightened if you did." He stands and reaches out a hand. When I stand to meet him, I find pride in his gaze. "Hard part's over." He brushes a hand along my cheek, and I lean in. "Are you ready?"

"Are you?"

He nods, but the motion's strained, and I can tell there is more beneath that he isn't saying.

At first, this was just a mission to assess if Tarak would be able to complete his trials so that we could cut him off. We need to get to him before Riann or anyone else does. We have to make him see reason so he can join our cause. But once I let Ari in on exactly how Tarak used his gifts on me, I knew that thought changed.

"He can't do that to me again." I mirror his expression, my hand reaching up to rest against his jaw.

His eyes close. "I know."

"I'm okay. I'm here," I try to soothe him with my words.

His answering smile is infectious. "I know."

His eyes open, and I find steely determination in their depths.

"Remember, once he's out, we have to catch up to him. He can't shift, so it shouldn't be a hard feat. Stay strong. Just facts. And we must be quick."

I nod.

"Okay. Let's go." He places an arm against my back as he guides us through another network of tunnels and caves. But this sight is far worse than what even the upper levels had to offer.

No light comes through from the surface. Instead, the open cave system is illuminated by flowing rivers of molten lava that seem to wait around every turn. Deep drop offs which lead to incomprehensible depths spring forth when I least expect them. And the heat all but overtakes me.

Just as I'm about to question how much further we have to walk through this hellish landscape, I feel a quick tug on my arm, and Ari brings us to a stop behind a nearby boulder.

At first, I don't see him. The rivers of lava have turned the floor into a vibrant, fiery maze, and the chaos of it all has stolen my attention. But then, just as I'm about to ask Ari to point out what he's found, I see him.

Tarak. Bent over and heaving.

"What's wrong with him?" I'm ready when the burning anger rises at the sight of him. What I don't expect is the pity that follows, now that I truly know and understand the life he has to lead.

"I'm not sure," Ari answers, confusion marring his features. "I don't see anything fighting him. Unless he just won."

"Maybe it's over?"

"No. Not–"

A wail of pain lurches out as Tarak falls backward.

"NO!" he screams out as his hands clasp his head, and I know there must be an invisible force we cannot see. He screams once more. The sound is so painful, I almost cower.

Then he falls forward as shadows leech from his chest and dance around his prone form. Colorful flames escape each obsidian silhouette as they move as one to ensnare the man I once believed I loved.

Languid tendrils reach out to his battered form, and I know he's been here battling whatever this is for far longer than we could imagine. As each one takes hold, I watch as his body becomes taken over. Moments of sadness turn into fits of rage. There's a point where he screams out his pain so loudly, I swear the cavern will crumble at the echoes, but then he curls in on himself as silent, shuddering sobs race through his body.

"They're playing his ability against him," Ari explains.

"What do you mean?"

"He can manipulate emotions. They're letting the emotions manipulate him. The trial is that he has to overcome them—fight them off.

I take a deep breath, uncertain how to reconcile what I now see with the man I know. Maybe this is payback for what he did to me. But even that thought seems to pain me.

XLIII

I watch unblinking as he battles each demon made from his own mind. My breath halts, and though I know I have no lingering feelings left, I still all but spring forward each time one reaches him and latches on.

The sight so ensnares my attention that, at first, I don't notice the change in temperature. I barely feel the heat start to recede and the cold begin to slither in.

A chilly breeze wraps around my legs before winding up to embrace my chest. A gurgling noise sounds at my side. I twist, ice pumping through my veins at the thought something may have attacked Ari, and I lunge forward to take his outstretched hand as a blackened shadow surges between us.

Instead of his hand, I grasp nothing but cold air. Ari, Tarak, the lava-filled cavern . . . it's all just . . . gone.

I stand and turn, taking in my new surroundings. This new cavern is dark, empty. Cold and dreary. Drops of water plunge down from far above, splashing into the inch-deep water at my feet.

I wrap my arms around myself to ward off the lingering chill, but nothing helps, and soon my teeth are chattering and my hands are shaking.

"You found me," the silky voice calls out to me.

I spin to find a figure hidden within shadows inching toward me. As it walks forward, the water below remains still. Undisturbed, even as my heartbeat reaches a fevered pace. With each step, a piece of its charred flesh falls away, nothing but ash on that eerie breeze.

I stand paralyzed by my terror, my lips unwilling to open on a scream. But who would even answer my plea?

"You found me."

The voice is so gentle, so reassuring, my muscles are nearly convinced to reach out to the mysterious thing.

"Who are you?" My voice is barely a whisper as the pitch-dark scorched form takes another step toward me.

It chuckles deeply. "*You don't recognize me?*" It spreads its arms, wisps of ash following the movement, gesturing around the room. "*You don't recognize* us?"

Hundreds—no, thousands of forms just like the nightmarish being that stands only yards before me are slowly moving closer.

"What is this? Where am I? Where's Ari?" My quivering words and chattering teeth betray the fear I am so desperate to hide. The being moves closer.

Its head tilts, assessing. "*Are you cold?*" it asks, now mere feet from me. The voice slithers along my bones as it begs to be let inside.

I long to step away, but that would only put me closer to others. My heart pounds out a violent warsong within my ribcage.

"Who are you?"

It takes another step forward, the curved edges of its grotesque face now slowly creeping into view. A sinister smile spreads across its half-missing face, and my breath freezes in my throat. This is the same thing I burned to ash in the underground tunnels of Reeves's palace.

This is the Shadow.

My head twists to find others so close, I can now make them out as well. Each one burned, charred. Some are missing large sections of flesh. Seared skin pulls away, exposing bone and muscle. Others are barely even formed.

"*Don't you recognize me?*" the first calls out again, now no more than an inch from me. My lips part and a shriek pours from my lips as the chorus of burned and broken souls rings out all at once.

"*You did this!*"

"*It's your fault!*"

"*Murderer!*"

"*Killer!*"

"*Celestra!*"

The bony hand covered in flaking skin claps my cheek, turning me back to face it.

"*Don't you recognize me?*" it calls out in earnest as the sinister smile grows, bits crumbling from its face with the movement. I can barely make out anything in its features other than what I know will forever haunt my nightmares, should I ever make it out of this hell.

My sobs drag on, my body quakes in terror.

The hand wraps around my jaw and tilts my head downward to face the reflective surface of the still water below.

"*I'm you.*"

My image mirrors the one before me, barely formed body, burned and charred. The flesh of my face melts away as screams heave from my chest over and over and over.

My hands and knees crash to the ground, water splashing, fracturing the image just as the other forms converge. I count the seconds, knowing I won't make it out. One by one they inch closer, slowed in movement by their missing and burnt limbs. But when I pull my hands from the water, soft, familiar feathers fill my palms.

Deep echoes reverberate through the caverns from somewhere in the distance. The army of charred forms halts mid-stride, waiting, calculating.

The only noises are those of my heaving breaths and the drumming of my heartbeat within my ears.

Then they come again. The echoes. This time louder. This time closer.

The broken bodies begin to pull away, as out of a crevice in the wall of black rock, a giant creature comes careening in. Its massive wings span tens of feet, and its talons shred those broken souls as it swoops downward to where I crouch.

Water splashes at its feet and cruel bellows promising pain and suffering ring out from its mouth.

"Anepi?" I whisper in awe as the bird's head dips in a gesture of reverence. Wide eyes slowly survey those lingering souls. When none move, a screeching cry peals from the anepi's throat in warning, and all turn away in fear.

But for me, there is only kindness in the bird's gaze. The feathered body tilts downward, great wings spreading out in the water, and though I have no reason to believe I'm safe, a wave of relief washes through me. Water splashes as I rush to the anepi's side. Just as my hand reaches out to stroke the neck, a silent thanks and plea to take me away, the world splinters and the room disappears.

My eyes peel open to find golden orbs dancing in my vision.

"Nera?" Ari calls out, pain lancing each word.

"Ari?"

"I'm here. You're here. You're okay," he soothes.

I twist, expecting to find myself in that water, those haunting forms surrounding us.

"Where am I?"

"Your bed. Reeves's palace." The words come out so swiftly, it feels as if he isn't sure how to speak.

"I'm back?" Tears burn my throat, chin quivering with the hope flooding my chest.

"You're back," Reeves confirms, her form slowly taking shape the closer she comes.

"What happened?"

"I'm sorry," Ari begs, and from the trembling in his voice, in his hands, I know it is taking everything for him not to break.

A tear falls down his cheek as the memory of what occurred barrels through me and I sit up, throwing myself to my side as the vomit surges and spills out onto the floor.

XLIV

"We don't have to go. We can call it off."

I almost laugh at the absurdity. I have been waiting for this meeting for too long to back out now. That would only serve to prove what a coward I truly am.

We lay there on the pillowy bed in silence as I contemplate how to prove I am fit to attend.

"I want to go," I declare with as much conviction as I can muster after a day spent in literal hell and a night with barely any sleep. I open my mouth to make a further argument when he nods and holds up a hand.

"Okay. If you're ready, then we'll go."

My mouth immediately clamps shut, if only from pure shock as I look over to him. He didn't question, he didn't pry, he irrefutably and undeniably believed me. He believes me.

He trusts me.

I lift his arm and wrap it around my head as I move my body closer to his, desperate for some sort of comfort. At first, his muscles go rigid, tense, as if any movement will shatter whatever gift I've just given him. But soon, he eases into the position, and I realize that our bodies fit together as if made perfectly for this very moment.

He sighs into my hair, and though his body becomes still and quiet, I feel a droplet of liquid hit my scalp. He's crying.

"Tell me what will happen," I say in an effort to distract his mind and quell the emotion I know is about to rise up within me. "What will they do?" I ask before I take a deep inhale of him.

"I'm not sure," he answers honestly. "There has never been a meeting like this."

"That's not very comforting." I chuckle, hoping to smother the building tension.

"In truth, I think they just want to see that you're here and alive. They need to see it to believe it, and they need to know that if you so choose, you will lead us again."

"I will."

"They're going to need to hear you say it."

"I know."

He shakes his head. "Nera, I don't want you to be anything other than who you are at this moment. I don't want you to try to be someone who no longer exists."

My brow furrows. "I don't understand."

"Just be you. When we're in there, don't try to act or present yourself in a certain way. I want you to just be you." He tilts my gaze up to meet a wicked smile playing on his face, and I know he is trying just as hard to calm whatever lingering nerve I might have stirring deep inside.

My hand lifts and traces the outline of his jaw, a healthy stubble forming.

I'm not really sure who leans in first. Maybe it's him, or perhaps it's me. But in the next breath, I feel his lips graze mine, and then he sucks in a breath of surprise.

"I missed you," he breathes against me.

"I missed you." I mean every word. I may not be able to remember him fully from before, but I know I missed him. I felt him—or better yet, I felt the hole formed by his absence every single day I was without him.

He only hesitates a moment once I press in a little further, as if making sure this is real. My lips are only on his for a heartbeat before he has flipped us and I am directly beneath him as he lays out a carefully placed attack.

A thousand pebbled kisses touch every inch of my face. It is slow and sweet, and yet still causes my entire body to light with flame and want. A giggle threatens to erupt as a flurry of emotions surges through me, but I somehow manage to hold it in.

It's at this moment that I think *I could skip the meeting for this* and smile as he nuzzles his face in my neck and inhales deeply.

I don't question it, but I swear I hear a whispered *"Mine"* pass his lips as he makes his way across my collar bone.

But just as I slide my hands slowly under the hem of his shirt, a knock barrels out from the door. His eyes meet mine as a silent apology hangs between us.

"It's time," he whispers against my lips.

"It's time," I whisper back.

The memory of this morning burns through me with such intensity, I find my eyes drifting upward as we walk down the corridor.

His hand is effortlessly placed on my lower back, and every now and then, I feel the quick brush of his thumb along my spine.

Combined with the thoughts of his lips on mine, that quick brush sends goosebumps spreading out to every inch of my skin. I wrap my arms around my middle in effort to dull the sensation, but of course he notices.

"Are you cold?" he asks, and I immediately shake my head, then glare at Dina as she bursts out laughing. Her gaze travels to my feverish skin. When she notes the placement of his hand, she eyes me knowingly.

"Shut. Up," I whisper as I roll my eyes at her and she cocks her head to the side in amused confusion. "Be quiet," I amend, realizing what phrase I used and refusing to acknowledge the memory the exchange brings forth.

She chuckles once more, indicating she understands my meaning, but still doesn't let up easily. "I didn't say a thing."

"What's going on?" Ari questions, oblivious.

A split second later, Dina and I both reply, "Nothing."

By the inquisitive smirk he now gives off, I know he doesn't believe us.

I turn my attention back to the halls we're passing through, marveling at how I can manage to still be surprised by the sheer size of this place. I have spent the last month moving around this palace, and I still feel as though I have only seen a small portion of what it has to offer. My days are spent within the confines of the east wing and training within the garden. Nights now begin with a massive dinner in the grand hall with all those Reeves deems trustworthy enough to let in on my arrival. It's only a small crowd, but still more than I feel comfortable getting close with.

Then, if I feel up to it, dinner is followed by a round of drinks and watching the others dancing in a side room.

These gatherings are so different from the parties Koreed held. Those were stifled with formal protocol and my own mounting confusion. Centra IV parties feel like a family has finally all come back together after a long time apart. Maybe that's exactly what they are.

I think back to the other night when I shocked both Ari and myself by finally agreeing to enter the side room following dinner. I still barely drank, and I never really danced, but I mingled, and that was nice. Freeing in a way I was desperately craving.

I spent the next two nights observing from the side as those I had come to know, and those who were still strangers to me drank, laughed and danced in the dim candlelight. Dina informed me that, normally, the palace grounds were open to and full of the citizens of Centra IV per Reeves's decree and her love for her people. Though she's a Celestra herself, she came from the poorest part of her centra, fought like hell in her Committence, and made a promise to never allow innocent people to go without again. And so these dinners and dancing nights were typically filled to the brim with people from all walks of life.

But now it's different. And that's all my fault. The entrance gate to the palace is locked, and the group mingling about is now smaller, more intimate. A simple lie of renovations keeps the citizens and the rumors at bay, but in reality, it is I who is the cause.

They have to keep me safe. They have to make sure there's no chance for Tarak and the settlement, or the Abolition, or Koreed and the Halabarian soldiers to learn of my location, and make their way inside the walls to take me once more. I still cringe at the possibility.

And even with the smaller group surrounding us, I know there are whispers of exactly who or what I am. I try to escape the rumors, but no matter how much I train my ears not to listen, at least once a day I hear someone comment on the state of mine and Ari's non-existent relationship, and the suspicion that I still harbor feelings for an enemy.

But that isn't it at all. Thoughts of Tarak in that manner quickly fled the moment his betrayal was revealed. My hatred for the situation he placed me in only grew more when I was far enough away from him to no longer feel the pull of his powers. And there is obviously nothing between Riann and I.

But Ari . . .

Ari's different, and that scared me—still scares me.

Ari feels real and true. More so than I can even comprehend. There have been moments when my body has begged me to lean further into him. To offer up whatever he would take. But then, sometimes when I'm all alone, the thoughts of him have felt foreign and benign. Frustratingly enough, while I've tried to shuffle through exactly what those feelings mean with little headway.

The only response my body allowed was the feeling of fear. Fear that I'm taking something from him. Fear that I'm keeping him from something. Fear that I'm not exactly who he believes me to be.

Those are the worries which circle my mind in the middle of the night when I wake to find him fast asleep in the chair by the window.

The picture of his finally sleeping and relaxed form curled up in the chair that is far too small for him is the final calm thought that rushes through my mind as we turn the corner and find the massive stone doors.

XLV

The creak of the hinges might as well be a warning of what's to come. As soon as we step across the threshold, my attention is drawn to the deep green and brown marbling in the smooth stone floors.

A myriad of guards seem to enter from every hidden space as they slowly align themselves with our group.

My feet mirror Reeves's gait as we walk. So much so that when she stalls before a new door, my body runs straight into hers. She turns back with a tentative glance.

"You alright?" she asks.

I nod in answer as I force my gaze not to meet those of Ari and Dina at my sides.

"These are our people," he urges, and I feel his fingers brush against mine.

"People who don't yet trust me," I whisper back as the final barrier door starts to open.

"They will," he promises. Without quite knowing why, as soon as he begins to pull away, I latch onto his hand and intertwine my fingers with his.

"You can do this," Dina assures just before she steps to the side. I'm half-tempted to clasp my hand within hers as well, but by the time I reach out, she has already fallen back to walk in behind us.

"She's not a Celestra," Ari answers my unspoken question.

And then we're inside.

The room isn't nearly as large as I assumed it would be based on the sheer size of the door alone. The small space is made worse by the fact that the atmosphere is thick with tension. The ceiling is covered in beautiful wooden beams with a large domed window at its center, and the floor seems to shimmer against the moving sunlight from above.

But what really catches my eye is the centerpiece of the room. A round table which sits four steps lower than the surrounding floor, directly below the dome. Eight high-back chairs encompass the golden stone surface.

When my gaze meets Ari's, I find a warm smile urging me onward.

With each forward movement, the anxiety from before slowly melts away as a new sense of ease settles upon my shoulders.

As if our bodies are one, we both just barely hold in the audible gasp of shock at the same time. Only four of those eight chairs are filled. Ari tries to hide the tension that rolls through him at the sight, but I catch the miniscule movement in his hand. I squeeze him back in comfort, not yet knowing what exactly I'm comforting him for.

But he never even bats an eye. He holds tight as we take the steps one by one until we reach the table. Once we do, he directs me to my spot as he and Reeves take the seats directly on either side of me.

"Good morning," Reeves says to the four sitting across from us. For some reason, I assumed many more would be present. I think Ari did as well. But it's only now, when the sun moves ever so slightly in the sky and the shadows shift across the room, that I notice the numerous people standing in the shadows. My breath hitches in nervousness as each one meets my gaze.

"Good morning." The man sitting directly across from me bows his head. The one next to him scowls at the gesture.

Ari clears his throat. "I assume everyone here has been fully apprised of the situation."

I watch as those standing a few feet away and slightly hidden by the shadows nod their heads in agreement.

The man with the scowl leans forward. "If you mean the information concerning Nera and her loss . . . " His voice is tentative and grave. ". . . then unfortunately yes, we have."

My response tumbles out of its own accord, and I silently applaud myself for this sudden brave stand. "Then you are aware that I am relearning most of what you already know, and that I have retaken control of my powers."

He nods, though I can see frustration filling his gaze.

I lift my chin, meeting his tone head on as I make my request. "In that case, would you mind reintroducing yourself?"

The first man gives a sad smile, the second looks repulsed. The other two are merely indifferent.

"My name is Kersack," the man with the sad eyes states, "and I am from Centra III. I was the previous sovereign before Ari took over last year."

My attention shoots to Ari in surprise. And while I've had my suspicions that this was the case, having it confirmed out loud for the first time causes my lips to turn up in a broad smile. An unexpected sense of pride swells within me.

"Is that right, Sir Ari?"

He coughs in order to hide the laugh that threatens to burst out.

Confusion flits across each of the faces at the table, but I don't miss Reeves's quick tilt of her head downward as she tries to cover the smile.

Ari clears his throat. "Kersack was a great mentor to us both. I am sure that once you two become reacquainted, you will find him to be a wonderful source of knowledge."

I nod along as he speaks, hoping to give off an air of ease and certainty, as opposed to the pulsing fear which threatens to bubble up.

Then my gaze shifts back to the other three unknowns. "Are all of us who are seated at the table Celestras?"

They each nod.

"And what gifts do you each possess?"

Kersack clears his throat before answering. "Mine are the same as Ari's."

"And who are you?" I nod my head toward the second, considerably less pleasant man.

He groans, not bothering to hide his annoyance. "I am Arthyr. Previous Sovereign to Centra IV."

I immediately shift my gaze to find a tense expression upon Reeves's face, and realize there may be a story hiding underneath that cool stare.

"And your gifts?"

"I could manipulate the elements."

"And you?" I nod to the much older woman next to Arthyr.

She stands before speaking. "I am Cyrs." Soft features and thinning white curls brighten her face. "I am also a previous Celestra to Centra IV, and I *used* to be a soothsayer." She looks to both Arthyr and Reeves before turning back to me. "Though that was a very long time ago." She gives me a knowing smile I can't help but return. "I am honored to have you back."

The youngest man beside her shifts awkwardly in his chair as our eyes meet.

"Fritz," he says swiftly. "I'm Fritz. I'm able to see one's past, but nothing else." He clears his throat, and I feel Ari place a hand at my back.

"Fritz is new to us. He's not a sovereign, but he is a Celestra from my home, Centra III. He's only a year older than you."

I look over to the man to find sweat rolling from his brow and staining his cotton shirt, and I smile, sensing the nervousness bouncing off the young man.

"It's nice to meet you."

He nods, ducking his head. If I were seated just a tad closer, I'm sure I would see him wiping the sweat from his hands onto the fabric of his pants.

"And all those standing around?" I gesture to the others, slightly impressed that my voice sounds so steady and commanding.

One woman steps forward, her frame now bathed in light from the dome of windows in the ceiling.

"We are the Restoration." At her declaration, all fifty or more who stand behind her move, and I quickly rise and twist in order to take them all in. As they come into view, moving into the streams of golden sunlight, their bodies alight as if carrying their own flames. Each is dressed so similarly to those from the settlement that I have to stop and take a breath to make sure I don't see any familiar faces.

Their hair is pulled back, and even those with short styles wear variously colored strands woven through their braids. But what gives me the most pause is the design stitched onto the front of their uniform across the chest. My hand instinctively rubs the mark on my wrist.

Ari taps me on the back to bring my gaze back to his. "Go to them," he whispers, and without hesitation, I move. He quickly follows suit with a hand placed at my back. "They fight for you."

My feet carry me around the table and through the flickering light pouring down before I meet the first woman in the group.

I open my mouth to speak, but uncertainty creeps in and the words halt in my throat.

"May the light drown out the dark." She dips her chin as her two fingers tap her chest, right over the emblem that I also bear.

I stand still, allowing the moment to wash over me. Goosebumps cover every inch of my skin, even my scalp, making it feel as though my hair stands on end.

Ari leans down, his long hair brushing my ear just before he directs, "Now you say it back," under his breath.

"May the light drown out the dark," I repeat, and in the next heartbeat, the room erupts into a flurry of thunderous excitement and chants as all repeat what we just spoke. But then I notice something else lingering in the noise. Another phrase I've heard before.

"Ebeli Mushari."

"Ebeli Mushari."

"Ebeli Mushari."

"What does that mean?" I look between Ari and the woman, not knowing who will answer over the roaring.

Ari gives me a soft smile before he cups my cheek. "It's the original language. Language from our Elders," he clarifies. "It means 'May the light drown out the dark.'" His hand comes to rest on my back as it did earlier. "You, Nera, have always been, and will always be that light."

XLVI

I'm not sure how I end up back in the seat around the massive table. I'm not even sure if I remember walking here.

One moment, I was standing in the center of this massive room, in what felt like a sea of people who were chanting what amounted to their declaration of loyalty for me. And the next, I find myself sitting in this chair, staring at my trembling hands, and wondering exactly what it is they see in me.

"I believe it is time."

My attention jerks up at the callus tone seeping from the man's lips. It takes a moment to realize he's staring at me, and another moment still to recall his name.

Allen? All– something? Art? Arthyr! The name finally bounces back to the forefront of my clouded mind.

"I'm sorry, Arthyr. Time for what?" My tone is undeniably steady and sounds more sure than I'm feeling at the moment.

"Have you been paying attention?" Arthyr rolls his eyes in exasperation.

Ari straightens. "You are speaking with Nera–" He quickly clears his throat. "You are speaking with Nera. I shouldn't have to remind you to watch your tone." His words are cool and calculated, but I can sense the boiling anger hidden beneath the surface. I reach out to intertwine my fingers with his below the table, and his taut muscles relax with the contact.

"I know who I speak with," Arthyr cuts back. "The question is, does she?"

I swallow hard at the implication.

"I know very well who I am." My eyes meet his straight on.

"And do you know where your loyalties lie?" He shifts to rest his clasped hands on the table, causing his navy tunic to open slightly. Just enough that the large golden pendant hanging from his neck becomes visible.

While this palace is quite large, it is abundantly clear that Reeves has no desire to flaunt her wealth. No, she would much prefer to share it with the masses. But this man . . . This man shares no such humility. His golden tunic is covered in gems and embroidery, and he wears more piercings and jewelry than I can even count. I haven't seen even a glimpse of such wealth since leaving Halabar.

"Very much so."

He nods my way. "I want to see it."

Dread settles in my core. I know this is why we're here. I have to prove what I can do. I have to show them that I've regained my powers and can lead them to victory. My fingers start to slide away from the comfort of Ari's grasp as I prepare to stand.

Ari stiffens at my side, his grip tightens, and I know he means for me to remain still.

"No," Ari states as he looks around the room.

"What do you mean, 'No?' I need to know what she can do!" Arthyr counters.

Ari shakes his head. "She is not a toy you can play with."

Arthyr grunts in frustration. "Unfortunately, none of us are soothsayers. If she wants to gain our trust, then she must prove to us what she can do."

"No," Ari grinds out. "She will–"

"Why do you need to see it?" I quickly cut in.

"I want to know that your gifts have returned. I want to be sure that when we fight, we will win." While he speaks true, there's something . . . off in the phrasing which I can't quite pinpoint.

"And what if they haven't returned?"

My question shocks him.

"Have they not?" He takes a deep breath in preparation for my answer, and I can see the thoughts swirling through his mind.

"That is not the question I asked. I asked, 'What if they haven't returned?'" He doesn't move, visibly unsure of how to respond. "It seems your tongue has become too heavy to speak. Let me elaborate." After a quick squeeze, I slowly release Ari's hand. My palms lift to match Arthyr's placement on the table as I stand, one opponent against another. "Does your loyalty only go to those you believe will win?" My opponent stiffens. "If so, then I don't believe you're someone I want fighting on my side anyway."

His nostrils flare in fury. "You twist my words."

I can't help but cut my eyes over to Kersack, who seems to be desperately trying to suppress the smirk threatening to erupt across his face.

I do my best to hold back a smirk of my own. But there's something off about this man, this conversation, and I have to find out what.

"How can I twist words which were never spoken?"

"Are you mocking me?" He leans forward, his anger building exactly as I expected it would.

"I'm only stating facts."

He heaves a shuddering breath. "What's your play, Nera?"

And in this moment, I know how to use my gifts without him even knowing I have. "I just want to make sure the people I have on my side are truly on my side. I don't like traitors."

Arthur recoils as if he's been slapped, and I know my prey has been caught.

"I am *not* a traitor!" he seethes through gritted teeth, and my blood turns hot as icy tendrils coil around my spine. I twist my hands around to grip the edge of the table, and hide my fingers as wayward sparks fly from their tips.

Ari's hand slides to the back of my thigh, holding me steady as I ground myself in the knowledge that I have just outed a traitor amongst us.

"I never said you were."

Arthyr's breathing becomes labored as his mind races through his next moves. Plotting his attack in order to mark me as the enemy. "You have spent the last few months, in actuality, the last few years, with the enemy. How do we know what side you will fight for?" But I am already paces ahead.

"You don't."

He stills, not expecting such honesty. "What are you saying?"

"Arthyr, I don't know what friendship you and I shared previously. As you know, I don't remember you or anyone else here at all. But what I do know is that when I bind myself with someone, with a group of people, I do so with my entire heart. And I do so in trust." He swallows at my words. "I had planned to show all of you that my gifts have returned. Now, I am not so keen to do so. Mostly because I do not trust *you.*"

Arthyr, who has had only moments to gather himself, violently stands, the chair falling over behind him. I don't move an inch. I barely breathe.

"Trust?!" His shoulders rise and fall with the intake of breath. "You talk of trust after you spent the last few months bearing your body and soul to those who wish to end us."

His words cut deep, but I know they are only meant to distract us from what I have exposed.

"Arthyr!" Ari pounds a fist on the table as he stands at my side. The hand previously holding my steady rises up my back and settles against my hip.

Arthyr's palms make a horrid sound as he slams them before us. "You!" He then points a finger toward Ari. "You weak man." The hoards of people standing around stiffen and ready themselves for the attack. "While you were out searching for her, she was letting the enemy bury themselves within her. She is the en–"

Ari shifts so quickly, he is gone from my side and standing over Arthyr before

I even hear the man's body hit the ground.

"Don't you dare. You know *nothing.*" Ari hurls the words with such violence, I swear it is not even his voice which speaks them. He then spits in Arthyr's face before grabbing him by the collar and lifting him from the ground. "Apologize to your commander," he demands.

"No!" Arthyr reaches up to push Ari back, but freezes mid movement.

Arthyr's gaze becomes unfocused, his face contorting first in fear and then anguish.

"Apologize!" Ari demands once more, his stance rigid, sweat beginning to pour from his brow.

A guttural, agonized moan escapes Arthyr's lips. He blinks rapidly, then closes his eyes, as if the sight before him is too horrible to bear. A moment later, his eyes shoot open as he comes back into himself. "No!"

"Ari!" Reeves bellows her warning while I stand frozen, unsure of what I'm seeing.

"I will not tell you again!" Ari whispers through gritted teeth. I can feel the pain which lances through him.

Cyrs and Fritz seem to mirror my current stance, while Kersack looks nothing if not pleased with the scene playing out before him.

But Reeves is having none of it.

"Ari!" She stands and slowly makes her way over to the two men.

"Apologize!" Ari seethes, then Arthyr slips back into the unknown, his face a mask of pain and anguish, before he quickly comes back.

Tears slip from Arthyr's eyes. "Stop," he whispers, and Ari stiffens. But before Arthyr can slip back to wherever he keeps drifting off to, he lets out a guttural, "I'm sorry."

Ari releases the shirt, and Arthyr sinks to his knees in relief. Ragged breaths race through both men.

"Don't insult her again. If and when she chooses to show you her power will forever be up to her. And yes, we had planned for today to be that day, but I don't believe that to be the case anymore."

Ari walks back to my side as I try to hide the stunned expression that covers my features.

"We are done for the day," he tells Reeves, grabbing my hand and leading us from the room.

The second the doors slam behind us, Ari wraps me in his arms and the world goes black. When the light trickles in again, I find us standing in my room at the palace. He pulls me into his arms and buries his face in my hair. His warm breath tickles my neck as he steadies himself.

"Ari?" I whisper but he says nothing. "Ari?" I plead for a response as I clasp his face in my hands.

"I'm sorry." His words are spoken as if a confession. "I'm sorry."

"It's okay." I pull back to meet his heavy stare as I try to decipher what he could possibly be apologizing for.

"I was wrong. I'm sorry. I was wrong."

My brows crease as my heart rate spikes.

"I don't understand. Wrong?"

"I have been preparing you and training you so that your powers will return—so that we can prove to them that you are ready. But I was wrong."

My heart sinks. "You don't think I'm ready?" It's barely a whisper.

He laughs as he realizes I don't understand his meaning at all. "You are ready. You always were. But you don't need to prove that to them. I shouldn't have put that weight on you, and I'm sorry."

"There is nothing to apologize for."

His head shakes as he holds my shoulders steady. "There is. I was so concerned with whether or not they would accept you again that I didn't see the truth staring directly in my face." He pauses as if waiting for me to catch up, but instead, I'm more confused than before. "The Restoration will always stand with you. You don't need to prove anything to anyone. Least of all me."

I think back to the way the members of the Restoration didn't even blink when I approached. They accepted me the moment I walked into the room. Gifts or no gifts, I am their Celestra.

Dina comes bursting into the room with a heavy breath as she rolls her eyes at the both of us. "You couldn't have taken me too?"

Ari pays no attention to her question as he leans his forehead on mine.

"What about Arthyr?"

Ari takes a shuddering breath. Before he opens his mouth to respond, Dina cuts him off.

"You don't trust him, do you?"

"I don't." My answer is immediate. "I don't know why but I–"

"You can feel it. You can feel that something is off with him. You can tell he lied when he said he wasn't a traitor," Ari finishes for me, and I nod.

"What does that mean?"

Ari runs his hands down my arms and intertwines his fingers in mine. "It means we may have just found out who has been supplying the Abolition with our plans." He purses his lips as he holds in the anger. But then he catches my gaze, and a soft smile spreads across his face. "It means we can officially begin."

I feel more confident as I stand before the wooden doors today. Ari at my side, Dina at my back.

She reaches out to repeat what both she and Ari have already said numerous times. "Remember, he can't know that we don't trust him. We need to act as if we have only been taking time to gather ourselves, and for Ari to calm down."

"I understand." I nod in her direction. "We need to feel him out. Get what information we can while making him believe Ari lost a little control due to our situation." I repeat the same phrase she has drilled into my head over the last few hours.

One part sticks in my mind.

Our situation.

That's how she referred to Ari and me, because saying anything more would lead to confusion and awkwardness on both our parts. We haven't spoken of that kiss, nor the one prior. We haven't truly explored what is between us. And I know that it's killing him more and more each day I let pass without fully acknowledging or accepting what he is—what we are.

She smiles in answer as I pull my thoughts back to center.

Ari keeps his sight directed straight above, readying himself to walk back into what could either make or break the plan we've devised.

After we first walked out of the meeting yesterday, Ari explained his thoughts and beliefs. He has never had much faith in Arthyr. The man has always been too cryptic, too unknown. Reeves mirrored the sentiment. But prior to my disappearance, I had not yet been able to discern lies, and thus we had no way to determine if Arthyr was being truthful or not. Once we realized I would slowly be gaining a version of each of the celestial gifts, we waited for that one to come, hoping it would help us determine if he was indeed the traitor to blame for the fact that the Abolition always seemed to be right on our heels. It didn't come in time.

But this time, I could feel it. I know something is off with Arthyr, and I have a sinking feeling it's because he's not truly with us.

It was then that I asked Ari exactly what had happened when Arthyr seemed to drift off from the here and now.

"I altered what he saw. I made him watch someone from his past die."

I gasped in shock.

"It was the only memory I could think of that would make him bend." The words were somber, and even though I know Ari dislikes Arthyr, I could tell he didn't like what he'd done.

"Who was it? What did you show him?"

"His older brother, Jonu. He died because we didn't get to him in time. Arthyr feels responsible for it." Ari rubbed the scars which line his forearm, and my stomach filled with guilt. "I showed him the death."

"That was cruel."

"War isn't pretty, Nera." He then placed his head in his hands before he stood, walked to the bathroom, and slammed the door.

The rest of the day and into the evening consisted of debating how best to handle Arthyr, as well as another history lesson for me of what exactly we would be doing now.

So here we are a day later, back with the others to figure out exactly how we will retrieve the remaining stones and end the four penances of this world. End the terrors I set loose upon the people all those years ago.

But when we walk to the table, I find one person missing.

"Where is he?" Reeves asks as soon as the doors close behind us.

"I don't know," Cyrs answers, her mouth a tight line.

"If I may speak?" The woman at the head of the Restoration steps forward.

Ari nods. "Missand, you are always free to speak in our presence," he clarifies with a smile.

My attention is drawn away as Fritz leans into Dina's side with a whisper I can't quite hear.

"He didn't come down this morning," Missand states. "We believe he left."

Reeves clears her throat. "I've already had his home and known locations assessed. If he's not in this palace, he is not in my centra." Her tone sizzles with barely restrained anger.

"I believe we've found what we've been searching for these many years." Kersack looks to me as he speaks. "And it took Nera mere minutes with him to pull the information out."

I shake my head, not knowing how to accept the praise.

"You startled him," Fritz pipes up, and from his sudden, wide-eyed expression, I can tell even he's shocked the words were spoken out loud.

I look at him expectantly as he clears his throat and takes a moment to shuffle in his chair.

"You are not what we expected," he says.

"Oh? What did you expect?" I ask.

"We were told you had entered a deep depression. You were somber and de-jected, you didn't care about anything or anyone, barely spoke, and spent most of your time drugged and asleep."

My chest rises and falls with the memory of a time when all of those things were true.

"That is what we've heard of your time in Halabar," Fritz quickly clarifies. "And that is what we were expecting. But you . . . " He finally looks up, and we lock eyes for the first time. "You are neither weak nor afraid. You don't appear somber or depressed. You are our leader, and today Arthyr realized that. And it scared him."

"Thank you, Fritz," Ari states as he squeezes my hand under the table.

Unable to speak myself, I mouth the appreciative words Ari just spoke to the young man. Fritz bows his head in reverence.

Ari turns to me before he stands.

"I had my assumptions as to how the meeting would proceed yesterday. Those assumptions dealt more with parading Nera around for you all to witness how strong she has become, how wonderfully made she is, and that her gifts have returned." He looks down, remorse etched on his face. "But I realized that she did not—does not—have to show you any of that. You will follow her just as I will, and I thank you for it. I have to admit, I am delighted at how things have progressed thus far. And now I wish to work through the next steps in our plan. Now that our leader has returned, I wish to discuss how we will take down that which aims to eradicate us."

There isn't even a moment's hesitation before the entire room erupts in the chant I now fully understand. And for the first time, I join in.

"Ebeli Mushari!"

"Ebeli Mushari!"

"Ebeli Mushari!"

XLVII

T he plan is quite simple, and yet somehow also grossly confusing and unattainable.

There are eight stones, and we must gather all of them. But finding them over the years has proven damn near impossible.

I sit silent, captivated as Reeves weaves the tale of how the stones came to be.

Each of the four elders created two stones; each stone a mirror to its twin.

Safar gave us the Eso and Omni stones. As we already know, Reeves is in possession of the Eso stone, which is red in color and helps to enhance the Celestra's ability to change the reality of what others see. The Omni stone is golden in color, and currently held by Ari. It's the very same I used to travel to Earth, and then back.

Amary created the Genesis and Ruination stones. Riann currently holds the Genesis stone. This stone is deep green and is used to strengthen the ability to create and manipulate the physical elements. The deep obsidian Ruination stone enhances the ability to destroy. Unfortunately, we have no leads on its location.

Haziar made the Seer and Patho stones. Himerak holds the Seer stone within his staff. It is deep blue in color and is used to enhance the ability for the user to see one's past. The deep orange Patho stone is supposedly used to see the past, though that gift has never made itself known, and the stone itself is as lost as the prophecy of what it can do.

Lastly, Elder *Balen* created the Afinity and Soothsayer stones. The Afinity stone is said to be a radiant lavender and is used to enhance the ability to alter another's emotions. It is believed to be somewhere in Centra II. And the Soothsayer stone, clear in appearance, enhances the ability of truth telling. They have no knowledge of its location.

"What happens when we find them?"

Kersack answers, "We forge them all into one. We unite the gifts, just as they are united in you."

Dina clears her throat when I give a questioning glance. "There is a story brought down from our ancestors. It relays the tale of a massive beast which roamed the lands thousands of years ago." The hairs on my neck stand at attention as she speaks.

"This was before the Ashclaw," Ari clarifies as he squeezes my hand.

"It's just a tale," Dina adds. "But it tells of uniting the stones and casting a weapon. That weapon is said to be able to slaughter armies in the thousands and beasts of any making."

"And we need to create it before they do," Ari cuts in.

"How do we find the rest of the stones?"

The entire group, save for Ari, seems to sink back at my question.

"We don't know," Reeves finally admits. "We've tried everything we knew to do."

"But now we have new information," Ari adds, and my head tilts in question. "We have you, and you have full use of your gifts. I think it's time we take advantage of that."

Ari

"They will find us," she states with absolutely no conviction in her voice. The cold winter wind blows in off the peak of the west-facing mountain. The barrier of sparsely placed trees growing between us and the tallest point I know does nothing to stop our bodies from shivering. She gathers her snowflake-covered hair and pulls it back.

"They won't find us," I counter, and startle when I look down to find a purple bruise under her newly exposed ear. My first instinct is to reach out and make sure it's real. She is so meticulous during our training that she rarely ever gets injured. She jerks away at my touch. "What's that from?"

Her hand covers the spot just as the hair that was being woven into a braid is dropped, and she shakes her head. "We should get moving." She nods toward the underground tunnel entrance we plan to use as our escape.

"Where did you get that bruise?" I tentatively grasp her chin and turn her face. When our eyes meet, I find only sadness in her gaze. A list of reasons why runs

through me. But it's only when her eyes shift away, in what I can only call a moment of shame, that the realization settles. Her silence is answer enough, and I can barely control the twisting of my features as fury slams into me at the thought. "You can say no," I command through gritted teeth.

"Can I?" She rolls her eyes. "And what would happen? If I suddenly stop allowing my betrothed to touch me, they will get suspicious."

A swarm of emotions I don't know how to handle settles in my stomach, and for the first time, it is I who feels the need to vomit all over the snow-covered valley.

"Ari." Confusion laces my name as she looks up at me. "You know I have to do this."

"No."

She shakes her head, but I see the truth in her eyes. "You're being irrational."

"Irrational!" I hiss as I grab her shoulders to turn her back to face me. "Irrational?!" Fury blinds my every thought. "He is—"

Her hand immediately clamps over my mouth. "Stop yelling or they will find us!" She jerks away as she surveys what's left of the Abolition's soldiers. "Don't you dare judge me!"

"Judge you? I'm not judging you! I'm mad that—"

"Mad that I'm doing my part? Mad that I am distracting him enough so he doesn't question where I go off to? Mad that I—"

"I'm mad at myself!" I cut her off as she stares up at me in earnest. "I'm taking too long." Regret laces each word. "I am taking too long at figuring all this out, and now you—"

"Don't make this about you." She huffs as she turns to put a few feet between us. "You and I aren't even together. What is there to be mad about?!" She hisses back before the rush of her feet brings her back to me. "We each have our parts to play."

"And now the price you pay far outweighs mine," I urge as I cup her face and take solace in the feel of her skin on mine.

"This isn't a contest." Her whispered breath mingles in the air between us.

"I know." I blink away the moisture before she can see.

"Ari?"

"Can you—" Bile coats my throat as the images play on a loop in my mind.

"I can stop," she finally relents.

My shoulders settle as relief arrives. But the feeling doesn't last long. Within a moment of her words, a crunch of newly-fallen snow comes from the right.

Our bodies shift as we ready for what may come. The leaves rustle and the ground crunches under unknown feet. I feel rather than see the heat form from Nera's hand as she prepares for the source of the noise that inches closer.

We barely breathe as we stand still and silent, knowing there is no time to run, and with my abilities drained from the recent battle, there will be no shifting to help us make a quick escape.

The leaves part and she heaves a relief-filled breath when, instead of Abolition soldiers bursting through the brush, we find a battered group. They recoil in fear the second their gazes meet ours.

Six unknowns stand before us. An older man and woman who seem to shake in exhaustion from what I can only assume was a long trek up the mountainside. A second couple stands to their side and are draped in bags and clothes that can only indicate a long journey ahead. The two women favor so much in their dark chestnut hair and slanted eyes that I know they must be related. And finally, a young girl and boy. The boy is so slender and gaunt, one may think he couldn't be much older than the girl at his side, but when he shifts his face slightly, the sunlight catches on the stubble that skirts his chin and straight jaw. My stomach caves as I see he is probably much older than he appears, but poor nutrition and a harsh life have done him no favors.

The oldest man, covered in wrinkles filled with dirt and grim, steps forward as he lifts his hands up in surrender.

"Take me," he calls out. "Let them go, and take me."

There is a muffled cry from the older woman standing behind him, and I can't help but notice the young man—who I can only guess is his grandson—stands tall and ready to fight, should either Nera or I make a wayward move.

Thankfully, Nera sees exactly what I do. The heat recoils within her hands as she takes a tentative step forward. "And where would we take you?"

The old man shakes his head in frustration as if we aren't understanding his plea. "Take me. Pretend you never saw them. Let them go, and I will comply." He drops to his knees as he shoves his hands out between us in preparation for the cloth we don't have. The five others behind him seem to tremble, not in fear, but sadness at what is sure to come.

I sheath the daggers as realization settles.

"The only place we would take you is to safety." I unwrap the leather binding around my wrist and show them the mark that scars my skin just as Nera pulls the twisted necklace from her shirt.

"We are Restoration," Nera explains, and the grieving woman falls forward in relief as a flood of tears dots the snow-covered ground around her.

There is a moment of muffled confusion. The young man who stood so firm in his defiance of what was happening, now shakes his head in disbelief.

"You're lying." He forces out the words as he makes his way in front of the old man, a well-placed dagger poised and ready in his palm. "The Restoration was demolished."

"Is that what they told you?" Nera almost laughs as she reaches into her sack to grab the two pieces of fruit she brought along. She tosses them at the feet of the

strangers and starts in on what I now know as her typical line of questioning whenever this type of encounter occurs. "How long have you been traveling? Do you need aid? Are there any more refugees? How many–"

"Give them a moment," I cut in, noting the shock still marring the faces of those before us. She huffs a breath and rolls her eyes in annoyance.

"You are truly Restoration?" the middle-aged woman asks as the young girl I assume to be her daughter takes a step forward. Her curious emerald eyes are trained on only me.

"I–"

"You're Arryn!" the young girl whispers before I can answer, and then looks back to her family in awe. "It's Arryn! Centra III! He can shift us to the Bend!" She shivers, her small feet seeming to bounce in excitement.

"Can you shift us?" The middle-aged man questions, and I see a flash of hope blooming in his gaze.

"I can, but not right now. I need rest." My features turn down at the confession.

Nera reaches forward, grasping my hand in support as she stands at my side. "Give him a few hours to recover." She looks back over our shoulders as wisps of smoke trail upward in the sky from the lives we just obliterated. "But we have a place we can hide you while we wait." She nods to the well-placed boulder which hides a direct route underground as confusion settles on their faces.

"I am Hamid." The older man smiles before turning back to his group. "This is my wife, Tani; my daughter, Kris; her husband, Reef; and their children, Fritz and Vessa."

XLVIII

As I run my fingers over the patchwork of vines, I find this door is unbelievably similar to the one in Halabar. A rush of memories I almost wish would vanish linger in my mind.

Ari clears his throat as he inches up closer behind me. "There are times in which I would give up every gift I possess just to know what thoughts fill that head of yours."

A small laugh erupts from me. "But then life would be far less exciting." I twist to find a beautifully wicked grin staring back at me.

The golden hue of his eyes appears darker than normal down here in the deepest part of Reeves's palace. Still, the flickers of life that swim within them seem to reach out for me, calling me home. His straight jaw, which previously only had a small hint of stubble, is now filled with hair, and I have to force my hand not to reach out and run my fingers through it. I almost laugh as I realize why he decided not to shave these last two mornings, knowing it was only due to my comment to Dina about my preference for the look.

"Go ahead." He nudges my shoulder forward with a laugh, and I jolt at the realization that I've been caught standing here staring at him.

"I hate you." I feign a sneer as I whip back around, and that small trickling laughter from moments ago turns into a torrent.

I feel his breath as he takes a step closer. My fingers skirt along the edge of the handle. "You most definitely *do not* hate me."

I focus on the shimmering mist that erupts from my wrist and collides with the handle at my touch, hoping to find something to concentrate on other than this overwhelming sense of urgency to turn around and claim what I know he would give.

The moment the door opens and we step through, I falter.

"It is exactly the same."

"As the one in Halabar?"

I nod in answer as I survey the entire room. An eerie memory of the last time I did this races through me, and I have to look back, if only to confirm it's Ari standing with me and not my father waiting on the other side of the door.

"It's so beautiful."

He reaches out to caress my cheek as he nods toward the center.

"What do you know?"

I look to find a room so similar to the one I already know. The floor appears to be a target with its four circular rings, each one laying a few steps lower than the last. The top is bare, but edged in never-ending bookcases I long to explore. The middle two rings contain eight tables with a glass bowl in each. Five tables on the higher ring, and three on the lower. But the final ring is what causes me to pause. Its beautiful table with inlaid vines and carved markings is so striking, I long to run my fingers along the designs. A single glass bowl sits on top and begs me forward.

As soon as my feet hit the second ring, I halt as the floor once again changes from solid wood to a beautiful sea.

"How?" the whispered question tumbles out as I reach down to once again confirm I won't be sucked within its wake.

"Think of this room as a middle ground . . . a place where the world converges and all its creatures can occupy. This is a place of peace. This is where we will save our world."

"Is it real?" I bring my fingers upward through the cool water to find the only wetness gathered there is a product of my own nervousness.

"Why wouldn't it be?"

"I can't feel it." I rub my fingers together, trying to force the feel of the cool ocean water to appear. It's an odd sensation, and I know my brain is tricking me as if this is just an illusion, but still, I can't take my eyes off it.

"But you know it's there."

I nod as I stand fully.

"Sometimes our minds and our bodies wage a war against themselves." He takes a step forward as he bends down, reaches into the nonexistent water, and causes a ring of expanding ripples to appear. "Sometimes our minds see things that aren't real while our hearts convince us they are. And sometimes it's our hearts that do the deceiving."

"That's oddly poetic."

"But sometimes our hearts guide us exactly where we are supposed to be, even when our minds tell us to run away."

I peer over at him as a beat of silence passes.

"I feel like you're trying to tell me something?"

He smiles dimly as he assesses me. "What do you see?"

I turn to survey the room, hoping the right answer will come, but then decide to respond with whatever answer comes to mind.

"It's a contradiction. It's as if this room is full of secrets, and yet it wants nothing more than to release every single one. It feels so familiar and yet so far away."

"It feels like home?" he asks, and I turn to find him now standing and staring down at me.

"Maybe?" I shrug my shoulders, not sure what answer I believe more. I shuffle my feet as I start to circle the second ring, mesmerized by the movement and ripples below. "You said I used to use this to travel to you?"

"You did."

"But Koreed said the first time I entered was with him?"

"He was wrong."

It's then that I turn to find him standing where I left him. "How did I travel?"

He smiles as he makes his way to the first table and water-filled glass bowl.

"Eight bowls, eight stones." He runs his fingers through the water of the nearest bowl.

"But there are nine bowls . . . " I look down to the innermost circle, noting the ninth and largest bowl among the group.

"Eight bowls coordinating with the eight Celestrial gifts." He pulls his hand from the water as he taps on the table. "The Seer stone was made by Elder Haziah." He walks around the table slowly. "Himerak currently has it, and it is used to enhance the ability to see one's past."

"I already know this." My arms cross in confusion. He has already told me this story many times. But Ari pays no mind to my words as he makes his way to the second table, and thus the second bowl of glistening water.

"Patho, also created by Haziar, is used to enhance the ability to see what lies ahead."

"And we have no idea where it is as no one has ever found it." I finish what I know he is about to say.

"You're catching on quickly." He smiles with each word as he moves on to table three. "Affinity. Made by Balen and used to–"

"Alter the emotions of others." Hot anger races through me at the memory.

He pauses to take a calming breath, and I know he too is trying to rein in every repulsive thought of the horrible things Tarak deserves for what he did. When he moves toward the fifth and final bowl on this ring, the one I am standing beside, he does so slowly and deliberately without ever losing my eye contact.

"The Omni stone made by Elder Safar." He lifts the golden jewel from his pocket and sets it down on the table beside me. "It enhances the ability to shift forward or backward in time or to various places. Though I believe you refer to it as *traveling*." He shoots me a curious glance before he reaches out to grasp my hand. The world shifts into sudden darkness, only to open up again mere feet away at the final bowl on this ring.

He catches my gaze before he taps the table beside us. "Soothsayer. Created by Balen and assists in truthtelling."

I nod in response as he walks a few feet down the stairs to the third ring. "Ruination. Created by Amary and—"

"Used to destroy." I roll my eyes as I answer.

He shakes his head as he moves on to the seventh bowl. "Genesis—"

"Made by Amary, and used to create. Riann currently holds it." I follow his path as I make my way to his side.

"Maybe I should let you give the history lesson?" He crosses his arms as I smile and walk to the eighth bowl.

I brush my hand across the table as I speak. "Eso. Made by Safar, currently held by Reeves and changes the reality of what people see."

"It's not only how I've hidden our home, but how I show you my memories."

I nod as he speaks, and then stare down to the fourth and final level. The ninth bowl stands still, alone and unmoving. I let my fingers trail the edge of the table as I dig deep for the answer to this one.

"What's this one?" My gaze shoots up to find Ari making his way to me.

"I thought you were the one giving the lesson, not me." He quirks a brow just as his feet meet mine. I playfully shove him backward at the taunt.

"You know I know nothing of this one. What is it? Why are there nine spaces, but only eight stones?" My fingers inch upward as I skim the bowl. Just as my fingers itch to skirt the enticing water, Ari pulls me back.

"This one is for you."

I catch his gaze as it lingers on me.

"That doesn't make sense?"

"It does." Reeves calls out from behind us, and I watch as she takes the steps downward, lifting the hem of her skirt from the ground as if on instinct to keep it from getting wet.

"Care to explain?" I ask as she finally reaches where we stand.

"You are the fifth centra."

"So I've been told." I look from her back to Ari. "But no one really has explained what that means for me . . . for us."

Reeves swallows as she reaches out and turns my wrist upward. "You are the last one of our kind." The words are solemn and tight. "But I think I mostly realized it, or better yet accepted it, once I saw your mark." I look down to the design on my wrist then, shaking my head in confusion.

"You have the same mark." I turn back to Ari. "We all do."

He shakes his head in answer as he slowly rolls up his sleeve.

Reeves clears her throat as she does the same. I stare at both of their marks, so beautiful and identical in nature, and then down at my own. All three look exactly alike. I furrow my brow in confusion, then Reeves lines her arm up with mine.

"My mark and Ari's mark are retreating. Yours is growing." She runs her fingers over the lines of my wrist, and it's only then I can see that she is correct. Where her mark ends, my continues on.

"Why? Is it because I'm not a sovereign yet?"

"No," Ari replies as he rolls down his sleeve. "The mark should never change. You are born with it, and you die with it. That is what has always happened. But something has changed in the last few years. Those of us with the marks have found them slowly retreating, almost disappearing as the years go on. But yours doesn't. It grows."

"What does that have to do with the ninth bowl?"

"Elithium speaks of a final test we will face." Reeves straightens as she stares down at the table before us.

"And a final Celestra who will either unite us, or destroy us." Ari reaches out to tuck a wayward strand of hair behind my ear. "The Celestras were a gift to this world. But the final Celestra is much more. The final Celestra will get to choose what happens to it."

"I'm the final Celestra."

They both nod in unison.

"And my mark grows because–"

"Because your power grows," Reeves answers as she circles us. "The tables in this room and the bowls that lie on top of them serve as a conduit of sorts. Just like the heartstone trees." She runs her hand along the deep mahogany surface. "You can use these bowls and the stones to gain knowledge, enhance your gifts, and–"

"To defeat the horrors we once created," Ari finishes for her. "While each specific bowl you see around you is tied to one gift, this one here"—he taps the glass and the water within ripples—"is tied to all of them. And no one but you can use it."

"The dome I create?" I ask, and he nods. "The fire light I can make?" He nods again.

"I have two extra gifts."

Reeves begins to smile as I put each piece in place.

"You are the final piece and we . . . " she looks to Ari as she speaks. "We believe you were sent directly from the Elders as the fifth centra."

I nod, though I'm not sure if I completely understand everything. "You know I'll do whatever I can to help."

She reaches out to grasp my hands in hers. "We know." Then she quickly shifts her attention to Ari. "Is the history lesson over, or is there more she has to learn today?" She quirks a brow.

"Over for now." He looks down to me. "Unless, of course, you want to try some of this out?" His hands sweep out to the room just as Reeves chimes in.

"Maybe later. Right now I need your assistance." Her tone shifts from playful to dread.

Ari furrows his brows in confusion.

"The Haze has made its way into Halabar."

I gasp as she speaks.

"My guards just returned with the news. Hundreds—thousands dead." She swallows as she speaks. "The palace is standing, but the city itself has turned to ash."

Ari reaches out to grab my arm, and I know in a moment's notice, we will be standing within whatever ruin is left.

"No," Reeves commands as she steps between us. "It happened last night and has since retreated. It's over. There is nothing there but death. No one left to save." Ari's hand slowly recoils. "My people have rescued those they can, and sent many to the Bend, but the Abolition now has control of the land."

Rage seems to roll off Ari as the seconds linger on.

"How were we not informed?" he seethes.

"I don't know." She pales in answer. "But if they have lured the few left living to their side, then they will surely outnumber us now."

Ari paces the small space as he runs a hand through his hair.

"What do I do?" I look between the two. I just promised to be of help, but here they are in the middle of something horrible and I have no idea how to aid them.

Ari stalls as he looks back to me. "They have overtaken Centra I. Which means they may have Tarak and his people." Dread coils in my stomach. "We need to infiltrate. We need to get into Centra I, possibly Centra II, and get those whom the Abolition took before they can be turned against us."

"They may already be against us," Reeves chimes in just as I speak.

"How?" I inquire as he cups my face.

"Go upstairs. Shift into your room. That will be good practice. Let Dina know what's happened, and I will get my people ready to fight," he urges.

"I'll get my people ready for refugees," Reeves adds.

And then, as if all three of us know exactly when it is time for the conversation to end and the action to begin, we let the darkness envelop us.

XLIX

Reeves barrels into the room just as I finish explaining the chaos to Dina.

"Is Ari back yet?" she questions as I stand to answer.

"No. But he's only been gone–"

"I'm here!" Ari walks into the room to meet Reeves, a newly worried look etched across his face. "I just heard."

"Heard what?" I question.

"Avandell is now under attack by the Abolition," Reeves replies as she looks my way and then back to Ari. "We have a change of plans."

Ari nods. "We aren't going to Centra I or II. We have to go to Centra III." He looks to me before cutting his gaze to Reeves and answering her unspoken question. "The Bend still holds," he clarifies, reminding me of the one place I have yet to learn about.

"Are the people okay?" Dina asks as she makes her way beside me.

Reeves clears her throat. "From the intelligence I've gathered, they remain secure. But they need reinforcements."

"We have to go," I command as all eyes focus on me.

"Are you sure you're ready? This isn't just a rescue mission anymore. This is running straight into an active attack." Worry seeps from Reeves's voice. I open my mouth to reply, but I ever get to answer.

"She's ready," Ari states his support while looking straight at me. "We won't be gone long." He turns back to Reeves. "I can get us in. We will take out all we can to dwindle the forces and allow the Avandell to do the rest. Then we will be back to help with the survivors from Halabar."

"If there are any left," Reeves whispers as she turns to face the window.

It's only when Dina is helping me dress in battle-ready clothing that I realize what I am about to do. She must sense it as well, because she grabs my shaking hands in her own.

"Muscle memory."

I furrow my brow in confusion.

"You've done this before. Your body will know what to do. You just have to trust yourself enough to let go."

"I don't even know what I'm walking into."

"The Abolition," she states the obvious as she reaches up to secure the leather vest and dagger hidden inside. "It's not their first attack on Centra III. But we always hold them off with very little life lost on our side. It's a power play for them. One they never seem to win."

"But they have more people now."

She pauses as she closes her eyes and lets the truth sink in.

"Do they ever attack Centra IV?"

"No." She leans down to lace up my boots.

"And the only reason they went into Centra I was because–"

"It was weakened by the Haze," she finishes my statement as she hides a second dagger in my boot. "Centra I is home to more Abolition allies than enemies, so they would have never truly attacked. They only went in to save the people they knew would stand on their side." She finally stands at her full height as she looks me over. "And they don't attack here because Centra IV would wipe them out before they even set foot on the land. Centra III is the only place they have the barest hopes of taking over."

"But they never win?" I wring my trembling hands.

"They haven't yet." She stills for a moment before squaring her shoulders in certainty and looking me in the eye.

"If they've never won, then why do they keep going back?"

"Because it's Ari's home, and it's where the Bend is, and they know what he means to you. And more than anything their goal is to anger you, to get you to lose control."

I take a deep breath. "What happens if I lose control?"

"Then they turn you into the monster they believe you to be, and fuel the lies that Celestras are the fruits of all evil in this world. If you lose control, all the lives we have saved will be at the mercy of those who want to see them dead."

My mouth becomes dry as fear races through me.

"What's the Bend?"

She smiles slowly and her lips open, but it's Ari's voice I hear from behind.

"I promise to show you once we eliminate the threat." He reaches out a hand, pulls me to him, and the world goes black.

The bite of the cold hits before my sight fully returns. But the shiver which runs through my body is more the result of the scene before me than the chill.

We stand on the edge of a mountain, miles away from what I assume is Avandell. There are no true buildings, only snow-dusted trees casting deep shadows. Dark smoke lingers in the distance as cries of pain bellow out.

"Where are your people?" I look up to find Ari surveying the sight.

"Underground. They're safely hidden miles from here."

"Then why is the Abolition here?" A thundering bomb explodes in the distance as white dust is blown into the sky. My body recoils on instinct.

Ari, though angry at what is happening, isn't fazed by the noise. "To draw you out. To trap you. They have more numbers, and now they want you to show yourself."

I take a step back as chunks of smoke and ash fall from the sky. "We are walking into a trap?"

He finally looks down to me, a sinister smile playing on his lips.

"No, dear Nera. I would never." His hand cups my cheek. "They have walked into ours."

He points to a ridge in the distance just as another bomb explodes. As the snow falls back to the ground, I barely make out the flickering of fires and scattering of people.

"Riann's not here. He never comes. But those people you see are his armies. Members of the Abolition. Those sworn to eradicate us. And if I was a betting man, I would wager to say he sees most of those souls scurrying as just bodies he can dispose of in order to weaken us."

The wind surges up the hill from the recent blasts and I have to shield my face from the hit of the cold.

"What do we do?"

He points back to the top of the mountain our enemies hold. "I doubt they

know it, but there is a lake on the other side of that peak. It's currently frozen."
He looks at me with no humor in his expression as he speaks the next words. "I
could shift in and take out their soldiers. But that is what they expect me to do. I
want to do something else."

I bore my eyes in his direction in question.

"I want you to crumble the ground and force the people back onto the lake,
then I want you to crack the ice, let them fall in, and then refreeze the water once
more."

I blink, unsure if I heard him correctly.

"You can do it. You're strong enough."

I shake my head. "I'll kill them."

"Yes."

I take another step back. "I don't want to kill them. I want to kill Riann. What
if those people aren't the enemy? What if they are just soldiers from Halabar who
lost their home yesterday ?"

"Riann's not here for you to kill. And I promise you these people aren't
newly initiated members of The Abolition. These are Halabarians who have been
against us since the beginning. By killing them, you are taking out the people who
want to kill us."

"But those people have families. What if they–"

"They are here to kill you, to kill me. They are here to kill our people." The
words are harsh, but I know he only means to push the urgency of the situation.

"I can't." My hands tremble in earnest now.

"Nera," Ari says my name as if it's a prayer before he holds my face in his hands.
"I told you once that if you wanted to run away from this, I would stand by you
and let the world burn."

"I don't want to run away."

"There is no middle ground. We run, or we fight. I will follow whatever path
you choose, but you must choose a path. Now."

"I don't want any more blood on my hands." I look down to find the creases
in my palms, wondering if they will suddenly turn red with the blood of all those
lives I have already taken.

"I know, and I'm sorry you have to make this choice."

"What if I'm not strong enough?"

"Imposible," he counters, "If you choose this, then I will get you as close as
possible to make it as easy as I can, and then I will shield us from view. All you
have to do is use your gifts."

I nod in answer before I even think through the thought. "Okay. For you. I'll
choose this for you." I smile.

He shakes his head. "No. For us." He reaches out to run his thumb across the mark on my wrist. "For them."

My hand slides so perfectly into his.

The sound slams into me. Screaming of orders and rushing of feet encircle us. A bomb explodes so close, my entire body rattles with the noise.

I barely remain standing, thankful for Ari at my side, when my entire form goes rigid. One, two, then three soldiers run right past me, none offering even a glance in my direction.

"Ari?"

"Shh," he whispers in my ear. "I'm altering what they see," he explains. "To them, we're not here."

I nod in understanding.

"Close your eyes." He shifts sideways and presses the front of his body into the back of mine. "I have you," he assures me. "Close your eyes. Move the ground. Make them retreat."

I stand still, steady, letting my thoughts drift away and my body take over. It's an odd sensation to relinquish control to the unknown. Even as I do, I hold tightly onto a small tendril to guide me back to the surface, just in case.

There is no sense of time or presence. For all I know, we could be standing motionless for hours as I fight against the barrier I have so beautifully constructed.

But finally, the heat takes hold. It starts in my palms, and with my eyes closed, I feel the small spider-web-like threads inching their way onward. I quickly pull them back.

It is a push and pull I haven't yet mastered—to grow my power, but not let it out. It spreads within me as it lurches up my arms in search of a target. Heat blooms outward as it fills my chest, and though my eyes are closed, I know my body must be covered in the same light Ari once caused.

"That's it," Ari's voice calls to me from somewhere far away. "Good girl."

I feel his fingers lace within mine as his breath tickles my skin.

The building heat reaches my feet, and I force my weight down into my heels as the light buries itself further. Tunneling, spiraling, inching its way down into the ground as far as it can reach. A corded swirl of light silently working its way through the dark.

And then it stops.

Cold, solid rock collides with the heat, and I feel my body recoil. I shiver as the ice lurches its way upward, fizzling out the heat I created as it moves. But I hold steady as Ari mumbles words I can't hear into my ear.

I latch onto what I can, hoping his presence, his words, his love will give me strength.

But this is an attack.

The cold shadow races through the ground below me as the dirt begins to rumble at my feet.

"Fight it." The yell sounds as if far away, but I know it's him.

I reach for the words which linger in the air, pleading with them to anchor me, but the heat I've built begins to retreat. It is then that I realize there's no amount of white light I can bring forth to fight this, because I have yet to fully accept that light and what it gives. Until I do, it will be useless to me.

Right now, all I have are the flames borne of anger and rage. I can only fight this force with the mirroring evil inside me.

I release his hand as I fall forward, my now-heated palms slamming into the ground.

My vision is all but gone as light surges outward, cocooning me in bright waves of death.

The building heat spreads as all that I have been through, all the death I have seen and caused bubbles upward.

"Nera?" Ari calls out, and this time I barely even hear my name. "Nera?" Worry and fear lace the utterance as I know my fire has created a barrier between us.

But my body remains steady. The heat surges on. I meet the cold as dark wisps intertwine within me, and I now know what I face.

"You have come back for me?" The now familiar voice, laced with deception and fear, calls forth, but for the first time, I am not frightened at the sound.

"I know what you are." My words linger in the distance. "I know what you want."

"And what is that, my dear?" Icy fingers trail up my legs and arms as I leech the heat from my body and let it surge into the ground below.

"NERA!" The panicked scream reverberates inside my frigid bones and I feel the icicles form on my skin.

"You want me," I answer, and a soft cackle sounds off. "You want me to give in to the hate buried inside. The hate built from everything I've done." My body shivers as more heat withdraws and is replaced with bitter cold. "You want me to surrender." My skin all but turns to ice as spindly fingers begin to encircle my own. My eyes remain closed, but I still see the Shadow lurch up from the depths of the dirt. "But I won't. Because I have something inside me that is stronger than hate or fear or anything else I now know you thrive on."

I open my eyes to find the white light swirling around me and soaring upward into the sky. Ari stands feet away, unable to reach me as he frantically screams a silent plea I can't hear. The soldiers who were previously unaware of my presence stand frozen in awe at the sight before them.

When I look down, I see the shadow of death coming for me. Clawing upwards from the snow-covered ground. I let it.

It inches upward as the swirling light comes closer.

"*What could be stronger than what I give?*" The voice is louder as the charred face I've come to know so well breaks through the surface to meet me.

"Love," I answer.

I pull all the glistening white light—light I know is only there because of him—back in, letting my body bathe in its magnificence as the heat of anger and rage bursts free. It surges from my body and into the waiting snow.

The wail of pain from the blackened mouth burns to ash as the ground begins to shake.

The white light becomes my protection, and no matter how hard the cold fights to get to me, it can't get in. The cold retreats below as heat and fire race through rock and soil, chasing it away. Massive craters split the world in two as the mountain crumbles at my whim.

Coils of heat again meet the icy rock so far below and fracture the foundation. Massive cracks splinter through the ground, and though I can't see, I can feel the heat melting away the ice which was once there. Flames of fury surge upward and out of the craters now littering the surface, turning everything they touch to nothing but ash and dust.

Ari races to me, a mixture of shock, awe, and love blazing in his golden stare. Soldiers race from me, terrified as to what I might do next.

And just as the snow-capped peak begins to quake with the hell I've unleashed, an avalanche forms.

"Nera." Ari leans his forehead against mine as I grab hold of the icy snow below. It easily crumbles in my hands. And without much thought, I race the avalanche onward, toward those who want nothing more than our deaths. They scale the short distance between us and the peak, and topple over to the other side.

"Break open the ice-covered lake," Ari calls out, his face less than an inch from mine, but his words are so very far away.

My hands slam into the ground as I feel the mountain, the glacier shatter.

The avalanche continues to surge onward, toward our enemy and now to us, the roar of racing snow drowning out the screams of those around.

"Shift us," I yell, aware of my body's sudden need to retreat, and knowing that there are only seconds before we will become buried as well.

Ari shakes his head. "Control it," he commands. "Turn it away from us, and bury them in the ice."

"I can't." My eyes flutter closed as darkness settles in.

"Nera!"

"I can't."

He leans forward as his lips brush mine. "Nera! You can. I believe in you."

The edges of the white cloud envelop us just as I feel the bitter cold of the ice swallow up its victims.

I wake to a smiling face.

"You're awake. Thank the Elders," the little girl whispers. Her face is so close to mine, our noses touch, and I feel the splatter of saliva which erupts with the effort to correctly say each sound.

I immediately pull back as I wipe my cheek and blink, hoping the sight will make more sense with the passing seconds. It doesn't.

"Who are you?" I whisper back.

She giggles in response, and before I can pose the question again, the door is flung open, and a familiar-looking woman comes rushing in.

"Ahriel! You aren't supposed to be in here! Nera, I'm so sorry," the woman grimaces in embarrassment as she scoops the little girl into her grasp. I force my tired body to lean forward on my elbows to better assess what exactly is happening, but a heavy arm holds me steady.

I turn to find a passed out Ari at my back. A gasp of surprise leeches out.

"Let him sleep," the woman says as she touches my hand, the wiggling child still somehow clasped within her other arm. "He has been up watching you all night. Just fell asleep in the last hour."

I stare at his beautiful face. The hard lines which seem to draw me in have softened in his sleep. He resembles more, I imagine, the teenage boy I once fell in love with than the man he is now.

I have a sudden urge to trace his lip, or brush back his long hair, but just as I reach out, I'm startled and go still at the sound of giggles which bring me back to where I am.

"Where are we?"

"Avandell." She smiles. "Are you hungry? I have a meal made up."

I unconsciously nod as I hear my stomach answer. We both let out a small laugh.

She waves me forward. "Come on. He'll be out for a while."

"What if he wakes up and I'm not here?" The thought of causing him any worry grips me with pain.

"It's okay. He knows you're safe with us." Her words ring true, giving me a moment of comfort.

"Who are you?" I question as I slowly slide my body from Ari's grasp.

She freezes at my question. A mixture of knowing and sadness settles on her face.

"I'm Elora. I'm Arynn's older sister," she whispers as her hand reaches out to squeeze mine before readjusting the small girl on her hip.

"I'm Ahriel," the ever-moving little girl proudly proclaims. "And you are my Aunt Nena!"

Heat floods my body at her words.

"Shh!" Elora admonishes Ahriel as she reaches for my hand to lead us out of the room. "Stop being so loud or you will wake Uncle Arryn."

As soon as we're down a darkened hallway, Elora shoos Ahriel away and leads me into what must be a central gathering room.

"We're in Avandell?"

"Yes." She nods as she fills a plate with meat and a bowl with soup.

"Where exactly in Avandell are we?"

"Lower levels of the palace in the city center. About a mile away from where you just took out the Abolition." A smirk fills her features, and I gasp as the last few hours come barreling back.

"The Abolition! It's gone!"

"Oh. No. Not completely." She shakes her head. "Just the soldiers they sent here. Who, if history repeats itself, were merely pawns in their game. They never send anyone of worth to Centra III. They know Ari will take them out without a second thought."

"I think I killed them." Remorse floods me at the admission.

"You did exactly what you were meant to do." She brings the food over and sets it before me. "Ari told me everything. He is so proud of you. We are all so proud of you." She once again grasps my hand and squeezes.

"How long have I been asleep?"

"Only about a day. I suspect the rest of the crew will mosey their way in here soon for dinner."

"Dinner? It's already night time?" I twist around, trying to find a signal of the time based on the sunlight, but there are no windows here.

"Yes. It's almost dinner time. You slept for well over thirty hours. I think Ari was beginning to get worried."

I'm sure he was. But what hits me most is the concern that Reeves, Dina, and all those in Centra IV must be feeling at our absence.

"Don't worry," Elora states as she cups my cheek. "You know, you never were one to hide your emotions. Everything you feel promptly lurches right off your face." She giggles a little at her own joke. "Reeves has been apprised of exactly where you and Ari are. She isn't happy about the delay, but she'll get over it."

"Why are we here?" I scoop the soup up as I try not to moan at the taste. But she catches my sigh.

"Spices, imported from–"

"Niser," I cut her off, nodding and remembering what Ari once told me.

She nods. "You're here because Ari knew you would be safe. It was the first place he thought of when he shifted you two out of the path of the avalanche."

I swallow at the memory.

"And you're his sister?"

"Yes." She loads up a second plate and bowl and places it down as she scoots onto the bench beside me.

"I knew you from before?"

"Very much so." She takes a bite.

"What do you remember? About me?"

Her laugh bursts out, reverberating against the thick stone walls. "Has Ari not shared his memories with you?" She quirks her head in confusion.

"He has, but I want to know what others remember, too, and not just him. I think he sees me through rose-colored glasses."

She laughs again, this time so hard she damn near chokes on her water.

"Well, it may have been years since we last spoke, but you haven't changed a bit."

Her statement causes me to pause. "What do you mean?"

"Blunt. Observant. Correct." She tilts her head my way. "Ari most definitely sees you through rose-colored glasses. How could he not when you are bon–" She stops herself, a worried expression etched across her features.

"It's okay. I know," I assure her, and she sighs a breath of relief.

Then her brows furrow in confusion. "He told you? Already?"

"He couldn't really keep it in. And I think I guessed it more than he told."

She turns a little to face me. Her previously relaxed features are now filled with worry and concern. "How do you feel about that?"

"About finding out I'm bonded to and have a history with someone I don't really know?"

She nods.

"No less shocked than I am about everything else I have found out in the last few months. I'm just waiting for the next surprise to be thrown my way."

She gathers my hands in hers. "I'm sorry for what you have gone through, but I want you to know you are strong, and you will persevere. You will meet whatever end you so choose. Your path is your own, don't let anyone else tell you otherwise."

I give her a small smile in answer, unsure of how to take her words.

"We didn't get along much," she blurts out the admission.

"What?" I turn to face her, the delicious food long forgotten.

"You and I. We didn't get along. I hope that since you no longer remember those feelings you harbored toward me, we can start anew. I would like a long-lasting friendship with my only sister." She beams in excitement.

There are too many statements to take in. My mind becomes muddled as I try to work through which question to throw back at her first. When I open my mouth, only one word spews out.

"Sister?"

Her face pales as my body becomes frozen at the thought.

"Nera? What all has Ari shown–"

"Elora," Ari greets her by name as he walks into the room. Sleep and exhaustion still play upon his face.

"You are supposed to be sleeping," Elora counters as she stands.

"So is she." He looks from his sister down to me. "Did she wake you? Did you have a nightmare?" he questions in worry, and I shake my head.

"No. She didn't wake me. Our niece did."

There's a moment where the entire room stands still, even the burning flames in the lanterns and the balls of fire light strung throughout the massive living space halt their movement at my words.

Our niece.

"I'll leave you two to talk." Elora swiftly leans forward and kisses her brother on the cheek. Though I can't know for sure, I believe there may be a whispered apology as she turns to walk away.

Ari runs his fingers through his hair as nervous energy escapes him. "Did you sleep well?" he questions, and for a moment I want to slap the handsome smile off his face.

"Are we . . . married?"

He opens and closes his mouth as if the answer is right out of reach.

"Ari, are we married?" I ask again. There's no malice in my words, only sheer curiosity, but from the tension in his stance, I can tell he's been dreading this moment.

"Yes." He swallows.

I take a step toward him as I place a hand on his chest. His beating heart is racing underneath.

"When?"

"A few weeks before you were taken."

I nod as I take in his words, solid and true. "I'm your wife."

He nods as tears fill his eyes.

"You're my wife." His voice breaks at the phrase.

"You're my husband."

"I'm your husband."

I cross my arms over my chest as the weight of that phrase settles in. "Why didn't you tell me? I already knew we're bonded Celestras."

He shakes his head as he takes a tentative step forward, then reaches out to grab my wrist, running his thumb over my mark.

"Being bonded Celestras was something that happened to us. We couldn't have fought that even if we wanted to. But being married was something we chose. Something we did together. I didn't want you to come into this with the assumption that you had to choose me again. I needed you to choose me because you wanted me."

His confession washes over me. He wanted me to choose. And he would have still accepted me if I never chose to accept him again.

"Okay," I state, and he pales in confusion.

"Okay?"

I roll my eyes and sit back down.

"Yes. I said okay." I don't look over, but he kneels down beside me and promptly turns my chin to face him.

"That's all? You don't want to yell at me or slap me or–"

My laugh cuts him off and then I am frozen by the sight of him. Every thought racing through my head dwindles down to one little word.

Mine.

Ari is mine. He always has been and always will be.

"I do want to slap you. A little bit," I tease and he starts to smile. "But only because I'm sad that we missed out on these last few weeks together. Ari, it was never a choice to make. It was always you. I just needed a second to let myself realize that." His laugh catches on a sob. I place my hands on his cheeks and wipe away the tear that begins to fall. "It wouldn't have mattered if I was gone for three hundred years. I know I would still choose you every time I came back. You are my other half. I don't feel lost when I'm with you."

Relief floods his features as tears slide down his face, and I slowly look back, almost embarrassed at the confession I just made. He doesn't let me get far before he reaches forward and pulls my face down to his.

I cut off the kiss just before it starts. "But I want to see it."

His eyes crease in confusion. "See what?"

"I want to see the memory of when I fell in love with you—the first time."

He smiles as his hand trails down my arm and his fingers interlock with mine. "I don't think there is just one. I think it happened over time."

I squeeze his hand in mine. "Then I want to see them all."

L

Ari

"You can't always rely on the bow," I whisper from behind her.

"And why not?" She straightens as she secures the hold and pulls back.

"Because bows are barely used today. The Abolition has bombs. What good will a bow do against a bomb?"

She quickly twists her body so the arrow is no longer facing the target but my chest.

"I won't be aiming at the bombs." She smirks, but I swipe the point away and step an inch closer.

"And who will you be aiming at?"

"You, you imbecile." She rolls her eyes as she tries to turn back, but I catch her wrist, stopping the movement.

"You would never shoot me."

Her head cocks to the side in defiance. "And why not?"

I give her a smile so stunning, even I know she can't hide from the brilliance. "Because."

"Because?" Her eyes go wide. "That's your answer?"

I leave the rest of what I want to scream out unsaid. I know what lies between us. She does as well. What I still can't seem to figure out is why she is so damn determined to fight it. "That's my answer."

"Imbecile," she whispers as she re-nocks the arrow and focuses ahead.

I reach around her, letting my left palm rest against her stomach as I slowly pull her back and into me. She immediately tenses in response.

"Stop calling me names you know you don't mean," I whisper into her ear. My hair falls forward to brush against her skin.

"I meant it." She breathes out the words as if speaking while in this stance is practically painful.

"Tighten your abs," I say as I flex my fingers into the skin of her stomach. *"And widen your stance."* My knee knocks against her thigh, causing her legs to open wider.

My right hand crawls along her outstretched arm as it meets her fingers. They tremble beneath my grasp. Her breathing becomes labored, and I can't help but notice how she slightly leans her body back into mine.

"Shoot straight," I command, and she lets it fly, only to have it miss the mark. She quickly pulls away from my grasp as I burst out into laughter. *"I hate you!"* she screams out as she shifts to retrieve the wayward arrow.

Ari

"Why!" She practically races to face me.

"Why what?" I ask just before she meets me. I know the basis of her question, but watching her work through the answer herself is far more alluring.

"Why did you do that?" She pushes against my chest as we collide. I barely move an inch and she grunts in frustration. I may not be able to best her at much, except sheer size and muscle. *"You . . ."* She pauses as if trying to gather her words, pacing a few feet in front of me. *"Why did you come?!"*

"I wouldn't miss it. Of course I had to come."

"No, you didn't."

"You looked pretty," I croon, and she rolls her eyes.

"I hate you," she confesses. This has been her most favorite saying as of late, and I may not be a soothsayer, but we both know it's a lie.

I burst out laughing. *"Yeah, yeah, yeah. I hate you, too. But truthfully, you did look stunning in that dress."* I'm not lying. She is an absolute masterpiece. It took every fiber of my being not to rush to her side and claim what I know is mine.

"I hate you," she states again.

"You already said that," I counter.

She crosses her arms over her chest. *"Well, I want to make sure you know it."*

I shake my head as I pull out a box from behind my back.

She stiffens at the sight. *"What is that?"*

"I couldn't walk up to you at the party and give it to you."

"What is it?" she questions in wide-eyed confusion.

"It's a birthday gift."

"I know that! But what is it?"

I push my arm out further toward her. "You have to open it to find out."

She shakes her head. "I don't want it."

"You don't even know what it is."

She finally looks up to meet my gaze.

"We aren't friends," she states. "You can't just bring me a gift."

"We are allies," I counter.

"How did you know it was my birthday? How did you know about the party?"

"You forget what my job is."

She rolls her eyes again as if she is suddenly remembering the fact. "Yeah, yeah, yeah," she mocks my earlier phrase. "Spy extraordinaire. You know everything about all of us. How could I forget?"

"I don't know everything about all the Celestras. Only you," I confess and she stills.

Her previously annoyed demeanor softens as somber confusion settles in. "I can't take it," she admits.

"Just open it," I plead. "If you don't like it, you can throw it at my face."

She doesn't move. The seconds turn into minutes, and my outstretched arm begins to ache in protest.

Just as I'm about to pull back, she reaches out and snatches the box from my hands.

I've seen plenty of women open gifts in my home. I do have a sister and plenty of cousins. Each time, they've been delicate and methodical, making sure to slowly peel back the wrapping so as to not tear the paper. Unsurprisingly, Nera is none of that. She violently rips away the paper with not a care in the world as to what will become of it.

Her fingers stall just over the latch, and then she finally slows as she opens the top.

I wait for a response, but she says nothing. Only stares at the contents open-heartedly.

"It's a snowflake."

"What?" Her chin juts upward, and for a mere moment I swear I see a gathering of moisture in her eyes. She quickly blinks it away.

I tentatively reach into the box to lift up the bracelet and show her the beaded jewel.

"It's a preserved snowflake," I explain as she gingerly takes it from my hand and lifts it to the light of the lantern hanging above me.

"How?" she asks in awe.

"It's from my home. We make these in winter." I step forward and reach out for her hand, surprised when she lets me tie the chain around her wrist. "Snowflakes are unique. One of a kind. No matter how many years pass, there will never be another like it. They are forged from what lies in front of them." I don't acknowledge the slight tremble of her lips. "They mean rebirth." I let go of her hand and she finally

meets my gaze.

"Thank you," she whispers as her fingers trace the beaded jewel with the snowflake inside.

"I also want you to know that it means I am with you." She looks back up. A lone tear falls down her cheek. And then, just when I think she's about to speak, she takes a deep breath and shifts out of view.

Ari

The dome explodes around her in a hateful fury as it barely misses me. The edge skirts along my shirt, burning the material as it moves.

"You almost got me!" I scream out, knowing she can barely hear me through the barrier.

She rolls her eyes. "You're fine."

"You would have missed me if I died."

"Barely!" she calls back, and I laugh.

"Would you have at least come to the funeral?" I question in mock seriousness as I circle the dome, making sure there are no cracks or weaknesses in sight.

"There can't be a funeral if there isn't a body," she replies. "Besides, we don't even know that it would kill you. Maybe it's truly just defense."

The structure falls to the ground just as I finish my circle.

"It has killed more animals than you care to admit."

She frowns as sadness seeps in. "I'm still not over that."

"Seriously?" I question as she takes the three strides to me. "You kill for food every time we meet up here. What's the difference?"

She halts directly in front of me, hands crossed over her chest, and a look that could kill. "Killing for food has a purpose. What my dome did to those little babies was horrific."

"It was three brelicks, and if you hadn't gotten to them first, I'm sure they would have come at you."

"You don't know that," she argues.

"It's a brelick. Its entire purpose is to breathe, kill, fuck, eat, and not be eaten in the process." She turns her nose up at my words. "Trust me, you are definitely on that list." I raise my eyebrows in inquiry. "At least in some capacity." Then I wiggle them knowingly.

She pushes my shoulder as she feigns a gag. "You're disgusting. They were just babies."

"Which means the mother was close by."

I lean down and pick up my pack, knowing we're done for the day. I'm just finishing up with stuffing the last of my items inside when she speaks.

"I practiced with the fire."

I freeze, knowing I could not have heard her correctly. "When?"

"Yesterday."

I turn to face her, confusion etched across my face. "You came out here yesterday? That was not a planned–"

"I was in the palace," she clarifies, and we both stiffen at her words.

"Nera!" I breathe out her name in warning.

"I'm sorry."

"You promised!" I admonish her.

She lifts her hand up in surrender. "I was alone. I promise. I tried to get down into the Soul Circle in order to get here, but there were guards, and I was stuck."

My pack drops to the ground. "That means nothing. You could have waited till today."

"You always get here before me," she argues as if it explains away every frustration I have over her recklessness.

"What does that matter?"

"I wanted to show you I could do it. I wanted to practice."

Her confession halts me, and I feel the smile lift before I realize I am doing it. Suddenly, every frustration and the bubbling anger melt away.

"You wanted to impress me?"

"What? No. I did not want to impress you." Her cheeks turn crimson.

"Yes you did."

"No. I just wanted to . . . I just wanted–"

"Show me," I butt in, and she covers her face.

I take a step forward and then another when she doesn't move back. When I'm right in front of her, I reach up and slowly remove her hand.

"Don't hide from me."

She crosses her arms over her chest and rolls her eyes. Gone is the embarrassment, and in its place is the attitude.

"I'm not hiding."

"Show me," I urge.

She takes a deep breath before reaching out to grab my hand.

"What are you doing?" I question as she laces her fingers within mine, the beaded jewel I gave her only weeks ago shimmering in the sunlight from above.

"I need to anchor myself to something. If I can hold onto something true, then it works."

"Am I some—"

"If you finish that sentence, I will punch you in the face," she warns.

I yield, lifting up the hand she isn't holding. "Okay. Anchor away."

She rolls her eyes before closing them, and after a moment of agony as I plead with the Elders for something to happen, sparks of white light surge out from her fingertips.

"Holy Elders!" I whisper as the tendrils snake across the ground.

"They're white."

"Like crystals or ice," I agree as we both stare at her right hand and the spectacular beauty that flows from it.

"I first noticed it a few weeks ago," she adds as she twists her hand in the air. I watch, enraptured as each coil silently obeys her command. "I was angry at my father and Riann." His name causes a stab of pain to pierce my chest. "I was so mad, and I could feel the flames starting to spark. I ran out of the palace and into the garden, hoping the air would help calm me."

"Did it work?"

"No." She flicks her wrist upward and the dazzling cords surge into the neverending sky. "I felt the fire come, so I fell forward to place my hands into the water's edge, hoping it would fizzle out. That didn't work either." She cuts her eyes to me. "But when I did that, I caught sight of my bracelet." We both look down to our clasped hands and the beaded snowflake she hasn't taken off. "I don't know why, but it calmed me. The next thing I knew, the budding flames fizzled out and this little white light was swimming in its place. It was small at first, only a few inches long. I made it back inside without a soul noticing, and then I played with it for hours." She pulls her fingers in, and I watch as the illuminated, crystal flames recede back within her. "I can make it come whenever I'm happy." She smiles, and I immediately look back down to our hands.

"What did you think of?" I question in hopes I already know the answer.

She swallows before pulling back with a nod. "Same time next week." Then she shifts out of view.

Ari

Her sudden inhale of breath steals mine away.

Her eyes open, meeting my frantic gaze, and then she is coughing and sputtering *as the water is forced from her lungs.*

"Ari!" she croaks out my name as she rolls on all fours. I cover her body, promising to never let anything take her again as I hold back her hair and brace her form on mine.

"It's okay. You're okay," I whisper to the back of her neck as tears spill forth from my eyes.

When she finally slumps toward the ground, worn out but breathing, I don't hold back. I twist her body within my grip pulling her as tightly as possible into me as I curl my body around her.

We sit in the damp sand, intertwined with each other for so long, I lose count of the seconds, minutes, hours, only able to note she is here and alive and in my arms.

"I drowned?" she finally asks. Her voice is hoarse and her short breaths tickle my neck.

"Never. I would never let that happen." My lips graze her temple.

She looks up to me. "You saved me?"

My hands grip her cheeks as I pull back to meet her gaze. "I'll always save you."

"But you hate me?" she says in between lingering bouts of coughing, and I burst out laughing.

"If there is only one thing I am sure of in this world, it is that I most definitely do not hate you."

Tears fill her eyes as her gaze searches every inch of my face, memorizing as she moves.

"You don't hate me?" Her voice quivers as her lips tremble.

I look down to her, tears falling from my face as they mingle with her own. "Not even close."

"You're supposed to hate me!" she hoarsely cries out, and I can feel the wall reforming as she tries to pull away. I hold her steady.

"Never," I counter with unyielding promise. "I never hated you. I never will."

"Please!" Her body begins to shake with the sobs. "Please. Hate me. Please. I'm a murderer. I'm what's wrong with this world. You're supposed to hate me."

Her plea bewilders me. I brush her soaked hair from view while I study her tear-filled eyes.

"Has that been your plan all along? To make me hate you?" She nods and I start to laugh. "Oh, Nera." I lean my forehead against her. "You've wonderfully failed at that."

"But– but then–" she doesn't finish the sentence before her body is racked with sobs.

I pull her in tighter, willing whatever pain she is in, both physical and mental, to subside. I have no idea why she would have thought I hated her, or why she thinks she is the reason for all of this, but I promise from this moment on to make sure she knows the truth.

I run my lips across her forehead from one temple to the next. Her breath catches, and the sobs start to slow.

"I don't hate you." I punctuate each word with a kiss. My lips linger on her cheek and my nose brushes against hers. "Not even a little bit."

When my lips finally brush against hers, she sucks in a ragged breath.

"I don't hate you either," she whispers, and I feel the tremble of her lips against mine.

"Good. Let's keep it that way," I say, all the while fighting the urge to crash my body into hers. Every nerve ending is screaming at me to strip her bare and let her know exactly how much I do, in fact, not *hate her. But she is injured and weak, and certainly sore from my efforts to keep her alive. I feel my body quivering with restraint.*

"Ari?" She pulls me from my wayward thoughts as she leans up just enough to meet my gaze.

"Yes?"

"If you don't kiss me right now, I'm going to–"

I lose the fight as I press my lips against hers. It's only a fraction of what my body is screaming for. But what I get is so much more.

Her kiss feels as though life itself has finally entered my veins. It takes an eternity for my own body to respond. In one respect, I have dreamed of this moment for so very long. But I never thought it would actually come.

She had spent far too much energy keeping us at arms length to ever allow the hope to take hold within me.

I was wrong.

This is real.

She is real.

And she is here. And she is kissing me as if her life depends on it.

I open my mouth just as she pulls back and gives me a stare filled with both curious optimism and growing embarrassment.

The sun has slowly hidden itself, and now her beauty is bathed in moonlight.

"Hi," she says.

I laugh as I feel my cheeks burn from the smile that reaches my eyes.

"Hi." I pull her to me as tightly as I can, further closing the gap between us. But when I move to lean in again, she winces.

"Nera?"

"I'm okay," she answers my unspoken question.

"You're in pain."

She vigorously shakes her head. "I'm okay." And then she reaches upward so our lips meet once more.

There is only a moment of pure ecstasy in her touch before I feel her entire body tense and I pull back.

"You're hurting."

She swallows down the pain, and my motives change.

"Where?" My hands make a frantic rush of scouring every inch as I slowly lay her back against the damp riverbank. "She winces when I brush past her ribs. "Here? It hurts here?"

She nods in answer, unable to truly speak the words. When I lift up her shirt, I find bruising already forming along her ribcage. A quick swipe of my thumb over the swelling area causes an immediate hiss of pain to escape her.

"It hurts to breathe," she admits between small shallow breaths.

I nod in answer as I try to formulate my next move.

"I think I broke your ribs." My eyes lift to meet hers.

"It's okay." Her fingers brush away a lone tear that escapes my hold.

"You need a healer."

She shakes her head in answer. "Don't take me back to–"

"You aren't going back to Halabar. I'm taking you to my home. I'm taking you to Centra III."

Her body stills, but then she gives a quick nod of acceptance.

"I'll have to shift us."

She nods again.

"It will be painful."

She closes her eyes, and I search the area for something that will give her even a small amount of relief.

There is nothing.

With a deep breath, I try to recall each and every one of my lessons. Unfortunately, I never cared too much to listen when the topic of the day was that of healing. All I ever wanted was to shred my enemy in two. I had no means for fixing someone back up once I was done.

My fingers flex around the hem of my shirt in frustration at my idiotic incompetence. My stupid stubbornness that will now allow pain to continue berating the one person who means more to me than any other.

But as I look down, knuckles turned white and covered in their own bruising from my attempt at saving her, I recall a small bout of information.

I need to bind her ribs. I need to secure them.

My hand reluctantly leaves her.

"I have an idea. Stay still for me, okay?" I ask, and she again answers with a nod.

A moment later, my shirt is stripped off my body as I rip the fabric into one long band.

"I'm going to wrap this around you. It'll be tight, and will probably hurt, but it'll

keep the injury secure as we move."

She nods again, a grimace covering her features.

I roll her shirt upward just to the line of her chest before I start.

"I'm sorry."

"Stop apologizing," she commands as the silent tears still roll down her cheeks.

I wrap the first length around her torso, pulling tight enough to secure, and cause a hiss of pain as I do.

"Stop being so stubborn all the time," I counter in an effort to distract her.

She laughs, and then immediately tenses as I begin the second roll around her abdomen. "Are you really about to admonish me for stubbornness when I'm injured? That's not very fair."

"Fair?" I shake my head in feigned annoyance. "It's never been fair between us, Nera. You've had me ensnared from the moment we met."

She balks. "You shouldn't have been such a menace, and maybe I would have liked you sooner." The words are short and clipped. "Besides, I had to make sure I was better than you at something."

I wrap the binding once more. Her eyes slam shut as she holds in the scream of pain I know she wants to let out.

"You are better than me at everything," I tell her.

"Not shifting. Not fighting." She takes a deep breath and winces at the movement. "You could send me to the Elders with brute strength alone."

"You could be within the throes of death and still carve me out a path to the Elders before you get there," I tease back.

She smiles. "You're right. I could still take you out."

Nodding, I laugh.

Her face suddenly stills. Her shallow breathing seems to hasten. "What if I'm in the throes of death right now?"

"You're not," I swiftly reply as I reach up to cup her cheek, not able to let the idea of her no longer being here go any further in my mind. "But if you were, I would ask that you do exactly as stated, and make sure I get there before you."

"And why is that?"

I secure the last wrap of the binding before pausing to find her eyes.

"Now that I know what it is like to live in a world with you, I hope to never have to know what it is like to live without you."

I stand motionless as the world slowly comes back into view. The discarded food sits untouched before me, and the massive room seems suddenly too small.

"Nera?" Ari asks as he brushes a hand across my cheek.

I instantly recoil.

"I'm sorry," he says as he brings his hand away, but I keep my gaze planted on the floor, unable to face what I just witnessed—what is standing before me now.

"I think I loved you," I blurt out, unsure of what else to say as the weight of what I just witnessed encompasses me.

He chuckles slightly. "I think so, too."

"And you loved me?"

His fingers tentatively reach out as they touch my chin, lifting my face to meet his. "I loved you then, just as I love you now."

Heat courses through my veins as I try to will whatever threatens to erupt back within me. But this I have no control over. I never did.

White light lurches from my palms and slams to the ground around us as tears stain my cheeks.

"I think I might love you, too." I whisper the confession I have held so tightly inside for all these weeks as my gaze shifts away, ashamed of the time I have stolen from us.

His thumb lingers on my bottom lip as he pulls my eyes back to his. "You love me, too."

The ribbons of white light reach out like ropes in the wind as they encircle us and bathe the room in glowing brilliance.

"I'm scared," I reveal as tears fall down my face.

"Me, too."

"What if I mess this up? What if I lose you again?" My vision becomes blurred as the reality of my fears settles.

I have lost everything I once thought I loved. Every person who has come into my life has been taken without warning. I barely survived each. And now that I have Ari, I know that losing him would be the final crack.

"You won't lose me. Not again." He steps forward, his body becoming flush with mine.

"What if I hurt you?" White light slithers in my periphery as I will it to my control.

"You won't." His words wash over me in calm serenity, and the white light slowly retreats.

"Ari?"

His brows peak in question.

"I love you."

The smile that spreads across his face is damn near blinding. He leans forward, letting his sleep-mussed hair fall around us.

"I love you, too."

His lips brush mine. It's tentative at first, but I don't let him linger as I surge forward, claiming his kiss.

He only hesitates a moment, as if making sure this is real, before he wraps his arms around my legs, lifts me up and back onto the table, and begins to devour me. The plates and bowls clang against the stone floor.

I can't keep track of where his hands venture as he lights a fire across my face and neck with kisses. I only know that everywhere he touches, sparks fly off.

"If you two keep going, I'm not eating on that table ever again." A voice calls out from across the room, and we both jolt in surprise.

Ari jumps backward and turns to face my newest enemy. I try not to laugh as he not so covertly readjusts himself as he moves.

"Do you want to die today?" Ari asks in all seriousness, and the man I now see leaning against the opposite doorway stands straighter as he laughs.

"Uncle Arynn!" A little boy screams as he runs past the man's legs and bolts straight toward Ari.

"Good thing I arrived before mother. She would have whipped you both for that little display," the man calls out just as the boy makes it into Ari's arms.

He quickly turns back to me as he ruffles the little one's hair and mouths a quick apology.

By the time I'm standing with my shirt readjusted and a half-hearted attempt at taming my hair, the unknown man is standing feet from me.

"What's the protocol?" He looks between Ari and me. "Am I re-introducing myself nicely, or do I just aggravate the shit out of her like normal?"

I burst out laughing as Ari drops the boy to the ground, pats his bottom, and shoos him away.

"Nera, this is my older brother, Calix."

"You call me Cal," Calix interjects with an outstretched hand. I survey his face to find so many similarities to the man I now know as mine. His hair, while not quite as long as Ari's, still has that shagginess that begs you to run your hands through it. His eyes are a deep brown, and his skin, while the same golden hue as Ari's, boasts no scars or signs of war. "So, nice introduction it is."

"You can aggravate me if you want," I chuckle as I shake his hand. "Actually you already thoroughly pissed me off by bursting in here just now."

Cal bursts out laughing as he wiggles his eyebrows in Ari's direction. "'Pissed you off'? That's a phrase I haven't heard before." He shakes his head, and I cringe at the thought that that small phrase is just another reminder of everything that has happened, and all the time I have lost.

"You better thank me." Cal crosses his arms in a jestingly stern stance then looks toward Ari. "Just keep it in your pants until mother and the littles head off to bed, and then you can mark the whole damn palace for all I care."

"Calix, go away." Ari shoves his brother backward toward the door he entered through. Though Cal pretends to fight back, I can tell there is no malice between the two of them. Simply two brothers who thrive on nothing more than frustrating one another.

"Who was that little boy?" I call out just before Ari has him across the threshold.

They both stop. Cal is the one to answer. "That was Elix, my son."

"And my grandson," a feminine voice rings out from behind me, and I turn to find the most regal woman standing not two yards from me. "Ari has been home for less than a day, and you two are already fighting?" she chides in the most motherly tone possible, and then clasps her hands in front.

Ari wastes no time as he gives his brother one last shove before turning back and walking right past me to his mother. Their resemblance is uncanny. While I can see the similarities in Ari, Elora, and Calix, it is obvious the latter two took most of their looks from their father, while Ari is a damn near replica of his mother.

"Mother." He kisses her hand, and then each cheek.

"It's been six months."

"I know."

"I hope it was worth it." She looks from him to me, and then turns before anyone else can offer up another word.

I am only in her presence for less than a minute, but that was enough to cause the darkest of dread to coil in my stomach.

"Don't worry," Cal whispers in my ear, and I jump in surprise at his closeness. "She never liked you, or Ari, or Elora, or me. So at least you're in good company."

"Leave, Calix," Ari states as he wraps his hand around my middle, pulling me in.

Cal takes a deep breath. "I wish I could. But I did come in here for a purpose."

That peaks my interest. "And what was that?"

"Dinner is being served in the great hall. Mother called in a few of the nobles, and they are waiting for you."

"Damn the Elders," Ari curses under his breath as his hand slides up the back of my shirt. "We are busy."

"Arynn." Cal steps forward, and though Ari must be at least six feet tall, if not more, Cal has a good two inches on him. He looks down at his younger brother with a look I know has been perfected over the years. "You are our sovereign. You have duties. Duties, may I remind you, that you have all but forfeited these last few months."

"I had other priorities." His fingertips tease the waistline of my pants as I pray to the Elders that the heat within my cheeks stays hidden.

Cal looks down to me, and then back to his brother. "I understand, but you are back."

"We aren't staying. We have to–"

Cal raises a hand in surrender. "Arynn. I get it. I really do." He places that hand on Ari's shoulder. "You don't have to stay for hours. Just eat a meal. Talk with the nobles for a few minutes, maybe dance with your woman to show them all is well, celebrate the fight you just won, and then go back and do what needs to be done. I have it handled here."

Ari takes a shuddering breath before removing his hand from me and pulling his brother in for a hug. "Thank you for what you're doing here."

Cal shakes his head. "You would do it for me."

"I hope our fight ends soon so we can return home."

Cal pats him on the back before turning to face me. "We never really hugged. It was more of a punch or a kick, sometimes you–"

I cut him off as I step forward and wrap my arms around his middle. I can tell how surprised he is at the action by the way he tenses before enveloping me in the tightest, most brotherly hug I could ever imagine. "I've never had a brother, at least not that I remember." I pull back and give him a smirk, and he laughs. "Best be ready for 21 years of pent up annoying sister vibes heading your way once all this is over."

He bursts out laughing, then squeezes Ari's shoulder. "She hasn't changed a damn bit." He looks down to me and then back to Ari. "I'll be praying for you."

Ari laughs as Cal turns to walk out of the room. He stops just before he crosses the threshold. "Send her up to El's quarters. I'm sure there is something she can borrow from her to wear to dinner."

LI

The dress fits me like a glove. Soft, white fabric with flecks of what look like golden diamonds sprinkled throughout the bottom and top. The bodice has a keyhole placed right above my cleavage, and if my earlier encounters with Ari are any hint to what is to come, I know he won't be able to keep his eyes off it.

It has a high neckline covered with golden jewels and a white cape which hooks onto my shoulders and around my arms, and flows to the floor below.

"This is . . . a bit much, don't you think?" I ask Elora as she helps me slip into the heels.

"It's not my fault you two decided to come by the same day as the nobleman's dinner." She looks up at me with a smirk. "This is the only event we hold in which extravagance plays a part. Most of these people remember a time when wealth was shared to some extent, and they still like to bask in that when they can." She huffs out a breath as our eyes meet. "But I have a feeling most will be far too excited about our recent win to care about anything else."

"Who all will be there?"

"Me, Calix, his wife Emory, you, Ari, Mother, and then various noblemen and a few citizens. I bet in total, no more than thirty. There have been times when we have had upwards of fifty, but it's too cold tonight for many to venture out. They would rather stay inside next to a fire."

I nod as she places what look to be golden diamonds on my ears.

"Besides, you are a Celestra and leader of the Restoration. They will expect you to look absolutely radiant now that you have returned."

I almost balk at the idea. A fleeting memory of being dressed up and attending dinners and balls with Riann comes to mind, and I almost tear the beautiful dress off right then.

I hear his throat clear just as Elora steps back. When I turn to find Ari standing a few feet away, it takes every ounce of strength I possess not to claim him right here on the floor.

"You look beautiful." His voice is an octave too low, and I can't help but notice how his breathing is more ragged than normal.

"You look pretty damn handsome yourself." I drink him in. His previously tousled dark hair is, for the first time, combed back into a low bun. The jacket he wears is black with a higher neckline similar to my own with a trail of gold lining the edges. It reaches just past his thighs. The black pants and boots fit him perfectly. I smile at the thought, and he mirrors the action.

"Like what you see?" he teases me as he takes a few steps forward.

"Very much," I answer, and hear Elora feign a gag.

"You two are ridiculous. Save it for later. Or better yet, save it for when you get back to Centra II." She rolls her eyes as she turns to leave. "And don't ruin that dress. It was a gift, and I haven't even gotten a chance to wear it yet," she states pointedly to both of us as she walks out of the room.

Ari extends his hand to me. I loop my hand behind his arm, but he shakes his head.

"What?" I question in confusion. "You don't want me on your arm?"

"I want you on my arm. I want you in my arms and my bed and my heart." He leans down to barely brush his lips against mine. I surge forward, begging for more, but he shakes his head. "If I kiss you how I want to kiss you right now, we will never make it out of this room, and we will most certainly ruin this dress in the process."

"You're such a tease," I whisper as I reach back out to him, but he shakes his head once more.

"We are Celestras. Let's enter as such."

He intertwines his fingers in mine and the world goes black.

Dinner is uneventful, as most everyone here is more concerned with ignoring me than anything else. It seems I am a contradiction they can't seem to piece together. Ari never leaves my side. I can't deny the parallels with this encounter and my previous dinners with Riann in Halabar. Except there's one distinction. Here I feel safe. Here I belong.

By the time dinner is over and drinks are poured, we are settled back into a corner making small talk with a couple whose names I can't recall. I laugh when they walk off and Ari comments that he can't either.

"I think it's time I sneak you out of here," he whispers in my ear as I tilt the glass to my lips. Goosebumps erupt across my skin.

"And where would we go?"

"I know just the place." He lets his hand slowly run its way down my arm before clasping my finger and shifting us away.

Soft music fills the bedroom. It is just a whisper of a melody. I close my eyes as Ari walks over to shut and latch the door we didn't come through.

The calm rhythm surges through my veins, dancing along my skin as I try to still my rapidly beating heart. A dreamy sadness fills my mind at the sound, and I let it overtake me.

There is only a moment of silence between one song and the next before I hear his near-silent footsteps creep back to where I stand.

My eyes stay closed.

The next song starts.

This time the tune, while still slow, is no longer sad, but sweet and peaceful. Though there are no words, there is a definite poetic inkling in what is being conveyed. It is hopeful. It is the beginning of a story. One I am sure has been told over a thousand times since it was first played.

Ari's hand reaches out. I feel the movement in the air before his fingers graze the tops of mine, sending bolts of electricity careening through me. When he finally intertwines his hand in mine, the bolts converge into a thousand lightning strikes straight to my heart.

The familiar tingles race along my skin. The rushing river of desire within spreads out as my heart begins its own race toward an unknown end.

My eyes open to meet him, a silent plea skirting between us. And though I know the answer, I don't speak it.

I want him to ask. Because last time, I said no. And this time, I want to say yes.

"Will you dance with me?" He gives a slight tug, effortlessly ushering me into his arms.

"I'm not a good dancer."

He shakes his head as he pulls me closer to the center of the room. "You're a wonderful dancer."

"I don't remember how," I counter.

"Just follow me." His left hand wraps around my waist as his right clutches onto my left for dear life. The fabric of the dinner gown does nothing to tamper the heated sting from his touch.

For far too long, we stand unmoving, unspeaking as he takes in breath after breath, letting the beat of the music somehow burrow itself deep within our bones.

It starts to build. The quiet optimism of the beginning slowly turns to turmoil. The beat ignites and the chaos ensues.

I start to smile, looking up to find his eyes trained on me. "On Earth, when someone is asked to dance, it normally involves some kind of movement." I give him the snarkiest smirk I can muster.

A voice begins to sing. There are still no words. Just a hint of something within, begging to be let out.

"Is that so?" he asks.

I nod.

He tightens his hold around my waist. "Well then, let's move."

At first, the sway is barely discernible. Just a slight move of our hips from one side to the next. It doesn't even match the beat. But then his left foot moves and then his right, and without even thinking, so are mine. He takes his time, and I step on his toes more than I care to admit. He never comments on it.

We circle the room.

Right foot, then left foot, then back again.

"I missed you," he whispers into my hair.

"I missed you, too." I smile up at him, knowing we mean the phrase in two completely different contexts. I didn't remember him, so how could I have missed him the way he missed me? And yet, I hope he knows that, in my own way, I did miss him.

He pulls me in tighter, and I let my body sink into his.

His forehead leans against mine as our breaths mingle and our bodies all but become one.

I stare into his eyes, mesmerized by the golden hue that pulls me in. "I'm sorry you had to wait so long."

He shakes his head as he stares back at me. "I would have waited ten thousand years for just a moment of your time."

The dam threatens to break with his admission, and I wonder what in the Elders' names I did to deserve a man such as this.

He suddenly stops, lets go of my hand, and reaches up to cup my cheek so tenderly, my heart clenches.

"Thank you for coming back to me," he whispers as his nose brushes against mine.

"Thank you for reminding me."

He lets out a subtle laugh before his lips melt against mine. It's a soft kiss, sweet and delicate, but exactly us. When he finally pulls back, a dazed, almost drunken expression on his face, he shuffles a step backward and surveys me.

"I'm going to kill my sister." He laughs. "I want nothing more than to rip this off of you, but she would kill me before the night's over."

I reach up and unclasp the cape portion, letting it fall to the floor.

"No killing you on my watch," I state as I slowly turn around, lift my brown curls out of the way, and say, "I need help with the buttons."

He lets out a ragged breath as he reaches out and runs his fingers along the spine of the dress. He takes his time carefully unfastening each one before placing a tender kiss to the newly exposed skin with each clasp he conquers. By the time he reaches the last one, I'm so wound up and my hands are gripping the foot board on the bed so tightly, my knuckles are white. My body is a sea of invisible sparks.

His hand trails up my spine as if surveying his work before he slips his fingers under the shoulders and pushes them down. The dress skirts along my arms and down my back so slowly, I know he is relishing every moment.

When it reaches my hips, he stops. I look over my shoulder to find him staring at the two small scars on the back of my arm I had all but forgotten were there.

"Who did this to you?" His thumb glides over the marks.

"Tarak injected me with something to knock me out a few times." I answer with the truth, and feel his body go taut.

He leans forward then to place a kiss to each mark. Then he brushes his nose against the back of my neck. From this position, I know he can look down and see my bare chest. And normally, that would embarrass me, but right now I want nothing more than for Ari to claim all of me.

"I'm going to make him pay for that." He forces out the words through gritted teeth.

"Let's not think about that right now." I twist my head back to quickly capture his lips in mine. "Right now, I want to think about us."

He settles his head on the back of my shoulder, as if trying to flush out all the anger that built at what he just saw.

"Ari. It's fine. I'm fine. It was just the stab of a needle." I reach back to intertwine my fingers in his hair. "I'm okay."

I feel his nod against my skin. "You're okay."

I smile sheepishly at his words and give a slight tug to his hair. "Now, get back to undressing me, or I will rip this dress off and your sister will come for both of us."

He finally laughs. "You are such a demanding little demon tonight."

The dress pools at my feet. I hear him step back slightly, and then silence pours through the room as he assesses every inch of me he can see.

"Turn around," he commands, and I immediately move.

I've never stood completely bare before someone. Most of my previous encounters, each driven by the need to feel one ounce of the love Ari is giving me in his gaze, were always quick tousles meant to satisfy a need—one that was never truly met. At least, not until now.

"Fuck," he whispers as he runs his fingers through his hair and slinks back into an ottoman.

"You're still dressed," I note, unsure of what my next move should be.

He nods before sliding off his dinner jacket and resting it across the arm of the chair. He sits, still and quiet for just another moment before he starts to roll up his sleeves to reveal the tanned and toned muscle underneath.

My eyes catch on his scars, and for the first time, I don't feel overwhelming anger at the thought of how they came to be. Instead, I have an urgency within me to soothe every ache he may have ever had.

"Nera?" My name is a question he can't seem to voice.

"What?" I close the gap between us, letting my bare legs slide up against his clothed ones.

He takes a deep breath as if preparing himself for the words he is about to speak. "We dabbled in a very . . . specific type of sex," he confesses and I swallow. "Not every time, but most." He leans forward and wraps a hand around the back of my bare thigh, pulling me in that much closer. "I need to know how you want this to go." His eyes are trained on the apex of my thighs as the pad of his thumb makes small circles on my skin.

"I don't understand." I reach down and tilt his chin upward.

He licks his lips as his hand runs the length of my thigh, from knee to ass and back again.

My body damn near explodes at the sensation as I feel a familiar heat bloom in my core and spread out to every inch of me. If just this small touch is lighting me on fire, I can't even begin to imagine what the rest of the night will bring forth. The thought crashes through me, and I can't hide the hint of a moan that seeps out.

He smirks at the noise.

"You are so very controlled in everything you do." He leans forward and presses a kiss to one hip. "You always have to make sure your emotions and your gifts are in check." His lips slowly run across the length of my stomach. "You can never let go. You can never truly be free." He brushes a kiss to my other hip. "But here, with me, it's different."

His lips and tongue slowly forge a path downward, teasing me as he moves. On instinct, my fingers sink into his dark hair, hoping to guide him where I am most desperate.

"This. What happens between us is the one time you get to let someone else control the outcome." His tongue swipes lower, just above where I desire it.

"Ari," I plead, no longer able to hold it in.

"When we are together, I am in control."

"You are in control," I instinctively repeat as he places kisses at the juncture of my right thigh.

"Do you want that? What we used to do? Or do you want this to go–"

"I want that," I blurt out, still not sure of exactly what it is I am agreeing to, but knowing that whatever it is will be heaven if this man is involved.

He nods once, then reaches forward to brush his thumb right across my sensitive swollen nub. I instinctively arch into his touch as the cry of pleasure is ripped from my lips.

"Shh," he coos as he slowly stands to meet my gaze.

My heart is pounding, and my hands begin to tremble as I reach out to unfasten his pants.

"No." He pulls my hands away, dropping them to my sides. "Tonight is about you. I have three years' worth of pent up, delicious torture to rain down on you."

My breath catches in my throat as I nod.

"Go lie on the bed." I immediately follow his command.

When I am lying ready, head placed on the pillows, hands by my sides, knees together and slightly bent upward, heart pounding in my chest, and body practically convulsing from need, he leans across the footboard, reaches out and lifts my left foot into the air before he runs the pad of his finger along the arch. The motion tickles, and I pull my legs up and back on instinct.

"Good girl," he purrs as his hands grip the edge of the footboard and he stares me down. "Now open your legs."

I swallow as I let my legs fall open. The windowless room is bathed in the soft light of flickering flames, which dances along his tanned arms. He runs a hand through his now-disheveled hair as he stares raptly at me.

"You are so damn beautiful," he says so reverently, it might as well have been a prayer. "And you are all mine."

I want to reply. I want to tell him that yes, I am. That I have always been and will always be his. But I bite my lip instead, unsure if speaking is even feasible at this moment. He immediately walks around to the head of the bed, reaches forward, and pulls my lip from the grip of my teeth.

"I'm the only one allowed to do the biting." He leans forward as he sucks on my lower lip, and then immediately clamps down just enough to cause a welcome sting. I fist the sheets as pleasure surges through me.

When he lets go, a small popping sound emanates, and I taste the metallic coating of blood in my mouth. He quickly leans forward to swipe his lips across the burn, soothing it with his touch.

"Was that okay?" he asks, and I can tell he still isn't entirely convinced whether or not I'm comfortable with the direction this is headed. But he couldn't be any further from the truth. This is exactly what I need.

"Yes, sir," I answer coyly, and his eyebrows peak in response.

"You've . . . never truly called me that before." I almost regret the phrase, until he admits, "I like it very much."

I run my tongue over my swollen and aching lip, silently pleading for more.

He smirks as he cups my cheek. "I know your body better than my own."

He leans backward, right hand still cupping the side of my face while his left pushes my bent knee down just a little more so the view of where I want him most is fully on display. I feel heat flood my face at his inspection.

"I know what makes you blush." He gives me a knowing look.

Then his hand moves back up my body, grazing the inside of my thigh, my stomach, the curve of my breast, just before he wraps it around my neck. "I know how to make you beg for it." He tests out the motion as he tentatively squeezes. My entire body tenses in excitement. This is something I have no memory of doing, but I think it is about to become one of my favorites.

His hand travels back down the center of my chest as he slowly cups one breast and then the other. "I know what makes you scream." He brushes across a peaked nipple, then squeezes so tightly, I damn near arch off the bed as the cry is ripped from my chest.

Then he sits beside me, lifts my left leg, and drapes it over his lap. "But most importantly, I know exactly how to make you let go." The flat of his palm slides down my stomach as his other hand caresses my outer thigh.

My head flies backward as I stare at the ceiling. He has barely even touched where I need him, but I'm so worked up, I know I'll come the moment he does.

When his fingers brush against the swollen nub, I let out a shuddering breath. I'm so distracted by the touch and feel of him, I don't even notice when his head drops downward.

I scream out as I feel the tip of his tongue lick upward, then in circles.

My hands instinctively move to bury themselves within his hair, but he pulls back before I even get the chance.

A groan of delicious misery is ripped from my throat.

"I've been thinking," he says as his hands roam my inner thighs, coming that much closer to my center with each passing sweep. I damn near grunt in frustration. "I normally would make you wait for it—make you beg for it. But I don't think I will do that tonight."

I almost cry out in relief.

"I'm going to let you come. And then I'm going to make you come."

"Please," I beg. My body practically lifts itself off the mattress in search of him.

"But tomorrow, and the next day, and the next day after that." His fingers slowly tease my entrance. "I'm going to make you work for it then. I'm going to let you lose control with me."

I nod in acceptance, knowing that at this moment, with this man in between my legs, I would willingly agree to anything he wanted.

He slowly adjusts so he's lying poised and ready at my center, and I swear he takes as much time as he can to settle, intent on torturing me in the process. His lips start at my thigh as they make their way to my core and languid sparks trickle down my legs. Just before he meets his mark, he leans backward.

"You've been such a good girl," he coos, and then his mouth is on me.

Long strokes of his tongue interspersed with gentle sucking threaten to rip me in two. If I wasn't holding on to the sheets so tightly, I'm sure I would somehow gain the gift of flight and take straight off into the heavens.

His fingers tease my entrance, and I cry out in relief, desperate for him to fill me. And when he does, deftly fucking me with his hand and his mouth, I cry out in relief.

The heat spreads, and for just a moment, as I twist and turn within the delicious torture, I swear I see a faint glow coming from him. Before I can fully take in the sight, he runs his teeth along me, and the wall I thought I would never break through with anyone finally shatters.

He crawls up my body as he covers my nakedness with his own. I'm not sure when he discarded his clothes, but in all honesty, I couldn't care less. I just hope that next time I get a front seat to that show.

"You did so good." His voice is pure heat as he lays down a gentle assault of kisses on my face. "Such a good girl," he whispers into my ear.

"Ari," I call out the only word I can functionally state at this moment.

"Shh." He brushes my hair back from my face as I feel his length run against me.

"I need you." The whispered words come out between pants as I ride out the high he just gave me.

"I'm right here." His lips caress my jaw as his hand toys with my chest. "I'm not going anywhere."

My hips lift on instinct, searching for more. "I *need* you," I beg, and he chuckles.

"So demanding." He places a kiss on my lips. "I'm going to have to fuck that defiance out of you again, aren't I?"

I grunt in approval as I nearly come again just from his words.

"Please." My hands search his body, desperate to feel him, but he quickly grabs me by the wrists.

"Later." He places both my small wrists in his hand and lifts them over my head. Then he looks down, surveying me. "Spread your legs," he directs as he nudges my thighs apart with his own, and then slowly begins to sink in.

For some reason, I expect a moment of pain. I can feel his size, and yet there is nothing but relief when he finally lurches forward and, in one smooth motion, buries himself within.

I open my eyes then, only to find him staring down at me. We both still, hearts pounding and chests heaving for air as he reaches up and wipes away a tear from my eye.

He opens his mouth to speak, but I quickly cut him off.

"I love you."

I can't help the smile that forms with the phrase as I gulp down air between each word. He smiles as he rests his forehead against mine.

"I love you."

And then he begins.

Every whisper of his warm lips against my skin is a claim. Every touch of his strong, calloused hands is a plea. Every thrust of his hips, an apology.

I'm sorry.

I love you.

I'm sorry.

I'm here.

I'm sorry.

I'm yours.

I'm sorry.

I love you.

I am yours and you are mine.

And I greedily take in every silent word he gives me. I let him consume me. I let him overtake me—mind, body, and soul. I drown out my worries and fears of the unknown in the moans that escape my lips.

The heat that never truly went away coils within me. My body shudders in anticipation. And when I finally feel the flame rise within, I call out his name as the room erupts into blinding white light.

LII

I wake to soft kisses trailing across my collar bone.

Three days of being consumed by this man, first in Centra III, and now in Centra IV, and I know that even if we are given eternity together, it would never be enough to satiate the need that grows for him.

Only him.

"Good morning," he whispers between my breasts just before turning his head to deftly lavish a hardened peak.

I grunt out a noise I hope lets him know it is most definitely a good morning indeed. The space between my legs still aches from the previous night, and I wonder if I'll ever get used to the feeling of him buried within me.

"Good morning," I whisper as his lips meet mine.

Sparks begin to flare out from under the covers, and I have to concentrate to pull them back.

"Reeves won't be too happy if you burn down her home," Ari coos at my ear as a hand finds mine.

"Then stop making them come," I tease, my hand reaching up to run my fingers through his hair.

He laughs. "I like making you come."

My grip tightens as I pull the strands upward so his gaze meets mine. "That's not what I meant." I squint my eyes in feigned seriousness.

He shrugs his shoulders as he falls back beside me.

"I think you like when I make you come, too."

I swat his arm in a fit of giggles.

It almost scares me how easily we fell back into this . . . bond between us. But in reality, it was always right there, simmering beneath the surface and begging to be freed. It just took my mind a bit longer to catch up to what my body already knew.

I twist to straddle his nakedness. He does nothing to halt the motion but intensely stares as the hard lines of his body seem to mold so perfectly into the soft curves of mine.

"So damn beautiful." The words are soft as he leans forward on his elbows then reaches down to situate himself perfectly between my legs.

"No playing this morning?" I tease, wondering why he's being so compliant, when the last two days have been spent in a blissfully torturous oasis as he shows me just how well he knows my body and how to take control over it.

He shakes his head. "I don't think I have the patience. At least not with you looking like a goddess on top of me.

We both laugh. Then that laugh turns into a mutual groan as he pushes himself upward, burying deep within me.

My lips part as I moan out his name. But before the utterance is even complete, a deafening knock that I know can only belong to Dina interrupts the noise.

"Stop fucking and get dressed! We're leaving in an hour."

Her words instantly cause the air to shift, and we both still. Gone is the moment I long for, and in its place I find a tension I wish would vanish.

"Fuck." He throws his head back as his hands find my hips.

"Does this mean we have to stop?" I roll my hips against his, savoring the feeling of him buried so deeply within me. He tightens his grip, and I know there will soon be new fingerprint bruises on my thighs and hips to replace the ones that are already fading.

"Not until you come." He gives me a wicked grin before swiftly flipping us over.

"I'm nervous." My confession stalls between us as we both catch our breaths.

"I know." He turns on his side, propped up on one arm and staring down at me as his hand finds my stomach. "But you've done a version of this a hundred times before. It's nothing new."

"Dina said Centra II isn't like here or Halabar. She said it was like a fortress—a prison."

He buries his face in the crook of my neck and inhales as I speak.

"She said many more go in than ever come out."

He nods. "Their main focus is keeping people in. Even when they want to escape." His breath tickles my ear.

"And yet here we are, preparing to voluntarily enter." I awkwardly laugh, because if I let out any other noise, it would be a strangled sob of apprehension.

"You don't have to–"

"Ari." I lean up and turn his way so that I'm looking down at him. "If you tell me one more time that I can leave or we can run or that I don't have to do something, I'm going to punch you in your stupidly beautiful face."

He laughs.

"You think I'm beautiful?" He wiggles his eyebrows and I roll my eyes.

"And annoying."

"Annoyingly beautiful?"

"Ugh." I reach behind, grasping the pillow and tossing it at his head. He quickly shifts out of its path, and before I can take another breath, I hear his whispered words in my ear.

"It's okay." I jolt at the noise and turn to find him standing completely naked behind me. "I think I'm beautiful, too." He shifts again as I reach out to swat him, but he isn't as quick as he thinks, and I shift directly in front of him.

"I love you," I whisper against his heated lips.

"I will never tire of hearing you say that."

"I love you." I reach up to my tallest height and kiss his cheek. "I love you." My hands grasp onto his hips as my fingers itch to explore what lies at the end of those immaculate grooves. He moans. "I love you." I swipe my tongue across the parted seam of his lips. "I love–"

"Thirty minutes!" Dina screams from the hallway.

Our eyes meet, and though neither of us says a word, I know there is an endless apology that races between us.

The last few days have been what I can only describe as actual heaven. Days and nights seemed to blur as we spent more time drowning within our moans than coming up for air. I spent hours relearning everything there was to know about his body and what he liked. And then I spent even longer trying to make up for three lost years.

But now, that hazy, lust-filled dream is over, and we are being thrust back into the reality we tried so desperately to hide from.

Once we arrived back in Centra IV, Reeves informed us that her people needed just a bit more time to secure the rescue mission, and then we would be on the move again. Neither of us seemed to mind that this time gave us three days to ourselves. But now they're ready, and so we must be as well.

"Can I show you something before we officially step away from this moment and into the next?" Ari tilts his head, pulling me out of my thoughts, and yet saying exactly what I'm feeling.

"More battle plans?"

He laughs. "No. Actually I was thinking about something last night as you were falling asleep."

"And what is that?"

"The first time we accepted each other. The first time we accepted the bond."

I furrow my brow in confusion. "I already saw the memory of the riverbank."

He laughs again as he stretches out his hand. "I promise this one is a little more . . . intimate."

Ari

"Put it up," I say as I throw my arms into the air in frustration.

"I have it up!" Nera screams, and I smirk back. I don't know why, but getting her flustered is my most favorite thing.

I think it's because she touches me more when she's flustered. Granted, those touches come in the form of pushes or punches or kicks, but still . . . they are moments when her skin grazes mine, and I will soak up whatever she willingly gives.

"You sure? Completely up?" I tease as I inch toward her. My skin prickles as if a thousand electric pulses are running through me.

Her eyes squint as the frustration grows, and she throws invisible daggers directly my way.

It doesn't deter me. If anything, it emboldens me. I am tired of this game. The kiss on the river bank unleashed something in both of us, and I am tired of hiding from it. I would have acted on it in that very moment had she not been injured, and there is a small voice in the back of my head that screams at the stupid chivalry that took hold when she let out that whimper of pain at my touch. I would have taken her for hours in that spot, and this push and pull game we have somehow fallen back into would have never even begun.

I inch closer and watch goosebumps scatter across her skin at my nearness. She couldn't fight this anymore if she wanted to. And, Elders, I love the way her body has started reacting to me.

"No little breaks in the lines?" My lips rise up in just the tiniest hint of a smirk as I speak. She has improved so much when it comes to mentally shielding, but she still can't quite get me out of her head. My body leans in closer . . . just a little bit more

with every word. "No little cracks for me to seep through?"

Her breathing grows heavy. She hates that I do this to her. She hates that I make her feel things she never thought she would. She hates that my little taunts and jabs and every single smile or smirk I send her way causes new emotions to coil within her. But she knows the game I'm playing. She knows because she made the rules. But now I think it's time to break them.

"Yes, Arryn." She bites out my entire name and I almost laugh. "It is up, and I don't let cracks or breaks in. You taught me that."

I lean in. Now just a breath away. "That's a good girl." I whisper so close to her ear, I know she can feel my words before she hears them. She shivers in response. "Get ready . . . "

She moves to step back, but her body hits the stone wall, and she knows there is nowhere else for her to go. She could shift. She could move five, ten, fifty feet away if she truly wanted. She knows how to, but she doesn't because she wants this.

"What's the ruse now? What's the point of this stupid little game you're playing?" she asks, but the only answer she will receive is my waiting smirk. A smirk which slowly widens into a world-shattering smile as I bring my body to hers. One arm reaches above her head to rest on the wall and the other snakes around her side. She reaches out to push me away, but I quickly inch my body closer to hers until we are flush together. Her fingers curl around the fabric of my shirt.

"You can feel it." I whisper as our noses brush.

It isn't a question. She knows. Even though she won't admit it, she knows.

"What?" The word is heavy on her tongue as she feigns ignorance. I roll my eyes at her stubbornness.

"Me. You feel me." I rake my hand up and down her bare arm as I let the warmth of our bodies heat the other. She knows what this is. The bond. The heat and life that moves between those lucky enough to experience such a thing. "Even with every defense you can muster up, you still feel me—feel us."

She swallows dryly as my words sink in. I am done hiding behind the walls of ignorance and denial she's put in place.

"You can choose to believe whatever you want. You can choose to ignore this"—my palm stretches out across her erratically beating heart—"but we both know deep down, and right here"—my fingers inch further north as I slowly wrap them around her throat, her pulse is rapid under my touch—"you feel me." I only pause for the briefest of moments as I feel her life under my skin, but my hand inches upward, and I stroke her bottom lip. "You love me. You've loved me since the beginning, and nothing will change that."

Her breathing hitches, and I watch as unshed tears rim her eyes.

"You love me just as I love you, Nera." A barely audible sob works its way through her lips, knowing I am done with the game, and she can no longer hide from this. "I love you, Nera. I love you. I. Love. You." I emphasize each word as if they will be the last things I ever say.

And then, when I feel the shield all but collapse with the weight of my admission, I have no other choice but to crash my body into hers.

She kisses me just as she did that day on the river bank. She kisses me with everything she has to give. Her hands find my hair and tug, but that is not how this is going to go. I'm tired of letting her lead. Now, it's my turn.

I grab her wrists and shove them above her head. She may be a Celestra—and in truth, so much more than that—but right now, she is mine to claim.

Next time I'll light candles and spoil her with soft touches and warm embraces. Not this time. This time, I will take what is mine.

My lips separate from hers and I sweep my eyes over what lies before me. Her lips are full and red, swollen because of me. There's a slight indentation from where I bit down only moments ago, and I quickly run my tongue over the spot as she moans at the contact. When I find her eyes again, I see only acceptance in them. But I won't do this unless she's absolutely certain.

"Nera." My voice is far too rough. I can barely focus enough to think straight with the way her body's pushed up against mine. I take a few breaths to steady the voice in my head that screams to take her right now, to rip every piece of fabric from her body and devour her whole. But that has never been me. "I need to know this is what you want. I'm done playing games."

She nods, her voice barely a whisper. "I want this."

"Are you sure? I'm not going to be gentle. I don't think I have enough restraint after holding back from you for so long." She moans in answer. "I'm going to be rough. I'm going to leave you covered in bruises. I'm going to mark you in a way so that my touch never leaves your body."

"Please," she says as she arches up into me.

The noise that escapes my body at her plea is inhuman.

I give her one more kiss, just to make sure this is really happening, and to allow her one more moment to turn away.

Our eyes meet. She stays steady.

My hand moves back down to feel the quickening pulse at her throat, and I squeeze, just a bit, in question. Her head lifts, giving me better access.

"You're mine."

"I'm yours," she finally admits as her lips meet mine.

I kiss her just as the shift takes hold, and when we land, I am lying on top of her in my bedroom at the underground palace I once called home.

Her body tenses under mine as she realizes just where we've arrived.

"Centra III?"

I nod in answer.

"Will anyone find us? What if they–"

"Shield the room." I all but command.

"What?"

"Shield. The. Room," I repeat, looking down at her face, her hair spread out like a crown atop her head.

She looks side to side as she takes it all in for the first time. This room has always been fit for a sovereign. It is ornate and built from the underground stone. The only light comes from the lanterns sparsely placed around. The west wall is covered in a floor-to-ceiling bookcase, and the east wall has various paintings. There are tables, chairs, and couches set around for lounging. The bed we lie on could hold far too many people at once, and is covered by a gossamer canopy. I blame my older sister for that touch.

She shakes her head. "It's too big. I can't shield the entire room."

"Nera, this is the only warning I'm going to give you. Shield the room, or the entire damn palace will hear you scream my name."

She closes her eyes, and I spend the moment she takes gathering up her power to count every one of the beautiful eyelashes rimming her eyes.

I feel the moment she sends it out. I can't truly see it, but a warmth spreads between us, and then surges through my body as it moves outward. When my gaze meets the wall of books at the far corner of the room, I can just make out a faint glow and a fractured seam, as if there's a thin but visible dome around us.

Her eyes sprint open. "Did I do it?" Her voice is still too breathy, and her hands are still clasped above her head.

I nudge her nose with my own. "Good girl." She sucks in a breath. "Now, you're mine."

I recapture her lips, and all but melt as I feel her tongue sweep out to meet my own. But I don't linger. While her lips are absolutely captivating, they are not where I plan to spend the majority of my time tonight.

My hands leave her wrists and skim her form, finding every inch of exposed skin I can. She seems to burn from the inside out. With every second that passes, I feel more and more heat pour from her body and into mine. I know it's the bond. It started the moment I brought her back to life on that river bank, and I have barely been able to stand being close to her since. The urge to soak into that warmth was always just a breath away from taking hold.

Now I don't want it to stop.

I drown in her whimpers as I explore every inch of flesh I can find. My lips make a fevered path down her neck, only stopping when they find the one spot that seems to send her back arching more than the rest. I lavish the area and force her legs apart with my knees when I realize she is trying to cause friction and her own release.

"Only me," I command as my hand cups the heated space between her legs. "You

come for only me." I gently squeeze the tender flesh through her pants, and she cries out as wayward sparks fly off of her and into the room.

I could torture this out of her, and maybe one day I will. I have built up far too many imaginary memories of things I wish to do to her, but I don't have the patience tonight.

My fingers trail upward and under the fabric of her shirt. She calls out, bucking her hips against mine as I play with my newfound treasures. Her hands begin a journey of their own as she reaches every bit of me she can. When I tease the hardened nubs, she lets out a slew of curses I commit to memory.

"Please," she begs just as my teeth replace my fingers through her shirt.

"Please, what?" I smile through the whisper placed against her rapidly rising chest.

"I want you." Her hands fist the hem of my shirt as she tries to pull it overhead.

The laugh bubbles up from deep within my core. "You are so needy." I tease as I move forward, letting my lips graze hers, and pulling back the second she tries to deepen the kiss.

"I want you," she repeats, this time practically panting with need.

I slip my knee between her legs, giving that one spot I know she is desperate for me to touch just enough pressure to relieve some of the build up, but still have her begging for more.

"You hated me last week," I retort.

Her shirt lands on the floor.

Mine follows soon after.

"I never hated you." Her legs tighten around my knee as she desperately searches for relief.

"You once swore to kill me if I ever touched you."

I unclasp the binding undergarment, not caring where it lands once she's finally free of it.

"I'll kill you if you ever stop *touching me," she promises as her hands find the buckle of my pants, and she quickly shoves them down my thighs.*

I want to reply with something snarky, something that will make her fight me for every inch of this. But now my lips and teeth have traveled back down to her breasts, and I find much more satisfaction in listening to her moans explode around us.

"Please," she cries out one last time as I forge a path across her stomach toward the one place I have yearned to be. I'm not even sure when her pants came off. Was it her or I who did that? I almost comment on it, but then her legs fall apart, and without another word, my fingers find her slickness.

I groan at the contact. So damn wet.

An array of sparks light the room.

I slide one finger inside as my mouth finds her swollen nub. If I thought her lips tasted like heaven, I have no true word to describe what is now before me. I lavish her in every way I can. I let all my desires take hold as I tease her orgasm out of her.

I shouldn't be surprised when she explodes only moments later. Her hands find my hair, and her back bows in ecstasy as she cries out in release.

It is only when the smell of smoke hits that I snap out of the deliriousness I found in just hearing her cries.

Dark wisps of smoke rise from the bed as sparks light a fire round us.

"Shit!" I crawl up her body as she, too, realizes what we have done.

"Oh, no!" She pants, her body begging for more oxygen than it can take.

Her shield crashes. The moment it falls, I grab both her and the headboard of my wooden bed, and shift.

The cold hits us instantly.

Snowflakes dance along our skin as the tall beams of the canopy to my bed become devoured in flames. But at least we're outside the walls of the palace. I don't even have time to contemplate what to do before a wall of snow is dropped on top of us. I close my eyes as air is pushed from my lips, and my body turns to ice at the touch.

When I open them again, we are standing not ten feet away, wrapped in what's left of the blanket we were once laying on top.

"You covered us in snow?" I whisper as tendrils of smoke fly into the air.

"Would you rather the flames have caught the forest on fire?" She cuts her eyes to me, and then buries her face on my chest.

She has a point.

"Maybe shift us before you try to freeze us next time," I whisper into her hair as I tighten the blanket around our shoulders.

"We're naked in the middle of the forest, aren't we?"

I start to laugh.

"You're naked." I move just enough to look down between us. "I have on socks." I try to wiggle my toes, but realize they have almost turned to ice standing in the frozen tundra. We both shiver as a wind bursts through the tree line. I tilt her face to meet mine. "I'm shifting us back, but I can't promise there won't be a plethora of guards in my room wondering what all the noise was." She laughs. "And also, I'm building us a home with everything made out of stone."

I lace up the leather boots and secure the daggers just as Dina has shown me when Ari appears in the doorway. I flush at the thought of the memory he gave me only moments ago. But when I meet his gaze, I only find seriousness etched within his features.

I turn back, not wanting to lose the playfulness of the last few days, but also knowing the only way we can truly return to that is to complete our mission.

"Can we go over it one more time?" I look back up to find his solemn stare pinning me in place.

He nods as he sits on the chair beside me, reaching out to still my shaking hands. Then he kneels as she unties and tightens up the lacing on each boot as he speaks.

"We'll shift in. Since you don't know the exact location and can't fully picture it in your mind, I will take you. Reeves is taking Dina, and Kersack is bringing Fritz."

"And then we meet Meric," I clarify.

He swiftly nods. "And the members of the Restoration who are already on the inside waiting for us."

"How many Halabarian refugees have they found?"

"Reeves said it was close to two hundred, but we aren't sure how many are actual Abolition sympathizers in disguise and how many are true victims of the Haze."

"How will we tell?"

He pulls on the strings, making sure they're completely secured before looking up and shrugging his shoulders. "I guess if they try to kill us or not."

"You two ready?" Reeves peeks her head into the closet we now occupy.

Neither of us says a word.

But even in our silence, she knows the answer.

"I thought so." She steps fully into view before handing over a long cotton gown in the most vibrant royal blue. "Ari will do what he can to alter what others see and disguise you two, but we all know our gifts can only be used for so long before we have to rest. Use this during your search when you need to hide your clothing but need time to build back up your gifts."

I throw the smooth fabric over my head, and Ari does the same with his before slipping into the garnet-colored fabric pants.

Our eyes never leave the other.

"Where exactly are we shifting?" The words break up the repetitive taps of our feet as we move down the twisting corridors inside Reeves's palace. I know he has told me, but I'm so worked up, I can barely remember my own name, let alone all the details of this day.

"A home of an old friend." Ari reaches back to pull his hair into a low bun, and I nearly falter at the sight. He gives me a wicked grin when he catches my stare before he continues on. "She lives directly in the city center, so it'll be a good spot to use as a base."

Meric, I mentally remind myself as he speaks.

"And what happens if we don't find the refugees?" I reach out to clasp my hand in his.

Dina steps in line beside us. "We will. And then we will take them to the Bend, and they will be safe."

I turn to Ari at the mention of the place I have yet to fully understand. "You never took me there."

He lets out a knowing breath. "I know."

"You never really explained what it was, either." I peer into his eyes urging him to answer.

He pauses our trek as he looks at me. "It's an underground city of sorts. It's where we hide those the Abolition hunts. It's a safe haven where Celestras can live freely, out in the open," He pauses as if he knows the wording doesn't fit. "Well, as open as they can. They don't have to hide what they are."

"The Bend is an underground town full of Celestras?" The surprise is evident in every word.

"About half are Celestras, and the rest are their families or others the Abolition may deem useful."

"If they're Celestras, then don't they have gifts?"

"Technically, yes."

"Will they not join us?"

He furrows his brow before understanding flashes across his face. "You mean use their gifts and aid the Restoration?"

I nod.

"Some would. But many can't."

"Why?"

He clears his throat. "You know the story of what your father did all those years ago?"

I square my shoulders, promising to not let the emotion of it all overtake me. "You mean when Himerak used that mind control on him and had him murder all those innocent children?"

Ari nods. "After, when the Elders gave forth an endless supply of Celestra children to try to combat that atrocity, that's when the Abolition really grew. That's when they started building up their own army and preparing to take us down. They saw the children as uncontrollable weapons that needed to be eradicated. Many Celestras weren't built to wield the gift they had been given. Many wanted nothing to do with it, and many others would only use it to aid themselves and further their greed. But just because they were given a hand at life they didn't understand, doesn't make them monsters. The Abolition wanted them all dead, but we intervened."

Dina twists so that she's now in my periphery. "Many like to pretend their mark isn't even there." I think back to the wrap Tarak wears over his. Didn't he say almost the same exact thing once? *If I can't see it then maybe it's not real.* "Many aren't trained, and so their gifts never developed."

"So we train them," I state, and both look at me as if I have somehow sprouted three heads.

"It's not that simple. We're helping them, but if we push too hard, they'll see us as just another enemy trying to use them for what they can offer and not seeing them for who they really are."

My shoulders fall in defeat. What he says is true, but still so frustrating. If we had an army of Celestras behind us, I am positive we would not only rescue these refugees, but also find many more hidden within Centra II, find the stones, and demolish every penance all before dinner.

"Nera?" Ari places a hand on my shoulder, taking me from the thought. "You ready?" He nods toward a window, and I turn to find Reeves, Kersack, and Fritz standing a hundred or so yards away, staring off into the watery expanse. The same expanse that lies between this place, which has brought forth my every dream, and the place that I am sure is about to become my worst nightmare.

The shift is quick, and as soon as the world opens back up, I find Ari spouting off every command I knew would come.

"Look around. Memorize this room. Memorize every detail." He secures a waiting bow on my back. "Hold it in your mind and make it true." A handful of arrows are shoved into the quiver as I nod at each command. "This is where you will shift back to if your power begins to drain and you need an out."

This is something we did prepare for. We spent the last few days, when not wrapped up in each other, shifting from one location to the next. Ari would take me into a new room, have me memorize everything I could, and then later, make me shift there. There were a few times in which I fumbled the task. And I know

Dina plans to bring up the moment I shifted into the servants' bathing chambers instead of the west garden pond for the rest of my life. Unfortunately, there were three very naked men already occupying the space when we suddenly appeared.

I shake the thought, discarding the memory as I focus on what is directly ahead.

The room is dark, only lit by sparsely-placed lanterns and familiar balls of light hanging on the walls. There are no windows, and if I wasn't already prepared for it by the memory Ari showed me, I would be very confused at the lack of a door. But I know the bookshelf hides our exit. The floor is stone, but covered in a wool-like rug that I know hides a secret room should we need it. I can just make out the faded blue that covers its surface. The table off to the right holds a few maps and writing utensils, and almost every surface is covered in at least a small layer of dust.

"It wasn't dirty in the memory."

He swallows as he nods. "We used to frequent this place much more than we do now."

"Because I haven't been here?"

"But you're here now, and that's what matters most." He cups my cheek just as the bookshelf starts to move. And though we both know it will be a friend, our entire group freezes in apprehension.

When the face I know from Ari's memories peeks around the corner, we all breathe a sigh of relief.

Meric looks between the group and shakes her head when she sees each one of us poised with a weapon at the ready. "Daggers? Did you have that little faith in me?" She smiles with the tease.

An ease settles as we each quickly reholster our weapons, and Meric finally walks in.

Though she looks just the same as before, I am surprised at her height. From Ari's memories, I pictured someone who would meet me eye to eye. I keep forgetting that being in his memories means I see the world from his point of view. Meaning I see the world from at least six feet off of the ground. But when I meet these people in person, that viewpoint is drastically different. Meric has to have at least four to six inches on me, if not more. And when she immediately makes a dash for me, I find my face stuffed between her voluptuous breasts as she wraps me up in the grandest hug I have ever received.

"Oh, Nera!" She seems to blubber for just a moment in my hair as I hear Fritz fail at hiding the laugh that bubbles upward.

Dina clicks her tongue. "Alright, alright. Don't smother the girl before we even get started."

Meric pulls back, giving me the most sincere look of love and adoration before her face twists into a mask of fierce defiance as she stares at the group behind me.

"If anyone gives me lip for any reason, I promise to personally send you to the depths of Shadow Isle myself."

I brace at the name of the place I have come to know and fear. The place we are headed.

Ari reaches forward, grabbing my shoulders and pulling me back, into his grasp. His arm reaches around my chest, just below my shoulders, and I lean back into his touch. "No lip from us." He promises before bursting into a smile and reaching out with his other hand to embrace my new friend.

"Are we good to go?" Dina wastes no time as she moves around the room, messing with various items and throwing a few in her pack.

"I have new counts," Meric states more to Reeves than anyone else. Reeves pales, but Meric quickly corrects the confusion. "No. No. No." Meric shakes her head. "No deaths. More refugees and innocents from Halabar, and if word is true, there are a few Celestras among the group now as well."

"Celestras?" Dina quickly turns, and I catch the light dim with the concern on her face.

"Yes!" Meric booms with excitement. "Two hundred and four of the original refugees are still accounted for, but apparently the Abolition found an entire group of hidden settlers on their way back. Thirty-eight people, including three more Celestras. And if the rumor is true, one may even be the new sovereign to Centra I."

The glass in Dina's hand shatters as it plummets to the ground.

"Tarak," she whispers as her panic-stricken gaze meets mine. "They have Tarak."

LIII

I t's hard to express the mix of emotions running through me at the reality that has been thrust upon us.

"Ari?" Dina's voice quivers with the unsaid plea.

He nods in answer. "If he's here, we'll get him."

"Where are they kept?" I shift my gaze to Meric, no longer able to look at the pain that Dina can't quite hide.

"Shadow Isle," Ari whispers. Meric nods.

"It's where they take anyone of importance that they capture," Dina adds.

My gaze shifts to Kersack and Fritz, who have remained silent since our arrival. Kersack appears ready for whatever may come our way. Fritz appears to be on the verge of vomiting.

"Are we going?" I look to Ari and then to Dina ready to get this started. They both nod in answer.

Once on the outside of the bookshelf-turned-door, I find the home to be rather simple and plain. The noises from the street, which were muffled within the secret room, are now blaring in through the window.

I step closer to the light that streams in from the street and reach out to push the curtain aside. I only catch a momentary glimpse of what we will soon enter into before Ari quickly closes the window and captures our attention with a few, much-needed reminders. As he speaks I know the words are mostly for me, and I hope he knows how grateful I am for each and every time he has repeated this.

"Shadow Isle is impenetrable with gifts alone. As you know, we just recently found out that the reason we were previously unable to shift directly into the location was due to the Esehtel river water Riann has surrounded the complex in. It's the same river that dulled the use of our gifts the night Nera was taken from us." He stiffens as he speaks. "So we have to enter through the underground tunnels." He lifts the beautiful golden stone from his pocket. "And the only way to use our gifts is with this."

I nod thinking back to the memory of Riann inside the cavern the day I shifted to Earth.

"But it isn't guaranteed." Meric adds. "The river is a fickle thing. That day you were sent away, Riann only had control of a fraction of the water he does now. I'm not even sure if the stones will override it completely."

She unrolls a map I've spent the last few days memorizing.

"There are three sets of underground caves between here and Shadow Isle. Only one is the correct path." She looks pointedly at me and Fritz. "This will be your first time entering. Please take heed of the walls. Do not touch them. They are connected to Caverns, and if what Ari has told me remains true, I would bet the Shadow travels its length, waiting to ensnare any who enter."

A chill runs down my spine at the memory of that horrible moment.

"Don't touch the walls. Got it." Bile rises, and I cross my arms over my chest. Ari's hand finds my lower back.

"The Abolition needs these tunnels for transportation, but they're smart. They never leave the same routes after a run because they know we have insiders who'll feed the map to us. Riann constantly uses his ability to change the landscape, and thus the correct path to Shadow Isle."

"How do we know which route to take?" It's the first time I hear Fritz speak out since arriving, and for just a second, I glimpse the strong and unwavering young man I met in the memory fighting for his family.

Ari clears his throat. "Like Meric said, there are three possibilities. So we go in three groups. One group will make it in, and the other two will make their way out once they realize the error."

"I don't like that," I repeat the same concern I've voiced for the past few days. "That's basically a suicide mission."

"It's not." Kersack takes a step forward as he peers down at the map outlining the coast of Centra II and the islands around it. "Three teams of four go in. One team should—if they do everything right—end up in Shadow Isle where the refugees are located. That's the easy part. The group that makes it in will need to get down into the lower levels where the refugees and prisoners are kept. Also, relatively easy."

Dina reaches out to point to a spot in the middle of the map, the place I now know as Shadow Isle. "The hard part comes when getting them out. By the time one group has reached the refugees, the other two groups would have realized they were heading down a decoy path that only leads back to the city."

I furrow my brow, knowing we definitely have discussed this, but unable to recall every single detail. "How will they know? Will they just pop back up on one of the main streets?"

"They will never lose the use of their gifts," Ari reminds me. "The closer you get to Shadow Isle, the more your gifts will start shorting out. It's best to tease your gifts just slightly every thirty or so feet to see if they still work when on the path."

Dina nods as she adds. "If they start shorting out . . . well, then you got the short stick."

"Right." I nod as the memory of the explanation surfaces. "And once in, the group will have to play a who's who game and make sure they only aid the refugees, and not the sympathizers that are staged there."

"That will be the first real challenge." Ari squeezes my hand.

Meric starts to roll up the map. "And by the time the group gets people to the top of Shadow Isle and away from the surrounding river, the other two groups will be there, ready and waiting to shift them out. That's why each group will take a shifter with them."

A knock blares into the room, and we all stiffen. But then, it happens again, a simple rapping that sounds distinctly like that of the beat of a heart. The group seems to finally take a breath as Meric turns to let the unknown person in.

Except it's not just one person, but six. I smile as a few familiar faces from the council meeting slide into place around the table.

Introductions are quickly made, and Penelopi and Benue step forward letting us know they will be joining Ari and I. Our eyes meet and they quickly bow their heads, a notion I don't think I will ever get used to.

We separate into our groups. Three teams of four, each containing at least one person who can shift for when the rescue occurs.

Ari, Penelopi, Benue, and I are team one. Reeves, Fritz, Carter, and Gia are the second. The third team is Kersack, Dina, Zenna, and Case. The six members joining us from the Restoration are all citizens of Centra III.

One night, after we lay still and satiated, I asked if it was because they would need to be able to communicate with one another fluently. Ari skirted my damp hair out of my face as he gave me a curious look.

"What do you mean?" he asks in confusion.

"If they were from different centras, then they wouldn't be able to speak to each other, so it makes the most sense that they're all from home."

"Why wouldn't they be able to speak to others from varying centras?" He scoots up a little, and I can tell he's immensely intrigued by this line of thought I'm working through.

"People from different centras can't communicate," I state, confused by what he

doesn't understand. "They speak different languages. Only Celestras can communicate with everyone."

"Who told you–" we both still as the truth hits. Tarak. Tarak told me that.

"I wonder if anything he said was true?"

Ari sits up a little higher as he cups my cheek. "I'm not one to defend the person I
would prefer never to take another breath, but . . . he may have truly believed it."

I shrug, not wanting to give the notion another thought as I pull the covers up to
my shoulders.

"Centra's have varying dialects and yes, some have developed their own phrases
and words but most can decipher the speech of another. It's not only the Celestra's
that understand."

"Why?" I swallow at the continued deception. "Why would he think that?"

"He grew up in a place where if you weren't an ally, you were an enemy. There
was no in between. Everyone who was not them was in the wrong. Maybe that was
just another piece to the story Himerak built in order to gain control."

At first, moving through the city streets is relatively easy. In pairs of two, we slowly
ride sykkels packed with supplies headed to Shadow Isle with the ruse of moving
shipments in and out. To the outsider, we appear as everyday working citizens.
We are anything but.

I keep my head down as we move further away from the city center and toward
our goal that lies at the ocean. This is the second true city I've ventured through
but there's nothing about it that brings me in. If anything, the atmosphere—the
putrid air, the gangly people, the faces of disgust and hunger seem to stare omi-
nously as they move about—makes my skin crawl. From the moment we stepped
foot onto the street, I have wanted nothing more than to escape.

We make our way down packed corridors and past open markets. A few locals
even try to stop our movement and barter with us from time to time, hoping to
get their hands on whatever treasure we have hidden inside. In their eyes, maybe
we carry weapons, or jewels, or maybe the containers are packed with enough
food to feed their starving families for a week.

My heart sinks as Ari portrays the perfect villain, pushing off the starving locals
as Reeves sends harsh words their way.

Ari warned me about this as well. Even so, the sight of those who are so needy
pleading for help we cannot give causes my stomach to knot.

"I want to help them," I whisper to Ari's back as we turn and move down another street.

"We are helping them," he answers, just as I catch sight of what I presume to be the dead body of a starved boy being carelessly flung on the back of some unknown man.

"They are starving. They are dying," I counter. "If we don't help them now, then–"

"They've been dying for years. This is the reality of Centra II and the Abolition." Ari slows the sykkel as we reach a relatively empty alcove, and turns to face me. I hear the sudden halt of the five sykkels behind me as they follow our lead. "The only way we get them out is to take this down from the inside. And that's what we're doing now. You can't save everyone. You have to be patient."

"Our patience will be the equivalent to complacency in their murder."

He shakes his head as frustration and anger settle within me.

"Nera–" he reaches around to cup my face. "I get it. I get the anger you feel right now. Six years ago, I was the exact same way. And you don't remember this because . . . well, you wouldn't remember it anyway because it was before we met . . . but six years ago, I lost people I loved by being stubborn and impatient, and trying to save everyone I could my first time here."

I swallow as his confession begins.

"I saved three people from the horrors of life here in Centra II. I got seven more killed, including my father."

"Ari." His name is a breath on my lips, but he shakes his head to stop whatever it was I planned to say next.

"I get your anger. I get your desire to help them. But you must wait. We will get the refugees out, and we will save Tarak and anyone else from the settlement, and then, as we take down the penances and the Abolition, we will save these people."

My lips tremble with all the emotion I unsuccessfully hold back.

"Fine," I relent and he nods before turning forward.

It's only another few minutes of travel before I notice a change in the scenery. The sun shines brightly in the sky as we weave through the turns I know I will never remember. On the last turn down a dingy corridor, I look up, preparing to ask a question I soon forget. The words die on my tongue as Shadow Isle rises in the distance.

The small set of islands off the coast of Centra II seem to create a barrier to the rest of Ithesin. There are three main ones with tall peaks that rival that of the caverns, and then sparsely placed smaller islands that cover the area as far as I can see.

The closer we get to the coast, the more thinned-out the population becomes. But off to the side, I notice a growing rumble of noise. I only catch sight of the chaos a few hundred yards away when we cut across a street that is so cracked and destroyed, I doubt it's been used in quite a long time.

"What is all this?" I whisper to Ari as I shake his arm, begging for a pause. I feel his shudder the second he brings us to a stop and sees what has captured my attention. The air is damp and hot, and I can feel the fabric of my leathers sticking to every inch of skin. The heat of anger only grows as realization of what I'm seeing settles in.

"It's the Celestra slave market." Benue answers as he moves up to my side, Penelopi driving the sykkel he's riding on. It's only then that I notice many of the people so far in the distance walk around sluggishly, as if drugged, and their hands are covered in a golden fabric I know all too well.

"Celestras?" I hold back the sob as Ari starts to move us forward and out of view of the sight.

"Celestras who didn't comply when captured, and are now under the control of other, more compliant Celestras, to do the Abolition's bidding," he answers.

I yank back, begging him to halt any forward movement. He slows just enough, and I slide from behind him, walking a few feet back to witness what I pray is just a fever dream. A barely audible sob leaches out as I stare at what I know could also be my reality if this doesn't work out the way we have planned.

I turn back to face my crew. "Are they not also who we are here to save?"

Reeves barges forward. Frustration lingers in her gaze, and she cuts off Ari before he can even begin. "Look around," she pointedly says through gritted teeth, and nods her head upward to the rooftops and buildings that line every road. Each are littered with various people dressed similarly to the others. At first, I'm confused at the sight. My initial reaction is that they must be guards of some kind, but they have no weapons and appear to be almost robotic in their movements as they scan the city streets. "We are dressed as citizens to this centra. They don't notice us because they aren't supposed to. But if you keep making a scene, they will figure it out and we will get caught before we even begin." She crosses her arms in annoyance. "Ari told me you were ready. Maybe he was wrong."

"I'm not wrong," he counters as he abandons the sykkel and steps between Reeves and I. Then he turns to face me, and pleads with everything he has to offer. "Please, Nera. We need to keep moving. There is a small window of time for us to enter, and once it's passed, we will have wasted all these resources for nothing." He glances at the market and the poor souls who linger. "The reason we chose today was because many of the nobles and higher-level guards will be out here, patrolling the Celestras and their buyers. There are less people to encounter once inside."

I have to force down the rising bile. I yank my arm free from his grasp as I scan our small group. And though they all know the plan for today, I also know they would follow me in a heartbeat should I choose to forgo it. I look each and every one pointedly in the eye. "Once this is over, once we have the refugees and the members of the settlement safely inside the Bend, I expect every available resource to be shifted toward getting these people free."

"We do that by getting the stones and harnessing the power," Dina tentatively answers.

"Then we get the fucking stones." I seethe under my breath barely able to contain my rapid breaths of determination. "No more training. No more planning. No more bullshit. We get the fucking stones. No more waiting," I urge. I expect some sort of pushback. Maybe there's another route I'm not seeing? Another barrier I don't understand? But instead of eleven pairs of defiant eyes glaring at me, I find admiration in each. I watch, as if in slow motion, each raises their left hand, two fingers pointed outward, and taps their heart.

LIV

I don't believe I fully breathe until we pass through the gate. The guards seem to barely even acknowledge us as they wave us through. They appear more concerned with the countdown to shift change and their upcoming moments of freedom than what we are up to.

I mentally picture the map as we abandon the sykkels and switch to pushing the empty carts through a darkened corridor. Water trickles down the dark slate walls, and I swallow as I realize we are now directly under the seabed. A previously unknown fear of drowning suddenly surfaces, and my skin itches to escape. I keep my feet in line with Ari's as we move.

"Passes?" The man's eerie voice causes every single one of our heads to spring upward, and when Ari answers, I note the twinge of an accent I only now realize was hidden under every word Riann once spoke.

"Certainly." Ari reaches into a pocket, and hands over a stack of papers.

The unknown guard balks in disgust. "More food?" He looks at the carts and then rolls his eyes as he hands the papers back. "If it was up to me, we would starve the bastards instead of feeding them just enough to keep them alive."

"I have to say I agree, but I don't get paid to have an opinion," Ari replies, and the man bursts out in laughter as he waves us by.

We don't see another person, and none of us speak a word for the remainder of the hundred yard walk. When we make the final turn that ends in three separate pathways, I know this is where we separate.

I catch each pair of eyes before we silently move into our places and with a quick two finger tap to our chests, we disappear into the darkness.

The pathway is unbelievably dark, with just enough scattered balls of dancing light placed around to give off a faint glow. Every few yards, I feel a nudge at my back and do my best to call forth just an inkling of my gift to test which destination we're headed toward. But each time, it comes with ease.

First, I make the droplets that span the walls of this tunnel congeal into a single band of water. A few moments later, I let a tendril of white light surge forward and watch as steam rises from the puddle it lands within. As we turn another curve, I shift a few feet ahead, only to turn back and find solemn expressions staring me down.

We walk for what feels like far too long. And I know before we even meet the end that this route can't lead to the refugees. We are headed back within the walls of the city. I clench my teeth to bite down the frustration that begs to be let free. But we never stop. Step after step after agonizing step we continue with the plan. Because at some point there has to be an end to this path and I pray that end leads to a new beginning. One where we shift to the top of the volcano like isle and then shift every innocent life away and into safety.

At the final turn, I freeze.

There is a light not far in the distance. One I know will open to a street and from there our mission can truly begin. I just pray that whoever did make it into the Isle made it there safely and is currently working to bring those innocent souls to the top.

We march forward but then stop as a cold breeze sweeps in from a secondary path, and when I turn to face Ari, I find confusion marring his features. The darkened pathway seems out of place and yet something in it seems to call me forward.

Our eyes meet. A silent question pulses between us. And then he nods, urging me forward and towards the unknown. This corridor, while dark and dreadful, is barely even fifty feet long. We make it to the end before I even fully think through what we are doing; the sight before me stops us cold.

Instead of solid onyx walls and cool droplets of water, this space is filled with old vines and dulled greenery seeming to burst in from every direction.

"This isn't Shadow Isle," Penelopi states the obvious as I reach out and run my fingers along the vines that mar the walls and door.

"But it's something." Ari mirrors my action before sweeping away a branch that reveals a hidden handle. A handle I've seen twice before.

It's a rich golden hue that matches so closely with Ari's eyes that I twist to find the specks of light flicking in his gaze. The carved design within the twisted handle begs to be filled, and I watch in awe as, when I reach out to grasp it, golden sparks seem to rise from my mark and fill in the surface.

"The Soul Circle?" I don't know if it's more of a question or statement, but I find my answer in Ari's awe-stricken face. "What do we do?"

"It could be a trap." He answers with a shrug of his shoulders.

"Everything could be a trap." I counter and he smiles.

"I don't know the location of the Soul Circle within this centra. But I doubt its entrance is placed at the end of a path only meant to keep those away from Shadow Isle.

He runs his hand through his hair in contemplation. Then he turns to face the others.

Benue clears his throat. "If it's real, then we"—he looks over to Penelopi—"won't be able to enter."

Ari nods and then we stare at each other debating what to do.

"What if it's a mirage. What if someone is using the same gift as you and altering what we see?"

Ari looks my way as he contemplates my words. But then his hands brush across the vines moving them in every direction. He shakes his head and answers, "You can't interact with something that isn't truly there."

A note of hope lingers between us.

"We won't know unless we try."

He smiles then grabs my hand. I state my name and we both gasp in awe when golden flecks rise from my arm and race towards the grooves in the handle.

A mixture of emotions slams into me when only Ari and I are able to cross the barrier and into the room. I marvel at a sight I have now witnessed three times. The beautiful circular expanse seems to beckon us forward and I smile at the familiarity as I run my hand along the banister of the top ring.

"What are we looking for?"

Ari's head seems to be cast on a swivel as he turns from one side to the next, taking in everything he can, searching for secrets we hope to discover. "Stones. Only Celestra's can enter so this would be a safe place to keep them."

"Genesis?" I think back to the emerald green jewel Riann once taunted us with.

Ari nods. "Maybe more."

We take the steps down to each level as we survey each table before moving on to the next. By the time we reach the center table and bowl, my eyes have become trained on the rising shelves that outline this magnificent room. I stare upward as I yearn for the shooting star I know will soon come.

It never does.

My gaze finds the floor, and it is only then that I note the deep stone in place of cool, flowing waters. I reach down, letting my fingers graze the surface only to find an odd heat buried within.

"Something's wrong."

Ari's gaze finds mine the second I speak the words. His hand hovers over the final bowl as small ripples flow to its rim.

"What can you sense?" He pulls his arm back as the water splashes out onto the wooden table.

I swipe my finger across the water I know will be there, only to find my fingers are still dry. I reach forward, plunging my hand into what should be cool water. Ari gasps when my hand seems to pass right through the bowl as if it's not even there.

The brilliant light from above seemingly made of a thousand dancing stars dims, and then, in an instant, is sucked upward as we are plunged into unending darkness.

Ari's hand finds mine the second I hear it.

A gurgle emanates from above, and when my eyes adjust to the blinding light, I look up to find the beautiful room transformed into a shell of what it once was. The basic structure is intact, but the tables and bowls are gone. The infinite rise of bookshelves has been destroyed by what I can only guess was fire as charred ends of paper lie at our feet and the crumbled stairway that I once dreamed of exploring is nothing but a slowly disintegrating mount of burnt rubble. Smoke lingers in the air, and when I shift my feet, I hear the crunch of wood that has turned to ash.

"Ari?"

"It's destroyed," he marvels as he leans down and swipes his hand across the ash-covered floor.

"Been this way for a long time." We both jerk upward as Arthyr's voice booms in from above. He sits on a piece of wood that's barely secured within the wall a few feet up. He is still wearing the same opulent clothing, and I want to immediately curl within myself as I watch the sinister smile play upon his lips.

But this time, Ari isn't taking chances. I move to secure an arrow but feel the shift the second his fingers lace within mine. The room disappears as I hear the echo of a laugh pierce the air.

The heat vanishes as the cool air of the corridor slams into us. When I blink my eyes, I find we have only shifted to the other side of the door. Panic surfaces, and I reach back out for Ari, desperate to move us further away, but instead of his hand, I feel nothing but air.

He is kneeling. Hands covered in blood as he scans the lifeless bodies of Benue and Penelopi left crumpled against the wall. A strangled gasp catches in my throat as my skin prickles in fear and warning. He checks for their pulses, but from the vacant look in both their eyes, I know they're gone. Probably have been since the moment we crossed into that room.

"Ari." I shake his shoulder and his eyes find mine.

"They know we're all here. They know our plan," he whispers as his eyes switch between me and the bodies before us.

I nod as the weight of his words settle.

"Dina," I breathe as my head turns from side to side, surveying the small corridor, and making sure the door behind us has stayed shut. "We have to get to Dina and Reeves."

"Let's go." His hand finds mine as he whispers a quiet mantra to our friends. Our fingers lift to tap our hearts in unison, a solemn goodbye to one of our own. The shift never takes hold as an explosion rings out and darkness consumes my periphery.

My body is thrown backwards, Ari's hand ripped from mine, as a cloud of dust settles in the space. Air is forced from my lungs as pain rattles my bones. My hands scramble to find purchase on the fragmented ground as my ears ring and my legs shake. I fall back, leaning against the wall as I wait for the rumbling, the falling debris, the clouded expanse to cease.

My mind tries to reconcile what I know is happening with what I can't quite comprehend. I've been through this once before.

Ari's form barely comes into view through the thick cloud between us. His blood-red lips part as silent words fill the space between us. His arms reach outward. Mine reach back.

Our fingertips brush as the wall at my back crumbles and my body falls into the unknown.

I brace for an impact that never comes as I fall through the expanse with his name on my lips. Unfamiliar fingers intertwine within my own, and I'm pulled forward and out of the freefall. Then, the darkness of a shift envelops me.

The soft grass bends under my fingertips. The smell of cool soil and damp air fills my nose. The light filters in as my eyes struggle to open.

Muffled conversation lingers above. But there is one voice I know. A voice I never thought I'd be thankful to hear again.

"Nera." Her cold touch rivals that of the ground at my back. I jerk away, but she holds steady as she lifts my head. I blink as they come into view.

She shakes her head as if my confusion at this sight is the oddity in this situation.

"Nera. I need to show you something."

"Alesia?" I swallow at the sight as the world fully opens up.

My hands grip the rich soil as I scramble to my feet and away from her touch. By the time I reach my full height, arrow knocked and aimed true, I find two pairs of eyes staring back at me.

"Please." Her gaze shifts between my shaking frame to the women now stepping up to her side.

"Where are we?" I search the area, finding no familiarity in the sight. "Where have you taken me?" I close the distance between us ready to fight. "Where is Ari?!" My palms meet her small shoulders as I push her back.

She barely maintains her footing as I push again. Heat rakes down my sides as my body begins to tingle with unabashed rage.

"Where are–"

"I need to show you something!" Her voice is frantic, laced with an edge I've never heard from her. Her hand reaches forward, and I brace for an impact. But instead, I find her pointing to something behind me.

There's only a breath between the moment I decide to turn and the moment in which I realize what I am seeing.

The sounds register first. Clanging of swords, explosions from what I can only guess are cannons, flying spears, and animals I can't quite place, a screaming and wounded soldier, and Ari dressed from another time and running headfirst into a battle I can't seem to make sense of.

My stomach plummets as he slices an opponent in two, blood splattering on his war-painted face. He turns for only a moment, and I find his dress and expression catches in my mind. Something familiar latches on and I search what little memory I have before it slithers away.

But then it surfaces, and my entire world all but shatters.

A scene of him from weeks ago when I entered the Soul Circle in Halabar. Two men, one with ice-blue eyes riding up a hill and begging for peace staring down another who was filled with malice. At the time, that unknown, malicious man meant nothing to me. He was just another mysterious piece in this chaotic world. But now that piece has been unveiled.

Ari . . . My Ari. The Ari who now wants nothing more than to fix this world and right the wrongs. Maybe, just maybe, that determination isn't built solely from a sense of good, but from a desire to fix his own demons. The demons of his past.

"What–"

"Our souls nourish this world." Her voice is low but exact as she creeps forward to stand beside me.

"That's Ari." My eyes are transfixed on the chaos ahead. My feet inch forward, but Alesia reaches out, grasping my arm and stalling the movement. "He is . . . he is . . ."

"He was the enemy," she finishes for me. "He caused a lot of what the Restoration fights against today."

"No." My lips tremble as I watch him slaughter life after life. The edge of his sword becomes an instrument of crimson death. He pauses for only a moment as he reaches into the breast of his leathers and pulls out two shimmering stones. Surveying the area, he watches as those around him fight. But what he doesn't know, that I now do, is that they are all fighting for the same thing.

Peace.

Then he slams the stones into the waiting dirt. The ground rumbles as dust and dirt fly into the sky. The field becomes a clouded maze as everyone stills. The grass, once flowing in the wind, splits and separates. Bodies fall into the chasm. Screams of agony bellow out in the distance. Smoke fills the air as a roar of triumph erupts from Ari's lips.

Agony settles in my core as realization of what that smoke will become dawns.

"We are in the Soul Circle. What you are seeing now is merely a memory from a different time."

"Ari?" I almost sob as the truth of what I see soaks in and I stare into Alesia's eyes. Confusion and anger at the unknown ripples from my skin.

"Ari and Tarak." She adds as she tilts her head forward and I follow her gaze. Blonde curls soaked with blood race through the battle. My heart convulses at the sight. "And Riann, Micel . . . me." She trails off and my eyes search until I find each one of those familiar faces mere yards away. Each is locked in their own fight for something I still don't fully understand.

"How?!" My feet move to take me there. I have to find a way to prove this isn't real, that what I am seeing isn't real. Her grip holds steady.

"This war has already happened. Nothing you do can change the outcome."

"This isn't a memory!" I counter. My head furiously shakes from side to side. "I've seen Ari's memories. This isn't how they happen!" I turn back to face the other woman standing and suddenly her face comes into focus. Her features settle in my mind as I recall my first escape from Halabar and my stumble through a streetside market. "You!"

Her gaze meets mine as she pushes the ebony braids away from her face. "I'm Eliza."

"You were at that cafe." Tears begin streaming down my face.

She nods.

"You're a Celestra, too? You both are?"

They roll up their sleeves, displaying a mark I know all too well.

"What is going on!?" My lips begin to tremble as I long for something I don't yet understand. "Take me back to Ari!" I yank my arm from Alesia's tight hold as I inch closer, making sure we are nose to nose. "Take me back!"

"Nera, please," Alesia whispers as she shakes her head, and I see true sadness in her eyes.

"This isn't real! You know what's happening at Shadow Isle!" I push her backward again when she doesn't answer. "You know about the refugees. You know about our plan. Riann knows our plan. This is just a distraction!" My fury grows.

"This is not a distraction," she counters as she finally stands tall and meets me eye for eye. "I'm showing you a truth. Your truth." She huffs in frustration. "Whether or not you believe me, I am not your enemy."

If I wasn't filled to the brink with absolute fury, I might laugh.

"Stop being so damn cryptic all the time. You have never once been honest with me. You hide and manipulate and . . . " I trail off as the weight of her previous deception settles and the tears continue to fall. "I once trusted you completely. If you want to gain that back, then show me something of use."

"Riann doesn't know I'm with you. He doesn't know I brought you here." Every word is smooth and precise with the edge of truth. "Celestras are reborn. Again and again and again. We live. We fight for truth and to mend this world, and then we fail, and we die, only to try again in the next life. But not you. You are new to us—new to this world."

I swallow as I will the lingering anger to subside. "Celestras are reborn?"

She nods.

"Does Ari know this?"

She shrugs in answer. "I don't remember my previous life. I only see snippets of it here." Her arm gestures to the raging war behind us. The same war I refuse to lay eyes on again.

"Why? Why are you telling me?"

She rubs a hand across her tired face as she wills the words to come. "I don't want to end this life as another failure. I've watched myself die a thousand times only to do it again. In this life, when I die, I want to know that when I once again wake, I will no longer be confined to a world filled with war and heartache. I want peace," she urges with so much truth my entire body sings.

"And you think I can bring that?"

She nods as her lips begin to tremble.

"Please forgive me?" Her voice quivers as she reaches out her hand. A lone tear breaks free of the hold and slides down her cheek. "I already broke your mother's trust. Let me make that up with you."

Her words slice straight to my heart. I stare at her outstretched hand as the seconds pass until finally she slowly drops it to her side.

"Are you saying you will help me? Help the Restoration?" Both women nod in agreement. "I need to hear you say it," I command.

"We will help the Restoration," they state in unison. Every nerve ending in my body sings in relief.

LV

The shift back is quick, and when the world comes back into view, I find the peak of Shadow Isle in my sights as we stand wedged between two crumbling buildings.

An alarm blares as people rush past. An explosion I can't quite see rings in the distance and the ground rumbles at my feet.

He knows we're here.

"The refugees are being held in the underground levels. There are guards placed at every entrance and exit." Eliza reaches into her boot to secure a dagger, and then looks around to make sure there are no prying ears to be wary of. "But Tarak and the other Celestras aren't there."

I shift my gaze to hers, hoping the unspoken glare is all she needs to elaborate. Another explosion, this time much closer. And the building at our side shakes in protest.

"They are in the palace," Alesia answers as she clears her throat. "I can get you in. But getting out with a handful of Celestras following me will be the hard part."

We cower behind a fallen pile of what was once a roof as a group of soldiers rush past and towards the mountain I hope to soon claim.

I turn back to Eliza. "Can you shift?"

She nods with a wince. "Barely. Mostly it's elemental manipulation. But I'm still early in my training, I don't have–"

"Can you get to Shadow Isle and relay a message?" I quickly cut her off.

She frantically nods. Screams ring out in the distance as another explosive detonates. The air becomes filled with dust and debris and we have to shield our faces.

"What's happening?!" I look around, trying to make sense of the scene.

"Riann. He now has Halabar, so this place is no longer needed," Alesia explains.

"He's destroying the entire city?" A mixture of confusion and awe mar each word.

"He can't let you get the Celestras."

"What about the people? The citizens? There are thousands of people here."

"They mean nothing to him. They're just a commodity. He will take those he wants, those who will be useful to him. But everyone else is expendable."

I think back to all the lives he wasted with the frivolous attacks on Centra III. Anger coils in my stomach.

"Eliza. Get to Ari. Make sure he is safe. That is your first priority." She nods at my command. "Then I want you to shift out as many of the bound Celestra's from the slave market as you can."

"I've never shifted with someone. I–"

"You're going to today." A sweat breaks out across her deep sepia skin but I continue as another explosion reverberates into us. "You are going to save those lives. I don't care if you only make it to the top of Shadow Isle each time. There will be someone waiting to get them to The Bend." She nods again. "Then, once every single life you can find on the street is safe, I want you to aid the others. Shift as many as you can to the top of the mountain. Ari and the rest of the Restoration will be there doing the same. Let Ari and the others know what's happening here. Let him know I'm okay and I'll be there soon. Alesia and I will go for the Celestras in the palace and anyone else we can." I look to Alesia only to find her nodding in agreement.

Screams peirce the air, and my heart lurches at the sound.

My eyes find Alesia's. "What can you do?"

"Alter emotions. Discern truths."

My chest sinks. I had a small hope it would be something else, but those will have to do. I reach out to grasp her hand, sparing only a moment to look back in Eliza's direction.

My eyes turn to slits as a let just a fragment of that fire skirt the surface of my skin in warning. "If you betray me, I will find you and I will slowly rip out every organ in your body, only to piece you back together and do it again."

"Yep." She nods in wide-eyed shock before cutting her gaze to Alesia.

"Don't test me."

"I won't," her voice quivers in fear, but her promise is smooth as it races down my spine.

"Good."

We pause just as the main palace comes into view. The explosions and fighting seem not to have made it here yet, but I can still hear the screams of the dying I know I won't be able to save. I only pray Eliza is doing what she can and saving anyone within reach.

The palace is encircled by a moat of sorts, and I know without asking where that water comes from. We won't be able to use our gifts once inside. At least not without a stone.

Alesia seems to sense my frustration and reaches out to shove a smooth, familiar gem into my palm.

"Where did you get this?" I roll Ari's stone between my fingers, knowing he had it on him only moments ago.

"Arthyr. He took it at the council meeting. What Ari has now is a fake," she answers and pulls out one of her own. One I have yet to see.

"Afinity?" I reach out as she places the gleaming purple stone in my palm.

"Afinity," she confirms as I hand it back to her. "Use your stone to get us in. I will alter the emotions of those we come across."

"Is that how you calmed those citizens you couldn't reach on the way here?"

She nods as she places the stone back into her waiting pocket and I think back to the last few moments of our shift. I stopped every hundred or so feet in order to keep from burning out my gifts, and thankfully that's when Alesia's ability became of use. I watched in awe as she calmed every citizen she could reach with not only her touch, but her words, hoping to drown out the pain and agony they were experiencing.

I make a note to thank her for that mercy later. Right now, I need answers.

"The memory of that war you showed me wasn't a memory." I breathe life to the notion that has consumed my thoughts these last few moments. And even though she has already voiced that truth, I need to say it out loud in order for it to solidify in my mind.

"No." Alesia shakes her head, unable to meet my gaze. We both stare ahead, waiting for the few guards left at the entrance to become distracted by the most recent explosion off in the distance.

As if on cue, the next one rattles the ground, and we stare in horror as those guards laugh at the screams that bellow out in the distance.

I make a promise to kill each one.

"It wasn't a memory," I state mostly to myself, swallowing as the pieces begin falling into place. "Eliza can shift and has elemental manipulation. She altered the corridor Ari and I were in, had me fall through the ground, and then shifted me back into the Soul Circle where you two used a stone to show me the past."

"Yes."

"Where had Arthyr gone?"

"My guess is back here." She nods ahead and to the palace I want nothing more than to demolish.

"And what you showed me was true."

"Yes."

Though I already knew what her answer would be, dread fills my stomach. "Ari killed all those people by creating the Haze."

"Yes."

"Why?" My lip trembles in a mixture of sadness and anger because I already know the answer. An answer he already provided me with.

"He wanted power."

I nod.

"Ready?" I ask and she reaches out to clasp my hand as the shift begins.

The four guards at the entrance are barely even a fight. I shift from her hold letting my dagger pierce the first one's heart. Life pulses from his eyes as his body falls limp in my grasp. Before he hits the ground, I shift again and behead the next while Alesia calms the other two and then slides a waiting dagger across each of their treacherous throats.

I barely register the feeling of warm blood trickling off my fingertips and marring the pristine marble-like floor as we shift inside the palace.

Inside is a maze of hallways and alcoves. We move a few feet down one before having to quickly twist into a hiding spot as a soldier rushes past. Most likely on a mission to find out who or what caused the deaths of those four guards. Not being able to picture the exact location of where we are headed, I have to rely on her guidance.

Four turns and we find the stairwell. We race downward, only encountering a few soldiers on our way. Unfortunately for them, none are prepared for me.

The first dies by blade, but the handle has become so slick with blood, I can barely yield it with accuracy, so it's quickly sheathed at my waist.

The second soldier burns from within as I let my coils of light snake upward and into his mouth the moment he calls for help. Ashes fall to the floor as his body disintegrates into nothing.

The third, who just saw what happened to the prior, flees into a room, only to find it has turned into a raging inferno. The flames engulf him from head to foot. When he rushes forward in an attempt to escape, I let an arrow fly straight into his heart, halting the movement.

I cross my arms and roll my eyes when Alesia leans forward, placing her empty palm to the marble floor, and uses her stone to calm his screams.

"I wanted to hear them."

She looks at me with a sideways glance and matches my stance. "If you could hear them, then so could everyone else."

"Fine," I reluctantly concede and turn to follow, taking the next stairwell at a rapid pace.

We only encounter two more obstacles in our path. Both look better as ashes on the floor.

"You're getting quite good at that."

I almost laugh. "Killing?"

"I was going to say using your gifts, but if you want to go with killing . . ." She shrugs as she trails off.

The bottom floor is cold and dark, and not a single soul occupies it. I almost cringe when I realize there is a moment of sadness at the thought that I won't get to take another life.

This isn't you.

I hear the plea with clarity and swallow at the thought.

"They're in here." She reaches for a door and then pulls out a key from her pocket. An unlit lantern hangs from the wall, and I reach out, letting my light ignite the flames.

Between one breath and the next, the lock clicks, and the door swings open.

The group shields their eyes with their bound hands as light pours in.

A beaten and bloodied Tarak, Micel, and Himerak lay crumbled against a wall at the back of the room. My feet move forward as if on instinct.

I reach Tarak first, finding confusion in his stare.

"Nera?" His voice is harsh, too dry and weighed down with something I hope to never experience.

"How do I get them off?" I'm frantic as my fingers fumble with the golden cloth.

"Ebeli Mushari," he whispers, and then pales as Alesia comes into view behind me. "Nera!" he tries to scream in warning, but I shake my head.

"She is helping us," I plead, and then recite the phrase I have come to love, "Ebeli Mushari." But nothing happens.

He coughs as Micel mumbles something I can't make out.

"It isn't working," I plead to Alesia as she makes her way to my side, her fingers beginning to work on Micel's binding.

"Wrap your hand around the wrist, right over the mark," she commands as she lets the phrase seep from her lips. The cloth parts and falls to the ground. Then she moves to Himerak.

My hands latch onto Tarak's wrist, still finding a comforting warmth in the skin I graze. "Ebeli Mushari," I whisper the plea and watch as the cloth falls.

I move backward as Tarak tries to stand. Obvious exhaustion and pain ripple through him with every move. I wrap an arm around his waist, lifting him further.

"Can you walk?"

He all but falls into my arms with each forward step. "Yes," he mumbles, the word grating along my skin as he hits the ground.

I stall as my eyes linger on the deep crimson covering my arm that once held him. "Fuck. They're injured. Badly." I look to Alesia just as her eyes meet mine. All three men are barely able to move.

"You're going to have to shift them out."

I nod in agreement as worry hits at what that much use of my gifts will do. We still have to make it to Shadow Isle and then to the Bend.

My eyes scan over every inch of the room, committing it to memory. I'll need to picture it to come back to. Maybe I can take two at a time.

"Tarak." I force his tired eyes to meet mine. "Help me get you to Micel. I'm going to take two of you at once."

He looks up to me in confusion.

I open my mouth to explain as the ceiling shakes and dust falls.

Even in the minimal light, I can see Alesia pale as realization hits. "They're coming."

"Shit." I've only ever shifted one person at a time, and for only yards at that. This time, I'm going to have to move four over a distance of miles.

"Just focus on the shift," Alesia encourages, and Tarak glances my way, shocked optimism gracing his features.

"You can—"

Pounding footsteps make their way down the stairwell as a rush of commands are yelled from one person to the next.

"I'll be ready to alter the emotions." She pulls a limping Himerak toward Micel as I drag a barely-moving Tarak in the same direction. "Just get us out of here."

I interlace my left hand within Tarak and Himerak's grasp, the golden stone trapped between our palms as I grab hold of Alesia and Micel with my right. I force the shift as it pushes back. An unimaginable weight holds me down, but I push through, willing the vision of that first room to take hold.

I gasp.

The room comes into view, but instead of a fully formed wall, I find a blasted out expanse, open to the war-torn street outside.

"Holy fuck." I stand.

The three men wail out in pain from the movement and their injuries.

I turn out of the way just as Micel heaves into what was once a rug covering a hideout, but is now just a hole in the ground.

"Where are the others?" Alesia rummages through what's left of the shelving, searching for something.

"The Restoration? Top of Shadow Isle," I answer before she can reply. I peek my head out of the massive hole toward the street to find most of the buildings have been demolished and the ground is littered with bodies as far as I can see. Dread curls within me at the inability to save them.

"Just get us there. Then you find Ari and the other Celestras can get us to the Bend," she pleads as she cradles Micel's bobbing head in her hands, forcing the salve he once used on me into what I now see is a gaping wound at his neck.

I rush back to the group and secure each hand in mine.

"Why?"

I pause as Himerak's gravely voice pierces the air.

My eyes meet his. "Because, no matter what you may think, I'm not a monster," I bite out as I grasp his hand in mine. "This will probably hurt," I warn just as I picture the top of Shadow Isle.

LVI

The rocky surface breaks my skin as we land. I muffle the scream of pain that threatens to erupt as the leathers of my pants shred and my shins become a maze of jagged cuts.

"Elders!" Her scream comes from my left, and when I force the energy needed to look up, I find Dina staring down at the five of us. She opens her mouth, a slew of what I'm sure are much deserved curses headed my way, but stalls as her eyes scan over to the mop of blonde curls at my right.

Reeves appears not five feet from us just as Dina falls to her knees beside him, her hands cupping Tarak's face.

"Addie?" The shock in his voice is palpable, and for just a moment, I catch a glimpse of a young boy finally finding home again.

"I'm here." Her voice breaks. She wipes the damp hair off his forehead and pulls him to her chest. The *thank you* she mouths my way is barely distinguishable from the trembling of her lips.

"You didn't follow orders!" Reeves yells out as she reaches down, ripping me away from the grip I had on the others to meet her eye for eye. "You didn't–"

"I forget," I cut her off. "Who gives the orders here? You or me?" She pales at my words before stepping back and nodding in acceptance.

"Then act like it," she seethes, bared teeth and hair flowing in the wind.

"Where is Ari?" I stalk past her, searching everything I can see. The picture Ari painted for memories pales in comparison to what is directly in front of me. The rocky surface we stand on can't be more than ten yards across and twenty yards wide. As I scan the area, the only ones I note are those I brought, along with Dina and Reeves.

"Down there." Reeves points a few feet ahead, her voice nearly drowned out by the howling winds from the altitude, and I slowly move forward to the top of a pit of what I can only guess was once a volcano. When I meet the edge, the noise from below rises, and I gasp as the scene before me plays out.

Ari moves from one spot to the next as he fights guard after guard while Kersack and Zenna lead a row of refugees, mostly children, to the top. It's obvious Ari is the last stand. He is the barrier between their freedom and their death. But he's worn down. His movements are slow and staggered.

"He's not shifting?" I yell down to Kersack, now only feet below me. As our eyes meet for the first time, relief melts his every worry at seeing me alive.

"Stone's not working." Kersack pants through each word as he lifts a child into my waiting grasp. "None of them are!" he calls upward from the ledge he's perched on, and though he may be old, his strong arms lift up child after child into waiting hands. Knowing I have the real stone, I almost move to shift to him, but the ledge he stands on inside this rim is so thin and fragile that I fear my weight would cause the entire thing to buckle.

"They're fakes!" I yell out over the roaring winds. Then search the area behind me to find Reeves poised and ready to take Himerak and Micel on to the Bend. Himerak holds an unconscious Micel in his arms as tears streak down his face. Dina and Tarak are no longer on there, and I can only hope Reeves has already shifted them away.

I reach down into my pocket and grasp the golden jewel just as a child is placed securely onto the ground at my side. Alesia doesn't hesitate as she rushes over to calm the frightened girl.

My gaze locks with Ari's the second the smooth gem is firmly in my grip. He stalls for just a moment at the glance. His entire body freezes, and then I swear he exhales so deeply he must have been holding his breath for the last hour.

"I'm okay!" I yell down knowing the words won't meet his ears as I grab Kersack's arm and help to hoist him upward.

He must be over a hundred feet down in this once volcanic structure. Charred, blackened rings and ledges encircle the inner edges with a half-broken staircase winding its way upward from a bottom so far below I can't make it out.

I pull Zenna upward next, a crying baby in a makeshift strap on her chest. Her feet just graze the surface when the reverberations of a far off blast rush through the air. She falls backward and toward the open top, but reaches out and latches onto my arm just as I shift us a few feet sideways onto solid ground. Relief races across her face as our eyes meet. And then I rush back to the opening.

Another explosion ripples through the world, maybe a mile away. Black smoke creeps upward, and I know if it weren't for the deafening winds, my ears would be filled with far off screams.

"Riann's demolishing the city," I yell to both Kersack and a now-returned

Reeves as I remove the crying but uninjured child from Zenna's arms and hand him over to Alesia. He instantly calms in her waiting hands.

"Go! Get Ari!" she urges me forward as she rushes back to the group.

Kersack grabs my arm before I can move.

"It's not just Riann!" His gray hair flies in front of his face.

"What do you mean?!" I implore and brace when the next explosion sounds off.

"The Haze." He looks toward the city, and it's only then that the black smoke born of explosions seems to take on a life of its own. Those familiar tendrils rise upward and then surge downward as if striking at a target with each move.

Terror settles in my core. Icy fear rushes into my sweaty palms at the idea of meeting that evil once more.

Kersack yanks my arm, severing the trance and turning my attention back to him. "Your father!"

"What?"

"Your father is down there." He points into the gaping hole at the center of the volcano. "With Riann."

I yank my arm from his grip. "How do you know?"

"I saw him. The only refugees left are either already dead, dying, or too injured to move. But he is there."

My chest rises and falls with an emotion I can't quite reconcile.

"Don't!" he urges. "It's a trap. I'm only telling you so you don't fall into Riann's waiting hands when he plays that card against you."

I mindlessly nod in hopes my false response will calm his fears.

"I have a real stone." I lift the golden gem in the air and Kersack breathes a sigh of relief. "Go with Reeves. Get the children out. Let me get Ari. We will meet you at the Bend."

He swallows then steps back, immediately following my command.

I move to peer over the ledge once more. Memorizing the charred edge Ari stands on as he fights off another attack. The fear of heights only takes hold for a moment before I toss it away.

"Holy fuck," I whisper as I take a few steps backward, then rush forward and dive into the gaping hole.

I let the shift take place at the last moment, saving what energy I have for what I know is coming, and feel the air rush out of my lungs as I land at Ari's feet. I move to stand on shaking legs. He reaches forward, grabbing me by the arm and throwing me behind him as his sword impales the guard who was moments from ending me.

"Thank y–"

His lips crash into mine as he yanks the sword out, blood spurting in every direction, and pushes me up against a crumbling wall.

"You're okay," he says more to himself as his eyes roam every inch of me he can see.

Another guard runs toward us from the left, this time I shift out of Ari's grip, resurfacing directly in front of the enemy, standing still and unwavering as he impales himself on my waiting blade. I twist sideways, letting the gurgles of his fading life linger in the air as I push forward and he falls down into the abyss. Before his feet fully leave the ground, I shift back into waiting arms.

"I'm okay." I kiss him back, not lingering as long as I would like, and instead pull back to survey his shocked and sweat-soaked face. "How many have you rescued?"

He huffs out a laugh and then his face falls as another guard's hands reach the ledge at our feet. I reach behind, pulling the arrow free and knocking it. The man's head pops upward just as I bend down and take aim.

"Bad decision." I smirk as his eye meets the arrow. His head falls backward and into the abyss. I throw the bow over my shoulder and turn back to Ari.

"You have no idea how sexy that is."

I roll my eyes in mock disgust and give him another kiss. "You can show me once we're home." I smirk and then my face grows serious once more. "How many are left?"

The playful moment melts away.

"All of the children and most of the citizens are out. I haven't found Tarak or any of the–"

Another guard rushes upward from a waiting stairwell. This time it's Ari who gets the kill. I pull backward and into the wall as Ari ducks at the exact right moment, barely missing the swinging sword. When he comes up, he brings his own blade with him, letting it find purchase under the man's chin. His blood oozes out as the cry is ripped from his lips. And then his body sinks to the ground. Ari stares for just a moment before kicking the lifeless guard off the ledge and turning back to me.

"I got the Celestras. They're already at the Bend."

He stills as my words register. Then insurmountable pride swells in his chest and races across his face.

"You're fucking incredible."

"I love you." I cup his bloodied cheek with one hand as I shove the real stone into his other. His brows crease in confusion as he looks between his face and the jewel. "Yours is a fake," I answer his unspoken question. He immediately pulls his own stone out to marvel at the similarities. "Arthyr took yours and Reeves's stones at the meeting." His jaw ticks in anger. "Alesia gave me the real one." Shock at that name permeates his gaze. "I promise I will tell you all of it later. But right now, use this. Get the rest of them out."

He nods as the entire mountain starts to rumble.

"My father," I whisper the unspoken plea, and he nods in immediate understanding.

"He's in the pit."

Screams tear through the air as black wisps of smoke fill the sky.

Ari tenses, and I recoil as recognition of what we are staring up at hits. "The Haze."

"The Haze," I confirm as the bright sky turns an ominous black.

He stares down at the golden gem, rolling it in his palm, but I can see the question in his eyes.

"We can go to the Bend," I urge as tears fill my eyes.

"Or we can go for your father."

I shake my head as my lips start to tremble. "We've done something similar before, and it didn't end the way we wanted."

"I know." He cups my face. "But it's your decision." He places a tentative kiss on my lips. "I'll follow anywhere you lead."

"He's my father," I say. The words contrast with the shaking movement of my head.

"I know."

"Was he alive?"

Ari takes a shuddering breath. "He was injured. Too much for me to move without the use of my gift. But yes, he was alive."

The world further darkens as the last of the light is stolen, and I know we have mere seconds before the Haze will find us and surge downward.

I take one last look in Ari's eyes, memorizing everything I can just in case, before I let the quivering words free. "I can't leave him."

LVII

H e never lets go as we dive into the depths and let the shift take hold. I wrap
my arms around his large frame, letting him guide us downward until
we find solid ground beneath our feet.

The first sensation is wholly unexpected. Putrid death. The air of soiled linens,
sweat, and vomit threaten to overtake me.

Groans from a hundred mangled bodies soon to meet death fill the expanse of
the hollowed out.

"Help me," a familiar croak of a barely audible plea lingers.

My head searches each alcove for the sound. I hold back the vomit that threatens to appear as I overturn each dead body, finding only lifeless eyes. Ari darts
from one side of the room to the next bringing to life every torch and ball of light
he can.

"Help."

I look down at the sound and instantly meet his tired eyes, a tortured sob
ripping from my throat as he suffers through unending bouts of coughs.

I can barely make him out in the wavering light. My father lies feet from me,
body soaked, twisted, and broken in an unnatural state. Dried trails of blood mar
his face, and his sweat-soaked hair clings to his scalp. The tattered crimson fabric,
nowhere near passing as clothes, is so far removed from the regal outfit he once
wore. He feebly attempts to move, and I catch sight of the patchwork of bruises
hidden underneath the tears.

I rush to his side, twisting him in hopes of offering some relief from the pain
but he bellows out in agony.

"You're okay." I let the tears fall as I cradle his face in my hands, brushing the
matted brown hair from his face.

"Help me," he mumbles between bouts of coughing as his confused eyes search my face.

"I'm getting you out. I promise." I kiss his damp forehead as Ari takes hold of my hands and we will the shift to come. Our bodies are pulled. The force of the shift is so strong, and yet a weight holds us down.

Ari and I stare at each other for a moment longer and then survey the area, trying to make sense of what's happening. There's no river that we can see, and even if there were, we have the stone to override it.

I swallow again, tightening the grip I have on both men, and will us to move. Nothing happens.

"It's not working," Ari seethes. Confusion crosses his face.

I try once more, this time it almost takes. But I stop the second my father screams out in pain.

Another sob rips from my throat.

"I'm sorry. It's not working," I plead into confused eyes that quickly shut as a moan of pain bellows from my father's lips. His color starts to drain, and his body becomes less taut.

When his face starts to roll to the side I grip his cheeks, urging his flickering gaze to find mine. "Dad! Please!"

He stares at me, confusion branded on his features.

"Dad?" His face twists in pain.

"Yeah." My voice breaks. Tears stream down my face as the realization that this may not end how I had hoped settles in. "That's what I . . . would have called you . . . on Earth." My voice quivers with each word, hiccups of sadness breaking up the phrase, as I try to smile through the agony of the scene before me. I force the rush of words to flow as I try to distract him from the pain. "I know you wanted me to call you father, but is it okay if I say dad instead?"

"Father?" He pulls back, the motion barely discernible, as his cold hand falls from mine. "Who are you?"

The question lingers between us.

"It's Nera. I'm Nera." My tears fall to his cheeks as he stares upward.

"Are you with the Restoration? Are you here to save us?" He looks between Ari and me as he searches for answers I don't know how to give.

"I'm your daughter. I'm Nera."

He shakes his head in answer, the coughing more pronounced with each move. The color drains from his lips as his body starts to shake. "I don't have a daughter." The words barely take hold as he turns, a rush of water-filled vomit surges from his mouth.

I don't even register what's happening before Ari yanks me backward and away from the liquid.

"Esehtel," Ari whispers, and I collapse to the ground.

"No!" I crawl over, pulling him back into my waiting arms. "I'm Nera Thesand. I'm Nera and you're Koreed. You're my dad. I'm your daughter." His waiting eyes stare blankly into mine. "You're my father, and Lenora was my mother."

He shakes his head. "Lenora?" The name means nothing to him. "I don't know you." He coughs once more. "Please help me," he pleads, and I shake my head as sobs rush out.

"I'm Nera." My body shakes as Ari tries to pull me back.

"Nera," Ari whispers as he tries to pull me back but I will not move. "Nera." His hand wraps around my arm but I feel nothing but the beat of my fathers heart slowing with every second that passes. "Nera!" Ari tilts my quivering chin in his direction but I barely even see him from the tears clouding my vision. "Look at him. He's been soaked in the river. They tried to drown him, same as you. He's lost his memory."

But the words don't register. They can't be true.

"Dad?" I turn back and plead into the eyes I had hoped to once again come to know. "Please."

The ground begins a familiar rumble. One I know we may not escape. Ari falls to his knees in desperation, placing his hands on my father's cheeks. I don't know his motives, but I fight him for every inch. If this is the last moment I have, then I want it as my own. I will not leave him down here to die with no one.

"We have to get him out!" I scream as my father's eyes still and his face sags. "What are you doing!?" I try to force Ari's hands away, but he's too strong, too steady, and within a second my father's eyes surge open, finding me.

Ari falls back onto his knees. "I just showed you the memories I have of the two of you," He explains and then looks at me. "Your seventeenth birthday party. The one you didn't want me to come to. You danced together."

"Nera?" my father questions, and I nod my head. "I don't remember." He starts to cry.

"I know." I cup his cheeks once more, finding his skin now cold and gray. "It's okay. I promise, it's okay."

He moans as the pain consumes him. His breathing becomes labored and his eyes start to waver.

"Dad?" Frantic worry rips through me.

His gaze meets mine as his cold hand finds my cheek. "Was I a good father?"

I instantly nod. "The best." The words are barely audible over my sobs.

"Did I love you?"

I can barely see through the rush of tears. "Very much."

"And you loved me?"

"Always."

"You came back for me?"

I nod and he smiles.

"Thank you." His hand falls from my cheek as his body turns limp and cold.

"No."

Ari pulls me back as the ground breaks apart and my fathers body falls into the bottomless crack.

"That was touching." Riann's seethes and we turn to find him holding Eliza, a golden heartstone cloth around her hands and a knife slowly slicing into her neck.

A trickle of blood seeps past her collarbone.

"Why?" Ari seethes as he positions himself in front of me. "You are a Celestra! Just stop this!" His frustration takes hold and I tighten my grip on his hand letting him know I am here.

Riann doesn't answer and Eliza gasps as the tip slices a little deeper.

The lingering sobs that still beg to be let free die out and in their place a raging fury burns. I reach back, securing the bow in my hands. The heat simmers just under the surface as I keep it from exploding into chaos.

My gaze meets Eliza, and I hope she knows we won't let her die. Not now, not ever.

"I want what's mine!" Riann screams as he paces the ground. The open crack separates us by yards and I know the only way to reach her is by shifting. My feet meet the edge of the broken seam as my body begs me to save her. The rumbling increases as the floor starts to quake. Small bits break away and tumble down into the expanse.

Ari cuts his eyes to mine. A knowing look. We both are well versed in what is soon to come.

"I already told you. Nera belongs to no one. Least of all–"

"I have no use for *her* any longer. I want the stone you carry. The one you stole from me."

I swallow and watch as Ari tightens his grip on the jewel in his palm. A rush of water surges in from a crack in the stone wall behind us, and a sense of the worst kind of deja vu hits.

"No," Ari commands, and Eliza screams as the knife is slowly slid across her neck just enough to weaken her and not allow the use of her gifts. The edge of her shirt becomes soaked in a deep crimson as the heat settles in my open palm.

"What about a trade? The stone for her." Riann jerks his one arm upward to grab hold of Eliza's ebony braid, yanking it backward and exposing more of her neck to the waiting blade.

The ground shifts again, and this time we almost lose our footing as a rock plummets downward, piercing the ground at our side.

Eliza screams out and the dam inside me nearly bursts.

"I don't trust you," I glare upon the man I once thought truly loved me. "You destroyed your entire city. Why should we believe you would care to save her or let any of us live once you get what you want?"

The heat rakes down my arms. Light surges forth and tendrils rush outward like illuminated wisps along the ground.

"Use that and she dies." Riann warns through gritted teeth.

Then he starts to laugh and I take note of the small movement off to the side. A familiar gray braid, matted with dirt, blood and grime slowly moves into the dim light. Himerak's pale face soon follows.

Ari stills in trepidation, but I yank on his arm as Himerak nods in our direction.

"Why are you doing all of this?" I urge. Hoping Riann will take the bait. Hoping he will keep his focus on me and not what is inching closer behind him.

"Why?" The word is filled with incredulous laughter. "You are the monsters here, not me! You"—he points the dagger my way before shoving it back against Eliza's throat—"created the Ashclaw." His menacing glare turns to Ari. "You created the Haze!"

Ari tenses, but I hold steady.

"And you killed thousands of innocent people with your bare hands. At least we are trying to right our wrongs!"

Ari looks down, shock and confusion etched on his face. But I don't respond. That is a conversation for later. Right now, I only focus on Riann and Himerak as he closes the distance between the two.

"I am trying to create a better world. One without the abomination of you."

I shake my head as Himerak hobbles to within feet of Riann and pulls out that familiar azure gem.

"We've been over this before. You said I was the same as you. Are you an abomination as well?"

His jaw tenses as he swallows.

"You've wasted your time. The trade is off." He tilts Eliza backward, meeting her gaze. "I like to watch the fight drain out of my Celestras. After I take your life," he cuts his eyes to us, "I plan to take theirs as well." He moves to plunge the dagger just as Himerak lunges forward and clamps Riann's head in his hands, the beautiful blue gem secured between his palm and Riann's temple.

"Drop it!" Though Himerak's voice is labored, there is a definite command in those words. The second they leave his lips, Riann's entire form stills, the dagger plummets into the abyss between us and Eliza falls from his grip, landing inches from what would have been a torturous death.

There is only a second between her weak attempts at scrambling to her feet and Himerak's cry of pain as Riann struggles and thrashes against his weakening abilities.

A crack splits in the wall mere feet from us as water begins flooding the space.

"Take it!" Himerak calls out, each word strained and deliberate. "Take the stone!" He forces the words through gritted teeth as he uses every ounce of remaining strength and will to halt any further movement from Riann.

Eliza looks to me, only feet away but grossly out of reach due to the bottomless crack between us. I grab Ari's stone, quickly shifting to her and removing the cloth. As soon as it drops, I turn to pry the stone from between Himerak's palm and Riann's temple. The second it's out of Himerak's grasp Riann starts to move.

I reach down grabbing Eliza's trembling form and shift back to Ari. He effort-lessly picks her up, cradling her in his arms as I interlace my fingers within his.

The shift takes hold just as Riann starts to break free of the control. It is heavy and cumbersome as the water rushes at our feet. Ari screams out in frustration, willing for us to move to safety. But the waters continue to rise.

"Nera!" Himerak's screams my name with abandon as we fight to leave this hellish place.

My eyes move to meet his and for the first time I find a knowing sadness in his gaze. With only seconds left before I know Riann will overtake him, Himerak reaches into Riann's pocket and steals away the emerald stone, tossing it across the fractured expanse and into my waiting palm. Riann lets out a deafening scream of frustration as he fights the mind control but Himerak has just enough left within him to prevail. He latches onto Riann's frame, holding him steady as he turns to face us.

"Tell Micel it was real. And I will find him again. I will meet him in the next life." And just as my hand reaches forward, a surge of electricity racing between us, he throws their bodies into the endless seam.

I barely catch my breath as we land in cool, ankle-deep water. My body immedi-ately tenses, and I move to shift us away before Ari stops me.

"It's okay. We're here." He nods forward, and I turn to find a massive cavern at least ten stories high and hundreds of yards wide.

But what takes my breath away isn't the size or the beauty, or even the massive city structure that seems to have been built so far underground, but the people who fill it. Thousands of refugees, citizens, and Celestras stand before us. Some old, some young, some still injured from the recent escape. One by one, they turn and stare, and I watch in awe as each brings two fingers to their chest.

Ari leans down and brushes a sweat soaked curl away from my tear-covered face as he says, "Welcome to the Bend."

Acknowledgements

I never thought I would be writing an acknowledgements page, let alone for my third book...yet here we are. After I released The Celestra, I had very mild hopes that it would do anything. Well, it did something, lol. And The Shadows Within became a reality.

As always, my biggest *thank you* will always go out to my husband who spent far too many nights taking care of our wild kids so I could hunker down in a back room and stare at a computer screen.

And of course my entire extended family (my mom, dad, sister Rachel, and my in-laws), who have been such amazing contributors and supporters throughout this new journey!

A big ass thank you to my newest bestest friends and co-hosts to The Rainy Day Smut Brigade, Ally, Ashley and Lauren (our behind the scenes guru) who entered into my life at the exact right moment. Spoiler alert...I killed them in this book lol. Let's see if you can find where.

A million hugs to my amazing editor/illustrator Marcia Godfrey and editor/alpha reader Rachel Bunner who spent countless hours on Facetime and Marco Polo while I worked through plot holes and detailed descriptions. I truly believe they know this book better than I do...maybe.

So much love goes out to my Beta team. So many of you have been there from the beginning, and a few I was able to gain on this most recent journey. Your guidance, love, and pep talks are more appreciated than you will ever know. And of course, everyone on the ARC team needs a well deserved shoutout. You all jumped in (some of you to 2 books and not just 1), and showed me so much love and support! Your texts, DMs, and comments bring a smile to my face every day!

Lastly, I want to thank you, the reader. None of this would be possible without your love for my story. To say you have changed the trajectory of my life is not an understatement. Thank you so much for joining me on this wild ride. I can't wait to see where it goes.

Printed in Great Britain
by Amazon